Eye of the Cobra

A big truck reversed into the garage and Suzie saw a lean, fair-haired man leap out of the passenger seat. He started shouting commands in English, and five other men jumped out of the back of the truck, all dressed the same way in jeans and T-shirts. And they all carried guns.

'Move it!' As he spoke the fair-haired man pulled a stop-watch from his pocket.

Suzie shivered as she saw the driver get out of the cab and move in a semi-circle in front of the others. There was a sub-machine-gun in his hands. What type it was, she didn't know, but she could tell from his manner that he was quite prepared to use it.

They opened up the container and hauled out the tyres. She could see into the back of the truck. One of the men started lifting tyres into the back of the truck.

They were swopping tyres, she realised.

It must be some sort of sabotage. She thought of Wyatt and Ricardo. A blow-out at high speed could kill them.

Christopher Sherlock is the author of two bestselling novels, *Hyena Dawn* and *Night of the Predator*. An advertising copywriter, he lives in Johannesburg with his wife and daughter.

Also by Christopher Sherlock
available from Mandarin Paperbacks

Hyena Dawn
Night of the Predator

CHRISTOPHER SHERLOCK

Eye of the Cobra

Mandarin

A Mandarin Paperback

EYE OF THE COBRA

First published in Great Britain 1992
by William Heinemann Ltd
This edition published 1993
by Mandarin Paperbacks
and imprint of Reed Consumer Books Ltd
Michelin House, 81 Fulham Road, London SW3 6RB
and Auckland, Melbourne, Singapore and Toronto

Reprinted 1995

Copyright © Christopher Sherlock 1992
The author has asserted his moral rights

*The characters, organisations and situations
in this book are entirely imaginary and
bear no relation to any real person,
organisation or actual happening*

A CIP catalogue record for this title
is available from the British Library

ISBN 0 7493 1323 4

Printed and bound in Great Britain
by HarperCollins Manufacturing, Glasgow

To Karen with all my love

To marry an idea, to remain faithful to it all your life, is a fine thing. It is much more difficult to remain faithful to a woman all your life – that is perhaps impossible.

Enzo Ferrari

1980

May
Monaco

Perhaps it was the smell of oil and gasolene – a smell that got right into your nostrils and stayed there. Perhaps it was the danger, the excitement. Whatever it was, its effect on him was always the same: it made him need to take risks, to prove himself.

After taking the world championship three times in succession, it wasn't the money or the need for fame that was driving James on. It was something deeper, less easy to explain.

He looked out across the flat expanse of tarmac and over to the Ligier machine on his right, then up at the dull grey sky. Damn. He hoped it wouldn't rain again. It wasn't particularly pleasant, driving in the wet, especially on a circuit like Monaco.

His six-foot frame barely fitted into the cockpit of the black and gold Chase Racing machine. The Cosworth V8 engine growled behind his head. His brother Danny leaned over, resting his hand on the roll-bar and giving him a few last-minute instructions. Danny was always there, giving everything he had to manage Chase Racing, the Formula One team they'd built up together. Further down the grid was their second machine, driven by the former Formula Two champion, Marcel Baudelaire, also carrying Calibre sponsorship. In a few years, maybe, James hoped his own son Wyatt might take that number two spot. Was he right to want that for his son? He pushed the thought away. Focus. Concentrate.

Danny moved away. James raised his hand in a final wave to Estelle, standing next to the car.

What was it Estelle had? He had never met another woman as attractive as she was. Now she was walking towards Reg Tillson, his chief mechanic for over ten years, who was in

3

conversation with Bruce de Villiers, the ambitious young South African who was the team's number two mechanic.

A giant of a man lumbered up behind them, came forward and put his arm around Estelle – Jack Phelps, the American entrepreneur, close friend and sponsor. But for how much longer? James asked himself. Sometimes, one could know too much about a person.

And there in the background was Wyatt, with the ruffled dark hair that swept back off his forehead, Wyatt, with the deep, booming voice. His dark eyes were set back deep in their sockets – restless, unafraid eyes that gave Wyatt the look of a hawk.

James could see Estelle behind those eyes. And already, though Wyatt was only seventeen, he could visualise in those dark eyes the succession of women who would fall in love with him. Passion was there, and so was courage – it made him fatally attractive.

God, how he wished he could be young again. At forty years old, with the first traces of grey in his hair, he raged against the advance of age. But now was the time to belie those telltale grey hairs – to prove to the world – and himself – that he could do it.

The one-minute signal came up. The scream of the engine directly behind his head blew the thoughts away, and he focused on the start, on winning. He rolled forward as the green flag and the thirty-second board came up, marking the start of the parade lap.

It was round four of the world championship. He was holding sixth place in the driver's championship with two other drivers. He wasn't going anywhere, yet.

Today, he was lying second on the starting-grid, after a time of 1 minute 24.882 seconds in the second practice on Saturday. Didier Pironi had stolen pole position from him by seven hundredths of a second. It had been dry and warm then, perfect conditions to race in. Today, most of Europe and his native England were basking in intense sunshine, enjoying an exceptional bout of hot weather, but here in Monaco it was grey, overcast and rainy.

4

His mind was clear as he swept around the narrow circuit, concentrating on the start. A few years previously, he had lost here, due to a bad start and a subsequent wheel-banging with another machine. He never made mistakes twice. That was how he'd stayed alive.

The start here was difficult. From the grid the machines would roar forwards into the tight right-hand bend called Ste Dévote.

He ran through his mental checklist – the basic elements – to drive as fast as he could but always steady, always controlled, never making hard gear-changes.

Above and around him were crowds of spectators, looking down onto the narrow three-mile street circuit on which twenty cars would do battle. He caught sight of a vivid red and blue poster advertising the Monte Carlo Show. He wondered what it was like to visit Monaco and not think of racing.

The starting-grid was in the narrow confines of the Boulevard Albert 1er. James knew the official starter, Derek Ongaro, would be battling to see the back of the grid, waiting for the green flag which would indicate that all the cars were in position.

Time telescoped, and he entered into another dimension of concentration. The start-light switched to red. Then the green light came on and his machine leapt forwards, just behind Pironi's first-placed Ligier.

He was through Ste Dévote, into second, and slightly sluggish on the uphill. Then the roar of another engine as Jones shot past him in the Williams.

Damn, damn, damn. Jones must have slipped back into first gear, giving himself the edge out of the bend. James had been thinking too much about Ste Dévote and not enough about what came after. It was a bastard to pass anyone on the Monaco circuit, now he'd be hard-pressed to regain the second place that Jones had taken from him. Besides, Jones was eight years younger than him, and had nineteen points, lying second in the world championship.

Dammit. He might be forty years old, but he'd show them. There was no other way to live except to drive.

*

5

Wyatt watched James fly off past the pits, holding second place, pushing hard against Pironi's tail. The black and gold Chase Racing machine's V8 Cosworth engine bellowed power.

She came up next to him. He was conscious of her femininity and her mesmeric blue eyes. She looked more like his girl-friend than his mother. No wonder his girlfriends were jealous of her.

He squeezed her affectionately, then kissed her on the cheek. He could sense the other men watching her, and he didn't like it. But he could never get away from the knowledge that she had this power over men.

Estelle moved out of his embrace and leaned back against the guard-rail that separated them from the pits. She shook out her blonde hair and winked at Wyatt. Blonde, yes, that was unusual for a Frenchwoman, but then there was nothing ordinary about his mother.

'Do you think 'e is ever scared?'

A throaty voice. He imagined her in a black evening-dress, turning heads, the diamond tiara glittering on her head.

'Would you be?'

'*Non*. I would be thinking only of winning. You were looking so sad just now, dahling. There is something troubling you?'

She touched his deeply tanned face very gently with her hand.

'It's nothing. I wanted to be on the grid.'

She smiled sadly. 'What has James done to you?'

Reg Tillson had a nervous twitch in his left eye when he was worried. Had they missed anything out in the preparation of James's machine? As always the night before he had meticu-lously checked it over, section by section. He tried to reassure himself with the thought that de Villiers had been with him all the time – Bruce was very, very good. Everything Reg knew had gone into the preparation of it; all the small but important details that he had learned over years of working in motor-racing.

But a perfectly prepared machine was just the beginning of the job. What counted in the end was the willingness of the

6

driver to take carefully calculated risks, to push himself and his machine just a fraction more than the man in front would dare to.

He liked James Chase, or Jamie as he preferred to call him. And he had grown fond of the boy, Wyatt. He hoped that he would see the day when Wyatt won his first Grand Prix.

Reg saw their sponsor, Jack Phelps, approaching. There'd been tension between James and Jack recently. Jack felt James should retire and put a younger driver in the number one seat. Jack had implied, but not said, that James was over the hill.

'I wonder if James can handle Formula One any longer?' Phelps said quietly in his strong American accent.

Phelps's eyes rested on Estelle Chase, mentally undressing her. Reg felt his irritation rising.

The sirens erupted. All around them was commotion. They looked down from the pit lane towards Ste Dévote. A massive pile-up had occurred.

Reg narrowed his eyes. 'They'd better get those bloody cars off the track fast or someone'll be killed – if they haven't been killed already.'

Wyatt felt Estelle's nails clawing into his shoulder. In the distance the marshals worked frantically, clearing the wreckage.

It had been a culmination of disasters. Derek Daly had ploughed into the back of Bruno Giacomelli, cartwheeled through the air, caught the back of Alain Prost and landed on the back of Jean-Pierre Jarier's machine. Meanwhile, trying to avoid the devastation, Jan Lammers had bounced over Ricardo Patrese's rear wheel.

Standing in the pit lane, Wyatt put his hand on his mother's shoulder. He wasn't scared for his father because he knew James would handle it. James didn't get ruffled, he just handled things. That was why he was such a good driver – because he never ever panicked.

Estelle was white. Wyatt knew she was always scared, but usually she didn't let it show.

*

The crane was hovering over the curve, lifting the broken cars from the track. The marshals were working very fast. In the distance – the roar of the approaching cars. No one wanted to stop the race, but no one wanted a serious accident either.

Estelle was crying now. Jack came across and hugged her.

'Don't worry, James'll come through OK.'

Wyatt knew that Jack was his father's best friend, but he didn't like Jack and he didn't trust him. Jack had been putting pressure on James to retire. And there was something in the way Jack was touching and holding Estelle that roused anger in Wyatt. Jack never touched Estelle like that when James was around.

The cars shot past, James's black and gold machine holding the third place behind Pironi and Jones.

'Oh my God,' Estelle said frantically.

But the track was clear and the cars swept safely round Ste Dévote. Reg didn't look happy and nor did Danny. De Villiers looked very cool, very much in control.

'Shit, Jones got past him,' Danny exclaimed.

'And he's not going to let Jamie return the favour,' Reg added. 'Pironi's certainly not holding back, either.'

'Just let him keep the pressure on Jones. This circuit is hard on cars, and ours is as tough as they come,' de Villiers said incisively.

Danny shouted the information into the microphone attached to his headset – information that was instantly relayed to the headphones in James's helmet over the direct radio link.

Estelle recovered her poise as if she had never lost it. There was a glint in Phelps's eyes, and Wyatt stepped forwards instinctively, blocking the big American from his mother. Just you try, he thought, hoping in a way that Phelps would. Wyatt knew he could take on anyone who tried to tackle him. He felt the callouses on the edge of his hands; he'd have to drop the karate soon, to concentrate totally on driving.

James kept the pressure on Jones's Williams-Cosworth. He wasn't going to risk an overtaking manoeuvre till later in the

8

race. He wanted to conserve his car and wait for a pit-stop to put on fresh rubber. After that, he would tackle Jones.

On lap twenty-five he saw the back of Jones's car begin to twitch, and moments later the Australian was out of the race with a broken differential. James swept past, elated that he could now move into second position and start pressuring Pironi.

By halfway there were only thirteen cars left in the race. On lap forty, James put in the second-fastest lap time of the race. He could tell Pironi was having problems, and he was going to make damn sure that the Frenchman didn't have a chance to solve them. He was in the rhythm of the race now, everything going very smoothly, everything under control. He just kept the pressure on the man in front.

Eventually, on lap fifty-five Pironi entered Casino a fraction too quickly and his car jumped out of gear, sliding out of control into the barrier of tyres. With his left front wheel splayed out, Pironi managed to keep going down the hill, and then reluctantly pulled off at Mirabeau.

James reeled in the laps now, taking advantage of the dry sections of the track. He backed off a little when the rain came down hard during the final laps, but when he crossed the line he was comfortably ahead of the second-placed Jacques Laffite.

He took the victory lap slowly, riding high on the elation of having finished first yet again. It crossed his mind that he should retire. Now was the time to pull out, while he was still winning.

Wyatt was buffeted by the crowds of people who stormed into the pit lane and embraced his father. Estelle was crying and hugging her husband.

Wyatt wanted that feeling for himself. He wanted to know what it was like and to hold on to it above all else.

His father came across and hugged him, then he was gone, appearing on the podium moments later, showering the crowd with champagne. Then he stepped across to the royal box and took the trophy from Princess Grace.

'Now that's what I call getting attention for my cigarettes,' Wyatt heard Phelps growl.

'Yeah, who cares about the racing,' de Villiers countered sarcastically.

In that moment Wyatt hated Phelps and loved de Villiers. He would remember the moment years later, when he learned to trust his instincts again.

It was much later, higher up in the hills, when he was able to talk again to his father. It was James's custom to go for a drive the night after a Grand Prix. Usually he went alone, but this time he asked Wyatt to come with him.

Outside the villa he handed Wyatt the keys to the red Ferrari. 'You drive.'

'No,' he said to his father. 'You said that it's good luck to drive hard the night after the race. It brings you victory again.'

James stood staring at him, and for the first time Wyatt saw his father for what he was – a determined, successful man. A hard man, with a body of taut muscle and a finely constructed face, his thin blond hair blowing in the breeze.

'I told your mother, just now . . . I'm going to retire from Formula One. I'm not going to race any more.'

Wyatt thought of his mother and how she'd reacted to the accident. He understood now. His father moved closer and held his wrists in his own strong hands.

'You're seventeen years old, not a boy any longer. You must make me a promise, Wyatt.'

He looked into his father's dark-brown eyes. 'As long as it's one I can keep.'

'You are just like your mother. I want you to promise me that when you start having fears, when you start having doubts, you'll walk away from it. Just walk away from it.'

'I promise.'

Wyatt took the keys, slipped into the driver's seat and gunned the engine. His father sat beside him.

'OK,' James said, 'let's see just how fast you can go.'

June,
Yosemite Valley, California

The walls of stone soared upwards, away from the pines towards the piercing blue sky. From far away they appeared smooth and insurmountable, but when you were close, right up against them, you could feel the roughness of them, the life in them. High up, Wyatt saw the brightly coloured dots against the stone, a thin umbilical cord of rope running between them.

He looked down at the earth beneath his feet, glanced at his watch, then dipped his fingers into the chalk-bag suspended from his belt.

He indicated to Suzie that she should start feeding the rope out to him from where she was belayed on the ground. A short sling attached her climbing-harness to a piton driven into a crack at the base of the rock face. She finished tying her long blonde hair into a pony-tail, and fed the two nylon ropes, one red and the other blue, through the aluminium figure-of-eight attached to her waistband.

'You're on belay, *ja*,' she said. Her English was precise, the German accent distinct.

He'd met her on another face the previous day. She'd been climbing solo, and he'd been impressed. He needed a partner for this route and everyone had turned him down. She'd accepted with a flash of those strange eyes – blue flecked with green. Maybe she was as crazy as he was. Apparently she was nineteen, two years older than he was.

He caressed the rock and moved rhythmically up the face, hardly pausing on the almost smooth surface. He began to relax as the danger increased and his mind focused on staying alive. There was nothing between him and the ground except the two thin ropes.

The exposure of the face provided the surge of adrenalin

that spurred him on as the pines began to look like model trees on a toy landscape.

He was alone, in control and doing what he loved more than anything else in the world – pushing himself to the limit. The thoughts that crowded into his brain disappeared, to be replaced by a total awareness of his surroundings.

There was a lot he needed to forget, especially one memory. Tracking the road in the darkness, pulse racing, body buoyed up with excitement – and then the loss of control. The lights twinkling in the harbour. The smashing and tearing of metal. His father's face at that moment, still, even calm, then his own head smashing hard into the steering-wheel.

He'd been lying in his hospital bed when she came in, her face red with crying.

'You killed him, you bastard! Oh God, I hate you. I hate you!' The words echoed round his brain.

Shit. He swung out, nearly losing his right handhold as he pressed his right foot against a tiny indentation in the rock. Shit, he was coming off!

Then he recovered his balance.

Focus. Focus.

He pulled himself in, his mind clear, and stared up at the route above.

The brightly coloured dots were now two people, climbing slowly above him. He felt exhilarated. He was making good progresss. It would only be harder later, when he came up against the toughest section of the climb, high up the face.

'Off belay!'

Suzie detached herself from the piton at the bottom of the face and untied the figure-of-eight from the ropes. The slack was taken in as he pulled in the rope. Then she looked above her, searching for this distracted young man she'd only known for a day.

There he was, spread-eagled across the living rock, hanging like some insect from the wall of a room, unconcerned and unafraid. She shifted her legs as she imagined him astride her. He would stroke her forehead, look into her eyes and then kiss her softly. Perhaps he would have a way of making love

12

that would make her lose control. Always she was in control. He was here for the same reason she was: to forget.

He had a long, lean body, with a boxer's legs. His hands were unusually large, but it was the grace and confidence of his movements that was most surprising. She thought of his face – the face of a hawk. Sometimes his face was an angry, troubled mask through which she could see nothing. But when he smiled, that was when she liked him most. The skin around his dark eyes would wrinkle up into faint crow's-feet and his mouth would lengthen into a devastating smile. She wanted to run her hands through his unruly dark hair.

Strength, that was the word that came to her mind when she thought of Wyatt Chase.

She felt the tug on the rope and cleaned her rubber-soled climbing-boots against the face. Then she started to climb.

He passed the other climbers just after midday – two men in their twenties. He understood their resentment; he was using less protection than they were, was less afraid of falling. And he was climbing with a girl who was better on the rock than either of them.

He understood them, because he had been like them several years before. He had confronted the fear of dying and overcome it. His father had taught him to do that. Oh God, he didn't want to think about his father any more. Sweet Jesus, why had his father asked him to drive?

'Fucking teenagers! Fucking lunatics!'

The words drifted upwards, muttered by one of the two climbers below him. He belayed himself at the next bolt and tugged on the rope for Suzie to start climbing. To block the thoughts of the accident that kept coming back to him, he focused on her progress.

The men were watching her, her body undisguised in black lycra climbing-skin. Her long legs stretched out against the rock, the muscles taut, pressing her hard into the face. She leaned out to reach up for another hold, licking her lips, and he felt himself going hard as he saw the form of her breasts pressing through the thin nylon.

Then she was next to him, tying herself onto the belay as he

13

moved up to tackle the next section, the midday sun burning into his deeply tanned face.

No one had ever climbed this route free. No one had ever dared. And he hadn't hit the worst of it yet. That came near the top, over a thousand feet off the ground, where the rock bulged outwards, forcing the climber to negotiate a terrifying overhang. But he didn't think about that. All that mattered now was moving. He was fighting himself in a race against time. He and Suzie would be at the overhang by four, and after that it was into the unknown. At that point most climbers would pull out the nylon webbing slings and move through the overhang, resting on them for support.

He would attempt this section without assistance. His name and Suzie's would go down in the route-book as having made the first ascent free of artificial aids, without using the slings for support.

Thoughts of the accident kept returning. He couldn't understand why he could remember so little about it. The doctor said he was suffering from retrograde ammnesia, blocking out painful memories. He just wished he knew what had caused him to lose control of the car and send it plummeting over the cliff edge.

He looked below him again. The other climbers would bivouac further down the face, suspended from the bolts driven into the unyielding rock. They would sleep, pinned to the rock face, recovering their strength to tackle the overhang the following day.

He looked up and found the first traces of fear in himself as he saw the overhang. That was why he had chosen this route, to challenge himself; to try and excise the guilt. Perhaps, even, to die.

She felt the sweat on the inside of her hands. She wanted to cry, and hated herself for it. He had reached the overhang. This was the moment she had thought would be so exciting.

A free ascent meant using the slings attached to the bolts as protection against a fall, letting the rope dangle through them via the metal snap-links called carabiners. To use the slings

14

for support or for leverage would invalidate the ascent as free. She knew other climbers would be watching them from the ground through telescopes, ready to challenge them when they came back, if they'd cheated.

She moved up to him and attached herself to the belay. The rock roof was above her head, stretching out far to the edge of the overhang.

He did not touch the bolts, placed in the overhang by previous climbers who had tackled the route with artificial aids. His ascent would be totally free. The danger would be just as much for her when she followed – if she came off, she would swing out into the void. But she did not protest. Everything in her despised weakness.

She watched him moving out, under the beginning of the overhang that ran out for over one hundred and fifty feet. He hadn't talked about how he was going to do it, she just knew that he wouldn't take any precautions. That was the way he was. It was all or nothing.

His foot slipped out of the crack that ran under the overhang. She gripped the ropes tightly. Could she hold him if he came off? She didn't want to think about it.

Fight it. Fight it.

He jammed his hand into the crack and pulled up, feeling the blood running down his arm. His knuckles were raw to the bone. He glanced across at the metal eye of one of the bolts in the face of the overhang and was tempted to push a carabiner through it, attach a sling and rest, suspended in his climbing-harness. Even that desperate attempt to connect up to the carabiner might bring him off the face. He looked down at the ground a thousand feet below.

No. No. No. He would not take the easy route, he was determined to climb this overhang without any artificial aids – whatever the risks. Damn Estelle. To hell with racing.

He swung his feet into the crack, jamming them up, level with his hands. He took a last look at the bolt that offered his final chance of protection, and moved on. One hundred and twenty feet to the edge of the overhang.

Hand-jam after hand-jam, everything concentrated on

15

moving forwards . . . His body was one single entity of pain. Then, without warning, came a loud screech that almost made him plunge towards the valley below and into oblivion. The bird burst from its nest deep within the crack and flew angrily around him, fluttering its wings.

He screamed at it, fighting his way on, focusing on the sky and the warmth of the sun-drenched rock that lay beyond the shadow of the overhang. He felt the crack narrowing and his grip reducing. This he had prepared himself for, because he knew that the last move out of the horizontal crack and up and out over the overhang was the most difficult of the entire climb.

Hanging on with his left hand-jam, he reached out into the sunlight and searched for a hold. There was none. His strength was running out, it was all or nothing. He had to reach further, so he loosened his left hand and stretched his right higher up. He knew the hold must be there, he had studied the route over and over again. It had to be there.

He further reduced the grip with his left hand, and felt himself coming off. Jesus, no.

He pushed his right hand up with one last, desperate movement and then shot off, suspended across the void as his right hand found the jug-handle grip he had been searching for. He pulled up on his right arm and his left hand shot up, searching the face, finding another grip. He moved fast, inching himself back onto the face, his feet finding a tiny ledge. At last the weight was off his arms. He found a bolt just over the edge of the overhang, belayed himself off it and then let himself down, so he could take in the ropes and guide Suzie towards him.

He felt better – and it suddenly came to him that he needed to distance himself from the world of motor-racing. There was the offer that still stood, the one he had been thinking of turning down before he went to Monaco. Then, he had thought he would choose racing rather than karate. Now he knew his decision would go the other way. Perhaps in Japan, he might come to terms with himself.

*

She felt cold with a fear she did not want to admit. She wondered what she would have done if he had come off. He would have cannoned down, smashing into the face. The ropes would have held him, but he would have been dead. Did he want to die?

For her, it would be different – less of a risk because he was slightly above her, taking the strain. If she came off, she would swing outwards into the void, the ground a thousand feet below her.

The rope tugged at her waist.

'Climb!'

The word echoed coldly against the rock. He was watching her with a detached expression on his face, hanging from the edge of the overhang, one hundred and fifty feet distant.

'If I fall I will pull you off.' She hated herself for admitting her fear.

'Climb!'

The rope tugged again at her waist. She felt terrified to detach herself from the safety of the belay, but there was no choice.

'Climb!' The rope tugged again.

'No!'

'I'll drop the ropes. Then you'll have to do it solo.' He started to untie the two ropes.

'No!'

He stopped. She detached herself from the belay, tears running down her face as she started jamming her way along the crack. He did not take the rope in.

'You bastard, take up the slack.'

Long loops of rope hung down beneath her.

'Take up the slack!'

If she fell, it would be one hundred and fifty feet – the full length of the rope. She knew what he was doing – not giving her a choice. She had to make it or they would both be killed.

Her hands jammed hard into the crack and she yanked herself forwards, her body shaking with fear and pain. He started to pull the rope in.

'Please, more . . .'

The rope stopped moving in when she hesitated. So she

17

fought on, every muscle in her body screaming as she moved along the crack, inching her way towards him.

The pain had reached a level almost beyond enduring when she felt his hand grab hers and yank her across him. She smelt the animal smell of his body. He clipped her into the belay at the edge of the overhang and climbed up the last easy section to the summit.

She regained her strength and followed. He said nothing as she pulled up onto the rock slab. She staggered up and onto her feet, and raised her hand to slap him across the face.

'You bastard.'

He gripped her hand before it struck, and pulled her towards him. She struggled, excitement rising. Then her lips found his and she clung to him as he peeled the climbing-skin off her.

She lay back against the cold rock and felt him rise up inside her and screamed out with the sheer ecstasy of it. At last. At last a man who would dominate her and possess her. At last a man who would make her feel like a woman.

He held her against him as the last rays of sunshine covered the rock face.

Enough. Enough.

He would not need to climb again, he knew that. He would sink himself into the discipline that karate demanded. He would train long and hard, punishing his body, driving the agony from his mind.

But this German girl. She was different, he needed her for this moment. He drank in the cool night air and looked down into the valley in the moonlight.

He was in love with danger – only when he took risks did the guilt go away and Estelle's voice stop echoing round his head.

He turned away from the broken rock of the summit, and they dressed quickly, then began to work their way down into the valley. He felt the tiredness in his limbs, but most of all he felt the elation that came from knowing where he had to go and what he had to do.

1991

January,
Amersham, Buckinghamshire and London

Danny Chase pulled himself up in the bed and leaned back on the pillows. Next to him, on a flexible arm, was a personal computer, and on the screen was the latest Reuters financial report. He punched in a few commands, studied the figures on the screen and groaned. Yet another investment that wasn't working out – why couldn't he get it right for once?

His body was in good shape, he'd made sure of that. At fifty-five, he took satisfaction in knowing that he had the physique of a man half his age.

She came in with a tray laden with toast, tea, orange juice and scrambled eggs. She had nothing on beneath the thin cotton dressing-gown, and this wiped the earlier thoughts from his head.

'Good morning, darling.'

She sat down beside him, rested the tray on the edge of the double bed and poured him a cup of tea. He took it from her gratefully, sipped it slowly, staring at her breasts. They were small and firm, the way he liked them best.

She sensed his mood and let the dressing-gown fall from her shoulders, glancing at herself in the mirror that ran the length of the opposite wall. They'd met in the gymnasium, gone out for a few weeks, and then she'd invited him back to her house.

Already he could sense she was losing interest. It was always the bloody same: he couldn't hold them. The problem, he guessed, was that women saw through him, saw the weakness. He ended up wanting them more than they wanted him, and the moment they sensed his desperation he was finished.

He stared at his own reflection. His hairless upper body, topped by an elegant head, looked like a statue of Julius

21

Caesar. His dark curly hair, tinged with grey, clung to his scalp. The face had many lines, especially around the eyes. He could see the bitterness there – and the weakness.

She bent down and began to caress him with her lips. It felt very good. He was hard now, and he grabbed her hair. She let out a moan, and he pushed her face into the pillow and raised himself up, above her pear-shaped buttocks.

'Please, Danny . . .'

The buttocks rose provocatively and he penetrated her smoothly, cupping her breasts in his hands. It was good. He watched himself in the mirror, shafting her, while the perspiration dripped from her face. Then the dullness came – the thing he feared most. He let out a sigh of passion. She must never know.

He lifted himself up and turned her over, sinking his face into the moistness of her crotch. Her scream of release taunted him, reminding him that he had not come.

Later they relaxed in the steam-room, and he watched the moisture on her body as she dozed beside him. The control he had over this beautiful creature gave him immense pleasure – but she would start drifting away from him, he was certain of that. If only he could hold a woman, as James had held Estelle.

When James died, he'd taken Estelle and Wyatt under his wing, tried to help them. But Wyatt had gone off to Japan and Estelle had met Carlos. The family had disintegrated. He'd managed Chase Racing alone for the last ten years, knowing that eventually Wyatt would come back. And he had, last year, and Danny had given Wyatt the number two drive in the team, hoping it would bring them closer together. But they'd argued, because Wyatt had dared to criticise Danny's management skills.

In moments of honesty, like now, Danny had to admit to himself that he couldn't run the team like James. He hadn't got James's ability to motivate people, and he constantly failed to get the team working together. True, Reg Tillson had hung in with him, but Reg wasn't enough to carry the team, and now his number one driver, Ricardo Sartori, was threatening to ditch Chase Racing in favour of a more successful Formula

One team. And Ricardo held their major sponsor, Carvalho tyres, in the palm of his hand: it was Ricardo they were backing, not Chase Racing.

Danny felt moisture on his palms. He was in deep financial trouble already, and Ricardo's departure, taking Carvalho with him, would break him.

He knew Wyatt had the talent to win. He'd tried to help his nephew, but everything had gone wrong that season.

Julia got up, kissed him on the cheek and went out, and Danny sank back against the wall and thought back to James winning the Monaco Grand Prix ten years before. He remembered the crowd cheering James as he stepped on the podium, and the kinship he had felt with his brother. James had always been there for him; whenever there was a problem, James had known what to do. Now, nothing went right. Last season Wyatt hadn't even qualified for a place on the grid at Monaco – the engine and the chassis had given constant trouble.

Perhaps, just perhaps, in the coming season he could give his nephew the machine he needed to win.

He stepped out of the steam-room and towelled himself dry. Then he flipped through the paper, turning as usual to the business pages. He studied the analysis of the previous day's activity on the stock exchange, then looked at the rest of the paper. On the second page from the back a headline caught his eye.

'Chase Quits Chase.' He muttered the words slowly to himself, hating the trite phraseology. He stared at the picture accompanying the story, reread the article carefully and then folded up the paper.

'Julia. Please, get me the phone!'

Danny waited in the oak-panelled boardroom of Chase Racing, scarcely able to contain his despair. He breathed in deeply and looked proudly at the pictures of himself and James in the early seventies. James had been a brilliant driver, and Danny knew Wyatt could be the same. Just one more season together and they could do it. And he needed Wyatt, not just as a driver, but as support. He'd given his nephew a tremendous break – letting him drive in Formula One even though he hadn't worked his way up the ranks – and now Wyatt had kicked him in the teeth. Wyatt had to see reason.

He looked at the framed portrait of James on the wall and decided he would appeal to Wyatt's loyalty. Wyatt couldn't desert Chase Racing, it was a family business; Danny owned half the equity and Estelle and Wyatt a quarter each. But he had never told Wyatt or Estelle about his financial difficulties; how, raising money against his share in the company, he had speculated in supermarkets and property – and done very badly.

He had been elated when Wyatt returned from his ten-year sojourn in Japan, eager to begin racing again. He'd certainly proved his ability – winning the Spanish Grand Prix the previous season – and Danny had reasoned that with Wyatt he could pull more sponsors. But the people he approached had been sceptical about the twenty-seven-year-old with no track record. They preferred to back young drivers who'd proved themselves in Formula 3000, they said. They argued that Wyatt's Spanish victory had been a matter of luck and not skill.

Danny was surprised Wyatt hadn't burned himself out – it had been a frustrating season for him. But instead it seemed he had more energy for racing than ever before. Dany knew that part of the problem with Wyatt was that he'd had to let Ricardo Sartori, the Formula One veteran and former world champion, drive the better of the cars. But that, and the ludicrously high fee he was paid, was the only reason Sartori stayed with the team. It was some sort of miracle that he was driving for them at all. Danny guessed that in his late thirties, money was more important to Ricardo than anything else.

Of course Danny had wanted Wyatt to win. Thank God the car had lasted at least one race to give him a first place. But he couldn't give Wyatt the best engines or the best chassis – those were kept exclusively for Ricardo. Wyatt's machine was basically two years out of date and constantly breaking down . . .

The door to the boardroom opened and closed softly, and his nephew was standing in front of him. Danny shifted back in his chair, avoiding Wyatt's dark eyes. Wyatt was taller and leaner than he was.

'Sit down, Wyatt, I want to talk.'

Wyatt slid easily into one of the chairs at the far end of the table. Every movement was precise yet subtle, reminding Danny of James. He looked across at Wyatt's enormous, calloused hands and thought, not for the first time, how much dedication it must have taken for his nephew to become the youngest Westerner ever to receive the Seventh Dan.

He could sense from Wyatt's stern expression that he wasn't going to be easily swayed from his decision. The dark hair was as unruly as the man, and his eyebrows were knotted in concentration. He was wearing his customary black windcheater and jeans.

Wyatt said nothing, forcing Danny to begin.

'I read the paper,' Danny said.

Wyatt arched his eyebrows. 'You're telling me you're surprised I'm leaving?' His rich, deep voice was heavy with sarcasm, his contempt for his uncle thinly veiled.

'You could have talked to me first, instead of smearing it all over the national dailies. I tried, dammit. You could at least have talked to me!'

'There's nothing to talk about. You've let me down – again and again and again! I would have qualified at Monaco if the bloody suspension hadn't collapsed.'

'Don't be a fool, Wyatt. I didn't have the resources. I had to put more into Sartori's machine – Carvalho insisted on it.'

'I'm not interested in your bullshit. My car was a dog.'

Danny felt the hairs lifting on the back of his neck.

'After all I've done for you . . . Look, I'll ignore your insults. Let's give it one more chance. It could be just like the old days with your father.'

'That's rich. He was the one who made the team a success. He carried you.'

Danny smashed his fist hard down on the table. 'You bastard!'

Wyatt remained calm. 'I don't have to take your bullshit any longer. I want out. I've negotiated a deal to buy myself into a new French team.'

Danny went white. 'You don't mean you want to sell your share of Chase?'

'Of course I want to bloody sell. The money'll buy me a decent drive. I'm not putting up with your incompetence any longer.'

'But Wyatt, your father and I built up the business . . .'

'Danny, I want to sell.'

Danny went over to the wall-safe and fiddled with the combination. He swung back the door, nervously pulled out the document and handed it to Wyatt, who quickly ran his eyes over it.

'Why didn't you tell me my mother owned a quarter of the team?'

'I thought you knew.' Danny's surprise wasn't faked.

Wyatt smiled stiffly. 'I thought I had fifty per cent of it. Anyway, just pay me out.'

'It'll take a month or so. I'll have to call in the auditors to work out the precise value of your shares.'

He had to buy time, that was all there was to it. Danny leaned forward across his desk, trying to look relaxed. Perhaps he could still find another sponsor and then persuade Wyatt to reconsider his decision.

'Look, if you should change your mind . . .'

'Danny. I just want my money. And I want it fast.'

Wyatt got up, walked out and slammed the door behind him.

After days of anguish Danny felt the tide of events was finally turning in his favour.

When Jack Phelps first approached him, he'd thought it was for old time's sake. Phelps had asked him how the business was doing, and Danny made out he had plenty of money and had only kept Chase Racing so that Wyatt could have a drive – though now, of course, Wyatt was leaving.

But Phelps had another agenda. He said he wanted to get involved in Formula One again, that he would sponsor the team. Danny had felt his spirits soar. He had always realised the strategic value of Chase Racing to anyone who wanted to get into Formula One in a hurry. James had built the company up out of love for the sport, but it had been very different in those days – not so much money and a far more select group of people involved. Now Formula One was an international business, ruthlessly competitive, with stiff rules and codes of conduct.

Danny knew Phelps had become incredibly wealthy. It was only logical that the American should want to resume his sponsorship of the team, a sponsorship that had lapsed after James's death. Danny knew Phelps would pump in the funds, just as he had in the past. And Phelps wouldn't monopolise the sponsorship – Danny had just negotiated a deal with Ricardo Sartori that included the Carvalho sponsorship. He knew that with a better car and big enough backing, Sartori could quite easily win the world championship again.

Danny had told no one of the possibility of Phelps becoming involved again. He wanted to keep it as a surprise, and anyway, he didn't want any of the other Formula One teams to know that Phelps was interested in sponsoring a team.

His secretary's discreet knock on the door told him that Phelps had arrived. He would hold the discussions in the boardroom. He fastened the inner button of his double-breasted jacket and walked smartly to the door. Now for some hard bargaining.

Jack Phelps leaned back and stretched his arms as Danny Chase finished his presentation. Good old Danny, the same weak-willed jerk James had carried all those years before.

Jack had done his homework – he knew Chase Racing was a disaster-story. But of course, the potential was there: Chase Racing had its own test circuit just outside London, and plenty of good equipment. Jack wanted to move in, strip out the weaker layers of management and take control. Chase Racing was exactly the way he'd hoped to find it – run down and deep in debt. Besides, he had sentimental reasons for screwing the Chases. He and James Chase had been good partners in the sixties . . . then James had got too clever for his own good . . . After James's death Jack had lost interest in the team – his other businesses had taken all his energy.

27

His eyes swept around the oak-panelled boardroom and then looked out across the grey skyline.

'Have you discussed my possible involvement with any of the guys on the team?'

Danny looked slightly put out. 'I wanted to keep it a surprise.'

'Don't you think they might be a little pissed off at not being involved?'

'Jack, I *am* Chase Racing. What I say, goes.'

Danny was feeling confident. He could sense Phelps was eager to close the deal, and he wasn't going to be pressurised.

'With your nephew's departure, you've only one driver left in the team . . .' Jack stared hard at Danny Chase, loosening him up for the big punch.

'I've just signed a contract tying in Ricardo and Carvalho,' Danny said with satisfaction. 'I'm not desperate for other sponsors.'

'Listen, buddy. I've just bought and taken over Carvalho. The deal you signed is void.'

Danny's hand tightened on the coffee cup, and Phelps moved in. 'Without that deal you're bankrupt. I'm buying you out!'

'I'm the owner and I'm not about to sell . . .' Danny parried desperately.

Phelps put his hands on his hips. 'Oh, really? I'm sure Wyatt and Estelle will sell out to me.'

Danny swayed on his feet. 'No . . .'

'Oh yes they will. Especially when they discover you're a million pounds in the red. Without the Carvalho sponsorship you can't roll your debt over. You're finished.'

'Oh God, Jack, be reasonable,' Danny stammered, avoiding Phelps's eyes. 'The audited value of the business is one-and-a-half million pounds in assets alone.'

Jack Phelps laid his hands on the smooth surface of the table. Then his voice filled the silence.

'When you're bankrupt, I'll buy everything you've got, including this building, the test circuit and all your equipment. Wyatt and Estelle will get nothing.'

Danny was shaking. Phelps had changed, or maybe he'd

never really known the American that well. He needed James now, and James was dead.

'What are you saying?'

'You sell to me now – all your shares – and I promise I'll pay out Wyatt and Estelle.'

'How much?' Danny stammered.

Phelps grinned. He reached inside his jacket, taking out a stiff manilla envelope.

'Your cheque,' he said, tossing it onto the boardrooom table in front of Danny.

Danny tore open the envelope and stared at the cheque.

'Fifty thousand pounds! Jesus Christ!'

'It's a lot, lot better than fuck-all. Estelle and Wyatt'll get the same. The other way, they'll each be liable for a quarter of a million pounds of your bad debts when the business goes down.'

Danny felt the room spinning. Phelps took out a printed agreement and laid it in front of him.

'Sign here and here. Very good. Now please, I think it's time you left.'

Revenge felt sweet to Jack Phelps. He might never have got the better of James Chase, but he'd certainly screwed his brother.

Wyatt ran his eyes over the woman in the too-short skirt at a nearby table in the crowded restaurant.

'So,' he said, 'now I get to be paid out in full for my share of Chase Racing.'

An uncertain smile crossed Danny's face.

'As stipulated in my father's will,' Wyatt continued.

Danny nervously pulled out an envelope and handed it to Wyatt, who tore it open.

'Fuck! What's this, a joke?'

'Wyatt, we're bankrupt.' Danny blurted out what he'd been too scared to say during lunch. 'The company was over a million pounds in debt. Jack Phelps bought out Carvalho last week and cancelled the sponsorship deal with Sartori. I couldn't carry the debt over, I had to sell. I've never been any good with money. Our creditors would have annihilated us –

they'd have taken you alone for over a quarter of a million. This way, at least you get something.'

'Fifty thousand pounds. The French team want at least two hundred thousand if I'm to get a drive with them. Fifty thousand? Are you crazy?'

'That's all Phelps gave me.'

'Phelps . . . You sold out to Jack Phelps! Carlos would have lent us the money. Why didn't you ask him?'

'Oh God, Wyatt, I couldn't . . .'

He watched Wyatt's hands open and close against the tablecloth.

'You jerk,' Wyatt said.

Danny got up. 'Don't you understand, I'm ruined.'

Wyatt remained seated and looked up at his uncle with contempt. 'Leave me alone. Just get out of here.'

Danny sat in the darkened room and listened to the sounds of the traffic. He felt totally alone.

Wyatt could at least have appreciated the fact that he'd saved him from debt . . .

He eased the service revolver out of the top drawer and laid it on the desk top. Then he pulled out a piece of paper, switched on the lamp and began to write.

It took him a while, and then he sat back, tears running from his eyes. All he'd wanted was a bit of bloody sympathy. Wyatt might as well have kicked him in the balls.

He picked up the revolver, eased back the hammer, pushed the muzzle into his upper palate and squeezed the trigger.

Wyatt felt almost as devastated as when his father had died. The emptiness was the worst part of it.

Perhaps he should have gone easier on Danny. But he'd been furious, he'd just never thought Danny would take it that badly. He couldn't help over-reacting in the restaurant – he'd been banking on the money from the business. With that money, he had calculated that he could buy a drive in the French team.

Formula One racing was expensive, and for the top five teams with the biggest sponsors, money was in plentiful

30

supply. But the other teams fought a continuous battle to raise enough cash to run their operation. If you had shown talent and were prepared to pay a substantial sum of money for the privilege, you could buy a drive with a team that was desperate for cash.

Wyatt knew it would only take him a year to prove his worth. But now that option was closed. He could not afford to buy the drive. He could not borrow money from his stepfather, his mother would never allow Carlos to support Wyatt in the sport she hated so much.

His chances of getting a drive in Formula One now looked about zero. Perhaps the lawyer facing him across the desk might turn the tables on Jack Phelps and get him his rightful inheritance.

John Farqharson, QC, took off his reading-glasses and stared at the powerfully built man opposite him. He'd watched James Chase win at Monaco – he'd respected the man for his talent and his friendship. James's death had come as a shock. Now, over ten years later, he was only too glad to offer assistance to his son.

Wyatt, he reflected, might not look like his father but he had the same strength of character. John drew in a deep breath, for what he had to say was not particularly pleasant.

'Wyatt. First, you mustn't blame yourself for Danny's suicide. I'm sorry, I understand how you feel, but it was his decision to take his life. And as to the other matter . . .

'Frankly, you'd be throwing good money after bad. A cursory investigation reveals that under your uncle's management Chase Racing was close to bankruptcy for years. If it hadn't been Phelps, it would have been someone else.'

Wyatt nodded grimly and rose. 'Thank you for your time, John.'

'Wyatt, a word of advice. You're well clear of Phelps, he's not a pleasant fellow. You're like your father – I know you'll make it.'

When Wyatt left the Inns of Court, the sky was overcast and a light drizzle was falling. He thought of all the times his uncle had been with him during his childhood. If only he'd known how Danny was feeling inside. His father must have known the weaknesses in Danny's character, that was why he'd always helped him.

First his father's death, now his uncle's. And he had been instrumental in both. It didn't bear thinking about.

He took lunch at a nearby pub and then caught a cab to the cemetery.

Wyatt nodded to a few close friends, then joined the pall-bearers at the hearse. He hadn't gone to the burial service: the stark ritual appalled him – and he didn't need to be reminded of his father's death.

The coffin was heavy. Danny had been a big man, but a weak one. Suicide, as far as Wyatt was concerned, was the coward's way out; everything in his own life had driven him to confront danger, not to avoid it.

It wasn't a long walk to the grave and he felt relieved when they let the coffin into the ground. The priest gave a brief service and then Estelle took the spade and threw the first sods over the oak case.

Wyatt stared at her. It was hard to believe she was his mother. She might be in her late forties, but she had the face and figure of a young woman. She was here on her own – Carlos wasn't with her.

She looked up and stared back at him – a hard, uncompromising stare. He couldn't resist his feeling for her, and walked over. He kissed her on both cheeks, but her look did not soften.

'Wyatt, why did you not come to the service?'

'I had business . . .'

'You are lying. You never tell me the truth.'

She stood very close to him, the long blonde hair falling across her perfect shoulders and the tailored black suit accentuating her curvaceous figure. He loved her. He hated what he had done to her by killing James in the accident.

Her blue eyes flashed, and she took his arm and guided him away from the rest of the party. He felt her strength, and he knew that she was as much a part of him as his father.

Behind some trees, she let go of his hand, then in a flash she raised her own, attempting to slap him hard across the

32

face. She didn't get near; he blocked her instinctively with a blow that bruised her forearm – an action that hurt him deep inside.

'*Merde*!' she spat. 'It is you who are responsible for this!'

'What do you mean?'

"'E left a note for me. 'E said you treated him like a dog and he was ashamed.'

Her throaty voice tore at him. 'It's not my fault that he was a failure,' he said defensively.

"'E loved you. 'E kept that team for you. You broke him, saying those things!'

Wyatt felt terrible, but contrived to appear cold and unmoved, unable to display the deep emotion he felt inside.

'And what did you think I felt,' he said, 'when you accused me of killing Father? How do you think I felt?'

She stood her ground. Most women were afraid of him when he was angry, but she was different, she always had been.

'You are strong, Wyatt. But you should have cared. Don't lie to yourself. You killed Danny with your words, as you killed James with your driving.'

Wyatt gripped her arms and drew her to him. He wanted her to say that she cared for him. Deep down, he still hurt from the things she'd said over ten years before.

'It was an accident.' He enunciated each word bitterly.

'You were driving too fast. That's what the police said.'

He let go of her hands, breathing deeply. 'You can't really blame me for Danny's suicide?'

'My God, Wyatt, do you think I am a fool? I can guess what you said to him. Don't you understand, he was no match for Jack Phelps. He was just trying to do his best for you, as he always did. Danny loved you!'

'I know, but I couldn't forgive him for wrecking the business.'

'He wanted you to stay with him, help build it up again.'

'I need to win. Chase Racing was losing.'

'Oh, it is so simple for you, is it not? There are winners and losers. It's just bad luck if you happen to be a loser . . .'

'I wanted a competitive drive, not a lame dog.'

'Is this the way they taught you to behave in Japan?'

He turned away from her and walked into the trees. He'd had enough.

She called after him. 'Wyatt, you're not a man. You don't have any feelings. I don't want to see you again unless you can learn to feel.'

The rain began to fall. A chapter of his life was closed for ever.

Sunday January 6th,
Bogota, Colombia

From the shelter of the doorway, Kruger watched the front doors of the church and glanced down at his wrist-watch. Nine o'clock. The bastard should be coming out any moment now.

He drew up the zip on the black windcheater and watched the vapour rise as his breath hit the cold air. His right hand felt inside the airways carry-bag that hung from his shoulder and touched the ice-cold metal of the barrel of the Browning Hi-Power.

Across the road, near the doors of the church, stood one of Ortega's two bodyguards – smart suit, dark glasses, and an Uzi carbine in his hands. A faint smile crossed Kruger's face. This was better than he had hoped for: he had been briefed to pull off a stylish job, but this was going to be good fun. 'Arsehole,' he said very quietly as he looked over at the other bodyguard, who was waiting in a doorway to his left.

In his ear, the tiny hearing-aid crackled. 'We're ready for him.'

Kruger smiled again. Two other men besides himself were to assist in the assassination; both were on the rooftops and armed with untraceable South African-made R4 assault rifles. Good men.

A woman walked past, a tiny child following her.

'Get out the fucking way . . .' Kruger willed them on, out of the killing-field. He had to admit it was fucking dangerous. But that was the brief – to hit the bastard close to home. There was no questioning this kill, it was logical and correct. This man deserved to be terminated, along with all the vermin who worked for him.

It gave Kruger satisfaction that few of the professionals would have taken this job. Ortega was dangerous. Kruger

knew that even if he killed him, Ortega's men would exact
their revenge on whoever had dared to take his life.

The church door opened and the smile went from Kruger's
face. The headphones crackled into life.

'Condition red.'

His hand closed around the butt of the pistol and he started
to drop down very slowly, ready to sprint. Other men would
have used a rifle or a machine-gun, but Kruger preferred a
pistol. He liked to get in close, to deliver what he defined as a
guaranteed termination.

First out of the church were the women and children; the
men would be talking to each other inside. The sound of the
church bells filled the air, and for a moment Kruger was
reminded of his own childhood, the lonely farm and the little
close-knit town.

Ortega was coming out, flanked by his wife and two other
women. Shit.

Kruger knew it was now or never. His two assistants were
ready to open fire the moment he gave the command.

'Go!' he screamed into the microphone concealed in the
lapel of his windcheater.

He pushed his feet hard against the tarmac, every nerve in
his body keyed up. He saw the bodyguard across the road
clutch at his chest and crumple to the ground – he couldn't see
the other one, but guessed he'd gone the same way.

The women were parting, he was closing, drawing, levelling,
seeing the fear in Ortega's eyes. Ortega's wife was coming
across his line of fire, silly bitch.

Crack.

Ortega's wife's face erupting in blood . . .

Crack.

The woman collapsing . . . Ortega reaching for his hand-
gun . . .

Crack.

Ortega clutching at his chest . . .

Crack. Crack. Crack.

Ortega dead.

Kruger felt coherent thought return as he sprinted behind

36

the church and onto the waiting motorcycle-scrambler. He smelt the fresh air. It was over.

Half an hour later a car drew up outside the back door of the church. The door opened cautiously and a man slipped out, darting into the back seat of the car. He whispered a command to the driver, who pulled away very slowly.

The man dropped down below the level of the window, and cursed silently. It had been planned so carefully, but of course they'd had to take the risk with his wife. It wouldn't have looked authentic unless she'd been there.

Ortega grunted. He was now officially 'dead', the price had been his wife's life and the life of the actor who'd impersonated him. Still, it had been a small price to pay. Now he, Emerson Ortega, owner of the biggest drug cartel in South America and perhaps one of the wealthiest men in the world, was free from persecution by the CIA. His wife's life – a small price to pay for such security. And the actor, well, he'd earned his fee.

February

Wyatt read the headline in a rage. 'Jack Phelps Set To Inject Power Into Chase Racing!' Phelps had really put one over Danny. And now Wyatt was sitting without a drive in Formula One, and with a pittance of a pay-out for his share.

He could not get a drive. He'd knocked on every door, but without money in his pocket, no one was interested. He'd have to go into Formula 3000 for a year – and that was a step backwards. The natural step up was a second year in Formula One. And he knew that a lot of people who made it in Formula 3000 never made it in Formula One. He didn't want to be one of those drivers. He'd be twenty-nine next year, he hadn't got time to play around.

Wyatt knew he could win the Formula One championship. He'd already proved he could finish in a totally uncompetitive and unreliable machine. He'd even won one Grand Prix in it.

He wondered who Phelps would choose as the new team manager – Danny had traditionally taken that role, though with a hands-off approach that appalled most people. He just wasn't around when decisions needed to be taken, or if he was available, he spent hours deliberating over a decision that needed to be made in seconds. Jack Phelps had said he was determined that the team would win the championship, so he'd be looking for a manager who was one of the top men in the business.

Phelps had already strafed the staff at Chase Racing, firing nearly seventy per cent of them. He was clearly intent on gearing up with the best people money could buy.

Bruce de Villiers sat in the back of the restaurant, sipping a glass of red wine. He looked through the letter again and stared across at the room, a faraway look on his face. It was a hard face that gave little away; clean-shaven, the skin slightly pitted, so that he looked his age – forty-three. His brown-blond hair was tousled unevenly across his forehead even though he had made every effort to comb it back. The hand that held the glass of wine was scarred and strong.

He had come a long, long way since he had worked as Reg Tillson's assistant at Chase Racing. He remembered those years well, and the way he'd pushed himself to the top of the Formula One ladder.

His hazel eyes scanned the typewritten pages for a third time. It was time to break off his contract with McCabe. He was the manager of the winning Formula One team – but that was all he was. He didn't have complete control of the operation; he didn't have a shareholding in the company – all he got was a salary plus incentive payments. He knew he could get a better deal.

He raised his eyes and thumped the table so that the china rattled. Several people looked round, and a waiter was over in seconds. Bruce de Villiers liked things done properly and bad service was something that really annoyed him.

'Another glass of wine, man.'

He looked down again at the letter. It was more than words on a flimsy piece of paper, it was a step into the unknown.

There was a typing error on the fourth page. It irritated him. Bruce de Villiers, for all his apparent lack of sophistication, was, and always would be, a perfectionist. He looked up again and saw a minor commotion at the entrance to the restaurant.

Bruce watched Jack Phelps as he swept past the tables. Phelps had the sort of face you knew you'd seen before, a strong face, with partially greying hair that came far down the forehead and was then swept slickly back. He was immaculately groomed in a hand-tailored double-breasted suit. Though he was over six foot six, it was his face, not his height that left the lasting impression – a face that reflected formidable determination and, above all, power.

Phelps's eyes locked on Bruce's. 'Bruce, how are you?'

'Good to see you, Jack.'

They shook hands and Bruce measured the American's grip. In his native South Africa the handshake was a subtle test of a man's virility and will-power. Phelps passed the assessment with flying colours. He remembered Phelps from Chase Racing, ten years before, but the man had changed with success; he was more confident now.

They exchanged pleasantries and ordered lunch. It was only over dessert that Phelps leaned in a little closer and got down to business.

He knew de Villiers was a different animal from himself. He had grown up on a wine farm in the Cape – an ambitious young man who wanted more than to inherit the farm that had been in his family since the eighteenth century. Phelps had decided that the only way to deal with de Villiers was to put his cards on the table. The man had to trust him, they had to work as a team. There wouldn't be much time: de Villiers would be under great pressure from the moment they signed an agreement.

The coffee arrived and Jack poured for both of them. His attention was caught by de Villiers' hands and arms, and de Villiers noticed.

'I started fixing tractors at the vineyard,' he said, smiling. 'Then it was racing-cars at the weekends. My father used to beat me when I went to the races. But man, once the grease gets into your skin it never really gets out.'

'How did you get into Formula One?'

'I wanted to be a driver. I still want to be a driver. But you know, there's always this little voice telling me I'm not good enough. I won some minor events in South Africa, but I realised I was better at making racing-cars, so I thought, if I can't be in the driver's seat, at least I can set up his car. I came here to England because that's the centre of Formula One.'

'So you became a Grand Prix mechanic – Reg's number two at Chase Racing . . .'

'*Ja*. And then I found that people came to respect me. They listened when I gave advice.'

Phelps had read a lot about de Villiers, about how the rough accent and behaviour concealed a sharp mind that missed nothing. It was de Villiers' fanatical attention to detail, and

40

his ability to manage people, that made him the best Formula One manager in the business.

'Jack, my man, I must make one thing perfectly clear to you. I'm only in this business to win.'

Jack laid his immaculately manicured hands on the tablecloth.

'You are a very direct guy, Bruce. I like that. You know much about me?'

'You've always been into racing – you sponsored Chase the last time I worked with you. You own the world's biggest tobacco company.'

Jack took a sip from his coffee and stared at a passing London taxi. How things had changed, he reflected.

'I started with nothing,' he said quietly. 'No education, no money. I vowed that I'd never be poor again, that men would respect me for myself. I, like you, Bruce, enjoy winning. I have never failed, and I will not tolerate failure. I want to win in our first season. No, not one race. The whole championship.'

Bruce watched Phelps. He had to trust this man. He had to be sure that Phelps was totally committed to his Formula One venture.

'So you'll keep pumping in the cash?'

'Whatever it takes to win, Bruce.'

Bruce felt a charge of excitement surge through him. This was the opportunity of a lifetime – more than that, it was a chance to be his own man. Then his heart plummeted. There was his contract with McCabe. He was locked in for the next three years.

'Listen, man. I've got commitments to McCabe.'

Jack held up his hands and smiled.

'Commitments are made to be broken. I want the best, and you are the best.'

Bruce stared at him, weighing him up. 'What are you saying?'

'I will buy out your contract – and you will owe me nothing except your determination to win the championship. You'll earn twice what you're getting with McCabe and you'll get twenty per cent equity in the team.'

41

Bruce whistled softly. Phelps didn't mess around.

'You have a deal, man.'

The stretch-limo pulled up alongside the huge New York office tower. The chauffeur stepped out and moved quickly round to open the rear door, then stood to attention.

Jack Phelps stepped out, not even looking at the chauffeur. His eyes were shielded by a pair of dark glasses. Irritated, he glanced down at his Piaget watch, then dismissed the chauffeur with a wave of his hand, and strode towards Phelps Plaza. Several pedestrians had to get rapidly out of his way: no one ever stood in Jack Phelps's path.

The doors to the office tower opened automatically as he approached them, and a smartly dressed negro in a white suit stepped forward.

'They're waiting for you on the top floor, Mr Phelps, sir.'

'Is everyone present, Royston?'

'Yes, sir.'

'You will make sure that we are not interrupted?'

'Yes, sir.'

Royston opened the door to the private lift and, with relief, watched Phelps disappear into it.

In the twenty years Royston had worked for Phelps he had learned to both respect and fear him. Phelps, he reflected, was like a bull-terrier: vicious – all six feet six inches of him. He kept very fit, and always cut an imposing figure in impeccable clothes. His smooth, dark, slightly greying hair was combed sharply back, exposing a definite widow's peak and heavy dark eyebrows. The lips were thin and defiant, the nose a shade too large, the jawline ruthlessly straight. Women, Royston had noticed, found him irresistible . . .

Phelps looked at himself in the lift mirror. Not a hair out of place, the way he liked to look. The pressure didn't show on his face, that was good. The problems in the Middle East, and the worsening United States economy hadn't been good for business; then there was that British journalist bitch, Vanessa Tyson, with her damning report on smoking. On top of that, his company was being sued in three different court cases for the effects of secondary smoking. Phelps's empire, Phelps Co., was in serious trouble. He'd been diversifying out of the tobacco business and had made many new acquisitions, all of which he intended to underwrite through new share issues. Now Phelps Co. shares were trading at an all-time low, and there was no way the market would support a new issue.

He wiped his forehead with a silk handkerchief. It was always the same, a tough fight to stay on top. But he had the means to stay in the market, a way of raising vast amounts of cash, quickly and efficiently.

And now everything was in place for the development of a much larger operation, one with enormous potential. He took a deep breath and prepared for action . . .

In the foyer Royston watched the light flash, indicating that the lift had reached the top floor. Royston reflected that while Phelps could charm anyone, he could also destroy them.

Royston turned the key in the control panel and stood rock-solid next to the lift doors. As usual, Phelps had made quite sure that he was totally in control of the situation.

Phelps stepped out of the lift on the fiftieth floor and stared across at the brunette in the dark suit.

'Lauren, is everything in order?'

'Yes, sir. They're waiting for you.'

He stared for a moment at her muscular legs sheathed in black nylon, then replied, 'Make sure that the whole discussion is recorded.'

'Naturally, sir. Is there anything else you require?'

'That will be all.'

He walked past her and through the black lacquered doors that led into the private conference room. There was a heated discussion in progress around the big black table. It stopped the moment he entered.

He waited a few moments in the doorway, looking up and down the lines of faces, making eye-contact with everyone, enjoying the chilling quietness. Yes, they were all afraid. He closed the doors behind him and took his place at the head of the table. He scanned the faces once more. Royston was correct, they were all there.

His eyes wandered around the room. Everything was black.

The walls had been specially prepared to his instructions: smeared in epoxy resin, they had been sprayed with tiny chips of black glass, so that the end result was a dark surface that sparkled in the intense light which illuminated the boardroom table. The table itself was a long oval of black marble. The room was designed to make people feel uneasy.

'I've called you here because I'm angry,' Phelps said quietly.

A few of the men shifted uneasily in their chairs, and he waited a moment. Good. Let them worry that they might lose their coveted positions. Divide and rule was his *modus operandi*. No man who worked for him could ever feel secure.

'This is one of the biggest operations in the world. We are known, we are respected, and above all, we are feared. But lately the distribution of our products has not been properly handled.'

A thick-set, grey-haired man wearing dark-tinted glasses raised his hand to object.

'Shut it, Ambrose. I know, you were going to give me a pathetic excuse. And I know what it is before you make it!'

Ambrose fidgeted nervously with a pen, not daring to make eye contact with Phelps.

Phelps said: 'Get out.'

'But, Jack, you're being unreasonable.'

Phelps hated Ambrose's strong southern accent. He found the long-drawn-out vowels intensely irritating.

'I said that you would come here to listen to me. You dare to try and speak, to make some pathetic excuse for your failure. Then you sit here twiddling your thumbs. Distribution was your baby, Ambrose. Well, you fucked it up. Get out!'

Ambrose got up and walked out through the double doors, his shoulders hunched forwards. The doors closed behind him. Phelps waited for a moment, letting the fear take hold of everyone at the table.

At last he said: 'I will personally handle distribution for the next year. I will show you how it can be achieved faultlessly, without problems. At the same time I will examine each of your areas of operation. If any of you are found lacking you will follow Ambrose.'

*

Phil Ambrose staggered towards the lift, his hands shaking. He noticed that Lauren was standing in front of the lift doors.

'Mr Ambrose?'

'I wanna leave, Lauren.'

'The lift is locked till the end of the session.'

'Jesus Christ!'

Ambrose had to wait for over an hour. Finally, the doors of the conference room opened and Phelps walked out. He ignored Ambrose and walked straight to the lift. As he was about to get in, he turned to Ambrose.

'You will wait till everyone else has gone. I don't want you holding up company business.'

'You're not gonna get away with this, Jack. I know things about yew . . .'

Phelps turned his back on Ambrose and got into the lift. The other men waited in the lobby. It was a rule that no one moved till Phelps had left the building, a rule that was never questioned.

Ambrose found his office stripped. Sitting outside was a new secretary in place of his own. He stared hard at her.

'Where are my things?'

'They've been trashed,' she replied with a sly smile.

'I demand to see . . .'

Two security men approached from the passage. 'Sir, you must leave the building.'

The secretary held her smile.

Ambrose made to resist, and the larger of the two men gripped his arms firmly.

'Out, sir. Now.'

A few minutes later he staggered out of the revolving doors of Phelps Plaza and took one final look up at its mirrored walls. Then he began to calculate how he'd get his revenge. He did not see a tall, blond man drop into step behind him.

Yes, with the things he knew about Phelps, he could cause a lot of trouble. Big trouble.

The light turned to green and he stepped off the pavement.

He never saw the car coming fast from the side-street, but he felt the punch that hammered into his back, and staggered forwards. As far as the watching pedestrians were concerned, he walked right into the speeding car.

The Pan American jet touched down at Narita airport in Tokyo at nineteen hundred hours. Aito Shensu, owner and founder of Shensu, one of Japan's biggest car manufacturers, stood on the tarmac waiting for the first-class passengers to disembark. He was dressed simply but expensively in a hand-tailored dark suit. He hated to admit it, but he was nervous. He didn't have much time. The deal that Phelps had proposed had to go through.

Aito Shensu was of medium build, with a lean, athletic body. His smooth skin and chiselled features gave him the appearance of a man in his early fifties, though in reality he was over seventy. He stood straight and moved determinedly.

As he caught sight of his distinguished visitor, his mouth broke into a smile, revealing his pearl-white teeth. He walked slowly across the tarmac, his two personal assistants trailing him, and stopped at the base of the gangway and stood at ease.

As Phelps walked down the steps, it struck Aito that he looked the typical American, well-groomed, tall and exuding confidence. Perhaps he looked a little like Richard Nixon?

'My pleasure, Mr Phelps.'

He bowed. Phelps followed suit – rather awkwardly. Aito knew how much he needed what this man had, but he did not want Phelps to realise this. Letting your competitors sense your weakness gave them an advantage – and for the moment Jack Phelps was competition.

'You will follow me please, Mr Phelps. Special arrangements have been made for your convenience. Please hand your belongings to my men. It is not correct that you should have to carry them.'

'As you say,' Phelps replied gruffly.

They walked briskly across the tarmac towards a section of the customs and were greeted courteously by the officials. Phelps showed his passport, its examination a mere formality, and his briefcase went through unexamined. Aito Shensu smiled at him yet again.

'I have informed the officials that you are a very important man. Jack Phelps, Tokyo welcomes you.'

Aito's English was faultless, with only a faint accent.

'I am most impressed by your welcome.'

'Now we travel to your hotel.'

Phelps felt better every minute. A relationship that had started six months ago, with a short phone conversation, had blossomed. Phelps was now confident of signing a deal with Shensu to co-sponsor a new Formula One racing team.

The benefits would be mutual. Jack wanted Shensu's technology – their engines and their design ability. He was offering a complete Formula One team in the UK, Chase Racing, and one of the world's greatest racing-drivers – Ricardo Sartori. He had just signed up Bruce de Villiers, the ex-manager of McCabe, whose team had won the driver's and constructor's championships for the last three seasons. As Jack knew, although the driver's championship was the one that the world really cared about, to the teams whose life was racing, the constructor's trophy was the highest accolade.

The prize for Jack was publicity for his cigarette brand, Calibre Lights – advertising that he couldn't buy for love or money elsewhere. It was also an opportunity for him to promote his latest acquisition, Carvalho, Brazil's largest tyre company. Carvalho was a rapidly expanding concern, and Phelps was determined both to challenge the international tyre giants who dominated Formula One, and to develop new markets.

For Aito Shensu, the benefits of the collaboration were clear-cut – the whole deal would be excellent publicity for Shensu, making it the world's leading motor manufacturer and the new driving force in the hotly contested world of Formula One.

And Jack had another ace in his pocket. He'd had long discussions with Alain Hugo of FISA, the world governing body of Formula One, and with Ronnie Halliday of FOCA, the Formula One Constructors' Association. Both men were deeply concerned at the way the McCabe team had dominated the previous season; audience levels were dropping, and sponsors were grumbling that the sport was becoming boring.

Both Hugo and Halliday were keen on Phelps's plan to challenge McCabe's dominance in the sport, and they sanctioned his buy-out of Chase Racing, its possible name-change, and the liaison with Shensu.

Aito Shensu ran his hand over the soft leather upholstery of the car they were now travelling in and looked directly, penetratingly, into Phelps's eyes.

'This is another Shensu product. Our finest. A worthy competitor for Mercedes-Benz, Rolls-Royce and BMW?'

'A worthy competitor. In fact, I have just ordered this model.'

Phelps was not lying. The Shensu Fuji was the car the world's toughest motoring critics could not stop talking about. At last, it was said, the Japanese had produced a luxury machine which surpassed the great European marques.

'Quality is all-important in our new venture. I would rather wait another year than go into Formula One with an uncompetitive team.'

'Yes. Naturally,' Phelps grunted. 'But you have no need for concern, I have the best of everything for you. Our tie-up will create a stir in the racing business. I can tell you that many teams are already apprehensive, even though our association is still only a rumour. I look forward to our partnership.'

'But first you must enjoy Tokyo.'

The car drew up outside the Okura, Tokyo's smartest hotel. Porters rushed from everywhere, vying for the chance to carry Phelps's luggage.

Aito Shensu bowed deferentially to him. 'I will give you a few hours to freshen up. Then we will paint the town red?'

Phelps smiled enigmatically, and Aito frowned. 'Did I say something wrong?'

'No. It's just that it's an English expression. I'm sure there's a better Japanese saying.'

'Ah. Let the evening be proof of that.'

'Well, I only wish I could speak Japanese as well as you speak English.'

'You do me a great honour. I will return at eight.'

As Phelps went up in the lift, he noticed the absence of a fourth floor. He knew from his researches that in Japanese the

48

number 'four' was pronounced in the same way as the word 'death', and was therefore considered unlucky. Thus buildings never had a fourth floor, and sets of anything like pens or teacups never came in fours.

He went to his room, took a quick shower, and then opened his suitcase. He took out a variety of pills and liquid concoctions, downed a selection of these and then lay down on the bed to sleep. He set his alarm clock for seven forty-five.

He was dressed and ready when he received a call at seven fifty-nine to say that Mr Shensu was waiting for him in reception.

As he'd expected, Shensu was wearing a different suit.

'*Ohaiyo gozaimasa, Aito-san*. Good day Aito,' Phelps greeted him.

'*Anato no nihongo ga jozu desune*. Your Japanese is very good,' Aito replied. It wasn't. Aito was just being a polite, well-mannered Japanese.

Phelps stared into his dark eyes and tried to find the reality behind the mask. He wasn't rewarded with even the smallest clue.

A chauffeur drove them away from the hotel in a Shensu limousine. First they went to the Caffe Bongo, a surrealist café on the ground floor of the store Parco. Jack stared at the bizarre combination of architectural styles, from minimalist to classical; above him was suspended a silver aeroplane wing and an engine. He was offered a baffling array of drinks and was surprised by how much alcohol Aito consumed.

There was a war of wills taking place. Aito watched with amusement as Jack tried to match him drink for drink. He knew from past experience that no Westerner could match his capacity for alcohol. It was an advantage he had used on many occasions to weaken the tongue of a prospective *gaijin* client.

From the Caffe Bongo they drove to Shiruyoshi, a restaurant with a reputation for serving first-class Japanese food in a distinctly Western atmosphere that appealed to tourists and foreign businessmen like Jack Phelps. They enjoyed *tempura* and *kaiseki* with a bottle of saki, from which Aito drank steadily. The dark eyes never lost their intensity.

At the end of the meal Jack was feeling unsteady on his feet. He could hardly credit the amount of alcohol Aito had consumed, without any apparent effect.

'Now for some real entertainment, Jack.'

Their next stop was a very, very exclusive club. As Jack had expected, the hostesses were beautiful, but he was wise to the ways of Japanese business and knew he would need all his energy and all his wits about him for the next few days of intense negotiation.

'Aito, I am tired after my flight.'

'I am a bad host. I apologise. We'll go back to your hotel.'

Round one to me, thought Jack. He knew the routine: drunk and sated, he would have talked, maybe a little too freely, to one of the girls. His revelations would then immediately have been reported to Aito Shensu. On his own territory he would have enjoyed one of these women, but here he was on dangerous ground and the stakes were high. He needed this deal far more than Aito – and he certainly didn't want the astute Japanese magnate to know that . . .

He collapsed on his bed at three that morning. Aito would collect him at seven. He downed some more pills and prepared himself for another brief sleep.

The next day was an intense and exhausting series of meetings with different members of Shensu's senior management team. Jack was impressed by the research and development that had already gone into Shensu's Formula One programme; the engines and gearboxes had been thoroughly tested. He wondered just how hard Aito Shensu would be when the time came to negotiate the deal.

Aito Shensu sat in his office, poring over a long series of reports on Phelps Co.. However, more interesting by far was the story of Jack Phelps himself. The man was the very essence of the American dream – a boy from Brooklyn who had made good in the motor spares business, eventually listing his company on the stock exchange and embarking on a meteoric succession of mergers and takeovers. There was no doubting Phelps's financial credentials – though the current low trading price of Phelps Co. shares was of some concern. As to Phelps's own personal financial health, Aito could not access any information.

Phelps had never married, but had courted most of New York's society beauties as well as a few film stars. This might explain his lack of interest in the women the previous evening, Aito reasoned. Clearly, a man who could have his pick of that sort of woman would not be interested in such entertainment.

The rest of Jack Phelps's life was shrouded in mystery. He only kept a few loyal men close to him, and they could not be bought. His passion for motor-racing had started at an early age when he had competed in his own machine on the American circuit. After that came his Formula One sponsorship in the seventies under the Calibre brand.

There was more to Jack Phelps than these papers could tell him, of that Aito Shensu was certain.

There was a knock at his office door and his secretary came in. 'Mr Mishima wishes to see you.'

'In five minutes.'

Once his secretary had left, Aito rose from his desk and walked through a door at the back of his office. He entered a mirrored walk-in cupbard that led through to an *en suite* bathroom. The cupboard contained many different outfits, and Aito now changed out of his elegant suit and into one that was identical, but slighly more worn-looking. He also changed his tie for a less distinguished one, and his glasses for an older pair. Thus dressed, he returned to his desk and pushed the intercom buzzer.

Mr Mishima entered the office and bowed low. He was a short, bald man who in some ways resembled the great humanist, Ghandi. The perfect employee, reflected Aito; a man whose loyalty he would never question.

Aito bowed slightly, then gestured for Mishima to sit down at his desk. 'How is he?' he asked.

'This American giant does not tire,' Mishima said.

'Take him to the research and development centre. Then take him to dinner with the development team. I want him to know just how far our development of the Formula One engine has progressed. But do not mention our design link-up or the progress we have made in that direction. Tell him I will see him at his hotel at six tomorrow morning.'

'Very good, sir.'

When Mishima had left, Aito Shensu leant back in his chair and let his mind wander. He would dearly have liked to run the team on his own, but Shensu was a public company and he was accountable to his shareholders and his board of directors. From his investigations he realised that the top teams in Formula One operated on unlimited budgets, and to embark on such a venture alone would be considered extravagant by his board, especially when rival Japanese manufacturers had already proved they could work successfully with European teams.

Shensu had already invested a small fortune on the development of an engine chassis and gearbox. By going to the board with another partner to shoulder the burden of further research, he would have more funds available to compete at the top end of Formula One.

Phelps would be totally exhausted by the time they came to tie up the deal. Aito planned to structure it with maximum benefit to Shensu . . . Yes, everything was proceeding as he'd planned.

Jack was more and more excited by what he saw. After inspecting Shensu's engine development facility he was pretty sure that it must be amongst the finest in the world. He also knew that this was Shensu's tenth year of building racing engines, but that they had never competed outside Japan.

The test area looked like a high-technology cathedral – a huge, airy room with gigantic stainless-steel pillars soaring upwards to a glass roof. Shafts of sunlight shone down onto a podium that looked like an altar. Noise reverberated through the room, more like a spiritual chant than the sound of machinery.

The glass and metal reflected the sunlight, creating a rainbow of grey and silver colours that seemed to flash before his eyes. The size of it, the financial investment it represented, took Jack's breath away. He had to have these engines.

There were ten on test, all V12s of 3500 cc capacity,

thundering away without a break. These units were forced to perform under the same loading and changing revs as an engine in a Formula One Grand Prix. A bank of computers transmitted information so that each engine was loaded and stressed appropriately.

If an engine broke down, it would be taken to the research centre and replaced with another one, all vital information having been recorded on computer. The goal was single minded – to produce the most powerful, most reliable Grand Prix engine ever.

After an hour, Phelps felt his concentration beginning to lag. He was pleased to see Mr Mishima walking swiftly towards him through the pools of sunlight, past the line of thundering engines.

'Thank you. Very impressive,' he said enthusiastically. 'Now I must return to my hotel.'

Mishima gazed across at him, exuding an almost missionary zeal. 'But Mr Phelps, a meeting has been arranged for you with our director of research. He is honoured to tell you that this will be followed by dinner.'

Phelps finally made it back to his room at half past two that morning and collapsed on the bed. He had never met people who could drink so much at a sitting. However, everything was going as anticipated, he reflected, as he dropped off into a deep sleep.

He awoke at five thirty and took a cold shower. He had no doubt that Aito would be at the hotel to collect him at six on the dot.

As he towelled himself down, he reread the details on his air ticket, just to make sure. Yes, everything was in order.

He dressed and waited. There was no call at six. He smiled. Aito was really cutting it fine.

Finally, at ten past seven, there was a call for him. He picked up the phone. Aito was waiting for him in reception. He took the lift down and prepared himself to look as agitated as possible.

'A thousand apologies, Jack. I was delayed in the traffic.'

Jack glared at Aito, reflecting, he hoped, a suitable level of irritation. 'My plane leaves at nine!'

'Don't worry. I have the agreement in my car. It is essentially the same as the one you drew up, with a few minor changes. You can check them on the way to the airport.'

'My bags?'

'They are being collected from your room. Shall we go to my car? We can discuss the final aspects of the contract on the way to the airport. Then you can sign.'

Once they were inside the comfortable confines of the car, Aito handed him the agreement – over two hundred pages of it.

'I have highlighted the important sections for you, Jack.'

'I haven't got time to read the whole thing.'

'It's not necessary, there are only minor changes.'

Jack read the beginning of the document very carefully. He circled anything that he found difficult to interpret, or unacceptable. He admired the way that Aito had had the whole thing carefully restructured – but some of the clauses were now a little too much in Shensu's favour for his liking.

The car was almost at Narita airport. Jack glanced across at the digital clock in the centre of the dashboard.

'Relax, Jack. Just read the relevant sections, then sign. I need to have the agreement for a crucial board meeting tomorrow morning. Otherwise, I do not know if we will make our deal before the season begins – then it will be another year . . .'

Jack ignored this and returned his attention to the agreement. Everything else ceased to be important to him, only the printed words mattered. This was what he enjoyed – playing out a deal. He admired Aito Shensu's artistry. Nothing particularly wrong with the agreement, just that it slanted all the advantages to the Japanese company.

He felt the car draw up, heard the noise of the arrivals hall. Did not look up but carried on reading.

'You'll miss your plane,' Aito whispered.

'I'll miss my plane.'

A faint smile crossed Jack's lips. He continued reading, sensing Aito's surprise.

'You wish to return to the hotel, Jack?'

'No, let's go to your offices. As you said, your board meeting's tomorrow and we have to be in agreement on this. I'm sure we can have it ready for then,' Jack said, his eyes still on the document.

The section on sponsorship was particularly interesting. The present structure of the agreement would leave him with little say in how the team was run. He ringed the whole section . . .

He finished his reading in Aito's office at half past ten. He turned to his host.

'In principle I agree with what's here. But I want far more say in the running of the team, and I also want to discuss the ambiguities that I have ringed. Once all that's resolved, I'll sign.'

'You will not sign now?'

'No. I will fax certain sections to my lawyers in New York, and they can work on them immediately. We can discuss the sponsorship section while that's being done.'

'But Jack, that will take days.'

'No, it can be done in twenty-four hours. Your secretary can fax my lawyers immediately. In the meantime, perhaps you can arrange a few more tours and dinners for me?'

Aito chuckled. When he turned to Jack, his face had lost every trace of oriental inscrutability.

'I see I have chosen a worthy partner in Formula One!'

Now they could get down to the hard facts of the business. There were only eighteen teams in Formula One. Jack owned one of them – Chase Racing, bought out from Danny and Wyatt Chase. He'd also bought Bruce de Villiers from McCabe, thus securing the best manager in the business. And through a separate deal he had Ricardo Sartori, the former world champion and that year's runner-up, signed up to drive for him in the next season.

Aito had Formula One engines and gearboxes that were ready to race. He had also done a lot of work on chassis and body design with a European consultant he refused to name to Jack.

They worked through the day and into the night, arguing

and negotiating. Chase Racing would lose its name, replaced by Calibre-Shensu. Phelps Co. would own forty per cent of the company, and get half of the surface area of the machine for Calibre Lights branding. Shensu badging would cover the rest of the machine. Shensu would also get a forty per cent shareholding, the other twenty per cent going to Bruce de Villiers.

They would appoint an independent consultancy to handle all the promotional work for their brands. The Shensu advertising account, worth five hundred million US dollars, would be handled by this consultancy, as would the Calibre Lights account. Phelps did not want any advertising agency involvement. There were people gunning for cigarette companies, and one of the main areas of attack was their advertising. If he wasn't seen to be advertising in the conventional sense, Jack reasoned, he would be safer from this kind of attack.

Aito insisted that he must have the final say on who the second driver would be. Jack argued this point for some time, then gave in. He realised that Aito might want a top Japanese driver in the seat of the number-two machine. He could understand that. Still, with Sartori in the number-one machine he didn't have anything to worry about.

They worked through the night, finally signing in the early hours of the morning.

Jack shook hands with Aito at the airport departure building.

'To winning, Jack.'

'To success, Aito.'

They bowed to each other, and parted.

Jack walked into the first-class lounge, well pleased. It was going to be a very profitable, very successful 1991.

Wyatt was awake at four in the morning. That was a ritual he had kept to since he was seventeen and had moved to Japan.

His house was part of a converted warehouse on the south bank of the Thames. The main room was enormous, with curving white walls that soared up to a vaulted roof of reinforced glass. The sprung wooden floor yielded as he walked across it to the bathroom. Everything was white, and he glanced out of the big picture window that filled one of the narrower walls, revealing a shadowy view of the Thames with the skyline of the city in the distance.

He followed the Japanese style. All the spare furniture in this room was against the walls, encircling the empty centre. The predominant motif through the house was circles. In Japanese decor, geometric mirroring and straight lines are practically non-existent; evil spirits, according to Shinto belief, travel in straight lines.

He stood for a moment, taking in the early-morning darkness and the silence. Then he looked up to where his Japanese water-colours hung on the high wall above him.

He took a scalding-hot shower, then turned the water on cold, feeling his body stiffen and resisting the urge to shiver. He stepped out and towelled himself dry. Then he slipped on the white robes, the *karate-gi*, tying them together with the black belt embroidered with the words of a language that was almost more familiar to him than English. That belt, signifying his status as a Seventh Dan, was the most valuable thing he owned. He had spent nearly ten years of his life earning it.

Then there came the moment he always savoured, the feeling of emptiness, the memories of the *dojo* in Tokyo and the *Shihan*, the supreme instructor.

He began with a series of warming-up exercises, then moved into heavier training for the next hour. After that came a session of punching against the *makiwara*, a long, sprung wooden plank fixed upright, its base planted in the floor. Then followed some work on a punch-bag that hung suspended from the rafters close to the window.

Then he performed a series of *katas*, formal movements against an imaginary opponent that focused the *karate-ka's* competitive and co-operative spirit. The swift, flowing movements were like a form of meditation to Wyatt, and his concentration never wavered.

At six he showered again, then changed into his favourite clothes, a black T-shirt and black cotton trousers. He made himself a simple breakfast and switched on the television for the morning news.

Through the procession of bulletins, he thought about his

fight up the racing ladder: the careful instructions he had received from his father; how he had won the British karting championship at fifteen; the travelling he had done with his mother and father, the glamour and excitement of it all.

Then the pain. The memories of the accident in Monaco. The turns of the steeply climbing road, the swift and determined gear-changes that took full advantage of the car's power in the corners . . .

But at that point the memories always faded, and the next thing he remembered was waking up in hospital, Estelle at the side of the bed, screaming hysterically as the doctor pulled her back.

He gripped the sides of his chair. The pain was still there, the words indelibly etched in his memory. *'You killed him! You killed him!'* And he had loved his father more than he loved anyone in the world. He still didn't understand what had happened on that lonely mountain road.

He thought of the German woman, Suzie, and the climb in Yosemite Valley, two months after the accident, when he'd made his decision to move to Japan. She had disappeared the day after the climb. He hadn't been able to find out any more about her, who she was or where she lived.

He left her memory behind and focused on the present. Now he was without a drive in Formula One. He had heard people saying he was past his prime – look at what he could have done if he was still in his early twenties.

Staying on with Chase in an unreliable machine for another year would have been a complete waste of time. But he had expected a lot of money from his uncle as a pay-out for his share in the team – enough money to buy him a drive with the French team. But he hadn't got the money and so he couldn't drive for them. He knew he was running out of time, and the frustration was getting to him.

He could go to the United States and compete on the NASCAR circuit. But that wasn't sport to him, going round in perfect ovals. He just wanted to drive in Formula One. And no one would give him a drive. No one would take him seriously since he'd driven for Danny's team.

Ricardo Sartori, the number one, had always got the better

machine. He'd nearly won the championship with it. And Wyatt had been far out of the points in what the outside world saw as essentially the same machine. Painful though it was, he had to admit that he was considered a has-been even though he'd won a Grand Prix in his first season.

The next item on the television news suddenly caught Wyatt's attention.

'Last month Jack Phelps, the American billionaire, bought out Chase Racing,' the newscaster said. 'This week, in a deal with Aito Shensu of the Shensu Motor Corporation and Bruce de Villiers, ex-manager of McCabe racing, Phelps formed Calibre-Shensu. The name Chase Racing will disappear.'

The picture cut to the headquarters of the Formula One Constructors' Association, with Ronnie Halliday, the president of FOCA, being interviewed.

'Yes,' he said. 'We're very pleased about this new team. I believe they will challenge the dominance of McCabe and Roger de Rosner. This move by Jack Phelps is welcomed by everyone in Formula One.'

The next picture was of Phelps, Shensu and de Villiers signing the agreement.

'This historic agreement was signed at Phelps Plaza in New York,' the newscaster announced. 'Phelps, Shensu and de Villiers are the founding members and shareholders in Calibre-Shensu, a formidable new force on the 1991 Grand Prix circuit. If the track record of any of these three men is anything to go by, Calibre-Shensu will be the team to watch in the coming season.'

The camera closed in on Bruce de Villiers, standing next to a reporter, and the interviewer asked: 'Bruce, how would you describe your involvement in this venture?'

De Villiers squared up in front of the camera. 'Look, I'm totally involved, totally committed. We are all very clear about our objectives in international Grand Prix racing. We want to win.'

'Isn't that being a bit optimistic on your first outing with a new team and a new engine?'

'Shensu have developed a superb V8 engine – we're already into our first week of development on a car.'

'But your old team, McCabe, has the best driver?'

'The best perceived driver. We have Ricardo Sartori, the former world champion. We're still looking for a second driver.'

Wyatt switched off the set. There was no doubt in his mind about what he had to do now.

The Lotus Super Seven, with a highly modified two-litre Ford Cosworth engine, shot down the narrow Buckinghamshire lanes at near suicidal speed.

Wyatt thought about Bruce de Villiers. The man was a fanatic. His meteoric career had nothing to do with luck and everything to do with determination. He had made McCabe the best Formula One team for five successive years. Wyatt was certain that Calibre-Shensu was going to be the new McCabe, and he wanted to be in on the team from the ground floor. This was his best chance – he knew de Villiers always got to work early.

He pulled off the tree-lined road and coasted down the tarmac drive. The memories came flooding back. He remembered his mother cutting the ribbon across this road; the sunlight filtering through the oak trees and his father smiling easily and talking to the reporters.

The old Chase Racing sign was gone. He felt a stab of bitterness that the last vestige of everything his father had built up had now been removed. But then he remembered the voice of his Japanese instructor, 'The greatest advances are made when, having accepted the tradition, you have the courage to break it.' Wyatt had severed his ties with the legacy his father had left him, but this place, the home of Chase Racing, was still a part of him.

The road dropped down and he looked out to see the building which had been designed in the early 1970s. It was typical of that time, with rough concrete finishes and lots of glass. His father had commissioned an American architect of considerable reputation to draw up the plans, and his wisdom was reflected in the fact that, nearly twenty years on, the building still looked impressive.

Behind the building was the test track, weaving its way in and out of the trees.

He pulled up in front of a set of high gates that blocked the road, flanked on each side by a wire security-fence. That was de Villiers' influence. A military-looking man with a neatly trimmed moustache and closely cropped grey hair stepped out. He straightened his black uniform and strode up to Wyatt's car, staring down at him.

''Morning, guvnor. Who are yer here to see?'

'Bruce de Villiers.'

'And your name is . . .?'

'Wyatt Chase.'

'Very good then, Mr Chase. Would yer mind fillin' in this form? I'll just check with Mr de Villiers that you've an appointment.'

He handed Wyatt a clipboard. Wyatt gripped his hand and stared into his eyes.

'I don't have an appointment and he wouldn't give me one if I asked for it.'

The man grinned. He leaned forwards and his voice softened.

'I know you. Weren't you driving as number two to Sartori last season? Your old man owned this place, didn't 'e?'

'Then my uncle was forced to sell.'

'Yes, I read all about it in the paper. I'm sorry about yer uncle.'

He waved Wyatt on. 'Good luck, Mr Chase.'

Wyatt pulled up outside the front entrance, his heart beating a little faster. This was a gamble and he knew it.

He guessed which office de Villiers would have taken – the one on the first floor with a sweeping view of the test track. He'd always liked that office. It had been his father's.

He walked up the stairs and was glad to see it was too early for de Villiers' secretary to be at her desk. One less obstacle to negotiate. Everything was neatly ordered, with no paper in evidence. Instead the desk was graced with the latest model of personal computer with a sophisticated laser printer. Again, hallmarks of de Villiers' style – to use the very best of what was available.

De Villiers' door was closed. Wyatt went up and rapped on it smartly.

'Come in,' a voice barked from inside.

Wyatt steeled himself. De Villiers raised his eyes from the computer monitor he'd been studying and looked up at him, then nodded his head.

'*Ja?*'

'I want the number two slot.'

'You've got a bloody cheek, Wyatt Chase. I haven't got time for inexperience. The answer's no. Get it? No.'

Wyatt took a deep breath. 'We think the same way. We want the same things. Give me a break.'

'Look, man, you don't listen, do you?' There was a menacing tone in de Villiers' voice now, but Wyatt ignored it.

'Danny never gave me a car that was competitive.'

Wyatt wanted in. He wanted de Villiers behind him, de Villiers' determination behind the cars he was racing.

'I buy results, not excuses,' de Villiers said. 'I'm not taking chances – that's why I'm not taking you.'

'Then who the fuck are you going to take?'

De Villiers rose up, his hands resting loosely at his side. 'I don't believe this,' he said, his hazel eyes narrowing.

'Let me help you develop your new car on the track while you're looking for a driver.'

'Get out!'

'Put my name on the list.'

De Villiers stared out over the track.

'You only get one chance in Formula One,' he said. 'You've had yours. Now get out!'

The door slammed shut and de Villiers punched in some more commands on the keyboard. Wyatt Chase had spirit, and that he admired. Yes, he needed a number two, but he needed a driver who had a string of wins under his belt, not just one freak victory. Chase was just too much of a gamble, and a little too old for a beginner.

He remembered his own parting from McCabe, two weeks before – telling the bastard he was resigning and seeing the surprise on his face. Then watching the surprise turn to anger as he told him he was leaving to start a new team. McCabe had attacked him immediately. 'You've got no chance, Bruce. It doesn't matter how much money there is behind you, you haven't got what it takes – you're not going to win.'

It was McCabe's smugness that had finally got to him. That McCabe didn't ask him to stay, that McCabe thought that without his backing, he'd fail. Well, he'd show McCabe.

The evening before, he'd spent four hours in heated discussion with Ricardo Sartori. Sartori had agreed to drive for Calibre-Shensu for what was probably the highest price ever paid for a driver – a cost that made Bruce shudder. But then he had realised: he wasn't working to a budget. There was only one objective – to win.

The phone rang. He snatched it up to hear his old employer, McCabe, on the other end of the line.

'You're a bastard, Bruce. Just listen to me. I'll give you your old job back and you'll have another year of winning. What's your answer?'

'I've got nothing to say.'

'After all our years together, you treacherous bastard.'

'Don't speak to me like that, man.'

'We had a contract. You broke it. I'll make your name dirt with FOCA and FISA.'

'I think you should concentrate on looking for a new manager,' Bruce said very softly.

'Go fuck yourself, de Villiers.'

The phone went dead.

Aito Shensu looked up from his desk as his personal assistant came into the office.

'Professor Katana wishes to speak with you.'

'He was not supposed to speak to me until Friday.'

'He said it was very important – that you would want to know about it.'

'Send him in, in five minutes.'

'Very good, sir.'

Aito waited until the door was closed, then got up to go to the dressing-room situated next to the bathroom suite at the side of his office. He rumpled his hair slightly, and replaced

63

his couturier suit with the official Shensu one. Shensu's corporate colours were black and white. Every Shensu factory worker wore a black and white overall, as did every member of the research team.

Katana's appointment to Shensu had been the result of an elaborate head-hunting exercise. Then professor of mechanical engineering at Tokyo University, Katana had been wooed to the company with the offer of developing a Formula One racing engine.

Aito adjusted his heavy, black-framed spectacles and then took his place behind his desk. A few moments later there was a knock at the door.

'Come in.'

Professor Katana bustled in through the door, a sheaf of papers stuffed under his left arm. A short, lean man who radiated energy, he was smiling from ear to ear.

They both bowed. Katana's sharp eyes, set in an ascetic face with perfectly proportioned features, probed Aito's face fearfully.

'Mr Shensu. I know we had a meeting scheduled for later in the week – but I had to see you.'

'It is always good to meet with you, professor. What is it?'

'First, the latest test results from the engine.' He handed Aito a sheet of printed figures. 'Just read this.'

Katana waited as Aito pored over the figures.

'You are sure they are correct?' Aito asked.

'I had them double-checked by three other engineers before I came to you, sir. I would not take up your time unless I thought it was of vital importance.'

He studied the figures more closely now – and felt his pulse racing. This was without doubt the finest racing engine ever to come out of Japan.

He stretched out his hand to Professor Katana. 'Well done. How is Dr Dunstal's project proceeding?'

'That is what I came to tell you about. He is already ahead of schedule.'

'Very good. It is time to begin testing in England.'

Professor Katana felt his spirits soar. Two years before, he had reduced his responsibilities at the university with some reluctance, in order to take on the Shensu project. At the time he had thought he might be making a big mistake: Mr Shensu's reputation for pushing people to the limit was legendary even in Japan, where most people lived to work.

Now all this was forgotten. The engine he had just developed would also be detuned and used in a road-going machine – a Japanese high-performance car that would usurp the great marques like Porsche and Ferrari.

He had enjoyed working with the mad Irishman, Dr Dunstal, whom Aito Shensu had brought out from Europe the year before under a veil of secrecy. Dr Dunstal had developed a chassis to match the engine and gearbox Katana had been perfecting.

Now he looked directly at Aito Shensu. 'Sir. Does Mr de Villiers know we have built the car as well as the engine and gearbox?'

'Not yet. It will be a pleasant surprise for him. I shall leave the revelation to Dr Dunstal – they are close friends.'

Bruce de Villiers was in a dark mood, seething with anxiety. It was less than two months to the start of the season. He could see himself missing the first couple of races while the car was still in the development stages.

At last Mickey Dunstal was free from his work in Japan and was here to see him. Mickey was the best there was – but two months was hardly enough time for him to develop a competitive car. The intercom on his desk sounded again, and he pushed the answer-button.

'Yes, Debbie?'

'Are you ready for Dr Dunstal?'

'Tell him to come through.'

Dr Mickey Dunstal came in through the door, a sinewy man with long blond hair which he wore in a pony-tail. He was wearing a Hawaian shirt in vivid colours, and tight-fitting jeans. He had a full beard, and his green eyes glittering with intensity.

Bruce had known Mickey for years. He remembered the face before the beard had been grown – it was wide-jawed and strong. He'd worked with Mickey often: a bit of a wild man, and a difficult person to control, but a genius.

'Top of the mornin' to you. It's been too long, Bruce.'

He took the outstretched hand and the grip was hard. Mickey Dunstal was certainly tough. He had to be, thought Bruce, to stand the punishment he meted out to his body. This was a man who could work for forty-eight hours without a break, then go out on a drinking spree that would destroy most people. Bruce had often thought Mickey had a death-wish – but he was still one of the most gifted and innovative designers of Formula One cars in the world.

The previous year he had just disappeared – gone out of circulation. There was talk that he might have returned to Lockheed.

Bruce watched the designer as he sank down into one of the leather couches and contemplated his boots.

'I was approached by Shensu,' Mickey Dunstal said at last. 'Long before he signed up with you and Phelps. I'd hate you to think I was imposin', but they contracted me to do the design before you came along. Aito wanted me to tell you.'

'You've made my day!' Bruce's face broke into a broad smile. This was better than he'd dreamed, a minor miracle.

Dunstal sat up, beads of perspiration on his forehead.

'Thank God, you're pleased! I thought you might be upset. I know you like to be in on the development.'

Bruce leaned back, a weight off his mind. He would have competitive machines for the first race of the season. The Irishman was the best. And he needed the best.

'OK, Mickey. Let's see what you've got.'

Mickey wiped the perspiration off his forehead. 'I want to tell you my thinkin'. The Shensu 3500 is a superb V12 engine.'

'But I'd heard it was a V8?'

'Yes. That was the smokescreen Shensu deliberately put out. I've been in Japan for the last year, working with Professor Katana – he's Shensu's newly appointed head of engine design and research. He's a clever little man, take it from me. Together we evolved the final design.'

Bruce sat hunched forward. He was listening now. Aito Shensu was smart; he must have known he and Mickey were friends. That must be why Phelps had approached him rather than any one else – to smooth the way for an equable working relationship.

Mickey continued: 'The engine produces far more power than previous designs, but the balance of the engine is awkward. In fact Katana told me they've found that strivin' to produce balance alone actually detracts from the power output of the unit.'

He unfolded his first plan on Bruce's desk, and Bruce sucked in his breath. It was beautifully drawn.

'This is what a conventional designer would have done. This was what I started off with. There are many flaws in this design once you realise two things: the new engine'll push the car very fast, and it'll have to corner quicker, handle well at higher speeds. In short, it'll need better aerodynamics and suspension.'

He now pointed to the section of the plan that showed the engine mounting points.

'Here's the weak point. The stress on the body is immense. It was me biggest problem.' He rolled up the plan and took out another.

Bruce had to respect this mad Irishman. At twenty-one Mickey Dunstal had left the Massachusetts Institute of Technology with a doctorate in aeronautical engineering, the youngest person ever to be awarded such a degree. It was presumed he'd join the Lockheed Aircraft Corporation, since it was they who had given him the grant to come out from Ireland and study at MIT.

Instead Mickey had returned to England and started his own sports car company. His first design had won numerous prizes and excellent reviews from the motoring press, and the car had sold well, making Dunstal an overnight millionaire. Then he was bought out, and Mickey had moved into the world of Formula One, producing brilliant designs, hopping from team to team. Then, a year ago, he'd gone out of circulation.

'Bruce, you know the ground rules as well as I do.'

Bruce nodded and leaned over the plan, watching as Mickey pointed out the different areas of concern.

'FISA sets them – the car's width, before and behind the front wheels, the front and rear overhangs, wing height, total height and fuel tank capacity. Then we have to have crushable side-pods, the front end must survive a twenty-two mph crash test without any displacement of the pedals. And to top it all, the fuel tank must be rupture-resistant rubber and mounted more than forty centimetres from the car's centre.'

Bruce grimaced. 'It's depressing.'

'Relax, let me get to the point. The rules say we mustn't weigh more than 1113·3 pounds before any fluids are put into the machine.'

He looked down at his notes again, his eyes glittering as he continued.

'Oh, and I nearly forgot – the driver's feet must fall behind the front axle line. And that's where me problems began. You see, the Shensu 3500 is twenty per cent longer than the average Grand Prix engine, but it gives the driver a lot o' fight in the corners.'

Now he unfurled a very basic design of car, but with not enough detail for Bruce to get the total picture.

'This is one of me first designs – just to show you the problems. Under the old rules I could just move the driver forward to accommodate the engine, but under the new rules I can't do that. So I've got seven and a half extra inches of car. And I can't gain weight.'

Bruce whistled softly.

'An' that's not the bloody least of it. The Shensu 3500's fitted with massive oil coolers as well as a bigger radiator. So I've got to fit enormous cooling-ducts to the car – the new engine is good for at least 780 bhp.'

Bruce looked sceptical.

'I had me doubts too,' the Irishman said, 'till I saw it on the test-bed. Which leads us to me next problem – the car has to be driveable. That power'll really hammer the driver. You see, it's not enough for me car to perform well flat out, she must also sail round the corners. Give the driver a bit o' fight.

'So I came to thinking, well, you've got a very different engine, so it sort of deserves a very different kind of chassis. But to lose weight I had to spend a lot o' Mr Shensu's money.

But he's a generous fellah, to be sure. Watch carefully, Bruce.'

Mickey unrolled a huge photograph. Bruce looked down, spellbound. Nothing was as he had expected it to be. Sleek and streamlined, the car set his pulse racing. She sat very, very low on the ground, and was squatter than an ordinary machine, with enormous cooling-ducts on either side. She had the look of a predator, an almost organic air of menace. The suspension system, even at a glance, was highly innovative – constructed from carbon fibre. At the front were anhedral wings, mounted either side of the nose cone to generate downforce to improve the machine's grip on the corners. Carbon-fibre disc brakes provided the stopping-power.

The whole machine was black, giving her a shadow-like appearance.

Mickey Dunstal went up several points in Bruce's estimation. 'Will she comply?' he asked.

''Course she will. I get a bloody headache from studyin' the regulations. Shensu have got their own wind tunnel, so she's as aerodynamic as a Formula One machine can possibly be. There's also pods on her back end, to generate even more downforce.'

'I don't want problems with the regulations, Mickey. Why does she look so different?'

'You're a smart boy. You see, the chassis and the cockpit are not constructed from kevlar or carbon fibre as you might expect. It's something else entirely.'

'What material?'

'XXT. It comes from Stealth technology – used to build the US's latest range of fighters and bombers. I've got this mate and he works in the development section of the Lockheed Aircraft Corporation. A bright lad. This compound features largely in the F-117A Stealth fighters. It gives me opportunities other Formula One designers haven't been able to explore.'

'She's got a completely different profile from a normal Formula One machine.'

'This is the most advanced design I've ever produced.'

69

'Mickey, I'm worried about the regulations. Where is this prototype?'

'I think I'd better call in Mr Shensu.'

'But he's in Japan.'

'No, to be sure, I saw him sitting outside.'

Mickey got up and walked to the door, opening it and leaning out.

'Mr Shensu.'

Bruce held onto the sides of his chair as Aito Shensu walked in. Mickey moved to one side.

'What's going on?' Bruce's curiosity was aroused.

'Mr de Villiers. I am a man with little time. I have been planning all this for a long time. The design Mr Dunstal has shown you – the car has been completed.

'I used all my resources to build the Shadow. There are four Shadows waiting outside in a transporter for you. Please, Mr de Villiers, I realise that this may come as a surprise, but . . .'

Bruce rocked backwards and forwards on his chair, a glazed expression on his face. At last he found the words he wanted.

'Mickey, we're going to massacre McCabe.'

Bruce de Villiers stood looking down at the tarmac of the test circuit and wondered if anything could ever be perfect. It was just that one tried and tried to get things one-hundred-per-cent right, and then there was always something that got in the way. What was getting in the way now was the man who owned forty per cent of the newly formed Calibre-Shensu team. The man who'd given him his job.

He looked up and saw Jack Phelps's helicopter coming down to land behind the main building.

Then Phelps was there, all six and a half feet of him, wearing a tiny yellow bow-tie, striding determinedly towards him. Impeccably dressed, his dark hair smoothed back from the high forehead, Bruce thought Phelps looked like the corporate axe-man. Yes, he was a well-oiled operator if ever there was one.

So far, the American had been far from co-operative, and had wanted far more control in the running of the team than he'd first indicated. Of course, he should have expected it, de

Villiers thought. Jack Phelps was a businessman and he enjoyed power. It was written in his cold blue eyes.

Now, in this continuing instalment of the argument, Bruce decided he was going to get in with the first salvo.

'Listen, Jack, I'm a perfectionist, and that's what kept McCabe in the number-one spot for the last three years. You only get out what you put in. I'm telling you that what goes into my cars is what makes them perform to their full capacity. And I choose what goes in.'

Phelps put his hands behind his head and looked out across the circuit.

'I know what it takes to succeed. I wrote the book. But I'm in this for exposure – it's marketing, pure and simple. You wouldn't be in this business if it weren't for the sponsors. I want to see Calibre branding . . . and of course Shensu branding . . . everywhere I look.'

Bruce relaxed. Perhaps Phelps had relented on the other matter.

'Bruce, we're on the same side,' Phelps said quietly, but with a distinct edge in his voice. 'Let's get one thing straight, buster. Without my sponsorship, you're dead.'

At that moment Bruce wanted to smash his fist into Jack's nose. The trouble was that Phelps could break him.

Bruce breathed in deeply and looked down at his hands – cracked and dirty, though he hadn't worked on a car for years. He thought about how he'd fought to get where he was. He thought of the vineyard, of the sun setting over the mountains and his father irate because he'd spent his weekend racing cars and not supervising the pruning of the vines. There was a time for losing one's rag and a time for holding on to it.

'All right, man. What do you want?'

'That's better, Bruce. I knew you'd come round to my way of thinking. Now, I can't have you talking to Zenith about tyres . . .'

Phelps turned away from him and stared down the long straight. There was something in his attitude that told Bruce that the full punch was still to be delivered.

'I own Carvalho tyres,' Phelps said. 'I want them on our cars, and Aito agrees with me.'

71

Bruce didn't hesitate. 'I've done my research. Zenith are the only choice with Mickey's chassis – if you want to win.'

'Carvalho have the best technical people in the world. I employed them.'

'Last year. They haven't had a chance to develop any new tyres yet. What will you say when we don't win because of the tyres?'

'Cool it, Bruce. You've got a chance here to develop your own tyres in complete secrecy. Almost everyone who raced last year used Zeniths, and this year it's going to be the same. Don't you see the advantages of what I've arranged? You're Carvalho's only customer.'

Bruce dug his hands into his pockets, desperately trying to control his temper.

'The tyres come direct to you,' Phelps went on. 'As many as you like for each race, not a set amount.'

He had to agree with what Phelps was saying. He just didn't like being dictated to.

'All right, we'll use Carvalho tyres. But I want to do extensive pre-testing. And if they're not good enough, we'll have to look for an alternative.'

Phelps pursed his lips, then relaxed. He scratched behind his right earlobe and avoided Bruce's eyes. 'Now let's talk drivers,' he said.

Phelps was going through every area of the operation. Of course, he had a right to, it was just very, very irritating.

They walked over to the pits. Bruce pulled himself up onto the concrete side-wall and sat upright, staring down at Phelps.

'Drivers?'

Phelps nodded, pulled out a cigar and trimmed it with a silver cutter. He lit up, blowing smoke in Bruce's direction.

'Sartori is going to stay,' Bruce said.

'That's very generous of him, for twenty million dollars.'

'He was your choice, Jack. You can't bargain with a man like Sartori. He's an arrogant son-of-a-bitch. He knows we need him more than he needs us.'

Phelps contemplated the glowing end of his cigar. 'And your number two driver?'

'Johan Claus.'

72

'He finished fourth in this year's season?'

'Correct. An excellent driver, precise and controlled. The ideal second man.'

'Hardly a glamour-boy.'

'And just what's that supposed to mean?'

Bruce was losing his cool again, and he knew that this was a mistake. If he allowed Phelps to get to him now, it would affect him for the whole season.

'Listen,' Phelps said. 'I buy Sartori. But Claus! Come off it. That'd give us two egoists. You know Sartori's attitude to commercial appearances; he's an old-style driver, and that means he does as little work as possible off the track. He's not into the promotional side – he doesn't understand its import-ance. Now, you may think I'm being difficult but let me again emphasise that what we're talking about here is sponsorship. Everything is paid for here because two people, myself and Aito Shensu, believe that this little effort can substantially enrich us.'

'Winning will put you on all the front pages.'

'Yes, but don't you understand, Bruce? People don't just want to see machines coming in first, they want to see the men who are doing the driving. Personalities. Claus comes across with as much pizzazz as a Nazi storm-trooper. The public want a man they can relate to, like Jackie Stewart. Now Shensu has the final say on the second driver and he doesn't want Claus. He's actually thinking of someone the Japanese people can relate to.'

Bruce got down from the concrete side-wall where he'd been sitting. The American was nearly a foot taller than he was – and he'd got him by the balls. He couldn't argue, not after he'd accepted the Sartori deal. And he was still worried about the design of the Shadow, she might just be pushing a little too far against the regulations.

'Claus is one hell of a driver,' Bruce said, 'even if his personality isn't to everyone's liking.'

'Listen, people were actually jeering last year when he led the field at Monaco for the first three laps. That guy isn't going to sell Shensu cars or my cigarettes – if anything, he's going to put people off them. From what I hear Johan hates product endorsements.'

Bruce breathed in deeply a few times. 'So I've got a problem. Drivers don't just fall out of trees. Money can bring them in, but only a certain amount of the way. Everybody's signed up for 1991, and to get another top-rated driver is going to be a bastard. Once the announcement gets out about Sartori, everyone's going to be watching us. To be honest, Claus is about the only choice I have.'

'Shensu is no fool. He wants to win as much as you do, if not more. But he doesn't need a big-name driver, he just wants a potential champion.'

Bruce wondered if he was hearing straight. It was almost unheard of for a driver to stand a chance in the championship if he didn't have a track record.

'So I suppose you told Shensu to make his choice from the top Formula 3000 drivers?'

'No, Shensu will make his own choice. I want you to think some more about it. We need someone who's showing promise.'

Bruce squared up to face Phelps. If he gave in on this he'd be on a losing ticket for the rest of the season.

'To take an unranked driver would mean that we'd only have one chance of winning, and that would be Sartori.'

'Listen to me straight, Bruce. Shensu also wants someone who is acceptable to the Japanese people.'

'Oh, for fuck's sake! A Japanese driver!'

'I feel our conversation is at an end. Either you agree to work with me on this or you're out.'

'You can't do this to me.'

Phelps moved in close to him, and Bruce smelt his expensive after-shave. 'Without Shensu we're going nowhere. Understand?'

'*Ja*. I've got no fucking choice.'

'You can always pull out. I'm going now. If I don't hear from you . . . Well, I'll know you've decided to co-operate.'

De Villiers watched Phelps's back as the man walked calmly off the track. He wanted to run after him, wind him one in the side of the jaw and then kick him in the balls. However, age had given him wisdom.

He walked back to his office and looked through the driver file.

Wyatt had been on the phone since early that morning. There was no way he was going to give up, but as each conversation turned out to be negative, he felt himself growing more and more despondent.

A season in Formula 3000? It wasn't what he wanted at all. He had nothing to prove in that arena. He'd been in Formula One for only a year: that was where he had to prove himself.

Each year out of Formula One would be a year lost. It was a race against his age more than anything else. He knew that there were a lot of other contenders for a seat in a Formula One car, coming up through the ranks in Formula 3 and Formula 3000.

At eleven-thirty he put the phone down, having called Ferrari headquarters and got yet another negative response. Almost as the phone hit the receiver it started to ring. He picked it up angrily.

'Chase.'

'Hallo, Wyatt.'

Then he recognised Bruce de Villiers' voice with its flat South African vowels.

'Yes?'

'I suppose you think I'm about to give you some advice?'

'Yes.'

'Well, you're wrong. One of our sponsors would like to talk to you.'

He felt his spirits soar. 'When and where?'

'In Tokyo. He said you'd know where.'

The coldness began to creep over him. 'Aito Shensu?'

'That's correct. You know him?'

He could not escape the past. He had to come to terms with it, just as he had to accept his part in his father's death.

'Is there a problem, Wyatt? The tickets are waiting for you at Heathrow. He said you'd know where to stay in Tokyo.'

'I want to think about this . . .'

'Wyatt, I told you that you only get one chance in Formula One. Now you've got a second one. Take it.'

The first-class cabin was almost empty, leaving him alone with his thoughts. He'd said he'd never come back, and now here he was returning. He remembered this same flight ten years before. Then he'd been at the back, crushed in amongst the tourists and lower-echelon businessmen. He had been as alone as he was now.

Then he'd been seventeen. He'd come back from Yosemite knowing what he had to do. It had been only a few weeks after the accident in Monaco, after his father's death. He remembered that Estelle had refused to speak to him. She had blamed him for the accident – of which he could remember nothing. They'd both loved his father, each in their own different ways. And there was nothing to fill the void after he'd died.

Yes, those times, ten years ago, seemed as if they were yesterday.

It had been in the London *dojo*, in the karate class, that he lost himself in the controlled moves of the martial art. He had pushed himself hard, because it was during the class that he forgot about what had happened. And in that forgetting he found freedom.

At seventeen he already had his black belt. In the free-fighting competitions six months before the Monaco accident, he had caught the attention of the *Shihan*, the chief instructor who was out on a tour from Japan. Wyatt had been invited to travel to Japan with six other *karate-ka*, the youngest six years older than himself. At the time he had turned the invitation down, but after the accident in Monaco he decided to give up driving and accept it. He had known even then that the experience would be an escape from the hell he was enduring. A week later he had been on a plane with the six others, bound for Tokyo.

Then he had been apprehensive, uncertain. He'd had no idea of what to expect or of how he would survive. He had felt apart from the group of six who travelled with him, both in age and experience.

So, ten years ago, the plane had landed at Narita airport on a grey, overcast day. They had milled around the arrivals hall, waiting to be met. But there had been no one there to meet them, so they had walked outside. A small van was standing next to the kerb and the driver hooted when he saw them. He gestured for them to climb into the back.

They were in a strange city, heading for an unknown destination. Eventually they had been dropped outside the *dojo*, and their driver disappeared without a word. Unsure of what was happening, they watched the last of the *karate-ka* leave. Then the *Shihan* stepped from the *dojo* and welcomed them inside. Wyatt remembered how rustic the place seemed, how primitive. Just a simple wooden building.

The place was virtually bare except for the *tatami* mats on the floor, and pairs of padded quilts – futons, but totally unlike what passed in England for futons. Here there was one for warmth, one to lie on.

Wyatt could sense the shock they all felt, but for him there was no disappointment. He enjoyed the harshness and the rigour of the *dojo* – it helped him to forget the past.

Japan. There he had come so far and been given so much. Why had he walked away from it all? That was a question that reverberated around his head now, as the Boeing 747 began its approach to Narita airport. The wheel had turned full circle, and now he was being drawn towards the culture he had tried to escape.

The plane landed smoothly, and he disembarked with his small kit-bag. Apart from that he had nothing. Outside the airport, the truck was waiting. He bounded into the back and relaxed, watching the lights flashing past in the darkness. They were all so familiar, the landmarks – the measured expanse of land around the Emperor's Palace, the illuminated Tokyo Tower, as elegant as ever. He felt that Tokyo breathed the life back into him. He found the place intoxicating, fascinating, because it was so unlike his own country and yet felt like a place that had always been part of him. For Wyatt, it could not be compared to any other place in the world.

When he arrived at the *dojo* there was no one to greet him.

A solitary candle burned in the centre of the floor next to some unrolled futons. He showered under one of the cold-water taps outside, then towelled himself dry and lay down to sleep.

Before the morning sun fell in broken lines across the floor of the *dojo*, he was up. He rolled up the futons, changed into a black Japanese smoking-jacket and pants, took his towel and toilet bag and walked outside.

On the street he stood out from the majority of pedestrians because of his size and height. Yet he did not feel a stranger in this place; in a way, it was more like a home than England. He paid for his ticket at the washroom and went inside.

He stripped, then went into the main area, joining the many men who sat facing the wall on tiny wooden stools. He moved over to a stool and sat down in front of one of the taps. He brushed his teeth and spat on the floor, looked into the mirror above the tap and studied his face. Then he opened one of the spigots and filled a bucket with hot water, lathering his face and shaving at a leisurely pace. Pouring the water away, he refilled the bucket with hot water, and then filled another with cold. He mixed the two and lathered himself all over, completely cleaning his body. Then he took the longer of the two hoses attached to the spigot and showered himself down. His ablutions finished, he stepped into the communal bath and soaked himself in the nearly boiling water with everyone else.

He was back at the *dojo* at six thirty. Usually it would have been full of students, but today it was empty. He changed into his *karate-gi* and performed a succession of warm-up exercises. He was charged with a new energy.

The door to the *dojo* slid back and in stepped a lean Japanese in *karate-gi* and wearing a black belt. Wyatt drew himself up and bowed. He recognised the man. Naoko, his former pupil.

'We fight,' Naoko said simply, in Japanese.

Wyatt understood perfectly. He had left the *dojo*, and that was a disgrace. Now, to return to it, he must prove himself worthy of the honour. But to fight, they should be under the supervision of the master.

The *Shihan* stepped through the door and Wyatt bowed to

him. It was then he understood that Naoko had taken his job, that of personal assistant to the *Shihan*. His return was a challenge to Naoko.

They bowed to each other again, then began the eye-contact and the waiting. The blow came before Wyatt could react, striking him hard in the solar-plexus. The breath burst from him and he staggered forwards to receive a hammering blow across the head that sent him flying across the floor. The anger rose up in him, but he fought it back, knowing that he must master his own emotions before he could outwit his opponent. Gradually he regained his self-control.

He felt blood running from his lip. His mind emptied, concentrating totally on anticipating the movements of his opponent. He had made the mistake of underestimating Naoko; he would not make it again. Naoko could have killed him, but in the controlled movements of *kumite* the intention was merely to prove that the opening had been left, not to cause serious injury. *Kumite* meant sparring, loose fighting in which both opponents held back from delivering the killing blows they were capable of.

Now they both moved with absolute precision, circling each other, striking and warding off the blows. Wyatt felt his confidence building, when a well-placed kick caught him hard between the legs.

He screamed out and toppled over. He wanted to crawl, regain his breath and wipe the tears from his eyes. Instead he rose again, controlling the pain and the anger, moving in on Naoko and timing three expert strikes against Naoko without hurting him. Each strike was carefully aimed to cause maximum injury, but each was held back a fraction in the controlled movements of *kumite*.

The *Shihan* called for them to stop. They both bowed, and then Naoko walked out of the room. Wyatt knelt down on the floor, ignoring the pain, and the *Shihan* sat opposite him. He spoke in English.

'You still train, Wyatt. You are still as expert as when you left here. I thought you would not train. You showed your superiority to Naoko by not striking him. I need you here. You were the finest of my pupils and I invested everything I had in your training. Then you left me. The void has not been filled. There was the other one, but he went on the path of evil.'

Wyatt was filled with guilt. He had had to leave to satisfy his need to race. That need still existed.

'I did not want to return here,' he said quietly.

'You still cannot accept your father's death?'

'I ran away. I have not proved myself yet.'

'You want to win the Formula One championship?' The words seemed out of place in the simple atmosphere of the *dojo*.

Wyatt nodded. 'I have to win to prove myself.'

'Then you will return.'

'Then I will return.'

'Aito Shensu says that you must meet him in his office.'

Wyatt rose and bowed to the *Shihan*. His body ached, but in his mind he was free from the guilt he had felt on leaving the *dojo*.

'Listen, Wyatt. Can you work with me? I mean, can you take orders and apply them? I'm hard. Fucking hard.'

Bruce de Villiers' words seemed out of place in the boardroom of one of Japan's largest corporations, but the man opposite de Villiers did not seem perturbed. Wyatt looked across to Aito Shensu. He stared into Aito's eyes and felt the power of them. The bond was still there – Aito had forgiven him for leaving – but then Aito was drawing him back. Aito was challenging him. Eventually Wyatt looked back at Bruce de Villiers and broke the long silence.

'I can take anything you give, Bruce.' Wyatt felt his spirits soaring. 'Why are you asking me?'

'You've got a drive with Calibre-Shensu.' Bruce swallowed as he spoke. He hadn't wanted Chase, but Aito had insisted. In a way, that left no room for negotiation.

Two hours later they signed the deal. Aito was in a reflective mood.

'I was under pressure from the board to choose a Japanese driver,' he said. 'I did a lot of thinking. I told them about you, Wyatt; that you were Japanese in spirit. You understand us and our culture, you understand we are centred here – ', he gestured to his stomach, ' – not here – ', he gestured to his heart.

Bruce looked puzzled not knowing that to the Japanese the stomach, or *hara*, is the emotional centre, the role Westerners assign to the heart. Bruce leaned forward. 'I'm not totally happy about this. Contractually, I have to accept your appointment, and so does Jack Phelps. It was Aito's decision. But I don't know if you've got what it takes, Wyatt. You've got a lot to prove. We want to be in the front all the way. The theory goes that it's twenty-five per cent car, twenty-five per cent team, twenty-five per cent tyres and twenty-five per cent driver. I'm going to give you that seventy-five per cent, so don't come looking for excuses.'

When Wyatt and Aito had left, Bruce de Villiers walked over to the big window overlooking the busy Rappongi district. He couldn't explain why, but he felt slightly more confident about Wyatt Chase than he had done before. Perhaps he was seeing things that he'd just never taken the trouble to notice.

He would keep pushing Wyatt, forcing him to cram into a month what it often took some drivers years to learn. And he knew that if he helped Wyatt to win, he'd hold him. As for Ricardo Sartori, that was another matter.

He lay on the beach, contemplating the dark hair covering his flat, bronzed stomach. A ball of sweat ran down his forehead and he turned over lazily.

'Maria!'

The big girl sauntered out of the beach house, naked, walking a little gingerly over the hot sand. Her body was as dark as his and her figure just as firm.

He stared past her at the glittering waters of the Aegean. This was paradise. The sun warmed and revitalised him. He wished the moment could last forever.

She knelt over him and massaged his back. He felt the last knots of tension disappear as her hands worked carefully down his spine.

Then, just when he thought it had gone, the nightmare vision returned. He was on the track in Detroit, coming into the first corner after the main straight. His foot was pumping the brake pedal, but there was nothing there. He was closing too fast, losing control, crashing into the concrete barrier.

It was all redness and pain. Blackness beckoned, and he resisted it.

'No! No!'

He couldn't get it out of his mind.

'I hurt you?' Maria asked softly.

He signed and looked out across the blue waters, narrowing his eyes. This villa on Skiathos had been a dream for a long time. He had bought it the previous year, but spent little time here since then. The racing circuit was demanding.

World champion. He had been world champion. But that was in the past. Since then, the fear had crept into his soul slowly, insidiously, but steadily. In a way, he wished he could give up. But he was greedy, as each season brought more money, more sponsorships and more fame. And this season it would net him twenty million dollars. Please God, he had to win for that.

He was addicted to one other passion besides racing – women. He could never have enough of them. Yet he had not found one he truly loved. He needed someone to trust, but there was no one. He had no family. Nothing.

Another girl appeared. Helena worked in the villa as a maid during the day and sometimes entertained him at night. She was a tall, lithe girl who moved beautifully on a windsurfer and was as wild in bed as a storm on the Aegean.

'Telegram for you, Ricardo.'

He pushed the big girl off him into the sand and got up. He liked women, and he had never had much problem getting them, but he found it difficult to keep them. Perhaps, he reflected, that was why he had never found a wife.

He tore the envelope open and saw that the telegram was in English. He hoped it was not another request to return to London. He had only come to the island yesterday, having signed the contract with Calibre-Shensu. He read it quickly. 'Second driver is Wyatt Chase. Will explain when you are in England. Calibre-Shensu. Bruce de Villiers.'

He felt himself shaking with laughter. Was de Villiers crazy? Wyatt Chase – inexperienced and hot-headed. He'd only got a drive because his uncle Danny had owned Chase Racing. He'd heard a rumour that there was some proviso in Wyatt's father's will that Wyatt had to get a drive if he wanted it. Ricardo had thought Danny was lucky when Wyatt pulled out, and most of the other drivers had doubted that Wyatt would ever compete in Formula One again. What the hell was de Villiers doing, giving Chase a drive?

He ran into the sea and started to do a fast crawl, pushing his body to the limit: he had to be fit for the next season. He knew that he had enough stamina to keep racing competitively for the next five years at the very least. The pain of the hard swim blotted out the last traces of the nightmare of the accident, and he thought again about Chase. De Villiers must be crazy to choose an inexperienced driver as his second.

He skirted some rocks and then pulled himself out of the water onto an isolated pier. He lay back on the wooden planking and looked up at the brilliant blue sky.

He knew very little about Wyatt Chase – the man was very much a loner – but he surmised that Chase must be soft. After all, he came from a wealthy family, so he hadn't had to fight to get where he was; he had ridden on his father's reputation and his uncle's money. Well, he would be in for a shock, working for Bruce de Villiers, Ricardo mused.

Ricardo was a fighter, and he intended to drive the best of the Calibre-Shensu machines in every race. He would receive the most attention – he would make quiet sure of that. Chase would certainly be the number two driver.

He would see a hypnotist in London to try and get rid of the dream; he had to purge it from his mind before it started to affect his driving. Getting to know the new engine and the new chassis would be a challenging exercise.

A shadow crossed his body and he looked up quickly, like a cat whose peace has been disturbed.

'Hallo?'

The voice was feminine, the body was light-skinned and succulent, with long, finely-muscled legs. The face was Nordic.

He rose lazily, keeping his eyes fixed on hers as he introduced himself. 'I swam over here from my villa. Ricardo Sartori.'

'You are the motor-racing champion?'

'The same. You haven't told me your name.'

'Mrs Olafson.'

'Mrs Olafson? What does Mr Olafson call you?'

'Helga.'

'How about a siesta over at my villa, Helga?'

'Ah. You are not just the world champion of racing. I've heard about you. Yes, a siesta would be very nice.'

There was silence for a moment while they looked at one another, then they both dived into the water. She was a strong swimmer and surged ahead of him. He let her get a decent distance in front, then turned on the speed.

He was back on the beach outside his villa ten minutes later. He looked back across the calm blue waters as she came up the beach, then screamed at his women to be gone, to stay out of sight. They disappeared, giggling. He went to the bar by the side of the patio and poured himself a drink. For Helga he prepared an elaborate cocktail.

She came up to him, the salty water still dripping from her costume. She pulled it off, then drank quickly, looking at him with appraising eyes.

'Siesta?'

Later, in the coolness of the bedroom, his lips worked their way down the lightly bronzed skin of her stomach and she started to cry out again.

No, he would not be returning to England in a hurry. It would be at least a month before the car was built and ready for testing. He had earned his pleasure, now he was going to enjoy it.

As for Wyatt Chase, de Villiers could have the pleasure of breaking him in.

Wyatt looked out across the polo field. He ignored the crowds of elegantly dressed men and women, concentrating instead on the players and their horses. A man in morning-dress with two attractive women companions walked across his field of view. They had no doubt just come from watching the racing at Royal Ascot.

He lifted his binoculars and studied Carlos's face. Carlos

was sitting easily on the snorting pony, but the casual smile on his face did not deceive Wyatt – he guessed his stepfather was swiftly calculating his next attack.

Carlos was captain of the visiting Argentinian polo team. With a ten-goal handicap, he was also the highest-ranked player on the field – his every move a cause for trepidation amongst the defending British side.

Wyatt panned the binoculars along the edge of the green field, searching for his mother, but he could not find her. The snorting of the polo ponies indicated that the next chukka was about to begin.

As the ball rolled into play and both sides galloped forward, one of the British players, Jeremy Flanders, closed in on Carlos, trying to cut him off from the ball.

Carlos spurred his pony forward and headed directly for Jeremy, who was already blocking him. Jeremy thought he was feinting, till their ponies almost collided and he had to back off quickly. Then Carlos was through, swinging his mallet and taking possession of the ball, sweeping it away from the English.

He pushed on at full gallop, swinging his stick backwards and forwards, each time cracking the ball towards the goal. The other ponies pounded down on him, but he refused to acknowledge their existence, pushing his pony harder and harder. Another rider pulled in front of him, but Carlos was not intimidated. He headed for him at a full gallop, making as if to run into him. At the last moment he diverted course slightly, and smashed the ball into the goal. A huge wave of applause drifted across the field.

Chukka after chukka, the Argentinians built up their lead, till by the end of the game they had given the English side a hammering. As they galloped off the field, the applause was deafening.

Wyatt felt elated. The excitement and the risk had been there, and he had really enjoyed the game. As he walked through the crowds, looking for Estelle, he felt a stab of regret that he had not played more often on Carlos's estancia when he'd had the opportunity.

He caught sight of Estelle, a glass of champagne in her hand, talking to a group of people.

'*Non, mon chéri*. Not at all. And it was the Argentinians' first day on their new ponies.'

He moved forward, his heart pounding, his mouth dry.

'Mother.'

Everything seemed to slow down as she turned round.

'Wyatt. To what do I owe this?' she asked coldly.

He wanted to say so many things, but he could feel the anger sweeping through him. He wanted to hit her for what she was doing to him.

He could sense her friends staring at him, assessing him. He was out of place amongst these people, in his black wind-cheater and cotton trousers.

'Wyatt, I would appreciate it if you would leave me alone. We 'ave nothing to discuss.'

She turned, and he felt the self-control slipping. Then he felt a hand on his shoulder, and he transferred his weight, pivoted in a lightning second, and moved to block and punch.

His eyes focused on Carlos. His body relaxed. To an outside observer he knew it looked as if he had just turned round. Only a *karate-ka* would know how close it had been; only a *karate-ka* would know the agony within him at the near loss of self-control.

'It was a brilliant game, Carlos,' he said, shaking his stepfather's hand.

They walked to the edge of the field in silence, away from the crowds of people.

Wyatt respected Carlos, admired his poise as a man. He didn't look his fifty-one years. The long, curling dark hair worn in a pony-tail, and the copper bangles on his wrists, set him apart from other men; on any other man they would have looked effeminate, but on Carlos they only added to the rugged texture. He was heavy-boned, with dark skin and a face that spoke of experience.

Only when they were out of earshot did Carlos speak.

'Wyatt. You must understand that she will never forgive you. I have reasoned with her, begged her to understand. But

86

your mother is determined, even obstinate – there is nothing to be done.'

Wyatt gripped the white fence that ran along the edge of the polo field and stared up at the forming clouds.

'I was only seventeen,' he said. 'It was ten years ago. My God, can't she ever forget?'

'She is a passionate and beautiful woman. I have never loved anyone, never will love anyone as much as your mother. You are so alike, and it hurts me to see this thing between you, but you cannot wipe out the past. She screams when she has the nightmare. She screams your name in hatred.'

Wyatt closed his hand and smashed it down hard against one of the poles of the fence – it splintered, and split down its length, and crashed to the ground.

Carlos was staring at him, not saying anything, looking at the broken pole.

'Leave this thing, Wyatt. It will never heal.'

'I wish I could remember the accident properly. I wish I could remember exactly what happened.'

'Perhaps you do not remember because you do not want to.'

The phone went at six, interrupting his training.

'Wyatt!' It was de Villiers' voice. 'Where the fuck have you been?'

'What do you mean?'

'I've been trying to reach you since early yesterday. The car is ready. Get your arse over here and show me how you can drive!'

'What, now?'

'Cut the questions. I'll see you in half an hour.'

Bruce de Villiers staggered out of the glass front doors of the Calibre-Shensu headquarters in the early morning sunlight. The newly built front entrance was his idea – a clean design incorporating concrete and glass. The effect was spacious yet functional. Things, he reflected, were taking shape.

He had worked through the night without a break. His wife Anna understood the need for such dedication and she didn't complain. She understood that all his energy had to go into developing the new team.

He had to have the right people. The people he chose could build up the spirit of the team, but they could also bring it down. He needed people who weren't shy of hard work, who loved Formula One racing with genuine passion.

It was tough if Wyatt Chase had to come in a month early, but he couldn't worry about Wyatt's problems – he had enough of his own.

In every person he selected he looked for the same dedication that he himself brought to the sport. He wasn't going to carry anyone. And he didn't want his people socialising with the other teams, he wanted his people to savage them.

Wyatt's Lotus roared up in front of the building. He leapt out and pumped Bruce's hand.

'So? Where's the car?'

Wyatt stared round the premises. Everywhere he looked brought back memories of James and Danny. Now this place was owned and controlled by different men. He felt bitter that it had come to this; but the last time he came here de Villiers had humiliated him, and now at least the man was treating him with respect.

It was strange that only a few weeks before he'd been out on his ear without a drive. Now the tables had turned and he was back in control. Well, he might be working for the man who'd destroyed his uncle, but he'd make sure he came out the winner.

'Come in Wyatt. Relax and have some coffee. I don't want you writing off the Shadow.'

They continued the conversation in Bruce's big, uncluttered office.

'I cannot emphasise what an opportunity this is for us,' de Villiers went on. 'Usually a Formula One team is stretched to the limit, designing, developing and refining its car, but Shensu has given us a completed car. All we have to do is to set it up properly.'

Wyatt couldn't wait to get his hands on the car. He was still having difficulty with the change in de Villiers' attitude. He owed Aito a lot for that, a hell of a lot.

'The Shadow's a brilliant design. Mickey Dunstal has created something totally different. Every loophole in the FISA
regulations has been exploited.'

'It's a gamble?'

'All designs are a gamble – but Dunstal has more flair and
ability than any other designer in Formula One. He's a lateral
thinker, an innovator. He's used materials developed for the
US Stealth fighter programme – that, and the way the car sits
low on the track, is the reason we've called her the Shadow.'

'How soon can I drive?'

'Relax, man. The car'll be ready in half an hour. Sartori
doesn't seem in a hurry to get back here, and his contract
specified he only had to start in a month's time, so the
bastard's giving me an uphill ride.'

'What do you mean?'

'You'll develop the car. She'll be set up to match your
driving style. And let me tell you, the moment Sartori learns
about that, he'll be back. He'll be bloody furious. You know
how hard it is to stay out front in Formula One.'

De Villiers couldn't say it out loud, but he wasn't going to
treat Wyatt as a number two. He would be given equal rating
with Sartori. Anyway, it wasn't his decision, it was Shensu's.

De Villiers got up and paced over to the window. He looked
down over the track, then turned to face Wyatt.

'This business is dogged by all sorts of problems. I've never
had so much handed to me on a plate. You have to deliver,
Wyatt.'

De Villiers wanted to say that he wasn't interested in
Wyatt's life outside driving. That his soul was part of Calibre-
Shensu; that he wanted to see him doing battle with Sartori –
challenging that arrogant son-of-a-bitch. That he wanted them
at each other's throats. But he didn't say it, because he knew
it would happen that way. He'd engineer it.

Wyatt stared hard at de Villiers' face. The manager had
given him all he wanted.

'I'll deliver,' he said.

'I want that car hammered. I don't want you to accommodate the car, I want the car to accommodate you. And you

won't be cramped. The cockpit's designed to fit a man of your height.'

De Villiers stirred his coffee, took a sip and then stared at Wyatt.

'I want you at the front of the grid. That means being fastest in the practices. It also means pushing your car and yourself to breaking-point. You've gone through the learning process for a year, but this is the real thing. You've got to score the moment you get out on the track. It's like a time-bomb, Wyatt. Every minute of racing determines the time you stay at it. Every driver wants to continue, to get to the top – and a few make it. They have the guts and determination to drive faster than the others; they have the ability to take high risks. Sartori is one of them.'

Wyatt gritted his teeth. 'For me, Sartori is just another driver in the way.'

Bruce smiled to himself. The ruthlessness was there.

Phelps sat in his vast private office suite, angrily drumming his fingers on the arm of his black leather chair. He stared out at the impressive view of the New York skyline in the early morning light. In the offices adjoining the main suite he could hear his secretaries hard at work.

He got up and slid back one wall to reveal a private swimming pool. It was a box made from reinforced glass, and the edge of the box hung over the top of the building, giving a spine-chilling view of the streets far below and the skyline he had just been watching.

He clicked his fingers, and Royston appeared with a white towelling robe and bathing-trunks.

Phelps swam the first length underwater. He liked the pool, enjoyed the feeling of power it gave him. No one else in New York had a pool like this, with a view of the city. It reaffirmed that he had made it – made it big.

He surfaced and switched to crawl, doing length after length, forcing the pace. Next to the edge of the pool were more doors leading to a jacuzzi, sauna, steam-room and small cinema.

Eventually he pulled himself out of the water and Royston

handed him a towel, then held open the door of the steam-room. Inside, Phelps tried to relax in the hot clouds of vapour, but it was useless. He was succumbing to his greatest weakness – impatience.

He glanced down at his watch. The time was passing so slowly.

Everything was in place. The car, according to de Villiers, was magnificent. Carvalho had begun producing the tyres. The two drivers had been signed up. The only difficulty was de Villiers – the man was uncooperative. And that could pose big problems.

Jack Phelps thought angrily about the fax de Villiers had sent to Shensu, telling him that he was prepared to test the Carvalho tyres, but if they weren't good enough, he was switching to Zenith. The bastard. De Villiers had gone over his head and got Aito's agreement. Well, he wasn't outman-oeuvred yet. He'd pulled in the best tyre development engineers in the business and send them down to Carvalho.

De Villiers would be using Carvalho tyres, that was all there was to it. The deal centred around publicity – publicity for Calibre lights, Carvalho tyres and Shensu cars. That was why he wanted drivers who could win. Only the cars on the front of the grid got extensive media coverage.

But Phelps knew he needed someone in on the ground floor, making sure that the three brands got the attention they deserved. So far de Villiers had only payed lip-service to that dictum – directing all his energies into head-hunting for the team and developing the new car with Mickey Dunstal.

There was no advance publicity – and already there should have been interviews. Calibre-Shensu was a big event, but it lacked an image. It needed well-co-ordinated visual impact.

He came out of the steam-room, showered, and changed back into his suit. He glanced at his watch. Good. She would be arriving very soon. He had seen the pictures in the international magazines like *Harper's & Queen*, Italian *Vogue* and *Time*. He wanted to use her.

There was a knock on the door. He almost purred with satisfaction – she was punctual, as he had expected.

'Come in.'

The door opened and in she walked. He baulked slightly.

About six foot, he estimated. High cheekbones, ice-blue eyes. Her hair was beautifully cut and hung around her shoulders like strands of fine gold.

His eyes took in her body – an athlete's body, but with generous curves in all the right places. The clothes were perfect: a black silk suit, with a white cotton blouse that rose to a high-buttoned collar. She wore a single strand of pearls and simple gold earrings, and her face was a mixture of haughtiness and sensuality. She was, in a word, delicious.

'Good morning, Mr Phelps. It is a pleasure to meet you.'

The accent was polished, though definitely German.

'Please sit down, Baroness von Falkenhyn.'

'Thank you. Suzie, please.'

'Of course. And call me Jack. Something to drink?'

'Perrier, please, with a slice of lemon.'

She was still standing. He wanted her seated – there was something about her that interfered with his usual feeling of control in such situations.

'Please sit down.'

She sat down on the leather couch and he caught a brief glimpse of her thighs. He wanted her, that was all he knew. But such a dalliance could not be rushed, with this sort of woman it would take attention and time.

He walked over to the drinks cabinet and handed her her drink.

'Thank you,' she said. 'Your office has the most beautiful view. In Munich we have few high-rise buildings. Our architecture is more classical.'

He felt the veiled criticism in her voice. 'Munich is, I think, one of the most beautiful cities in Europe,' he said.

'You know Munich?'

'My cigarettes are sold in your country, and I set up an office in Munich to handle the marketing and distribution. I must tell you that it was more because of my fascination with the beauty of the city than because of its location.'

She seemed unmoved by this statement. 'You are a busy man,' she said. 'I thank you for your interest in my country. Let me begin my presentation.'

Baroness Susanna von Falkenhyn was as he'd been told – precise and to the point. He would play along with her, get her into his power and then mould her very slowly to his way of thinking. It would be a gradual process, like reeling in a marlin.

'You read through the brief I provided for you?' he asked.

'Yes. It was most comprehensive. The project would provide me with the broad canvas I always look for.'

'Believe me, Suzie, the brief was tightly composed. Your proposals, if they are the ones that win . . .'

He made a significant pause. He must make sure she knew she was not the only one in the running for the job – that she would have to fight for the account. It would be his first opportunity to assert his control over her.

'. . . will be followed through in their entirety,' he went on. 'They will dictate the way the advertising and promotion is done.'

'Excellent. First, I would like to put forward the philosophy of my company – Zen.'

She opened her portfolio case and placed a parchment board in front of him.

'In Germany we have often been accused of being too regimented, too dogmatic. It is, in fact, not true. Throughout history, German art and music have been among the most creative and avant-garde in the world. That is why I chose the name Zen – because my company considers design to be a way of life. Thus I make no presentation.'

Phelps felt as if he had been given a slap in the face. 'You're not going to show me *anything*?'

'You expected to be shown something? You gave me words written on paper and you expected a visual response? I see you're angry. I apologise, my response is not meant to be an insult but rather a mark of respect. As I said, I make no presentation. Instead I will tell you of the philosophy of my company.'

Phelps came round and sat beside her on the couch. She was intriguing him more by the minute. He gestured for her to continue.

'I studied design at school; however, I did not study it at

university. Instead I studied film at the University of California. I realised that film was the communication of our time. Thus, all design that is seen must at some point be seen on film. Design must be related to the images created by the movies of our time.' As she spoke, she took some pictures from her case and handed them to him.

'How do you know these men?' she asked softly.

'I've seen them winning races. On TV.'

'Exactly. You know them through film. Or through pictures.'

'So?'

'I am still a designer. Now I design images for companies that want to be seen in a certain way. A successful image is the one that is best suited to the personalities of the people it represents. Your racing team has two key personalities, the two drivers.'

'Ricardo Sartori and Wyatt Chase.'

'Correct. And in order to project the Calibre-Shensu image, I first have to know them, understand them, feel them . . .'

He wondered if that included sleeping with them.

'Why are you smiling? You find my approach amusing?'

'No. I admire your nerve. What would the fee be for this appraisal?'

She shifted slightly and pulled her skirt down to her knees. His eyes left her legs and refocused on her eyes. She took a moment to compose herself.

'You do not understand, Mr Phelps. Either you agree to my way of doing things . . . or you don't. If you agree, then I go ahead and draw up a plan of action. If you don't – I go.'

He took a deep breath. She was not only one hell of a looker, she was also a very shrewd businesswoman.

'All right. I'll consider your proposals. I'll give you an "in principle" decision by the end of this week.'

She lay back on the couch and her skirt rode up, revealing her legs almost as far as her crotch. He sucked in his breath and she looked at him with a subtle smile on her face.

'I have dealt with many businessmen, Mr Phelps. Time is used to achieve a certain advantage. I have a number of projects which will occupy me till the end of next year. I do not have the luxury of time to wait for your decision.'

He was excited by her aggression, it was actually a challenge to him. He knew she was good – perhaps the best in the business. He looked her straight in the eye.

'All right, I'll give you the job on one simple condition.'

'And what is that?'

'That we have dinner tonight.'

'Mr Phelps, we have, as you Americans would say, a deal.'

She left the building elated. She had always been fascinated by Formula One, now here was a chance to experience it at first hand.

Jack Phelps was both interesting and charming. She also sensed that he was attracted to her, and had used that to her advantage. Exploiting her sexuality had never bothered her, it was merely part of her ammunition. Later, she argued, her work would speak for itself.

As a rule she acted in a supervisory capacity for the projects Zen undertook, but on this one, she decided, she would be totally involved. The scope and difficulty of the exercise excited her. She had a very clear idea of the way in which Calibre-Shensu's image should be projected, and she was determined not to compromise on her vision.

She would begin with the cars, then focus on the team. The drivers and the pit crew would all be outfitted in matching designs – a totally integrated look that would reflect the electric atmosphere of the Calibre-Shensu team. The clothes would be easy to wear and comfortable – always an essential feature of her designs. Suzie believed that 'the look' should come from within as well as from without.

The concept would then be sold to the public – a range of Calibre-Shensu clothing that would break for the European summer as the Grand Prix season got underway.

Phelps was the perfect backer. He understood the nature of promotion, and that, together with his advertising knowledge, would ensure that all her plans were followed through. He would guarantee that she had the full co-operation of the team.

Of course, it wouldn't pay to let Phelps become too aware of how excited she was about the project. She sensed that he was one of those men who loved to manipulate others. Her aloof professionalism was an elaborately painted mask that protected her from such people.

Suzie knew all about Phelps's reputation with women. The rumour went that once he had slept with a woman, he lost all respect for her. She looked forward to the challenge of manipulating him, for she was sure she could do just that.

Now, back in her hotel room, she went to an enormous amount of trouble to make sure that she looked her best for the evening. She made up three times before she was satisfied with the way she looked, and experimented with her long blonde hair – finally deciding to let it hang loose around her shoulders. Her evening-dress completely covered her bosom in black velvet but left a gaping V at her back that ran right down to the curve of her buttocks. It had a long skirt, generously slit to reveal a daring mini beneath. She scrutinised herself in the mirror and was pleased.

Slipping on her high-heels, she looked down at her watch and saw that it was almost time to leave.

Jack Phelps bathed carefully. German women, he had heard, were fastidious about hygiene, and he did not want to be found lacking in this respect. He shaved slowly, making absolutely sure he did not nick the skin of his throat. Then he smoothed on the after-shave – specially prepared for him by America's leading couturier, Rudy Washington. He laughed quietly, imagining the way Rudy would react when he learnt that the Calibre-Shensu job had gone to Susanna von Falkenhyn.

He chose his finest black-tie suit from the big wardrobe adjoining the bathroom, and stood in front of the mirror, hand-tying his bow-tie. He had seen the flicker of Susanna von Falkenhyn's ice-blue eyes when he gave her the contract, and he would exploit that weakness to the full.

He thought of her now, sitting alone. He would arrive at the restaurant late.

*

The noise of conversation, the glow of candlelight and the dark forms of the waiters created an atmosphere of rich exclusivity. As Phelps walked into the crowded restaurant he caught sight of Suzie sitting at a table. She was talking to another man. He kept in the shadows for a few moments, watching them together. Then he walked across to her table – and was rewarded with a faint smile. He took his hand and kissed it.

'My apologies, Suzie.'

The man got up. 'You shouldn't be late for a lady like this,' he said, 'you might find she disappears.'

Phelps gave the man an icy stare, and he moved away.

Then Phelps kissed Suzie on the lips, enjoying the scent of her perfume. Roses, jasmine – a hint of sandalwood? She was delicious.

'Perhaps I might wish you had not come so soon . . .'

Phelps coughed uneasily. Susanna von Falkenhyn didn't respond to normal tactics. He'd underestimated her.

The meal passed in a delirious succession of intimate moments. They drank a bottle of Tattinger Rosé, and soon the lateness of his arrival was forgotten and she was relaxed and laughing freely. Almost despite herself, she was enjoying being with him.

Her leg brushed against his under the table. It was the right time to make a move.

'Suzie, why don't you come back to my apartment for a drink? I've just had it redecorated by Rudy Washington . . . I'd like to know what you think of it.'

He saw her eyes light up. 'I didn't know he dabbled in interior design. I'd like to see what he's done.'

Sitting close to her in the silence of his chauffeur-driven limousine, he could feel the warmth of her body. She rested her hand against his shoulder. She wanted to see just how much she could control him.

'It is an achievement to live in such style,' she said. 'Is it all showmanship, or do you really enjoy it?'

'It's the only way to live in New York.'

As he'd expected, her eye was critical. Rudy Washington had furnished his apartment entirely with Queen Anne furniture, collected from auctions around the world. He guessed it wasn't her taste.

'You like antiques, Jack?'

'Well, the choice was Rudy's – but it was the investment angle that appealed to me. What can I offer you?'

'A Cognac.'

He poured her drink, and then a Pernod for himself. Sitting on the couch, they touched glasses.

'To success, Jack.'

'To the most beautiful woman in the world.'

To his satisfaction, she giggled. 'You're not serious!'

'I have never been more in earnest.'

He put his glass down and kissed her on the lips. She responded, and the next moment she was in his arms. A long, lingering kiss.

Carefully he undid her dress. It slid off easily, the velvet crumpling softly down beside the couch. His eyes drifted around the apartment. The curtains were closed; the room was completely sound-proof. No one would hear a thing.

He pushed her down so that he was over her, her naked buttocks rising as she attempted to get away. She tried to resist, but he increased his grip around her waist.

'You're hurting me.' Desperately, she tried to wriggle loose.

'Stay where you are.'

Her strength surprised him, but he grabbed her shoulders and forced her back down.

Suzie couldn't quite credit what was happening. The cultivated veneer was gone and Phelps was revealed as a savage animal. Desperately she tried to break loose. God knew what he planned to do to her.

'You bastard!'

He lost his grip then, and her hand caught him hard across the face. He felt the blood running from his lips. 'My God!' He yanked her hair and twisted it, forcing her face down below his waist.

It was then that the memories came flooding back to her and she sank her teeth into him.

He lay on the floor, sobbing, and she quickly pulled on her dress.

'Jack, you could have had me, but you chose the wrong woman for your perverse fantasies. From now on it's just business.'

She turned on her heel and he heard the door slam. He staggered to his feet. This was just the beginning, he told himself. It would take time, but he would get total control of her.

You could hardly tell it was dawn. It was still almost dark, and it was raining hard. The weather matched his mood. Bruce de Villiers rolled open the metal garage door and switched on the lights. He stared at the Formula One car crouched on the concrete, and his spirits lifted. She broke all his preconceptions of what a Formula One car should look like.

She was beautiful, a work of art – a reflection of Dunstal's design genius. He knew she was based on some sketches that James Chase had made long ago – James had always had a flair for design. Bruce couldn't wait to see her perform. But until the test track was dry he wasn't going to give the Shensu Shadow her début run. And he didn't trust Jack Phelps's Carvalho tyres one iota.

Looking up at the black thunderclouds, he thought of Ricardo Sartori. Sartori was still on his island, he hadn't responded to the telegram. Sartori, he surmised, must have someone very pretty keeping him occupied. It was a problem. But short of sending some strongmen over to Skiathos, there was little he could do except wait.

Wyatt Chase was a different animal. He was champing at the bit to drive the Shadow. He'd hit it off perfectly with Mickey Dunstal at their first meeting. That was important, because if the driver could communicate well with the designer, then the car could be set up perfectly.

He rolled down the door and locked it, then walked back through the pouring rain towards the main building and his office.

The morning paper did nothing to improve his mood. As he turned over its sodden pages, he found that the weather forecast did not look in the least bit promising.

The international news didn't interest him. He turned to the

99

stock market prices for the previous day. The block of Shensu stock he'd got as part of the deal had been performing well.

His eyes zeroed in on an article with the magic words 'Formula One' in the headline. He skimmed through it. The story amused him. A German couturier would be designing the outfits and promotional designs for one of the Formula One teams. It was going to be a fashion statement. He smiled. A team that had that sort of help wasn't going to be taken seriously. Probably one of the teams that had nothing much going for it. He preferred a neutral image, neat and orderly but not over-conspicuous.

There was a knock on the door and his secretary walked in with a cup of coffee for him. She modelled herself on Madonna, and the excruciatingly tight pencil-skirt she was wearing didn't leave much to the imagination.

'Debbie, you shouldn't dress like that.'

'Don't you like it?'

'A little too much.'

He glanced down at his diary and saw that it was only minutes before he was to speak to a representative of Jack Phelps who would, as the American magnate had expressed it over the phone, 'look after his interests'. This person, Phelps said, was to be given full co-operation.

'There's someone here to see you.'

'Must be the consultant Phelps was talking about.'

'It's Susanna von Falkenhyn.'

'And who the the hell is she?'

'Her *prêt à porter* range was the talking-point of the Munich shows.'

'I don't bloody believe this.'

Susanna von Falkenhyn came in through the door and he was conscious of a delicious fragrance. He felt slightly disconcerted as he stood up for the blonde vision in front of him. She made Debbie look like a tart: perfectly made-up, with long blonde hair that cascaded around her face, and dressed in a stunning navy-blue suit.

'Miss von Falkenhyn? Please sit down.'

He felt ill at ease. He did not want anyone else interfering in the running of his team.

'It is a pleasure to meet you. I have read so much about you.'

'So how can I help you, Miss von . . .'

'Please call me Suzie. I prefer it.'

'Sooz . . .' he said, trying to exert a little control over the situation by giving her a nickname.

'No. Suzie.'

He settled back, and his eye caught the article in the paper. Suddenly he put two and two together.

'Hell,' he muttered under his breath.

'I'd like to start immediately,' she said crisply.

Bruce cleared his throat. 'I'll be straight with you,' he said. 'This is a racing team. We need to concentrate on what we're doing, which is racing.'

'Yes?'

'I am busy developing our new car. I employ the best drivers. I run this operation like a rugby team.'

'I think we are going to get on well together.'

He felt disconcerted again. She smiled.

'Look, Suzie,' he tried again, 'let me make myself clear . . .'

'No. Let me make myself clear. I know, as the Americans say, where you're coming from. Well, I am coming from nothing. You can help me or, I suppose, you can make my life impossible.'

'Look, fashion and Formula One just don't go . . .'

'Your philosophy will become an essential part of my designs. I admire your approach, your fanaticism.'

Bruce coloured.

'I will make you what you want to be,' Suzie pressed on. 'I am handling all your publicity and design work. I wanted this job and I am going to keep it.'

'OK, I get the point,' Bruce replied drily. Something told him he wasn't going to get the better of this number.

'First, Bruce, I'd like to tell you a little about the way I work.'

He liked her spirit, he decided.

'So what do I have to give you?' She leaned back and looked him straight in the eyes.

He laughed. He couldn't help it. There was no way he was going get one over her.

Suzie laughed too. 'I think we will work well together, Bruce.'

Over the next hour he was exposed to the Zen culture, the fascinating design business of Suzie von Falkenhyn.

'So you really want to be a part of the team?' he said at last.

'I will not get in the way. I just want to develop a feel for the way you function. Clothes and colours are a part of life. If I am to design for you, I must become a part of you.'

'You'll do that in a spirit of co-operation?'

'As I said, I want to help you, not bring you down, as you seem to think I will.'

He stared out through the window at the falling rain. It was going to be a very difficult year. Nothing was going as he expected it to. However, this woman seemed intelligent, and anxious to make a contribution. If he didn't accept her, Phelps would force him to, and then his relationship with her would be strained. If he co-operated she would be more manageable.

'All right, Suzie. You're part of the team. When do you want to start?'

A broad smile broke across her face. 'Tomorrow morning. I should like you to introduce me to everyone, and after that I promise I will not get in your way.'

He pulled open the drawer of his desk and handed her a set of keys.

'Everyone who works here gets these. This isn't a nine-to-five job. I trust everyone.'

She took the keys and put them in her handbag. 'You know, I did some research on you before I came. I expected a fight.'

'I appreciate your honesty,' he replied, slightly taken aback at her candour.

'And I want your stamp of approval on everything I do.'

He showed her out to her car – a navy-blue Aston-Martin convertible.

'I like your style,' he said.

She kissed him on the cheek. 'Thank you for accepting me.'

His senses reeling, he watched her drive off. He didn't think there'd be anyone objecting to having Suzie von Falkenhyn around.

She drove away fast. She didn't know how she'd kept so composed – he'd made it so difficult for her at first. But she liked Bruce de Villiers. It was going to be a challenge, working with him. She could tell that his approach was very similar to her own – he was a man who didn't accept compromises.

She thought back to the evening with Phelps. She had been disappointed in him – but she was still excited about the project and relished the challenge it presented. Why was it she could never find a man who measured up to her expectations? A man she could love.

Everyone thought her life had been one easy ride on the roller-coaster of success – that as a member of the German aristocracy she had come from money, and all the advantages that money had made available to her. Nothing was further from the truth.

The truth was something she did not talk about. After the Second World War her family had been penniless, and during the time of the reconstruction her father had worked as a labourer. He was an arrogant man, Baron Ludwig von Falkenhyn; a gentleman of leisure. He had never entertained the thought that he would ever have to work. Before the war he had amused himself with the scores of beautiful women who fell natural prey to his saturnine good-looks. He had evaded conscription by keeping in socially with the Nazi chiefs-of-staff, but they had demanded heavy payments from him towards their cause and had expropriated much of his land. By the end of the war he had nothing.

Susanna had been born in 1959, her parents' first and only child. Her mother had adored her and so had her father, at first. By the time she was born he had managed to gravitate from his position as a labourer to that of senior clerk in a leading German bank.

He never brought anyone he worked with home. Susanna's mother knew this was because he had created a false picture of the way they lived, telling everyone they owned a huge country estate. In reality they eked out a meagre existence in a two-bedroomed flat where the plumbing leaked continually.

Susanna worked hard at school, determined to earn enough money to support her mother – to take her away from her father. He treated her with callous disregard, laughing at her excellent results and saying that only ugly girls had to succeed academically.

She remembered the night her life changed. It was late, and her father had slammed in through the front door. Her mother had come out to greet him. Susanna heard the sound of the blow as he hit her, then the sobbing.

Susanna had been working on a drawing in her bedroom, but immediately switched off her light. She heard his feet falling heavily on the floor, and waited to hear the noise of the mattress springs in the next room as he collapsed into a drunken stupor.

Instead she heard the handle of the door to her room being turned, then the light was switched on. Her father closed the door behind him and locked it. She pretended to be asleep, and smelt the schnapps on his breath.

'Hallo, Susanna.'

He shook her so that she had to open her eyes. He was staring at her fondly.

'Kiss your father goodnight.'

She rose up and kissed him. He held her, and pushed his tongue into her mouth. He kept on kissing her and enveloped her in his arms. Obviously, she thought, he felt guilty about the way he had been treating her.

She felt his hand come up between her legs and start stroking her pubic hair. She shivered involuntarily.

'You're almost a grown woman now . . .'

'Please, father. I want to go to sleep.'

'I must teach you how to please a man.'

He pulled her hands down behind her back and with his other hand unzipped his trousers. There was a masculine smell now, and she stared down to see his erection.

She tried to struggle free, and he became angry. He ripped off her nightdress and began to fondle her breasts. He put his mouth to them and licked them. Desperately she tried to kick

104

out with her legs, but he leant on her with his full weight so that she was powerless.

'You're not going to lose it gracefully, are you?'

She screamed as he forced her legs apart. He laughed. She closed her eyes as he penetrated her. It was worse than any nightmare. All she could do was cry.

It was the beginning of a bizarre relationship that had lasted over a year. She felt she couldn't talk to anyone about it, especially not her mother. Susanna was torn between the guilt and the longing.

Then one night, when she was lying in her father's arms, there was banging on her door. She heard her mother's voice.

'Ludwig, what are you doing with her?'

The banging intensified, and he got up from the bed, his face red with rage.

'Shut up, you bitch!'

He unlocked the door and her mother burst into the room. She stared at Susanna, naked on the bed.

'What have you done?'

He hit her hard, and Susanna screamed out again as her mother collapsed on the floor.

Her father climbed back on the bed and forced her legs apart again. 'Come on. Show your mother what we do together.'

She closed her eyes tight and heard the sound of breaking glass. Her father collapsed on top of her, bits of glass falling everywhere.

When she opened her eyes she saw her mother holding the neck of a broken bottle. Her father's body rolled off her and fell heavily onto the floor, and her mother gathered her in her arms, sobbing.

'You must get away from here!'

She had stared silently at her mother, hardly comprehending.

'Come,' her mother said, 'I have some money saved for you.'

Her mother watched as Susanna dressed quietly, then packed her few clothes into a small suitcase.

'Don't come back, Susanna. Don't write. Just get away from here . . .'

The rain was drumming hard against the windows of the car, a truck was coming straight for her. Suzie pulled the wheel over hard, breaking out into a cold sweat. How long had she been driving like that, thinking of the past?

She composed herself. She wished she could wipe that time from her mind, but it would never go away. There had been men in her life but never love. Sex was merely a physical act, a momentary pleasure.

She concentrated on the road ahead. She was going to make a success of the Calibre-Shensu sponsorship. She was determined to succeed at it, as she had at everything she had ever done – except at love.

And she liked the idea of calling herself Suzie. It was one step further away from the past.

Wyatt jogged slowly round the test circuit in the early morning light. Today he would drive the Shensu Shadow for the first time. He knew the circuit intimately – the exact nuance of every curve, and the straights where he could coax the car to go a little faster, a little more smoothly.

It was vital for him to be fit. He needed to keep his weight as low as possible and his reaction times razor-sharp. He alternated between slow jogging and fast sprinting. He liked the silence of the track in the early morning, the dew on the grass, the freshness of the air.

He sprinted down the straight and then relaxed into a jog as he approached the esses. In the distance he caught sight of someone in a black tracksuit and immediately upped his pace. Perhaps it was someone snooping around. Other teams were always anxious to catch up on the opposition's secrets.

The figure drew closer. Very athletic, the man was a natural runner. The proportions seemed almost feminine, though; perhaps the backside was a little too curved.

It was only as he drew level with the runner that he realised it was a woman, a very attractive woman. He gestured for her to stop. Instead, she increased her pace. He knew he could outrun her, it was just a question of wearing her down, so he kept level with her until she finally stopped sprinting at the next curve.

'Leave me alone,' she said in a German accent that seemed vaguely familiar.

Her blue eyes flashed angrily, and her features were thrown into relief by her blonde hair swept back in a long pony-tail.

'This is private property,' he said.

'I know. I like to run on my own. Privately.'

'Who are you?'

The face was so perfect, he was almost driven to kiss it. She frowned, facing him squarely, and he admired the athletic stance of her body, the firm breasts pushing hard against the thin material of her tracksuit.

'My name is Susanna von Falkenhyn,' she said.

'Haven't we met somewhere before?'

Her face coloured at the memory. She crossed her arms, holding her shoulders with her hands, but he took the hands and gently pulled her arms apart, drawing her close to him.

'You bastard,' she murmured.

He kissed her, and her body softened. Her arms wrapped round his back and he felt himself swimming in the warmth of her sensuality.

'Last time,' she said, 'I think I made it a little too easy for you. This time I want to get to know you better.'

He relaxed his arms around her. She sighed, her breath turning to vapour.

He felt scared. He never lost control like that. It went against all his training.

'I only started work today,' she said. 'What do you do here?'

She started to run again and he kept pace with her, still talking. 'I'm Wyatt Chase.'

She stopped and stared at him. 'We're going to be working together,' she said.

'You own Zen?' He felt his perspective changing. He had read about this woman, was fascinated by her interest in Eastern culture. 'You'll be handling all our promotional work?'

'Everything will be a statement. Your clothes, the colours

and logos on the Shensu Shadow, all the publicity material and the way we present ourselves to the public.'

Wyatt's eyes widened. 'Bruce agreed to this?'

She nodded.

'But whose idea was it?'

'Mine and Jack Phelps's.'

At seven o'clock a big motorcycle roared up in front of the Calibre-Shensu headquarters. It was a unique machine, modified for higher performance and handling. Mickey Dunstal rode without a helmet, his long blond hair in a neatly plaited pony-tail. The infectious grin behind the curling beard indicated that he was as excited as the rest of the team.

He spent a few minutes discussing some details with Bruce, then turned to Wyatt.

'Ready?'

Wyatt nodded.

The sun was up now, casting a pale, warm light across the vegetation around the track. There was a freshness in the air, and the horizon was bright blue, with a few distant clouds.

Wyatt followed Bruce and Mickey into the workshop bay in the pits. The Shensu Shadow was hidden under a white dust-cloth, standing in the middle of the big room, the rays of early morning sunlight falling down on her.

Even covered up, she had the air of a predator. She was his weapon for the year, Wyatt thought; with her he'd fight it out with the other drivers and machines in a dangerous war of attrition and nerves.

Wyatt changed into his racing gear, pulling on the layer of Nomex fire-proof clothing and balaclava helmet that would protect him from the immediate effects of burning if the car crashed or blew up.

With one energetic tug Mickey pulled off the dust-cloth. Wyatt stared at the Shensu Shadow in rapt surprise. Her body was an ominous black, and she was flatter and wider than the Formula One car he'd driven over the past year. He could tell he'd easily fit into the cockpit, instead of being cramped. Formula One cars were generally designed for much smaller men than him.

He stared at the steering-wheel and the selector switch that actuated the gears on the electronically controlled gearbox. He walked around her, and had to admit he was taken aback. Somehow Dunstal had managed to overcome the FISA dictates of shape and produce a car that was truly and originally forbidding. The front – the wide shark-like nose – was the best part of all. The anhedral wings were neatly sculpted in beneath the nose, and at the back the pods that would add to the downforce looked like giant extraction-pipes.

'She's beautiful – like a jaguar,' Wyatt said quietly.

Mickey was close to her now, examining the engine placement.

'I'm pleased with her line, but it's her performance that'll really knock yer down.'

He lifted the light cowelling to reveal the Shensu V12 engine, a mass of injection-pipes, coolers and electrical equipment. 'Five valves per cylinder, each actuated by compressed air,' Mickey continued reverently.

Wyatt eased himself into the cockpit as the pit crew took the tyres from the warmers and the wheel-on men attached them onto the car with pneumatic spanners. The pneumatic starter was pushed into the air-hole at the back of the engine and it roared into life with a deafening wail. Wyatt felt the excitement coursing through his body as he dabbed the throttle, listening to the engine respond with a feline growl. One of the pit crew rolled up the garage doors that led onto the pit-lane.

As Wyatt was slipping on his helmet, Mickey leant over the cockpit.

'The lower profile will make her devastatingly quick round the corners. Be careful – she's different to anything you'll have driven before. It's up to you now, Wyatt.'

Wyatt was lying further back than usual, but he felt very comfortable. That was important. He was about the biggest driver in Formula One and it was hard to find any car that would accommodate him.

This was perhaps the most important moment of his life. If the car wasn't up to his standard he would spent a season of frustration and heartbreak on the circuits.

His foot touched the accelerator pedal and the engine erupted with a deafening snarl – the tacho needle shot up to ten thousand. Impressive, on such a cold engine. The sound – strong and enveloping – was also extremely enervating.

He engaged first, shot out from the pits and onto the track. Glancing at the digital gauges, he saw oil and water temperatures were exactly right. In response, he raised his hand to indicate to the pit crew that everything was functioning perfectly.

He took her lazily down the main straight and into the esses. She responded well, bedding down nicely through the bends, feeling very positive.

As Wyatt continued his first test lap he could feel the excitement building inside him. He had never driven a machine that felt as positive as this. She demanded to be driven hard and fast. His heart was beating fast as the temperature gauges indicated that the engine was now ready to be opened up.

At first, he thought of taking it carefully, but then de Villiers' words came back into his mind. He could hear them quite clearly, as if Bruce were next to him. 'Don't go easy on her. There are too many other good drivers. You must push her to the limit.'

He pressed down hard on the accelerator, the revs shot past 13000 and the engine screamed out a high-pitched wail. Wyatt was forced hard back into his seat as he passed 160 mph in under eight seconds.

Now he was living, the world passing him by in a vivid assembly of colours and images as he came to the end of the straight and pulled the car hard over to take the first corner in a perfect line. She was rock-solid – he couldn't believe it.

Into the next curve, laying down the power and pushing her to the absolute limit. Just as he felt her breaking away, he backed off the power and thundered into the next bend.

She was a driver's car, feeding him the information he needed through the fluctuations in the chassis. As he rounded the final corner back into the main straight, he realised he hadn't explored the limits of the engine's potential.

He rocketed down the straight and saw Dunstal with

another figure next to him. Obviously they were timing him. Sartori held the lap record for the circuit with a time of 2.566 minutes, achieved in the previous season.

Wyatt pushed her hard through the corners, close to breaking-point, the engineer screaming. He knew what he was up against – Sartori was one of the quickest drivers through the curves, and this circuit was all curves. But Wyatt knew the track better than Sartori ever would. This was the track his father had taught him to race on. Wyatt could almost drive around it with his eyes closed – he didn't have to think, he just went on instinct.

The main straight came up again quickly, and he shot down it at over 150 mph. He had never approached the last bend as fast before.

He glanced up at the speedo and saw the needle lick over 200 mph as the bends came up again. He didn't just like this car, he loved her. Though the thought of going eighty laps in her was faintly terrifying. She was so fast, so agile. She demanded to be driven hard.

At the end of the next lap he steered her into the pits. De Villiers would want to examine the car closely, to pick up any faults.

Mickey was up and shaking his hand. He pulled off his helmet and fire-protective balaclava. The air cooled the sweat off his face. He felt bruised and exhausted.

'You did it, Wyatt!'

'What?'

'You broke the lap record by two seconds!'

He felt exhilarated. For the first time he was driving a Formula One car that was competitive.

'You're a genius, Mickey. She handles like a dream.'

Mickey ran his eyes over the Shadow. 'Yer goin' to have to keep pushing her, lap after lap as if yer were racin'. We have to prove that she can handle the strain of a race, especially the engine and the automatic box. The lads from Shensu want to strip her after she's done a genuine eighty laps. Now tell me, how're those focking tyres?'

Wyatt stared down at the tyres. He knew Mickey's and

111

Bruce's concerns, but as far as he was concerned the Carvalhos were good – they'd proved pretty sticky.

Dr Jorge da Silva, the head of Carvalho's research and development team, stepped forward. A short, distinguished-looking man, he ignored Mickey.

'We change the tyres every ten laps. Each set has a slightly different compound – just tell us which gives you the best handling.'

Mickey was about to say something to Dr da Silva but Bruce punched him gently on the shoulder. 'Easy, Mickey, Wyatt's not unhappy with the tyres.'

The Irishman shrugged his shoulders and went over to Professor Katana to discuss some technical matters.

Bruce pumped Wyatt's hand. 'Keep that up, and you'll be at the front of the grid for the whole season. We'll continue testing this afternoon.'

At the end of the day Bruce de Villiers sat in his office alone. He was very, very pleased with Chase's performance.

He switched on the intercom.

'Debbie, get me Ricardo Sartori.'

'It'll take a bit of time, Bruce, the exchange on the island is operated by a Casanova – he tries to chat me up every time I put a call through.'

Bruce chuckled. He looked down at the development schedule for the Shadow. They would fly to Kyalami, in his native South Africa, for extensive tyre-testing. The conditions there were ideal – hot, dry weather and excellent marshalling around the track. For tyre-testing, the high altitude of Johannesburg was an added advantage, and the privacy of the circuit appealed to him – he'd be assured that other teams wouldn't be watching. He didn't want them to get a close look at the Shadow till the first official Grand Prix.

Wyatt was fired up, and already earning his fee. However, Sartori wasn't, and every hour he spent on Skiathos was sapping their chances of victory.

The phone rang, startling him. He hadn't expected the call to go through so quickly.

'Ricardo?'

'He not here,' a female voice, dark and husky, replied in poor English.

Bruce lost his rag. 'I don't give a flying fuck where he is. Get him here and get him now!'

He heard the phone drop and then lots of shouting. He hung on, feeling his irritation grow.

''Allo?' Sartori's voice was clear and melodic.

'Ricardo. It's de Villiers. You've . . .'

'You insulted my maid.'

All right, thought Bruce, I've now had quite enough of this prima donna.

'Stop buggering around. The car's ready. Chase has just broken your lap record by two seconds.'

There was a lengthy pause.

'The car. She must be very good, eh, Bruce?'

'Chase is a brilliant driver. Every day he's getting better.'

'I am better.'

'Prove it to me instead of sitting on your bum in the sun!'

There was another pause. Then: 'I'll see you tomorrow, Bruce. Then I will a show you how fast your car really is.'

Bruce put the phone down. Now Ricardo would start earning his fee – the twenty million they had had to pay to hold him.

Bruce was quite certain that Sartori would break Wyatt's record.

He slammed the phone down and felt the sweat trickling down his face. He looked out through the window with the vines round its edge. The Norwegian woman was lying outside in the bright sunshine, her body brown and sensuous on the white beach-towel. He would have to leave her.

The competition never went away. Perhaps he might have underestimated Chase. He had given him an advantage already, but not much of one.

He made another quick call to the airport, asking them to have his plane ready, then he walked through into the master-bedroom and threw his essential clothes into a leather holdall. He always travelled light, buying new clothes wherever he went.

113

She came in through the door and he noticed the droplets of suntan oil clinging to her pubic hair.

'Vat are you doing, Ricardo?'

She irritated him now. 'What do you think?'

'The phone call, it was bad?'

He ignored her question and continued packing. At last he relented. 'I have to go to England tomorrow to begin training for the new season. There's also a driver I have to put in his place.'

She put her hand over his buttocks. 'I will come too?'

He had plenty of women in England, he didn't need another. Besides, she was part of Skiathos, and he liked to forget about it when the pressure was on.

'No. I will go alone.'

She started crying. It was so predictable. He didn't need her.

'Bastard,' she said.

'I promised you nothing. You understand? I live to drive. Motor-racing is my wife.'

It was the standard excuse, and he got the standard reaction. 'You can chust fuck off!'

He zipped up the bag and put on his jacket, checking his passport.

'I don't need to hear your crying,' he said. He went up to her, kissing her briefly on the mouth. 'You . . . are a very beautiful woman.'

He walked quickly out of the front door and jumped into the front seat of the jeep. As he started the engine, she ran out, pulling on a towelling robe. 'I will come with you to the airport!'

'As you will.'

He drove fast, revelling in the fact that she was scared. The jeep slid through the corners of the narrow dirt road that led away from the villa. It launched into the air several times – then he hit the tar road and floored the accelerator. In the distance he saw the small airport, and on the runway his jet, its windows twinkling in the bright sunlight – his pride and joy.

Minutes later, he pulled up next to it. He leaned over to kiss her, but she pushed him away and stared at him angrily.

'I am coming to England. Even if you don't want me.'

'I don't want you. I don't love you.'

He tensed up, his face becoming a map of fascinating wrinkles. His eyes stared off into the distance. He had to shut himself off from this, he did not need it in his life.

He jumped out of the jeep and she drove off. He watched as she disappeared into the distance, feeling relief as the space between them increased. Then he turned to the jet and began his pre-flight inspection. The holiday was over. It was back to business, and he was determined to do what he had always been so good at. Winning.

Suzie watched Wyatt come round the corner for the fortieth time and accelerate down the long straight, the engine erupting into a bloodcurdling scream.

She imagined his eyes, the dark eyes that never seemed to rest. She had spent the whole day in the pit. She'd had never realised what a tightly-knit organisation a Formula One team was.

You had to earn respect. You didn't become a part of the team automatically. Bruce's secretary, Debbie, was a great support. She'd introduced Suzie to everyone and offered to help her in any way she could.

She kept thinking of Wyatt's leanly muscled body – the hard, sculpted face and the tangled dark hair. There was a confidence in the way he moved . . . She had never seen a man so much in control of his actions.

Now, mesmerised by the car flashing past, she imagined him making love to her. Perhaps she should have given in to him on the race track that morning. All she knew was that she wanted him.

In business she had often admired men for the power they radiated, but this was different. There was something more here – because in this place a man could die. Here, cars and drivers competed against each other for victory. It was an activity that ate up nearly half a billion pounds a year, and for her it held a magnetic attraction.

She took out a sketch-pad and made a few rough drawings. She worked quickly, in sharp, well-defined pencil strokes.

'You draw so beautifully.'

She turned round to Debbie. The men couldn't keep their eyes off Debbie's short, tight skirt that revealed a stunning pair of legs.

'I saw your latest collection in *Vogue*,' Debbie went on. 'Wyatt said he'd give me one of your dresses.'

Suzie smiled. She'd been right not to give in to him. There were plenty of other women in his life and she was determined not to join the procession. She wanted Wyatt to respect her, she knew that was the only way she'd hold him.

The car shot past again, and they both stared at the driver's helmet.

'He's magnificent,' said Suzie. 'Have you met Ricardo?'

'Yes. Very charming, but with the looks of the devil.'

They walked over the track on the steel walkway and Suzie gazed off into the distance. She could see the Shadow snaking through the bends. Suddenly she was aware again of how dangerous it all was.

'Have you ever seen an accident?'

The faint smile that had been on Debbie's face disappeared. 'We don't talk about them. It's bad luck.'

Mickey Dunstal came over to them, dressed in his regulation white shirt and jeans. 'And what might you two beauties be looking so concerned about?'

His Irish charm always caught Suzie slightly off balance. He defied categorisation, he looked like one of the prophets in the storybooks, his thick, long blond hair caught up in a pony-tail.

'Nothing,' Suzie answered quickly.

'''Tis a tragedy to spend your life thinking o' nothin'.'

She laughed.

'I believe you'll be decorating me car,' he said.

She nodded, and he pinched the back of her arm affection-ately, and whispered in her ear: 'As long as it doesn't affect the aerodynamics, you can do what you like with her.'

*

116

When Mickey returned to the pits, there was a new electricity in the air. Everyone was frantic. De Villiers was glowering at the mechanics.

'This isn't a holiday camp. If you want to win, you've got to give the job one hundred per cent! Wyatt's on his fiftieth lap, and when he comes in for fresh tyres I want them changed in under eight seconds. Got it?'

A young mechanic turned to him. 'This isn't a bloody race.'

'Get out, Ryan!'

'What?'

'Get out and don't come back. I'm not carrying anyone, and if anyone else feels the same, they can join you.'

Ryan was shaking with rage now. He walked up to de Villiers. He was nearly six inches taller than Bruce, and holding a spanner in his right hand.

Mickey stepped forward. It looked as though it was going to get ugly. Then he felt Reg Tillson, the chief mechanic, restraining him. Reg whispered in his ear: 'Bruce can look after himself.'

Ryan raised his arm. 'Fuck you, you fucking South African fascist!'

Before Mickey realised it, Ryan was lying spread-eagled across the floor of the pits and de Villiers had the spanner out of his hand.

'Get out, Ryan. Or I'll break the other arm.'

Ryan staggered to his feet and walked out of the pitch, clutching his right arm. De Villiers turned to the rest of them.

'I want you all with me. If you're not in this business to win, get out. It's Chase who'll end up in a coffin if any of you fuck up.'

His eyes searched the pit, catching the attention of everyone around him. Only when he was certain that all eyes were upon him, did he continue.

'This is a hard business. Especially hard if you're running cars that don't finish every race or don't get first place. To beat everyone else, you've got to be better than everyone else.'

He turned and pointed at Reg.

'Reg is one of the best. And you know why? Because he

117

never stops.' He paused, his eyes locking into each one of them. 'You know the circus. There are always distractions. But if you get distracted, you'll fuck up. So if you want a screw, do it before the race, do it after the race, but don't think about it when you're working on my car. If you kill one of my drivers – you'll live with it till you're dead.

'I want each of you to ask yourself a question each day: What have I done to help Calibre-Shensu to win? What have I done to earn my salary – to deserve my place on this team?

'I'll tell you something. I work so hard that when I get home, I want to vomit on the lawn. And it's only when you start feeling like that, that you have any right to say that you work for Calibre-Shensu.' He looked up as he heard Wyatt's machine coming into the pits. 'Under eight seconds lads. Get it?'

Everyone was silent, poised as the Shadow screamed up to them. Bruce de Villiers leapt back, stop-watch in hand.

'Go!'

The whole pit area erupted with noise, and in swung the Shensu Shadow. The mechanics swarmed over the car like bees and the wheels were changed at lightning speed. De Villiers raised his hand to Wyatt and the machine blasted out of the pits.

The silence after the deafening noise from the engine was disturbing. De Villiers grinned.

'Seven point five seconds. And I'm sure we can get it down to six.'

Wyatt pulled in after eighty laps. He was wet with sweat and feeling totally exhausted. His neck muscles were finished, the pressure of the G-forces inside the Shadow as he was cornering had taken their toll.

He pulled off the steering-wheel and was helped out of the cockpit by some of the pit crew. Wyatt pulled off his helmet and then the fire-proof balaclava, as Mickey peppered him with questions.

'How did she handle, me boy? Wasn't she like a dream?'

'Better, Mickey. It's just that I've got to readjust myself.

I've never driven a car that goes so quickly through the corners, it's as if I'm learning to drive again.'

'You were very quick.'

Wyatt saw de Villiers walking towards them. He noticed that there had been a change in the atmosphere in the pits since he'd started. He guessed Bruce had laid down the law.

'Are we going to win, Wyatt?' Bruce's hard voice was in stark contrast to Mickey's sing-song Irish brogue.

'I'm going to have to work on my neck muscles. The Shadow really goes through the corners – the G-forces are hammering me.'

'You'll handle it. How's the engine?'

'Magnificent.'

'Sounds too good to be true.'

'Professor Katana will be stripping the car and the engine, Bruce,' Mickey said. 'We'll be giving you a full report by tomorrow mornin'.'

'You'll work through the night?'

'Well, Bruce, we get the impression that if we don't you'll be after us with yer fists.'

Early the next morning Bruce was reading through Dunstal's and Katana's analysis of the Shadow's performance, when the door to his office burst open.

'You make a complete fool of me!'

He put down the report and looked up to see Ricardo Sartori in front of him, boiling with rage.

'That's because you spend your time in bed, rather than on the track,' Bruce replied, leaning back in his chair and folding his arms behind his head.

'I was world champion three times! I am the greatest driver in 'istory!' Ricardo screamed, almost on top of Bruce. 'You make a complete fool out of me!'

Sartori was a powerhouse. His short body was as lean and supple as a cat's, and his dark eyes glared intensely from his deeply tanned face, which broke into a thousand intriguing wrinkles with every change of expression.

'You let that fool drive your new car! You are crazy!'

'He broke the lap record.'

'Big deal! Do not insult me. I, Ricardo Sartori, will tomorrow give you a demonstration of how that car can really be driven.'

'Your car will not be ready till Friday.'

'I tell you, I don't know why I drive for you! You know that? I think I leave.'

'Forfeiting your twenty million dollars, and your reputation?'

Bruce was angry now. He was not prepared to put up with the Italian's histrionics.

Ricardo knew he was cornered. He needed the money. His dark eyebrows began to twitch out of control.

'No one has ever dared to speak to me in such a manner before. Whadda you think I am?'

Bruce wasn't scared of Ricardo. You couldn't manage drivers if they intimidated you. Supremely confident, they were hard to control and used to taking risks.

'What do I think you are?' Bruce paused a second, and then looked Ricardo in the eyes as he delivered his body-blow. 'I think you're a superb driver who's punch-drunk with success.'

Bruce wasn't sure for a few seconds if Ricardo was going to hit him. Then the Italian sat down in the chair opposite his desk.

'I apologise. All right?' He spoke quietly now, the anger gone from him.

'OK. Now let's get down to business,' Bruce said, relieved. He was always amazed at the way the Italian's temper could suddenly disappear, like a flash storm in the Mediterranean.

'The new car, she sounds very good.'

'Better than good. We're going to win the championship. Wyatt says that the Shadow handles very differently to the usual Formula One machine.'

'What does he know? He's driven one car for one year. I have driven for fifteen!'

Bruce stared up at the ceiling. Shit. Was he going to have to put up with this sort of behaviour for the whole season? He would just have to get used to it.

'Wyatt knows plenty,' he said. 'Don't underestimate him.'

'Huh.' The Italian shrugged his shoulders. 'When will my car be ready?'

Bruce looked up as Mickey strode into the office. The Irishman gave Ricardo a scathing look.

'In about three days, me boy, so you'll be twiddling your thumbs till then.'

'And who are you?' Ricardo stared at Mickey as if he were seeing some distasteful object.

'Dr Mickey Dunstal.'

Ricardo rose from his chair and shook Mickey's hand. Every driver on the circuit had immense respect for the mad Irishman and his brilliant cars. 'I am honoured to meet you,' he said graciously.

Bruce was taken aback by this sudden outpouring of charm – then realised that, most of the time, Ricardo was acting. What the Formula One champion really felt was very difficult to gauge – but he enjoyed drama, that much was clear.

Bruce laid his big, gnarled hands on the table. 'Look, till your car is ready you can drive Wyatt's, all right?'

'Thank you,' Ricardo replied, 'but I will rather wait for my own car to be ready.'

Bruce gave him a veiled smile. He had the Italian worked out.

On Friday morning the sun was shining brightly through the beech trees that surrounded the circuit, and the cool winter air was crisp. In the pits there was an atmosphere of excitement. Everyone involved in the running of Calibre-Shensu had turned up, and people were standing round drinking coffee, and talking in hushed tones. Steam rose from their mouths. The feeling of expectation was almost tangible.

Today was the first drive in the Shensu Shadow for the former world champion, Ricardo Sartori.

Wyatt had tried talking to Sartori over the previous few days, but the man had always snubbed him. He sensed a new hostility in the Italian's behaviour, and resented it. The previous season he'd had to endure seeing the Italian get the better car every time, under his Uncle Danny's watchful supervision. Well, there was certainly going to be no camaraderie between them this season. He guessed that was because Ricardo now knew they were evenly matched.

Ricardo pulled on his helmet and Wyatt saw the look of fiery determination in his eyes. He was determined to prove he was faster than Wyatt – that was all that mattered to him.

Again Wyatt realised the truth of what Bruce had told him a week before – that there was no such thing as holding back on the circuit. Every driver desperately wanted to prove himself.

Wyatt watched Ricardo settling down in the cockpit. The Italian raised his hand to indicate he was ready, and Bruce leaned over him and whispered something in his ear. Wyatt wondered what it was, then mentally shrugged it off. As they would say in Japan: *Shikata ga nai*. It can't be helped.

The big engine roared into life and the Shadow shot out of the pits and onto the circuit. Wyatt felt his blood-pressure rising. He lowered himself into his own machine. This was war. His engine roared into life behind him and he screamed out of the pits, hot after Sartori.

Bruce watched the Shadow come down the main straight towards the starting-grid, then bellow as Ricardo floored the accelerator. Bruce admired the way the car moved. She looked superb.

He glanced down at the electronic timer and watched the seconds tick by. There was no doubt in his mind that Ricardo would be going for a record time.

The seconds ticked slowly past and everyone was quiet. Wyatt's car shot past, completing its warm-up lap. In the back of Bruce's mind was the thought of the accident that Ricardo had been involved in the previous season. Would Ricardo be afraid now, and would this slow him down?

Every head turned as Sartori's car appeared out of the last corner and came into the main straight. The engine had a wonderful sound to it, almost singing as it shot up to maximum revs. The dark shape shot past the pits and Bruce again glanced at the timer.

'Incredible.'

Everyone was looking at Bruce's back, waiting to hear Sartori's lap time.

'One second faster than Wyatt's new record. The Italian hasn't lost his touch.'

Bruce gestured to Reg Tillson to hold up the board to let Wyatt know his lap record had fallen.

'Now let's see what this man's really made of,' he said to himself.

Wyatt looked up at the board as he shot past the pits. He became cold, as well as angry. Ricardo would be amongst the front runners that season, but he was determined to beat him. And that meant going faster.

He accelerated into the esses. The surface of the track was invisible to him, all he saw were the contortions of the circuit in front of him. 'Take more chances.' He repeated his father's words to himself, over and over again.

He was in a trance-like state by the time he completed his second lap, and watched for the sign that would prove he had beaten Sartori. This was what he enjoyed doing. This was what he lived for. There was no place for fear. Suzie's face flashed before him, then disappeared. He was almost cold now, taking the bends faster than he'd believed the Shadow was capable of doing. He flashed past Ricardo and down the straight.

Drops of water splashed against his visor. Shit. It was raining.

He pulled into the pits on the next lap, furious that he couldn't go on, but knowing that in the wet he'd never beat Sartori's time. As he got out of the car, Bruce slapped him on the back.

'You bastard! I've never seen driving like that on the test circuit.'

The slow realisation that he must have broken Ricardo's record lifted the weight from his shoulders. 'I beat his time?'

'You knocked another two seconds off it!'

Ricardo walked silently out of the pits. He hated Wyatt Chase more than any other man on earth at that particular moment. And in the pit of his stomach there was fear. The memories of last year's accident had not gone away: he had not been able

123

to go faster. But he would have to, or Chase would be ahead of him. There was no such thing as a final victory in Formula One, only the prospect of another race to be won.

Wyatt sank down next to Suzie on the settee in Bruce's office.

'I want you to feature in all our publicity,' Suzie said.

There was a forced smile on Bruce's face, and Wyatt laughed, but Suzie remained serious. 'It's not a joke, Wyatt, and you're going to have to model for us.'

'No way!'

'It's in your contract.'

'And what about Ricardo?'

'I – a refuse to model clothes,' Bruce said, imitating Ricardo's voice perfectly.

Suzie got up, her eyes resting on Wyatt's. 'It always amazes me how afraid men are of their masculinity. Come, I want to measure you.'

Wyatt didn't say anything. He just returned her stare, and Suzie swallowed.

'It's going to take me just a couple of minutes. It means you'll have clothes that fit you perfectly.'

Wyatt gestured for Bruce to leave, which he did with a smirk on his face. Suzie felt her confidence evaporating as the door closed behind de Villiers. She could feel the sexual electricity between herself and Wyatt.

'You feel by being measured we will destroy your image? It must be pretty fragile.' She tried to sound assured but she was almost stammering.

'Are you going to make me a dress?'

'You want one? You have a good figure – nice legs, slim waist.'

He didn't laugh. He hadn't realised that she had a sense of humour. She also smelt delicious, some fragrance he couldn't quite recognise. He caught her eyes and saw them flicker as she tried to retain her image of controlled professionalism.

'Measure me,' he commanded.

'You are a clothes-hanger, Wyatt,' she said as she drew out her tape-measure.

She was close to him now, and she felt scared. She could

124

smell the maleness of him. Then, without warning, he drew her to him and kissed her.

The pretence was useless, she wanted him so badly she was almost crying with desire. They tore at one another's clothes, kissing, touching, stroking.

He kissed her all over, then ran his lips up the inside of her thigh, pausing before the blonde hairs at the top.

'Oh God, please.'

But he didn't oblige. Instead he continued to arouse her so that she tore his racing-suit from his body. Then she kneaded his buttocks and drew him inside her.

She started shaking, out of control, the orgasms rippling through her body, feeling as free as the wind.

'Oh my God, Wyatt, I love you, I love you!' she screamed. Then she felt him explode inside her.

She awoke later, lying naked in his arms on the couch. How long had they been sleeping? She looked at her watch on the floor and saw it was after midnight.

Wyatt opened his eyes as he felt the tape-measure against his body.

'The way you are proportioned' she said, 'means that clothes will always sit well on you.'

'I could have told you that.'

'Ah, but it was fun finding out . . .'

She drew away and made a final note. He noticed that her handwriting was sloping and extravagant, reflecting the passion that lay behind her precise, ordered exterior.

Her face turned serious.

'Is it true that you offered to buy Debbie one of my dresses?'

'And if it is?'

'It is a very personal gift. I am not one of a procession of . . .'

'You think, after we made love like that, I would want to make love to someone else?'

It was as she had expected. She would never get a commitment from him.

'Suzie, what I do is dangerous,' Wyatt said. 'I cannot take

125

risks for someone else. I must face the world alone. There has been too much pain in my life already.'

He folded her in his arms and kissed her softly, but after a time she pulled away.

She would make certain he chose her, not Debbie, a dress.

Emerson Ortega took another pull of the large Havana cigar and walked past the chimpanzee cage. He grimaced with pain. Even the action of pulling on the cigar hurt his face.

He had always enjoyed visiting the zoo when he was small. Not that he ever went with his parents to the zoo, like other children; at nine he didn't know who his father was and realised he couldn't rely on his mother – she was more interested in turning tricks then educating her only son. So he fought on the streets, stole cars, traded drugs, killed the people who crossed him, and developed an instinct for survival. Now he had his own private zoo, stocked with animals from all over the world. He earned over $350 million a week and was arguably one of the ten wealthiest men alive. And he was no longer Emerson Ortega.

He was slim and dark, five foot ten inches tall, with smooth black hair. And he was very scared.

He touched his face. It still felt very sensitive. He had not dared look in the mirror yet. His moustache had disappeared before the operation and he would not grow it back. He would look younger, the surgeon had told him. Ortega said he did not care, as long as he did not look like himself. But of course he did care – his looks had been his trademark. He had liked the fact that he was known, and feared.

Emerson Ortega was wanted by the United States authorities on cocaine production and smuggling charges. The CIA had tried to kill him on three occasions. On the last one they had succeeded. Emerson Ortega was now officially dead.

But he had some unfinished business to conclude. Several months before, the United States government, through the CIA, had put pressure on the government of Bogota and got them to sign an extradition treaty. That meant anyone involved in smuggling drugs to the US, or making drugs for the US, arrested in Colombia, would be deported to the US.

This ruling was a disaster for the drug barons, because in Colombia there was always someone they could bribe to get off a sentence. Failing that, they could kill off whoever got in their way with impunity. But to face US justice was another matter altogether – which was another reason why Emerson Ortega had felt the need to disappear.

There was one man behind all this, a man Ortega hated more than anyone else in the world. He was an ex-Argentinian who could not be bribed: David Ramirez, the new head of the Colombian Palace of Justice.

Emerson Ortega wanted to get even with Ramirez. Emerson Ortega believed that in Colombia he should have been lauded as a national hero for bringing his country wealth and prosperity. He had been close to getting a seat in the Colombian parliament, until David Ramirez had started undermining him. He was quite sure that Ramirez was also behind all the CIA assassination attempts on him.

The killing at the church, the killing in which Ortega had supposedly died, had been perfectly set up. His double had taken the bullet intended for himself.

The double had been an out-of-work actor they'd located in Brazil, who looked exactly like him. He'd told the actor the whole thing was to sort out a problem, that the idea was to convince the local minister that Emerson regularly attended church, and thus increase his standing in the community. Emerson told the actor that he hated church and was willing to pay the actor a large fee to go in his place each Sunday. The actor had readily agreed, pleased to find such a simple way of earning a good living.

Emerson had heard of the plot to assassinate him through Rod Talbot, an American who was helping him develop the cocaine business.

Normally, Emerson would have had his would-be assassins captured, and then tortured to death – this time he had decided it would be better if they succeeded. Emerson knew that the time would come when he would not be able to stay one step ahead of the CIA – that it was time for him to disappear. Carmen, his wife, had agreed to go through with the charade. He had loved Carmen, and the fuckers had killed his wife as well.

It was ironic in a way. She was the one person – apart from his non-identical twin brother – who could have led them to him; the one person who could have blown the new identity he had now assumed.

No longer would he walk the streets of Bogota as a man of standing. Now he must live as Antonio Vargas – a nonentity. Emerson guessed that if the CIA found out he was still alive, they would try to kill him again. But now they would never know they had killed the wrong man, because his wife was the only person who could have told them.

Today he was faced with a serious and growing problem. He could produce cocaine, but he could not ship it to the US. Every avenue of supply he had used in the past had been effectively blocked, including Panama and the Bahamas.

However, he was now possessed of a huge advantage. He was unknown, forty years old and in excellent shape. He did not drink, smoke or take drugs – those things had become less and less important to him as he made more and more money. He had ruled his empire through fear and intimidation; it was the only way he knew how to control people, and it was very effective.

He walked away from the zoo, across the lawns of his eight-thousand-acre estate, glancing at the gun towers in the distance. A vast wall ran around the property, constantly patrolled by armed guards and tracker-dogs. A complete aerial surveillance system combed the sky – should anyone dare to invade the airspace above his property, a jet-fighter and helicopter gunship were on standby.

A thin smile crossed his face as he came closer to an assembly of people gathered on the main lawn. Above them towered a gallows from which hung a solitary rope. Two of the men broke from the group, both armed with Uzi sub-machine-guns.

'Pablo, Emilio, how goes it?'

The fatter of the two answered.

''E is ready, Mr Vargas.'

Even those who had been closest to him, failed to recognise him.

'You have a camera crew?'

'They are all in place.'

Emerson waved the men aside and walked into the group, which parted to reveal a handsome man in his mid-forties standing beneath the gallows, the hanging rope around his neck.

Emerson waved, indicating that the others should go away. He waited in silence, studying the Minister's face. When the men were out of earshot, he whispered softly to his captive.

'It is I, Emerson Ortega, risen from the dead.'

'Ortega,' the man mumbled in a strangled voice.

'The CIA killed my double. I know you led them to me, and for that you must pay with your life.'

'You will never get away with this, Ortega!'

He spat the words out, an impressive figure in his dark-blue suit, a big man with a broad forehead and open eyes that commanded attention. David Ramirez, head of the Colombian Palace of Justice.

'Oh, Minister, I think you talk very big for a man who is about to fall a few feet.'

Ramirez laughed – a dry, empty laugh.

'Shut up!' screamed Ortega. 'This is a solemn moment. Mr Ramirez, you have an appointment with God.'

The estate was deathly quiet. Ortega turned to the still face of the head of the Palace of Justice.

'Do you have a last request?'

The spittle, David Ramirez' answer, landed on Emerson Ortega's face. He wiped it off slowly.

'I take a video of this event, Ramirez,' he said. 'I take it to your wife and children as a present. I let them see your last moments.'

'No.'

'Oh yes, and the noose is set so you die very slowly, eh?'

Ortega held Ramirez stare for a minute, then pulled the lever that released the trap door. Ramirez uttered a strangled cry.

'Your last word, sir. But it will take half an hour for you to pass out. A good length for a short film. If you don't mind, I will sit and watch.'

Ortega stepped back and sat down in the chair placed beside the gallows. From out of his shirt he took a pet marmoset and stroked its head softly.

'It is boring watching you die, sir. But when I think how many of my men you have sent to jail and to death, I feel it is worth the wait. A copy of this little film will naturally be sent to your colleagues in the government. Perhaps then they will think a little more carefully about the extradition treaty they have signed with the United States government, eh?'

Ramirez' face gradually turned purple, much to Ortega's satisfaction. He knew what this would mean to the nine thousand people who worked for the Ortega Cartel. These people had begun saying that the Ortega Cartel had lost its power, that they were afraid of the Colombian government. Well, thought Ortega, this little gesture would show them who really held the power.

A little later Ortega looked at his watch, then called one of the guards. The man came up at a jog.

'Call the doctor.'

The sun was setting across the beautiful jungle as the tall, white-suited man strode over the immaculately cut lawns that surrounded the gallows.

'Good afternoon, Mr Vargas,' he said, slightly out of breath.

'Yes, it is very good. You have met the head of the Palace of Justice?'

'No, sir.'

'Would you tell me if he is dead?'

The doctor put down his bag and examined the body suspended from the gallows.

'He is very dead.'

'Very good. Now we must send him back to his family, I'm sure they are wondering where he has got to.'

The doctor was quiet – an unassuming man with white hair beneath his panama hat. 'Isn't that a little excessive?' he asked in his languid American drawl.

'How do you Americanos put it? Nothing succeeds like excess, eh?'

The doctor did not laugh, but he managed a tight-lipped smile.

Emerson Ortega got up and stretched. 'You may go, doctor. I must check that the animals are being properly fed. I am a man of deep compassion. It was Emerson Ortega's last wish that Ramirez should die.'

The doctor was silent.

'Have you lost your tongue?' Emerson snapped.

'Mr Vargas, sir, you are the most caring person I have ever met,' the doctor replied contritely.

'Ah, that is nice to hear. You like to live a little longer?'

'Please.'

'We understand each other so well.'

The helicopter flew low over the dense green jungle and powered on up the river. The pilot, a Vietnam veteran, kept a tight hand on the controls. His new employer, Antonio Vargas, who sat in the cabin behind him, paid him more in a month than he'd have earned in a year back home, but Larry Sykes knew that if he had an accident, Vargas would kill him. This wasn't just supposition: he'd seen Vargas kill ten men in the last two weeks. One had actually been thrown out of this very chopper.

This was a regular journey they made at least four times a week. Larry kept his eyes open. He remembered all that was going on, but he resisted the temptation to get part of the action for himself. He was sure that if he proved his loyalty, Vargas would trust him more and more. Then he could just exert a bit of leverage – subtle blackmail – and get a very generous retirement package.

He dropped down as he found the clearing, slightly to the left of the Vaupes River. He eased the chopper onto the landing-pad, and men armed with Uzi carbines burst from the surrounding buildings, quickly standing to attention.

Larry turned back and watched Vargas step from the cockpit, followed by Jules Ortega. What a pair. After them came five young women, aged between fifteen and seventeen, all wearing too little clothing and too much make-up. He knew what they were for – entertaining the staff. They never left the women there, instead they brought in a new batch each time. Very clever, thought Larry, then turned away as Vargas shot him an irritated glance.

Antonio Vargas, alias Emerson Ortega, looked angrily around the manufacturing plant, then walked briskly to the main office, followed by his twin brother Jules.

It was more comfortable in the big air-conditioned room. Jules sat down at a large desk, with Emerson seated a little to one side. It irritated Emerson that with his new identity he had to assume the role of subordinate to his non-identical twin. He tried to console himself with the thought that Jules had to be seen to be in command. Nobody must realise that he, in the person of Antonio Vargas, was silently pulling the strings that ran the Ortega Cartel – the biggest cocaine dealer and manufacturer in Colombia.

A dark-skinned, black-haired man with a heavy moustache entered, carrying a sheaf of reports. He stood to attention, his laboratory coat immaculately pressed for the occasion.

Jules Ortega leaned back on his chair, legs open wide, hands clasped behind his head. He liked his new role, with his brother in permanent disguise and himself in control.

'Speak, Dr Estevez, and it better be good.'

'Everything is in place. Whenever you want to move, you can, sir. It will only take a few days,' Dr Estevez said hesitantly. 'But I have one major problem. Though we have more than enough raw material, we don't have the chemicals we need for the refining process.'

Jules Ortega smashed his fist against the table. 'Well, order more chemicals, you stupid bastard!'

The doctor paled. 'Our usual suppliers can no longer help us.'

'What do you mean, fuck-head?'

'The Americans, they know what we use those chemicals for. They have been prevented from renewing our contract.'

Jules hunched his shoulders, glancing at his brother, who gave him a slight, imperceptible nod.

'But the chemicals are for industrial use . . .'

'Sir, the Americans, they are not so stupid.'

132

'But then, arsehole, you look for another source.'

'I have looked, sir. Germany is a possibility – but these things take time.'

Jules Ortega got up and walked round the table. Without warning he slammed his fist into the doctor's solar-plexus.

'Every time I come here, you talk shit!' he shouted. 'You think 'cos my brother's dead, you'll get an easy ride? You have one month. If things are not working properly by then, I bust your balls.'

'But sir,' Dr Estevez groaned, 'I can't get the chemical.'

Jules kicked him in the back, scoring a direct hit in his kidneys. 'Stop worrying. We will get you the chemicals. My new source has promised them.' And then, as Dr Estevez staggered to his feet, 'Now show Mr Vargas and me around.'

Emerson relaxed. Jules was doing a fine job. All he had to do was prime him, and things would carry on the way they'd always done. It was just that he was now the man in the mask, the unknown controller of the operation.

This manufacturing plant had always made Emerson feel uneasy. He was glad they had planned to move it. True, the plant was hidden in the jungle near the tiny settlement of Mitu, on the Vaupes River, some four hundred miles south-east of Bogota, the capital of Colombia. And it was only accessible by air or by water, sailing up the dirty brown waters of the Vaupes from the town of Mitu.

Mitu, now largely unoccupied, had once been a rubber boom-town. Now it was a line of painted wooden houses that broke the unending carpet of green covering south-eastern Colombia.

The plant made Emerson feel insecure because it wasn't quite secret enough. Word had already got out in Mitu that there were good work and good women available in the strange new factory up the river, so at least labour wasn't a problem. And even if it were, people could be taken by force – could just disappear, no questions asked. Emerson imagined what it had been like when the area was exploited by the Casa Arana, a rubber company financed by British and Peruvian backers. They'd used the local Indians as slaves; they'd raped the women, and they'd cut the hands off anyone who

133

challenged them. He understood how the men of Casa Arana had operated. He liked their style.

Emerson had come from nothing, a petty thief from the slums of Bogota. As a young man his talent for killing those who got in his way had become legendary, and he had rapidly established himself in a position of power. In those days, big business meant handling a couple of kilograms of cocaine. Now, with advanced processing equipment, it was tons he was producing, not kilograms.

Cocaine was a wonder-drug. People who tried it couldn't have enough of it, so the American authorities to the north were continually attempting to prevent the supply of cocaine to their shores. They had tried to limit the cultivation of the coca leaves in Ecuador, Peru and Bolivia. Fools! Because it was cocaine that kept those countries alive . . . They might as well have asked the people not to breathe.

Now the Americans had taken steps to destroy the cocaine processing plants. So far, they had failed. It was ironic, thought Emerson, that during this period he'd managed to increase production while at the same time lowering the street price. The market was growing every day.

The Americans were getting more and more frustrated. They could do nothing. Through a complicated network of bribes, the police were also in on the action, taking a cut. The power of drug money to corrupt was absolute.

But it was the other world markets, not just America, that now interested Emerson – because in Europe cocaine could fetch three times the price it did in the United States. And in the Old World, the authorities weren't as wide awake as the Americans to what was happening. The opening up of the Eastern Bloc also meant a huge new pool of potential users.

What was more, the Japanese market was also expanding rapidly. So demand was shooting up all over the world.

Emerson had set up this processing plant after a couple of laboratories in Bogota had been bombed under mysterious circumstances. He sensed that the CIA had orchestrated the attacks. But he knew that even this plant on the Vaupes river, hidden from prying eyes, and with all essential staff flown in, was not secure enough.

Of course, his employees knew the risks if they talked. If they gave out information that led to the discovery of the factory, they would be found and killed. The Ortega Cartel was famous for finding and punishing those who dared to betray its secrets.

The Vaupes plant was equipped with the finest technical equipment, and every step was taken to ensure the quality of the product. True, street dealers might debase it, but it would still be better than anyone else could supply. The factory had been running smoothly, producing tons of cocaine every week, until this problem with sourcing the chemicals used in the refining process.

Emerson turned to Jules. 'How's distribution?'

'We have some problems. But we'll soon be able to fly product direct to the States.'

Emerson chuckled. This was a new and unexpected development, organised by the man who was assisting in the construction of the new factory – Rod Talbot.

Emerson trusted Talbot. After all, it was Talbot who'd told him about the CIA assassination attempt and saved his life.

Distribution was Jules's responsibility. He was always coming up with new ideas for smuggling cocaine. This was important: as one door closed, it was essential to open another. The fall of Panama had been a big disaster for them; even their shipment-points in the Bahamas had been uncovered.

'We will have to be careful, Jules.'

'Talbot has arranged for us to land our planes in a US army private military base. There are no customs people there. No questions are asked because it's all top-secret.'

'I don't quite believe it. Why should they allow this?'

'Talbot says they want to move a lot of weapons into South America – and they need to do it quietly. If the transport's provided, they don't ask questions.'

'I don't trust those fuckers, Jules.'

'But you can trust Talbot. He found and killed Kruger, the man who thought he'd killed you. He got the chemicals we needed – and he also obtained all the hardware for the development of the new labs. Best of all, he's opened up a supply route to Europe that is totally dependable.'

'And if the fucker turns on us?'

'My brother, do you think I am stupid? When Talbot has done everything – then we kill him. Nice and slowly, like you did Ramirez.'

They left the office and strolled along the corridors, looking into the large, air-conditioned dining-room on their way. It was almost full, and gales of laughter rang from the tables.

Jules arched his eyebrows. 'The men think between their legs. The girls are doing a good job, and naturally they will find out what everyone is thinking.'

'Yes, there are always a few who get a little too big for their boots, eh? Then we fly them home early. We push them out without a parachute, and they disappear into the forests . . .'

Emerson looked out of a window, surveying the steamy jungle that surrounded the camp. Since the last attempt on his life, all he could think about was security; he was fast becoming paranoid on the subject.

'Jules, I do not like this place. I will be happy when we move – the other plant is almost ready. It will increase production and it will be very, very safe.'

'How much do you expect to be able to move out?'

'At least thirty-six tons per shipment . . .'

'It can be done. Talbot says he can do it.'

'Can you trust him?'

'He's only interested in money. He told me he used to work for Air America, doing crazy flights for the CIA in Vietnam.'

Emerson smiled briefly. 'I like it more and more. We only have to trust one man – Talbot. We use him, then we dump him.'

'We think alike, my brother.'

The helicopter flew on through the clouds of spray, the huge waterfall invisible below it. Water droplets covered the plastic screen and he switched on the wipers. This wasn't dangerous, this was fucking crazy. In the mirror, Larry Sykes watched the American's face. The guy was no arsehole; he knew how risky this flight was, but he wasn't showing or saying anything.

The American was blond-haired, with emerald-green eyes that missed nothing and a very pale, freckled skin. He was dressed in a green military jacket, khaki pants and black running-shoes. He looked an athletic forty, and on the ground, every movement he made was purposeful. But there was a coldness in the emerald eyes that scared the hell out of Larry.

They'd shaken hands briefly, and Talbot's grip had been like a vice-jaw; his hand was still aching from the contact. Larry was having reservations about talking to anyone about this particular operation. He didn't like the look of Rod Talbot one bit, and he didn't know who he was working for.

Talbot was sitting between Antonio Vargas and Jules Ortega. God, the three bloody musketeers. And what a hell-hole. He looked down at the map. Where the fuck were they? With all the bloody mist rising up from the jungle, it was impossible to see very far in front of you.

Next minute, the rock wall loomed in front, and he yanked hard on the cyclic-stick and the machine shot upwards. He could smell the fear on the men behind him.

The stone wall seemed endless in the mist, and he was scared he'd lost direction. Then, without warning, they burst out of the whiteness and into blazing sunshine. Larry sucked in his breath. It was incredible! The giant plateau stood high above them, surrounded by sheer rock walls. A lost world in the middle of the jungle.

'This is where you've built our processing plant? You are crazy!' he heard Jules Ortega cry out to Talbot.

'Yes, right here,' Talbot replied, without a trace of fear in his voice. 'Don't worry, gentlemen, the landing strip's coming up.' Then, more loudly: 'Over to your right, Larry.'

It was a challenge to find the place. The plateau was covered in lush vegetation that lay like a thick carpet over its surface. In the distance Larry caught sight of a concrete slab in amongst the green, ending abruptly at the cliff edge. He put the chopper down carefully.

This was what Ortega employed him for – to fly him where few other pilots would dare to go.

*

137

Talbot climbed out of the cockpit and was assailed by the wet, sticky heat of the plateau. He glanced back at Jules Ortega, who he guessed might be too thick to realise that this was the perfect location.

'You can't be serious, Rod,' Jules muttered from behind him.

'I think we should listen to what 'e 'as to say,' Emerson said quietly. Until now he had remained silent.

Talbot had already figured out that Vargas was Emerson after plastic surgery, but he kept up the charade. He wanted the Ortegas on his side. Anyway, Vargas was coming across as much more than Jules Ortega's personal assistant.

'Thank you,' he replied, clearing his throat. 'I have undertaken to handle distribution for you, but to do that you have to guarantee supply.'

'So?' Jules Ortega muttered angrily.

'Your installation on the Vaupes river, I have it on good authority, has been located by my countrymen. It has probably been bombed by now.'

Jules glowered. 'How do you know this?'

'Unimportant. What matters is that it's true.'

Jules nodded his head grimly. 'Yes . . . yes, they have bombed our installation. But we got all the equipment out beforehand.'

'So. I have built you a plant they cannot find. And even if they do find it, it is almost impossible to bomb.'

'But how do we get in and out of this place?' Vargas quickly asked.

Larry Sykes moved forward, eager to get in on the action. 'Easy. This short runway, right on the cliff edge. It makes take-off simple, and landing . . . well, you've got me, Larry Sykes.'

Talbot stepped across and hit him hard across the head. Larry never even saw it coming.

'Jesus!'

He fell across the concrete, his head ringing.

'Shut up,' Talbot snarled. 'You're here to take orders, not to show off.'

Jules Ortega roared with laughter. 'I like you, Mr Talbot. Come, show us the installation.'

They walked down a long concrete tunnel into the bowels of the mountain. Talbot gave them a commentary as they went deeper and deeper.

'This place is built to withstand a full-scale nuclear attack. In short, it's impossible to destroy with conventional bombing. Located around the perimeter areas of the mountain is an aerial surveillance system, so that any hostile plane can be blown out of the air before it even gets in sight of the place. This is an impregnable fortress. The runway you saw from the air can be covered up in less than a minute, making the whole installation invisible.'

He opened a huge door at the end of the tunnel and it swung back to reveal what looked like the entrance to a luxurious penthouse. A fountain played into a marble bath, set in the centre of a white tiled floor. Small ceiling-mounted spotlights gave a gentle illumination to the whole area.

'I like, I like,' Jules exclaimed.

'Through these doors are the master-suites. These are for us. Please follow me.'

Talbot led them through the dining, cooking and exercise areas to the massive bedroom suites. Each room looked out onto a balcony. Talbot slid back one of the big picture-windows and they walked out onto a cave-like patio that looked out over the cliff wall.

Emerson peered nervously over the edge. There was no railing. He stared at Talbot.

'These rooms,' Talbot went on, 'are invisible to the outside world. There are no railings because they might be visible to someone on the ground with a very high-powered telescope. We're not taking chances.'

Emerson nodded and stepped back quickly. The drop made the soles of his feet tingle.

Talbot led them back through the executive suites and into the plant itself.

'This laboratory area is completely sealed. The air supply comes through the air-conditioning system: should hostile elements intrude into this area, a simple flick of the switch can introduce a nerve gas which will kill anything living in less than a second.'

Talbot caught Jules's eyes. 'And should you want to – how shall I put it? – renew your staff, the same procedure can be applied.'

Jules puffed out his chest. 'We think along the same lines, Rod.'

Emerson, alias Antonio Vargas, scratched his nose, then touched Talbot's arm.

'So, you build us this facility, you provide the distribution network . . . What's the catch?'

Rod Talbot looked closely at Vargas. He was still the brains behind the operation and always would be. He was far too clever to be second-in-command to a dumbo like Jules Ortega.

'The catch, Antonio, is the rent.'

'Rent!' blurted out Jules Ortega.

'Yes,' replied Talbot. 'It's fifty million US dollars a week.'

Jules moved up to Talbot, to grab the lapels of his jacket. Instead, stinging blows caught the sides of his arms and he felt himself lift off the ground, fly through the air and hit the sidewall of the laboratory. He lay on the ground gasping for breath, furious.

'*Bastardo*!'

'One more word, Jules, and I'll kill you.'

The atmosphere was ice-cool. There was fear in Jules's eyes noted Talbot, but not in Vargas's. Vargas was the killer, he knew that. And as he expected, it was Vargas who broke the silence.

'And if we do not agree to this "rent"?' Vargas asked quickly.

'Then you build your own laboratories again and again, because wherever you put them, the CIA will find them.'

'The rent is extortionate.'

'When you clear three hundred and fifty million dollars a week?'

Anger flashed in Vargas's eyes. 'We pay.'

Wyatt Chase did not like sitting behind a desk, but there were a few technical papers from Shensu he had to read. He also had to look through Suzie's clothing designs for himself,

Ricardo and the pit crew. He liked them, they had an oriental feel.

It had been another exacting day on the test track. He found the silence of the night soothing after the animal noises of the engine that had filled his ears all day long.

He heard a noise outside the main building and looked out of the window.

'What's going on, Wyatt?' Suzie asked from behind him.

He turned and pulled her close to him.

'Just another delivery of Carvalho tyres.'

Wyatt watched the driver of the truck being directed across the track to the area behind the pits. They would put the container down so that its doors opened directly into the rear of the pits.

'Bruce has been worried about the tyres,' Wyatt said softly. But he wasn't thinking about the tyres. His hands were working their way under Suzie's dress and starting to caress her between her legs.

'Please . . .' The word was a gasp.

He eased her round so that she was pressed against the darkened glass of the window. She wore only stockings and a suspender-belt under the dress.

As her hands unzipped him and guided him towards her, another Carvalho truck drew up outside. Bruce came out and directed it towards the slip-road running next to the track. There must be some other storage facilities, Wyatt thought distractedly, that he hadn't seen.

He started to withdraw. 'You bastard,' Suzie sighed, turning round to face him.

'I only have one real obsession,' Wyatt said. He unzipped her dress as he spoke. Then he raised her up onto the desk, parted her legs and began to kiss her.

Her hands worked their way through his hair and he felt her body convulsing. Every part of her was beautiful, he wanted her to have pleasure.

Her head arching back, her blonde hair cascading around her naked shoulders, Suzie screamed out as sensation soared through her body. Wyatt rose up and plunged inside her. She lost control as he rode her, memories and feelings coursing

141

through her mind. Then suddenly she had only one vision: this dark-haired man astride her, mastering her, possessing her.

She felt him pour into her, then sank into his arms. Within a few minutes she had fallen into the most delicious sleep she had ever known.

Ricardo came in without knocking. Suzie woke suddenly, embarrassed, crossing her arms to cover her naked breasts.

'Wyatt, you should spend your time learning to drive, eh.'

It was a deliberate taunt. Suzie got up and slipped on her dress while Wyatt faced Ricardo squarely. 'Perhaps someone should teach you some manners,' he said.

The Italian was bristling. He was shorter than Wyatt but unafraid.

And then, before Wyatt realised what was happening, he was gripped from behind – two arms came round his torso.

There was nothing he could do to stop what happened next – the reactions were inbred. He dropped slightly, and felt his unknown attacker sag forward; then he pivoted, drove his right elbow back hard and hit out with the left.

Now Wyatt saw Ricardo closing in and drove his right fist out, striking him on the side of the head. Ricardo left the ground and flew against the desk.

Wyatt was still breathing normally as he regained his focus. Suzie was staring at him in astonishment; Bruce de Villiers was lying on the floor, clutching at the edge of the chair; and Ricardo was pulling himself up from the desk, retreating nervously backwards.

Wyatt helped Bruce to his feet. 'Don't ever surprise me like that again. I could have killed you.'

Bruce coughed and drew in his breath. 'I was trying to stop you fighting Ricardo.'

'Don't interfere.'

Ricardo was staring at him, hatred burning in his eyes. Wyatt loathed himself for losing control.

'Beat him on the track not here, Wyatt,' Bruce managed to cough out.

The instant Wyatt's guard was down, Ricardo picked up the

ashtray from the desk and hurled it at him. Wyatt caught it in mid-air.

'Ricardo, try that again and you won't walk for a month.'

Ricardo's eyes ran scathingly between him and Suzie, then the Italian driver turned on his heel and staggered out of the office.

'Take it easy, Wyatt, you'll beat him,' Suzie said softly. 'Are you all right, Bruce?'

De Villiers managed a smile, and Suzie gave him a quick kiss on the cheek. 'I'll leave you two alone for a while,' she said, and smiling at Wyatt, she left the office.

Wyatt was glad to see that Bruce was fine. He offered him a chair. 'I saw we got more tyres,' he said.

'That's the new compound from Carvalho. Dr Jorge da Silva believes it's a perfect match for the Shadow's exceptional cornering power. I want you to take her out tomorrow and put those new slicks through their paces – show Ricardo a thing or two about driving.'

Wyatt was pleased. It would be a good opportunity.

It was past midnight, and Suzie lay next to Wyatt, staring around the big room and then out of the window that looked over the Thames.

She didn't have to look for reasons when she was with him; it was enough that he was there. No man had made love to her the way he had earlier at the office; she hadn't thought she was capable of feeling so much. And then Ricardo had come in and there had been that explosion of violence. Suddenly, a lot of pieces had fallen into place. She'd heard about the ten years he'd spent in Japan.

He was everything she'd been searching for in a man, and the terrifying discovery was that it was the physical thing she craved after all. She needed his strength, needed to draw from it to make herself whole.

She was in love in a way she had never dreamed possible. The thought of life without him was too terrifying to contemplate. She thought of children, and other things that had remained essentially foreign to her for so many years.

He turned over and held her in his arms, still asleep. Fear

starting gnawing at the pit of her stomach; fear that she might lose this man. She thought of the money backing the Shadow, and of Wyatt's all-consuming desire to win. She thought of the team's determination to win the championship, whatever the cost, whatever rules had to be broken.

She sensed he could not make a commitment to her yet, but she knew he would be faithful to her. That would have to be enough.

But in a week's time they would be testing at Kyalami, almost ready for the first race in Rio. She was so afraid of losing him . . .

She closed her eyes, smelt the animal huskiness of his body and concentrated on the present.

Bruce stared at the screen of the Cray computer and the design of the Shadow projected on it. Mickey was next to him, punching in commands, making subtle yet significant alterations – the result of the testing.

The test results were beyond expectation. The Shensu V12 had surpassed itself. Stripped and rebuilt again and again, it now appeared to be flawless. Usually it took months of driving, then months of analysis to develop the machine to its full potential.

Mickey turned to him. 'Let's call it a day. There's nothing more to be done.'

Bruce could feel the excitement surging through his body. They had a great car. They could win the championship. He slapped Mickey on the back.

'She's a winner. A piece of real genius. But I don't like to challenge the rules, so I hope she complies with all the regulations.'

'Oh, she does, to be sure.'

'How's the development of the sports car going?'

That day Mickey had received the full go-ahead from Shensu. He had already made a few tentative sketches of how he envisaged the machine would look – a road-going car based on the Shensu V12 engine.

'Well, Bruce, the Italians have always led the field in design,

144

but now the Irish will show them a thing or two. With a little help from the Japanese, of course.'

Bruce stretched, and felt his bruises. 'Our German designer,' he said, has fallen for our number two driver.'

'All the bloody luck for Wyatt.'

Bruce settled down into the leather armchair next to Mickey's.

'How's her work, do you think?'

'Good. Very good.'

Mickey handed Bruce Suzie's drawings, and he spent some minutes evaluating them. Bruce's opinion of her rose. There was a lot more than just a good understanding of design principles here; the curving shapes that she had placed on the bodywork genuinely added to the graceful lines of the car.

'She understands our intentions very well,' he said at last. 'I thought it would be a bastard to make the branding look good, but I think she has succeeded. Maybe, though, it's a little too subtle to satisfy Jack Phelps?'

'I thought that was the last thing you'd be concerned about. But then look who's payin' the bills.'

'Let me see what she's going to have us all wearing.'

Mickey handed him a drawing-book and he paged carefully through it. She was plainly a master-craftsman. Every drawing was finely executed – and he noted that Wyatt featured in most of them.

'Think they're good?' Mickey asked after a while.

'What do you think? You're the expert.'

'Bluidy good.'

Mickey thought of Suzie close to him, showing him the sketches the previous day. He had been aware of the fragrance she was wearing, slightly musky and very alluring. Her blonde hair was swept back, revealing her distinctive forehead; her lips, precise yet sensual, beautifully painted, were pursed up tightly, waiting for his judgement.

'You have a natural talent. I don't think anyone else could have done such a fine job of work,' he had said.

'You think Wyatt will like them?'

'That I cannot tell you, me luv. You'll have to ask him.'

Now he stared at her drawings again, lost in thought.

145

He felt as if he were walking on a tightrope. Everything was perfect – but it could so easily disintegrate. He had devoted himself to his work, but it wasn't enough. Sometimes, like now, he felt very empty. He was tired of the one-night stands, the fleeting relationships.

There was a fire of passion burning in Suzie, he could feel it. He envied Wyatt.

Bruce put his hand on Mickey's shoulder. 'You're tired. Go home. You'll feel better tomorrow.'

When Bruce had gone Mickey sat staring at the wall for a while. Then he picked up the drawing of a sports car and studied it. Gradually, with a huge effort of willpower, he removed the image of Suzie von Falkenhyn from his mind. In his hand the drawing-pencil began to weave its magic.

In the woods behind the circuit, the massive silver-bodied truck drew quietly to a halt. Two men, dressed in black tracksuits, came out of a side-door. They were both armed with silenced weapons. They fanned out into the undergrowth and assumed a silent vigil.

After a few moments the driver stepped out, similarly dressed. He moved towards the old air-raid shelter and opened the big doors quietly. Inside it was deathly still and there was a strong smell of damp. He switched on the light and looked across at the container of Carvalho tyres that stood in the centre of the concrete floor. He went outside and flashed his torch twice.

The rear doors of the truck opened and a fork-lift truck emerged from the back on a platform. The silence of the night was broken by a sound like the air brakes on a big lorry, and the fork-lift truck was lowered to ground level. The driver stepped up into the driving-seat and operated the controls to lift out a large container, identical to the one in the old air-raid shelter.

In the space of five minutes he exchanged the containers and then gestured for his men to return to the truck.

The blond-haired driver pulled out a cigarette as he drove away, taking the silver petrol-lighter from his top pocket

146

and lighting up. His green eyes flashed in the light of the flame.

It was all going perfectly.

Jack Phelps watched the morning sun rise above the horizon as he floated in his pool, staring through the transparent panels. Steam rose up lazily from the surface of the pool, while outside everything was shrouded in a blanket of white snow.

Testing in Kyalami. He couldn't have chosen a better location himself.

Wyatt was driving the Shadow. The circuit shimmered in the heat-haze. Beyond the watery image he could see a distant line of low hills.

This was a high point for all of them, the culmination of all the work they'd put in together as a team. Everyone had been in a holiday mood when they'd arrived at Jan Smuts airport, but the moment they got to the circuit the tension had returned.

He thought about the Shadow coming out of the container into the warm sunshine, and how it had felt to know he'd be driving her. That had been yesterday.

He was feeling a lot more comfortable now than he had been during the first few laps, and the new rubber gave him marginally more grip in the corners. He had analysed exactly those areas of the track where he could go slightly faster, and knock another second off his lap time.

There was the crackle of static in his headphones, then he heard de Villiers' voice, loud and clear. 'One minute, nine-point-o-two seconds. That's equal to the lap record. Good driving . . . but not quite good enough. Remember, you'll be faster when the ambient temperature goes down this afternoon.'

So he'd touched the record. But he wasn't taking enough chances – wasn't pushing himself hard enough. He was going to have to drive even faster.

The sunlight caught the visor on his helmet. He moved off the main straight and into the first corner. He braked late, taking a tighter line, going through faster. He kept cool. The Shadow had held. He would take each corner this way.

Through the next bend he almost lost control, but then he was through. He was learning a lot more about the Shadow, understanding her capabilities at the edge – the minute communications that she fed to his body through silent movements.

The esses passed quickly by, characterised by the pull on his neck of the G-forces. He was vaguely aware that someone was speaking in his headphones, but he wasn't listening. He was concentrating on the next curve, coming up hellishly fast. He resisted the instinctive urge to back off, and somehow the car still held. His body was battered, his neck stiff with tension.

He came out into the main straight. The Shadow rocketed forward, the engine an electrifying scream. The power kept on coming. He was in a trance, he felt he could go even faster.

The pits came and went in a blur. The disembodied voice in the headphones was screaming, and the words broke through into his consciousness.

'Fire! Fire!'

He touched the brakes. Then he felt the heat behind him, smelt the burning and the hot petrol.

He kept the terror under control. It would be over in less than a second if the tanks caught. He'd only done ten laps, so the tanks were full.

The brakes were dead. He overrode the automatic box and changed down, angling the car into the concrete, knowing that the seconds spelt the borderline between life and death.

He screamed as he felt the burning on his back. He tried to activate the fire-extinguisher and the oxygen as the smoke burnt his lungs.

Nothing happened.

Oh my God, please no.

He was spinning, smashing into concrete, his body yanked hard against the harness.

Then he was still, and screaming.

He sensed the marshals moving in, the smell of the foam, his harness being unbuckled, the steering-wheel coming off. Then he was pulled out.

The burning became pain and he rolled on the concrete, grabbing the legs of one of the marshals.

The coolness hit him as the marshal squirted the foam over him. He breathed slowly, feeling like death. Then he staggered to his feet.

He was all right.

The Shadow exploded before his eyes, blowing over two of the marshals who were desperately trying to put out the blaze. Bruce and Mickey pulled up in the pace car.

Wyatt dropped to his knees as the burning pain hit him again, and Bruce held him as the surgeon and ambulance men arrived.

'Wyatt, for God's sake stop moving!'

The doctor was taking out a syringe. He didn't even feel the jab, just the sudden calmness. There was Suzie's face, the *dojo*, his mother, and then his father screaming as the car went over the edge of the cliff . . .

Debbie held Suzie as she vomited again. Up to now she had always thought of Suzie as someone who was in control. She was a woman who had taken on challenges that would make most men afraid – the story of her climb with Wyatt years ago had somehow got around the office. But Debbie knew now that Suzie was also human, and that she was desperately in love with Wyatt. Her eyes were red from crying.

The director of the circuit came over, a big man with brown hair and a weather-beaten face, Doug Gibson. They'd had dinner with him the previous evening. He took Suzie's shoulders in his big hands.

'Calm down. He's all right, nothing serious. I'll take you to the hospital.'

Suzie felt stronger as she got into the Mercedez-Benz and they drove through the flat grasslands towards Johannesburg. Doug looked across at her, glad to see she was regaining control. He knew she was a tough lady.

'I didn't realise how close you were . . .' he said.

'He feeds off the danger. He lives for it. I understand that.' Suzie's voice was high and taut. 'But it's the fear of losing him. I can't deal with that.'

Doug gripped the wheel tighter. He would never tell her how close it had been.

Bruce examined the burnt-out wreck closely.

'The fire-extinguishers didn't work, nor did the oxygen.'

Mickey was ashen-faced. 'I'll make sure they bluidy work the next time!'

Bruce grimaced. 'There almost wasn't a next time.'

'He was pushing her to the limit. The cooling-system couldn't handle it.'

Bruce felt the sweat dripping from his face. It had been too damned close.

'We'll have to talk carefully to Ricardo. He's still recovering from his accident of over a year ago. He's going to freeze up if he thinks the Shadow is dangerous.'

The press meeting was called in the control tower at Kyalami. Over seventy-five reporters and TV cameramen were there. Suzie was supervising the PR function for Calibre-Shensu, but she'd hired a veteran motor-racing journalist and PR man, Don Morrison, to deal directly with the press. He bore more than a passing resemblance to Graham Hill, and was very British. He touched his nose and then his moustache as he took the podium. The room went silent.

'I am sorry that our first press conference should be taking place in this atmosphere. I must tell you that the hospital has informed us that Wyatt Chase has serious burns. At this stage, the prognosis is that he'll be out of action for a month. Naturally, that means he won't be competing in the first race of the season.

'We'll resume testing tomorrow with our second car, with the former world champion, Ricardo Sartori in the driver's seat.'

As Don spoke he caught sight of a striking woman with auburn hair in the front row. What, he asked himself, was Vanessa Tyson doing at a motor-racing event? He sensed trouble.

'Bruce de Villiers would now like to explain the cause of the accident,' he concluded.

Bruce stepped forward and stared hard at his audience. He didn't like this sort of thing, but he knew it was the life-blood of the business. Phelps wouldn't be pleased about the accident, and it was his responsibility to make sure it wasn't blown out of proportion by the press.

'Today's accident was caused by the Shadow's Shensu V12 engine overheating,' he said. 'Wyatt was driving the machine harder than ever before. He knocked three seconds off the current lap record.'

There was a stunned silence. It was an incredible achievement, and Bruce had calculated on its having just this effect. His attitude was always to try and make a victory out of a disaster. He moved on quickly.

'We now realise that we'll have to make certain modifications to the cooling-system which will overcome the problem.'

Don tried to pull Bruce down as he saw Vanessa Tyson rise to her feet. Tall and buxom, she definitely had presence. The man next to her was focusing his video-camera on Bruce, and Don caught sight of the WWTN emblem on the side.

'Jesus Christ,' he mumbled to himself. 'Not now.'

'Mr de Villiers,' Vanessa Tyson said in her crisp London accent, 'I have a quote here from an interview you gave a year ago at McCabe. "Drivers are much like engines. Every once in a while they blow up. I've had people who've died on the track, but that's something one has to live with. Hard, but true."'

Bruce was seething as he listened. 'You are quoting me out of context.'

'You failed to mention that the fire-extinguisher and the oxygen supply systems in the Shadow failed to operate.' Vanessa Tyson paused for a moment before delivering her punchline. 'If Wyatt Chase had died, would that have been "out of context"?'

Don tried to catch Bruce's attention, to persuade him to get off the podium, but Bruce was concentrating too hard on the Tyson woman. 'He knew the risks he was taking,' he said.

'What, that the machine was dangerous? That the safety equipment wasn't working?'

'No. But he knew the risks he was taking.'

'So that you could have greater publicity? You're on record as saying you're going to win the driver's and the constructor's championship, whatever the cost. Is that cost measured in body-bags and cancer cases?'

Bruce was furious. 'Motor-racing is dangerous – that's the attraction.'

'Yes, and you and your sponsors make big money out of it. You and Jack Phelps will just bury as many people as it takes to get you to the top!'

'You don't know what you're talking about. You've got a bloody cheek coming in here with that sort of sanctimonious crap!'

Don Morrison got up. He had to get Bruce off the podium.

Vanessa Tyson smiled softly. 'Ah. Here comes Don, the protective PR man. Am I getting a little close to the bone, Mr de Villiers? Isn't it about time someone asked why millions and millions of dollars are spent each year on a sport that is as mindless as bullfighting?

'You need deaths, don't you, Mr de Villiers? You need casualties to attract attention and keep sponsors interested.'

Ignoring Don Morrison's desperate gesticulations, Bruce squared his shoulders. 'I don't know what point you're trying to make. Everyone is here of their own free will.'

Vanessa gave de Villiers an icy smile. 'I suppose you are free to choose when and where you die. I'm just saying that you're all here to make money. Isn't it true that Wyatt Chase gets twenty thousand pounds for every point he makes?'

'That's part of his contract,' Bruce replied stiffly.

'The closer he comes to death, the more money he makes and the more publicity he gets for his sponsors.'

The room was deathly quiet. Bruce felt the rage building in him, wild and uncontrollable. But he knew the TV cameras were rolling – and Jack was counting on him, Aito was depending on him, so was the whole team. Don moved in front of him, grabbing his arm, pulling him away, then took the microphone himself.

'I think you caught Bruce at the wrong time,' he said smoothly. 'I'll answer your questions as clearly as possible.'

Vanessa Tyson didn't hesitate. 'How do you feel about

people dying of lung cancer?' she said coldly. 'About the millions of young people who are suckered into buying cigarettes because they see Calibre branding on a Shensu racing-car? Are you into death?'

Don Morrison wasn't fazed. He was paid to handle this sort of situation. 'I am a full-time employee of Calibre-Shensu,' he said. 'Wyatt Chase demanded the cash-for-points clause in his contract. It's a normal arrangement for an up-and-coming driver. As for our sponsors, they're just capitalising on the world's most popular sport. I think everyone here today would agree that Formula One racing is the most exciting business in the world.'

Vanessa gestured to Max, her cameraman, to stop filming. Don was the wrong target, she wanted de Villiers, not this professional.

'Thank you for being so open with me, Mr Morrison. I think Mr de Villiers has stated your team's views quite succinctly.'

Everyone in the room burst into conversation. The press conference was over.

What was he doing here? He hated the effect of the drugs, he hated losing control. If only the bloody fire-extinguisher had worked. Now the Shadow was a write-off. He was losing time, time that could be spent practising.

He tried to get up, and felt a hand push him softly down. It was a doctor, dressed in the regulation white jacket.

'Easy there. You'll be back on the track in a day's time, I've no doubt. But now you need rest.'

The doctor filled a syringe, then injected him. He felt the drug begin to take hold and thought of Suzie. Where was Suzie?

He drifted off into unconsciousness again.

She waited outside the foyer, enjoying the sounds of the African night. There was the constant buzz of the crickets, the occasional croak from a bullfrog and in the distance she could hear a dog barking.

The roar of the high-powered engine in the distance signalled his arrival. Ricardo pulled up smartly in front of her and leapt out of the car. He was wearing a white tennis-shirt, black trousers and mocassins. There was a flurry of activity in the reception area as people recognised him.

He opened the passenger door of the Ferrari quickly, and Debbie eased herself down into the low-slung seat. Then he was in, next to her, and pulling away.

Ricardo smelt of exotic after-shave. His hand rested on her thigh – it felt very good. He had a power about him, an easy confidence that was very attractive. She liked his openly aggressive nature; it was a constant challenge to her.

'You are envious that Wyatt took three seconds off your fastest time?' she said.

She waited to see how he would respond. She liked men who could stand up for themselves – that was why she'd worked for Bruce de Villiers for the past three years.

'He drove very well,' Ricardo said. 'I cannot deny that. There is no question of his ability.'

'But can you drive as fast?'

'It is one thing to perform well in practice, it is another to achieve victory in competition. He will be slow now. At least for another couple of weeks, eh?'

'How do you know?'

'I know. He will be scared.'

Debbie knew that Ricardo was staying with friends, that he didn't like the hotel – too many people staring at him and too many reporters getting in his way. He didn't need them.

He slipped his arm around her waist, squeezing her play-fully, and she felt uninhibited, like a young girl again. He was raw and elemental: she wanted to be naked against him. She looked at the black curling hairs on his chest revealed by the open buttons of the T-shirt.

He drove very quickly but she wasn't scared. He was always in control, and she watched the dark hairs on the back of his wrists as he changed gear. He flicked his eyes over her, taking in the dress she had chosen for the evening.

'You are very beautiful.'

She laughed softly as he ran his hand over her dark-stockinged thigh again.

*

The restaurant was exclusive, set in lush gardens beneath an office complex. Ricardo looked up and the *maître d'hôtel* came across to them smartly.

'Good evening, Mr Sartori.'

He handed Ricardo the wine list and ran over the restaurant's better dishes. Ricardo ordered a bottle of Dom Perignon, and Knysna oysters for both of them. 'Champagne is all that the beautiful should ever drink,' he said.

It was the most exotic food Debbie had ever eaten. Afterwards they walked out to the Ferrari, and he said: 'You spend the night with me.' It was not a question.

She lay her head against him as he drove. She felt scared of herself, of the sexual desire she'd never been able to control. She wanted him, that was all she knew.

Later, he pulled up at the end of a long tree-lined drive, next to a black-walled house. The architecture was clean and modern, greenery clinging to the plaster around the big, square oak door that was set deep into the wall. Inside, they stepped into a huge, marble-tiled hall; through a picture-window the northern suburbs of Johannesburg could be seen twinkling in the distance.

She wanted him to make love to her and she wanted it to be good.

His hands moved gently over her body. He knew almost instinctively what aroused her.

'Don't stop.'

She whispered it softly in his ear as his hand unzipped the back of her dress. Now she wanted her naked body next to his, to feel that darkly tanned skin against her own.

He pushed her over one of the white raw silk couches, her legs parting in anticipation. He dropped his trousers in a single movement.

Then she felt him, hard and big. She could no longer control herself. She pushed back against him as he thrust deep within her. She needed to be possessed.

'Oh my God.'

There was now a masculine smell about him that excited her even more, and she came again and again. Then he exploded within her and she sank down, satiated.

155

Later, they lay naked on the tiles. She placed her head on his stomach and he stroked her hair.

'Did the accident scare you?' she asked softly.

It was some time before he answered. 'Perhaps,' he said.

She wondered what Wyatt would be like in bed. There was something about racing-drivers that turned her on. She'd slept with some of the best, but always there was a new conquest to make.

He ran his fingers teasingly across her upper lip.

'You are afraid of Wyatt?' she asked.

She felt his body tense up. She enjoyed the sensation, enjoyed the power she felt she had over him.

'Am I afraid?'

Already she could feel herself wanting him again. She parted her lips and worked her way down his torso making small kisses.

'They say he has the makings of a great driver.' She enveloped him with her lips.

'He does not know how to control a car. Look what happened today.'

She felt the sap rising within him and his hand ran through her hair.

'I want to beat him,' Ricardo said, 'show him that I am the fastest. Yes, he is a challenge.'

She tasted him, and it was almost too much for her to bear. He lifted her up, and then thrust, and exploded again within her.

God, it felt good. But she had to have Wyatt as well.

She could never have enough.

The hunter took another drag on his cigarette and contemplated the meaning of life. He supposed he should be pleased. The spectacle he was about to witness would net him around twenty-five thousand dollars, but there was something that made him feel slightly guilty about the whole business.

He'd spent days trailing this animal, working out its habits and finding when it drank at the waterhole. Then it had been a matter of setting everything up and bringing in Mr Phelps at the right moment.

156

Mr Phelps wanted to bag a rhino, and that he would certainly do. Whether it could be called hunting was another matter.

He inhaled again and hoped to hell Phelps wouldn't belch or do something else to scare the animal away.

Jack watched the rhino walk up to the water's edge as the sun rose in the cold air of the morning. He liked the atmosphere of the bush, the rawness of the environment. He'd wanted to do this ever since he was a kid.

He looked through the hairlines of the sight and hugged the rifle closer to his shoulder, then let his finger stroke the trigger softly.

The huge animal faltered on his hooves, then staggered back and let out a snort of pain.

Jack smiled. The bullet had caught the right front knee. He felt the hunter's hand on his arm.

'*Meneer* Phelps, let me finish this.'

'Leave me alone. How I kill him is my business.'

He loaded up and fired again. The body of the rhino collapsed forward, both front legs crippled. The cries of pain echoed across the bushveld.

Phelps laid down the rifle and pulled out a cigar. The hunter raised his own rifle.

'I don't want your money, *meneer*. But believe you me, this'll be in all the papers.'

The hunter's first shot killed the rhino instantly. Then he felt the cold of Phelps's rifle-barrel against his ear.

'Go and see the kill, Mr du Plessis.'

The hunter staggered forward.

'Now you can find out what it's like to be hunted,' Phelps said furiously.

Du Plessis broke into a run, pulling the sheath-knife from his belt. Phelps raised his rifle and aimed again.

The bullet hit du Plessis in the centre of the neck and flattened him against the veld.

Phelps lit his cigar, sucked the rich smoke into his lungs, then exhaled, enjoying the soft warmth of the first rays of sun against his back.

The bush was just like the business world; the weak always got savaged.

Suzie looked aghast at the doctor. 'What do you mean, he checked himself out?'

The doctor moved uneasily in his chair and stared again at the beautiful blonde woman sitting opposite him. He could quite understand her anger. He hadn't wanted to let Wyatt Chase go, but then he hadn't had much choice.

'Miss von Falkenhyn, this isn't a prison. We can't force a patient to stay here against his will. Besides, he threatened me.' The doctor took off his glasses and cleaned them on the side of his coat.

'Threatened you?' said Suzie, not believing what she was hearing.

'He said that if I knocked him out again he would break my arm when he came round.'

'But surely you didn't take him seriously?'

The doctor looked again at the open file on his desk.

'Look, Wyatt Chase is a good athlete. He's tough. If he wants to leave, that's his decision.'

'I do not believe this,' Suzie shouted angrily.

'Dammit. He got out of bed, he knocked one orderly over – and I was not about to take him on,' the doctor replied quickly.

Suzie got up, red-faced. 'I am sorry. I didn't realise. You don't know . . .?'

'Where he is? Well, he left this note for you.'

The burns stung. The pain was terrible, but he was mastering it. He swivelled round again, his bare feet moving softly across the wooden floor of the *dojo*.

His first attacker moved in, lightning-fast. He pivoted, blocked and then punched, aware of the second attacker approaching. The blow came before he could react, striking the burns on his back and he screamed out with pain as he retaliated, knocking the third man flying off his feet.

The three men surrounded him, trying to find another

opening but not succeeding. Then the whistle went, and they bowed to each other.

Wyatt walked across the floor to the *sensei*.

'I thank you. It has been a pleasure to train with you.'

The *sensei* bowed. 'Your style is not ours, but I heard much about you in Tokyo. From what I have seen today, what I heard is true. You must come here every day till you leave Johannesburg. It is an honour to train with you.'

Wyatt bowed, then walked across the floor of the *dojo*.

She was waiting at the side, her blue eyes never leaving his. He took her hands and kissed her softly.

Later, as they drove to the hotel, he told her about Japan, about the years of training.

'Pain is something you live with. It's a challenge, Suzie. A hospital is a place for the sick. I am not sick – and the drugs do not help me to fight the pain, they make me weak.'

'Promise you'll rest, Wyatt.'

'No. I'll drive again today.'

Wyatt walked casually up to the side of the Shadow and stared over the Kyalami race-track at the setting sun with a vague, dreamy smile. As if it were the most natural thing in the world, he eased the packet of cigarettes out of his black jumpsuit. Looking straight into the camera, he shook the pack, slipped out a cigarette and put it gently to his mouth. Then he struck a match and inhaled deeply – and broke into violent coughing.

'Cut! Cut!'

Wyatt threw the cigarette down on the tarmac with disgust. The director glared at him in consternation from his chair, and turned to the crew.

'Move it, guys. We've only got thirty minutes more light.'

He came over to Wyatt, a thickset man with tiny spectacles that made him look like a grown-up Billy Bunter. 'How many times have I told you – don't inhale and you won't cough.'

'It has to look real. You told me that.'

'Fuck, but you're stubborn.'

Wyatt stared at him. He wasn't impressed by this arrogant bastard of a commercials director. He handed him the pack.

159

'Why don't you shove them up your arse.'

Then he heard Jack Phelps's voice in the background. 'Cool it, Wyatt.' The calm, assured tones of the professional businessman. 'Damion's only trying to do his job.'

The director looked despairingly into Wyatt's eyes. 'The James Dean pose looks good. Just light up, and take the smoke into your mouth.'

'I really feel great, endorsing lung cancer.'

'If you don't like it, Wyatt, choose another career.' Phelps's voice drifted across the tarmac.

Wyatt stared across at him. He was still sore from the burns, but Ricardo had not bettered his times and he could tell the Italian was itching to prove himself the better driver.

Suzie walked up to Wyatt, while Phelps ran his eyes up and down her body, mentally undressing her.

'Relax, Wyatt,' she said. 'It's not difficult. As Damion says, don't inhale. Watch me.'

Damion was glaring at them, red-faced and angry. Time was running out, the sun had almost set. Wyatt knew the commercial was already over budget, but he disliked the director intensely.

Suzie lit the cigarette, placed it between her full and perfect lips, then drew in her breath very slowly. The cigarette glowed, she lifted it elegantly from her mouth.

'Too much for the great Wyatt Chase?'

He laughed. Phelps wasn't amused, but there was a smirk on Damion's lips. Wyatt stared at him, aching to wipe the smile off his face.

'OK, Damion. I'll try again.'

In a few minutes the crew were ready, and Wyatt sauntered casually across to the car. Phelps was watching him like a hawk. He was trying to figure him out, much as he would a company he was about to take over.

Wyatt looked across at Damion sitting nonchalantly back on his wood and canvas folding-chair. He crushed the cigarette pack in his right hand.

'Shit!' Damion's voice cut through the air. 'Jesus, Wyatt! That box has been specially prepared. We've only got one more – wreck that, and we'll have to can the shoot.'

Suzie was at his side again. He smelt the familiar fragrance as she handed him the other packet.

He held it in his hand.

'Go on,' she said. 'Crush it.'

Everyone looked on, horrified. He stared at her for what seemed a long time. She was testing him – she wanted him to do it. And then he relaxed.

Damion fidgeted in his chair and wiped the beads of perspiration from his forehead. 'OK. Action.'

The set went deadly still, and this time Wyatt went through the actions perfectly – he sensed Suzie was watching him, judging him. He took the cigarette to his lips and inhaled softly. Then he blew the smoke out and stared coolly into the camera.

'Cut.'

There was applause, and Damion was up.

'It's a wrap.'

Wyatt walked away from them, down the track. He stared down the straight. This was all irrelevant. It was only the racing that mattered, the rest was superfluous. The rest was a game.

The trick was to concentrate on the driving, not to let the other issues distract him. It was only two weeks to the first Grand Prix in Rio. Tomorrow they would fly back to England, ready to make their final preparations.

Someone came up behind him. 'Wyatt, don't let them piss you off.'

It was de Villiers, hands in his pockets, looking haggard.

'It does piss me off.'

'Jack's happy. You've just made his day.'

'The publicity seems more important to him than winning.'

He walked further down the track with Bruce alongside him.

'Listen, Wyatt,' Bruce said. 'Let me give you some advice. If you handle the sponsors well now, you'll make it easier on yourself when the racing's on. And let me warn you, too. If you won't go along with him, Phelps will dump you.'

Wyatt nodded.

Bruce said earnestly: 'You, me, Aito and Ricardo, we all have the same objective. We want to win.'

Wyatt looked above the line of blue-gum trees and saw some birds in the distance, flying across the red sunset. He thought back momentarily to the *dojo* where he had trained in Tokyo. Then the memory was gone, and his mind was clear. He was in Formula One for the same reason as Bruce. To win.

Back in London, Suzie wasn't quite sure what to make of what was happening to her. Suddenly she had achieved celebrity status through her liaison with Wyatt.

Jack Phelps was particularly happy about the publicity. There were stories about her and Calibre-Shensu in most of the major international magazines, and she'd been invited to appear on a prominent television talk-show. Also, her *prêt à porter* range had sold out within five minutes of the Paris opening, and she'd been approached by several large clothing manufacturers to lend her name to a new label. Now she was sitting in her London apartment, awaiting a team of journalists from *Time*.

The phone rang. It was Jack Phelps again. He wouldn't leave her alone. He'd insisted on helping her set up the New York office of her design company through the acquisition of an American group.

'Suzie dear. Everything is in order. I've successfully negotiated your take-over of Morgan Design. You get a fifty-five per cent controlling interest, and their name changes to Zen, as you requested.'

Suzie sighed. Phelps was setting her up in big business – whether she liked it or not.

He continued, his tone confidential, 'I've set up a meeting for you tomorrow with Lawrence Simons Junior, their executive president. He seems to be most amenable to working for you.'

'What if he isn't?'

'Then he'll get the laughing heave-ho.'

'What?'

'A handshake and a parting cheque. Listen, Suzie, with your new celebrity status there are plenty of top creative

162

people here who'll leap at the opportunity of running the New York arm of Zen.'

'I'm sure Lawrence will be fine. The reason we chose his company is because his philosophy has always been similar to mine.'

The doorbell rang insistently. 'Jack, I'll see you tomorrow, the reporters from *Time* have arrived.'

She slammed the phone down. There was a price to pay for everything in life, and Phelps was hers.

Aito Shensu sat on the *dojo* floor, facing the *Shihan*, the chief instructor. Each day it became harder and harder to move through the training exercises. The disease was creeping over his body and he was unable to resist it. No one except the *Shihan* and his doctor knew of the leukemia that had attacked his blood cells.

Despite the disease, he remained focused on his life philosophy – Budo – the way of the winner. He had reached nearly all his goals. Only two remained – perhaps only one could be achieved. He wanted Wyatt to return to the *dojo*, and he wanted victory for the company he had started thirty years before.

He rose to his feet with the *Shihan*.

Dishonour had shaken this *dojo*. Their two greatest disciples had left. The one he would not think about, not talk about. As for Wyatt, he had his promise that he would return.

They bowed to each other, then stepped back.

The first blow struck Aito hard beneath his heart. It was a harsh, fighting blow. He looked into the eyes of his opponent. The *Shihan* did not treat him like a sick man and they fought like men.

It was not over. It was just beginning.

March

Bruce de Villiers surveyed his cars as they came off the jumbo at Rio airport. It was always an anxious time for him. He just hoped that nothing had been lost or mislaid, because the actual business of transportation was out of his hands. The airlift of all the Formula One teams to South America was a huge operation, co-ordinated by the head of the Formula One Constructors' Association, Ronnie Halliday.

Bruce had two spare cars in addition to those he'd prepared for the Brazilian Grand Prix, but they weren't the cars he'd set up, they were unknown, untested.

He only relaxed when everything was on the ground and it was clear that it was all in perfect shape. The customs people seemed to take forever, then a hydraulic hoist loaded the cars and equipment onto the waiting trucks.

The Brazilians always worried Bruce. He didn't quite trust their good-natured conviviality.

More and more equipment came out of the plane, and he looked aghast at the four pallets of tyres Carvalho had insisted he bring with him. He had argued that they could supply him direct from their factory, just north of Rio, but they had insisted that he bring existing supplies.

He walked out of the airport customs area an hour later, more than a little annoyed. The customs officials had insisted on going over one of the cars very carefully, and he'd been terrified that they'd damage something. He couldn't understand a word of Portuguese, and the one official who could speak English wasn't interested in playing interpreter.

Now he headed back to the hotel and a fresh set of worries, the first of which was keeping a close guard on his team. The temptations of the city were real. Again he cursed the nature of the Formula One circuit – almost all the events took place in the most glamorous possible locations. But at least he had little to worry about with his drivers. Ricardo had a lot to prove, and he was having an affair with Debbie, who seemed to be balancing out his Italian wildness. Wyatt was already at the circuit, itching to drive.

Bruce entered the hotel foyer and was immediately conscious of much shuffling and bowing – the Shensu factory mechanics had arrived. After shaking hands and exchanging pleasantries twenty times over, he slipped into the hotel bar and ordered a Scotch on the rocks, hoping to find sanity in the familiar amber liquid.

Tomorrow could only be better, he promised himself. They would be down at the track and he could get on with doing what he knew best – pulling his team together and focusing their attention on winning.

Bruce drank alone, studiously avoiding the managers of the other teams. As far as he was concerned, they were the opposition. He maintained his view that he wanted to savage his competitors, not drink with them.

He was pleased that Wyatt had recovered well from the accident at Kyalami. He knew that Wyatt's mind was totally focused on the race; he wasn't taken in by the glamour of the sport, he didn't want to be a prima donna. In that way he reminded Bruce of James.

Bruce knew he had a lot to be pleased about – but there was something that was making him nervous, though he hadn't admitted it to anyone. The journalist Vanessa Tyson was definitely stalking Calibre-Shensu. Fortunately, her interview with him hadn't been given much air time in England, though he knew that in the US it had received wide coverage. She could cost him Phelps's sponsorship and she could do Formula One a whole lot of damage. But, strangely, Phelps seemed unconcerned about her and said that he'd sort Vanessa Tyson out.

Ricardo lay back in the water and contemplated the bronzed goddess who'd been watching him for the last half-hour. There was nothing shy about the way she'd been assessing him; in fact there was almost an open invitation in her eyes.

He glanced across at Debbie and realised that she hadn't even noticed what was going on. With her blonde hair, she was natural prey for every Brazilian male on the beach. He doubted if she'd ever had so much attention in her entire life – and he knew she loved it.

He closed his eyes again and thought about the Shensu Shadow. His marriage with the car was a hard one, and not yet entirely resolved. The Shadow refused to respond directly to some of his commands – the two of them were still fighting, still unsure of each other. He didn't trust the automatic gearbox, and was scared that it might malfunction during the race; he knew that more and more of the teams were making the move to automatics, but he preferred the simplicity of a fully manual shift.

This season, there would be more competition on the track. For the first time in years, many of the cars would be equal in their levels of competitiveness. Even if he did have the best car, it would still be only marginally better than the rest. Of course, Wyatt would be driving the other Shadow, and he was certainly gunning for top place.

Ricardo looked at the goddess again, then at Debbie. Why could he never be content with one woman?

A dark-skinned Adonis had sat down next to Debbie, and was getting a little too interested for Ricardo's liking. He turned over and swam for the shore. By the time he reached them, the man already had his hand over Debbie's.

'Eh, she is my lady.' Ricardo glared at the man, who seemed totally unfazed by his arrival.

'The charming young lady is talking to me,' he said.

To Ricardo's annoyance, Debbie didn't say a word, nor did she try to extricate her hand.

'Why don't you take another swim,' said the stranger. The tone of his voice suggested there would be a fight if the suggestion was not taken seriously.

'Fuck off!' Ricardo yelled.

The Brazilian rose, and Ricardo swung a hard left into the

man's jaw. He toppled over into the sand, and suddenly the beach went very quiet.

'Ricardo, you . . .'

He stared at Debbie and she shut up. The Adonis dragged himself up, wiping blood from his mouth, and Ricardo sat down next to Debbie and examined the broken skin on his left hand. She slapped him on the face, an unexpected, hard, stinging blow.

'You bastard!' she said. He'd never seen her so angry. And suddenly she started shouting at him. 'So you lie there eyeing that Brazilian bitch for the last half an hour, then I decide to talk to someone and you hit him!'

'He was holding your hand . . .'

'Sometimes,' she said, 'you're just beyond belief.' She got up.

'I suppose you're leaving?' he said, not moving.

She walked off the beach without turning round once, and he smiled to himself. If she thought he was going to tolerate her seeing other men, she had another thing coming.

His mind was quickly distracted. The dark-skinned goddess he'd been watching earlier was walking slowly up the sand towards him.

'I see you're alone.'

The voice was husky and attractive.

'You see very well,' he said.

She sat down on the sand next to him and then stretched out, exposing herself to the sun.

'You have a fight with your woman?' she said lazily.

'She is for me, not for anyone else.'

'But you can have who you want?'

He laughed. Slowly at first, then out loud. She was very perceptive, this woman. He turned on his side and stared into her dark eyes. 'Are you a mind-reader?'

He couldn't keep his eyes on hers for long, instead they moved down to inspect her beautiful body, the svelte torso, the fecund hips and the long, long legs.

He moved forward and kissed her on the lips. It was going to be an enjoyable afternoon.

*

The television studio was filled to capacity, and all eyes were on the woman who held the floor.

'I believe that your legal system has exposed itself to a level of abuse unprecedented in the history of civilisation. The facts I have laid before you show that you have become slaves to an obsession with money, rather than the servants of justice . . .'

The Senator from California looked up at the woman with the hypnotic voice and cursed the day she had decided to investigate what her programme series called 'The American Way of Justice'. Who the hell did this British bitch Vanessa Tyson think she was, a knight in shining armour? That was the way the majority of US television viewers saw her, and it made her a dangerous adversary.

She was a difficult woman to handle. Her face was arresting with dark eyes and full, almost pouting lips; her body was, in a word, voluptuous. But she was a tough professional through and through – anyone thinking she was a pushover because of her sexy looks should think again. Vanessa Tyson was a formidable reporter with an incisive mind.

'Far from making you a strong nation, your laws have crippled you. Ridiculous liability claims have prevented manufacturers from spending enough money on research and development to evolve better products. My findings suggest that serious and major reforms in your legal system are a necessity.'

The Senator shuffled his feet uneasily and eyed his female adversary cautiously. 'You may have a point, Miss Tyson, but I think you are using specific examples to undermine the overall strength of our legal system,' he said in his deep, sonorous voice. As well as being a Senator, Burt Calhoun ran a prosperous legal practice that specialised in liability suits. They had a high success rate that brought in millions and millions of dollars each year.

'Might I suggest that you're scared you'll lose business, Senator?'

His face reddened. He scratched at the deep dimple on his chin. 'I'd like to tan that fat bitch's hide,' he muttered under his breath, and then, out loud: 'No. But I am afraid that ordinary people who are protected by those very laws you seek to attack, may once again become victims of unscrupulous manufacturers if those laws are repealed.'

'"Unscrupulous manufacturers", Senator?' Vanessa said sarcastically, her eyes sweeping across the studio audience. 'Like Jeff Sutherland, whose new car plant was closed down by a claim represented by your legal firm? A claim that would never have been made if one of your attorneys had not approached the owner of a Sutherland sports car and encouraged him to move against the company – providing he paid your company fifty per cent of the settlement?'

'That's a downright lie!'

'A downright lie that closed down Jeff Sutherland's factory, put the five thousand men who worked for him on the street, and personally bankrupted him. All because your client had a bad accident after a heavy drinking spree. Is that justice?'

'The man is a cripple. He needed that money to survive.'

'Seventy-five million dollars for him and seventy-five million for you? I would hardly call that survival money.'

'He can't walk.'

'Neither can thousands of Vietnam veterans who fought in a war you pushed for, a war that your son did not have to fight because you got his call-up deferred.'

'That's irrelevant!' the Senator yelled.

'No, that's politics. It's what suits your needs, your back pocket, Senator. Not the needs of your people – the American people. Your committee is a sham, like you. You are protecting laws that keep you in business while closing down the American economy. Jeff Sutherland shot himself yesterday. He could have been a future Henry Ford. You, with your great legal system, destroyed him!'

Vanessa Tyson rose, indicating that the live debate was over, and the audience clapped loudly. Her attack on the US legal system over the past year had culminated in this opportunity to put her views to Senator Calhoun, live.

She left the studio quickly and made her way outside. Reporters and spectators were waiting for her.

'Miss Tyson, how did it go?'

'Watch my programme at six tonight on WWTN and find out.'

'Senator Calhoun says you're seeking media hype and nothing else.'

'Senator Calhoun is destroying this country. I'm trying to keep it where it belongs, on top.'

In front of her she saw Max, her assistant, pushing people away so that she could get to her car. Thank God. She needed to be away from all this. The interview had been far rougher than she'd expected; Calhoun had frightened her – though she refused to show it. He was like a mountain bear on the rampage, scared of no one and not afraid to strike out.

Max closed the car door and she stretched out, safe behind the dark-tinted windows. She gestured for her driver to pull off and began to compose herself. Her secret was to bring emotion into her arguments, constantly pushing her opponents to react.

As one of the highest-paid television reporters in the United States, she had an important reputation to uphold. Because she was a Londoner, some called her an alien, interfering in American matters, but she loved the United States and its people. What she did not love were the big wheeler-dealers who were destroying all that was good about America.

Calhoun had played into her hands, and she knew that evening's programme would put her in an unassailable position. Her objective was to motivate major reforms in the American legal system.

She closed her eyes and relaxed.

Senator Calhoun poured himself a stiff Bourbon and eased into one of the leather button-backed armchairs in his office. 'That bitch needs a good fuck,' he roared at his chief aide.

He'd asked Cleaver to ask the men on Capitol Hill some questions. In particular, Calhoun wanted to find out how the President was reacting to his chairing of the Senate Committee that was investigating possible flaws in the American legal system.

David Cleaver was a thin, bespectacled, twenty-five-year-old Harvard legal graduate, with a nose like a hawk and a mind like a razor.

'So, David, give me the low-down.'

'Well, sir, the President obviously knows that you and he are closely allied in the eyes of the voting public – the public believe that whatever you say is endorsed by the President. The economy is in poor shape, we're being annihilated by the Japanese in our traditional export markets, our motor industry is under attack. Now, you are seen as having destroyed Jeff Sutherland . . . Of having sided with the big corporations to take out a young entrepreneur.'

'It was perfectly legal,' Calhoun snorted. 'The man didn't protect himself from liability action.'

You bastard, thought David Cleaver. But he said: 'He would never have had the capital to open his factory if he had, sir. That's what the President is saying. Sir, I think compromise is the order of the day.'

'Jesus Christ! What the hell is this country coming to when some fat British reporter who looks like she needs a first-rate fuck can dig holes in our great legal system?'

David Cleaver refused to answer his employer. Personally, he thought the Senator had played right into Vanessa Tyson's side of the court.

'So, David, what do I do?'

'I think, sir, you should announce that the committee has found there are certain areas that require special investigation, and that if these areas are found to be problematic, changes should be made.'

Calhoun's glass was shaking, the ice rattling noisily.

'The bitch has beaten me.'

'This way, sir, you come out clean. You never told me about your son evading a Vietnam call-up. What other dirty linen will she dig up if you don't back down?'

Calhoun looked away from his aide. What other dirty linen? Cleaver was right – his only way out was to back down.

'All right. Phone her up at WWTN and tell her that I've decided she has a point and we will be reviewing certain laws in a serious light.'

'You've made the right decision, sir.'

'Just shuddup and make the call.'

*

171

Vanessa walked into the main office, smiling from ear to ear. The head and founder of Worldwide Television News, Jay Levy, was waiting for her.

He'd asked her out many times, but had always received a pleasant rebuff. He had to admit he was infatuated with her. She wasn't attractive in the conventional sense, though the camera loved her: the full, sensuous lips, the dark arched eyebrows and her olive complexion made her irresistible on the screen. But he longed to know what lay behind that incisive mind. He guessed she might be passionate, but she certainly didn't show it. And he also knew that she didn't have a lover. Yet every time he made the slightest effort to get closer to her, he had received that ever so pleasant, ever so polite rebuff. It was frustrating, to say the least.

He kissed her softly on the cheek. 'Congratulations, Vanessa! You've done it again!'

'Thank you, Jay, but really it's Burt Calhoun we've all got to thank. He played right into our hands,' she said softly.

You could get anyone to play into your hands if you just used your looks instead of your mind to win an argument, thought Levy.

'Well,' he said, 'our ratings have never been higher.'

'Jay, the point is, I was right. There are genuine holes in your legal system. I hope that what I've done goes a long way to repairing them.'

That was one of the reasons why Jay had hired her. She wasn't in this for the money and the fame, she was in it because she believed in what she was doing.

'So, Vanessa, what about your next assignment?'

'Ah ha. Formula One. Smoking and death.'

Jay nodded, wanting to hear more. Her first report from Kyalami had researched excellently. It was media dynamite.

'It's controversial, don't you worry. And it's something I've been interested in exposing for a long time. We're off to Rio tomorrow.'

'But Burt, surely you know how to handle her?' Jack Phelps thought Burt Calhoun seemed to be making a helluva fuss

172

about nothing – but the Senator's reply wiped the smile off his face.

'What do you mean, you can't help me with this one?' Jack roared. 'Hell, I pay you a fortune in legal fees every month – you're making a fortune off all these claims smokers are making against my company.'

Jack slammed down the phone. He wanted to strangle Vanessa Tyson. He guessed the fat bitch was out to cause havoc. He'd never known Calhoun to be so cautious.

Well, Vanessa Tyson had better watch out, because he wasn't going to be a pushover.

He picked up the publicity reports that Don Morrison had sent him, a broad grin spreading across his face. It was paying off. All the effort and all the work were showing a handsome dividend.

He reread the *New York Times* item on the forthcoming Brazilian Grand Prix – a full-page article. They were playing up the competition between Sartori and Chase, and there was a full-colour picture of the machine – in jet-black livery with silver highlights. Suzie von Falkenhyn's design work was faultless, but the byline on her affair with Wyatt made him furious. He wanted Suzie himself; he needed to have her.

He lay back in his chair, contemplating the New York skyline and the success of Calibre-Shensu. Aito Shensu had proved to be the perfect business partner. The man rarely asked questions, and when he did, it was only about technicalities. Aito had been as good as his word, so that he, Jack Phelps, was the one who was running the team. The only thing that still rankled was Aito's appointment of Wyatt Chase.

Jack checked his watch. He would be in Rio in twenty-four hours' time, ready to watch the Saturday practice and make sure everything was running smoothly.

He switched on the video unit that was hidden behind the end wall of his office and watched the endorsement commercial that had just arrived from his ad agency. It was good, very good – the work was of outstanding quality. He always let the creative director have total control; he found he got a far better product that way. If he didn't like what was produced, he just the fired agency and appointed another one. Advertising people were simple to control. One fed them money to keep them thinking, and fired them when they stopped delivering.

Of course, the commercial was basically supposed to support Shensu, because cigarette advertising had been outlawed from the TV networks years before. Quite why, he had never been able to understand; he felt that freedom of will should include the choice to smoke or not smoke. One's death was a personal matter. But the commercial was deliberately designed to look as though it was for Shensu rather than for Calibre.

He watched it through once more, and smiled. Wyatt Chase might not be world champion, but he was a natural television star. He would exploit Wyatt to the full. Besides, Wyatt had Suzie, and he wanted Suzie. Forcing Wyatt to make commercial appearance after commercial appearance would pull him away from Suzie, giving Jack a chance to move in on her. Contractually, he had Wyatt by the shorts.

With Ricardo it was a different matter. His contract was far more specific, limiting the number of commercial appearances he had to make. Wyatt's contract contained no such protection and obliged him to do almost whatever Phelps wanted him to.

He'd get Suzie von Falkenhyn. It was just a matter of timing. He smiled, and watched the commercial through again.

Debbie got back to the hotel after having a cup of tea at the circuit with the rest of the team. She was still smarting from Ricardo's behaviour on the beach that morning. She went straight up to their room, and saw to her annoyance that the bed still hadn't been made. She reached for the phone to call room service, and then decided against it. She didn't want to have to sit around waiting for the maid to come and make up the bed.

Anything that smacked of disorder irritated her. She hated Ricardo's messiness – though she had to admit he did dress perfectly. She pulled back the duvet cover and straightened the sheets beneath it. Next she plumped up the pillows, and arranged the duvet beneath them. As a last touch, she pulled the duvet out at the edges. It was then that she felt something beneath the duvet cover.

Carefully she undid the buttons that fastened the cover and reached down. Her hand found something and pulled it out. She was looking at a pair of pale-blue silk panties, and they weren't hers. There was a noise outside the door and she realised that Ricardo had returned. She threw the panties on one of the chairs and went to the mirror, pretending to make up her face.

Ricardo burst into the room. Obviously he had been planning to tidy up the bed before she returned. He turned with shock as he saw her at the mirror.

'Debbie?'

'Yes?' she replied, as demurely as possible.

'You surprised me.' He came over and kissed her on the back of the neck.

'Have you been busy?'

'Er, yes. I've been shopping,' he lied.

'What did you buy?'

'Er, window-shopping. You understand.'

She saw his eyes dart around the room and eventually light on the panties, lying brazenly on the chair. He sauntered towards them.

'Ricardo.'

She rose, forcing him to turn his gaze to her. She could see the agitation on his face. She touched the dark skin of his cheek and looked into his eyes. Now she wanted to see him lie.

'Do you love me?'

'But of course. There has never been anyone quite like you.'

Not quite like me, thought Debbie; but similar, apparently. She could see his eyes, looking at the panties. She walked over to the chair and picked them up.

He coloured. 'I can explain!'

'Explain what? That the cleaners must have left them here?'

'No . . . Yes . . . You're right. I'll phone the manager and complain.'

As she watched him make a fool of himself on the phone,

she quietly undressed and got into the bed. If he was going to make love to anyone else that day, it was going to be her.

He put the phone down angrily. 'They said they already cleaned the room, can you believe it?'

'No. Come to bed . . .'

If she hadn't known, she would have never guessed that he had slept with another woman only hours before. She gripped the headboard in ecstasy. Sure, he was a bastard, but an irresistible bastard.

The sun rose over Rio, the Sugar Loaf mountain standing supreme over the city; the slums lay sprawling the distance. This was a world where poverty and wealth walked hand in hand.

The car-crazy locals were expectant. The glamour of Formula One attracted them – especially to cheer on the three Brazilian drivers. The searing summer heat added to the carnival atmosphere, and cars raced madly along the bumpy road towards the circuit.

At the Autodromo Internacional do Rio du Janeiro, Baixada de Jacarepagua, conditions were perfect for the practice session.

Bruce de Villiers looked down at his non-existent fingernails and cursed his nervousness. So far, everything was fine. The two cars looked immaculate and so did the team, out in their livery for the first time in public. The press photographers were loving it. Bruce had to admit that Suzie had done her job very well. He felt entirely comfortable in the jet-black and silver jumpsuit; it breathed well, and despite the heat he didn't feel at all restricted. Ricardo and Wyatt were keeping their distance from each other, like two fighting-cocks, eyeing each other out before the contest.

He saw Mickey Dunstal strolling over to him, clipboard and calculator in hand. He liked the way Mickey got involved with the pit crew and didn't stand aloof from them. His long blond hair was not plaited up as usual, and he looked like a rock star about to grab a microphone and give a performance.

'Nervous, are you, Bruce me boy?'

Bruce laughed. Mickey had just as much to be concerned about. 'How could I be worried, with your car?'

'You're a sly fellah, to be sure.'

Wyatt came over to them, and Mickey slapped him on the back. 'Tense?'

'I just want to get going. It's bloody hot.'

Bruce looked closely at his driver. 'Everything OK for you, Wyatt?' he enquired casually. 'Just take it easy to start with.'

'Relax, I'm not going to put your car into the concrete.'

Bruce shuddered. Even the thought of it was bad enough. In the distance he caught sight of a bevy of Brazilian beauties handing out packets of Calibre Lights to the spectators.

'When they die of cancer in forty years' time, who will they have to thank?'

'Wyatt, would you stop being so cynical.'

'Call it professional pride. Jack tells me the TV commercial is a winner.'

'Congratulations, Wyatt,' said Mickey.

'I want to win races, not cigarette sales.'

'This year you'll do both.' Suddenly, Phelps's American accent boomed out behind them.

Shit, thought de Villiers, the bastard's arrived early. They all turned, and there stood their sponsor, perfectly dressed in a double-breasted suit.

'Everything A-OK, Bruce?'

'Yes, Jack. We're confident of good times today.'

'Aito arrives tomorrow. It'll be a nice surprise for him if both cars are in the front-runners.

'That's the idea.'

Bruce glanced over at the dozen Japanese mechanics in the pits, all looking very determined. 'How are the Shensu crowd?' Jack asked, following his gaze. 'Are they any good?'

'To be honest, Jack, I've never had a better team. Discipline definitely has its rewards.'

Bruce watched Wyatt climbing into the Shensu Shadow. This was the moment of truth. Further away, Ricardo strutted out towards his machine, a number of dark-skinned Brazilian women with autograph-books chasing after him. He stopped and signed them, giving each of the women an affectionate kiss.

Bruce turned slightly and saw Debbie watching Ricardo. The look said it all. He chuckled. He wouldn't like to get on the wrong side of Debbie. If Ricardo didn't behave himself, he'd have to look out.

There was a mechanical scream as Wyatt's engine erupted into life. Bruce raised his hand and Wyatt shot out of the pits onto the track. The Japanese mechanics weren't smiling, and Bruce knew why. This was the acid test.

Ricardo had an ugly sneer on his face. He had followed Wyatt's progress out of the pits and was now settling down into his own car. This tension between Wyatt and Ricardo was exactly what Bruce had wanted. Now all he had to pray for was that they both performed.

Two front-runners, that's what he wanted. The way it had been at McCabe – except he wanted it even better. The press were complaining that Formula One had lost its excitement, that drivers like De Rosner dominated the races. Bruce sensed that Wyatt would be the one to challenge them.

It was hotter inside the Shensu Shadow than Wyatt had imagined it would be. He would have to get used to that, forget about it. Eighty laps in this heat – he was going to sweat a lot. A helluva lot.

The other cars were grouped close by him. In front of him was the Ferrari driven by Hoexter, and behind him, De Rosner in the McCabe: the two greats of the sport. Somewhere in the distance would be Ricardo, hungry for his blood.

Only now did the excitement really grip him. The engine was stronger than ever before; he had marvelled at the expertise of the Japanese mechanics as he watched them tuning it. These men were in a class of their own. The intricacies of the telemetry – the electronic tuning and monitoring equipment – were beyond his comprehension; but all that mattered was that they could extract from the engine the kind of performance he needed.

On the main straight he followed the rest of the cars as they weaved from side to side, bedding in their tyres, getting them warm. This was fine. He could still think. But after this it would just be reaction and concentration.

As he turned the corner into the main straight, for some unaccountable reason Suzie's face came into his mind. Then it faded as he saw the rest of the field accelerating hard, ready for the first timed lap. He would prove himself today or he would kill himself.

He pushed his foot down hard, and the Shadow leapt forward. All around him the noise was deafening. The other machines were a blur.

The first corner was fine, not too sharp. Easy to keep the speed high. The automatic gearbox allowed him to concentrate totally on driving. He was aware of the other machines surrounding him. Everyone was vying for a place high up on the starting-grid in two days' time.

A succession of curves, and then came the really sharp 180-degree curve before the main straight. He cut the line of the corner and wove his way through a succession of machines, barely keeping control. Then he was into the main straight, the engine running flat out as he passed over 200 mph, thundering down towards the next corner, more gentle than the entry to the straight.

He passed another five machines. The signage of the corner came up as though it were blocking his way, but he took a good line and passed easily round the corner.

The Shadow was going beautifully. She was responding well to the track, almost relishing the challenge.

He was in a trance. Every second counted in this practice. He was setting up the Shadow for the main event. He could make mistakes now which he could not make on Sunday.

No one had passed him. He was faintly surprised. He knew he was going quickly, perhaps faster than before. But what really mattered was the number of cars he was passing – cars that were disappearing behind him in a blur.

The engine's reserves in the corners appeared to be limitless – he knew he was going over 13500 rpm and that there was more to come. He was discovering new depths to the car's responsiveness. It was just a question of getting a good balance

179

between the output power of the engine and the outer limits of adhesion of the Carvalho tyres.

The laps went by with gruelling regularity. When his head-phones finally crackled into life he resented the intrusion, as if his private world had been invaded by some alien force.

'Come in – great drive.'

De Villiers' enigmatic tones did nothing to reassure him. All he wanted to know was how his times compared with those of the rest of the field. He did not relax his pace until he came up to the 180-degree curve before the pits.

He drove in, and people converged on the machine. He pulled off the steering-wheel and then levered himself out of the cockpit. The helmet felt like an immense load, and he was glad to pull it off.

Everyone was clapping. He stared round, uncomprehending. Bruce came up to him and shook his hand warmly.

'Your best lap time was one minute twenty-six seconds on the dot.'

'I don't believe it.'

'Well, it's officially recorded. No one else has come close. You'll be first off the grid, I bet.'

Suzie kissed him on the cheek. He gradually felt he was coming back to reality.

He went over to Mickey. 'She's wonderful – and I still believe there's more in reserve. At the edge she handles magnificently.'

'It's the race, Wyatt . . . the race that counts.'

'Yes. But this is a great start.'

'That it is.'

Suddenly he felt drained. Jack Phelps loomed up in front of him and pumped his hand.

'Great driving, Wyatt. The Carvalho tyres are delivering.'

Wyatt kept quiet. He didn't want to get involved in Phelps's private battles. If Bruce and Mickey were happy with the Carvalhos, then he was.

Phelps turned his back on him and walked across to the stands. A mass of press photographers seethed past him and headed for Wyatt. Now Wyatt was blinded by an avalanche of flash-bulbs, and then the shutters fell like rain.

'Can we predict a win on Sunday?' An eager reporter stared

at him, pen poised above notebook. Wyatt knew this was where he had to prove his mettle to his sponsors.

'I'll do my best,' he said. 'Calibre-Shensu is right behind me. As a team, we aim for victory. That's what we're in this sport for.'

A woman reporter moved forwards. She looked familiar, and she had dark eyes that he found strangely alluring.

She said: 'Are you scared of dying?'

It was too much. It was too close to home. He turned his back on her and stormed into the workshops. Who the hell was she?

He sat down on a bench in the shadows and stared for no particular reason at a wheel-spanner hanging on the wall. Someone sat down next to him. He didn't have to look to see who it was; he smelled the fragrance, and was grateful.

'It was a stupid question. She's a big bitch,' Suzie said softly. He thought how different she was from the hard-nosed British reporter.

'You can't know what it's like,' he said. 'To be . . .'

'Hush,' she said. 'I do know.' He felt her hand on his. 'That's Vanessa Tyson,' she said. 'She was the one who went for Bruce after Kyalami.'

But he didn't care who she was. He took Suzie's hand and walked out with her into the sunshine.

Flying to the hotel in the helicopter, Wyatt took over the controls from the pilot. He needed to clock-in hours and experience before he could get his licence and buy his own chopper. Suzie was with him. She was looking particularly lovely, he thought; her blonde hair bleached by the sun and her skin more tanned than usual. She wore a light shade of lipstick that gave her lips a lustrous quality. He leaned over and kissed her.

'You know that Debbie's attracted to you, Wyatt? Mmmm, I think I'll have to watch out.'

'She's just playing around.'

'She should keep her eye on Ricardo. From what I hear, he's still having affairs.'

'The lecherous Italian.'

'Do you ever think of me when you're driving?'

'Yes.'

He felt more relaxed by the time they got back to the hotel, but the image of the circuit would not disappear from his mind.

Suzie undressed in front of him, and he started by licking her nipples, then worked his way to the lustrous blonde hairs, crisp and curling, lower down. Now he was rock-hard and he could restrain himself no more.

She shuddered as he thrust into her wetness, feeling the tension released from his body. It was frightening – knowing that she was more in love with him than he was with her – knowing the power he had to hurt her. But she needed him, there was no escape for her.

She would not let him go. Everything he did turned her on – it almost scared Wyatt, the power he had over her body.

'Wyatt, please, please . . .'

Her orgasms went on and on, and he felt aroused again. This was the part about Suzie he loved. Earlier, there'd been a barrier within him that prevented him from getting close to her, but now, through the sheer joy of sex, he had managed to break through that barrier. She was a woman who loved to take risks, but who needed constant physical attention.

'Just hold me, Wyatt. Hold me tight.'

He held her – but already his mind was far away, thinking of Sunday and of the challenge.

Debbie had never seen Ricardo so angry. Now she would get her revenge.

'But you did well,' she said, watching his distraught face.

'Don't you understand? "Well" is not enough.' He looked menacingly around the pits.

'There's another practice tomorrow,' she said. 'You've still got a chance to show Wyatt you're faster. After all, Bruce says your cars are identical.'

His eyes burned like hot coals in the darkness. 'I will put him in his place. He has a cheek.'

'What, the cheek of being better?'

He glared at her, ignoring the people around them. Then Bruce stepped between them, and she smiled.

'Relax, man. You did bloody well. Wyatt's just got more to prove than you have.' Bruce tried to seem concerned when in fact he was overjoyed. Wyatt's performance had destroyed Ricardo's complacency.

'He has a better car than I have,' Ricardo said in a low voice.

Debbie could see the vein that ran across Bruce's forehead, bulging with irritation. Bruce had the build of a street-fighter – a short, stocky body with strong arms. Even though there was grey in his hair, he had the physique of a young man. Now he said roughly: 'You're talking bullshit, Ricardo.'

'You've set me up.'

'You've lost your nerve.'

It was cruel but effective. Bruce was the one in control. He had Ricardo and Wyatt worked out – he was doing everything he could to get them at each other's throats on the track. He knew he would get faster times out of them both that way.

Ricardo squared up in front of Bruce, his perfectly honed body rigid with anger. The curly black hair on the imperious head was wet with sweat. 'Now you insult me,' he spat out. He'd always proved himself with his fists – that was still the best way.

'If you were the fastest there'd be nothing to insult. You're the best driver in the world? Prove it.'

Ricardo backed down. Bruce had called his bluff.

'I will prove it where it counts,' he said gruffly. 'In the Grand Prix.' He turned his back on Bruce and took Debbie's hand.

But Bruce hadn't finished with him. 'To win, Ricardo, you'll have to go faster than Wyatt. And you can't walk away from that.'

Ricardo stormed away from the pits, scowling at some reporters who tried to speak to him. He turned to Debbie.

'Who does he think he is?' he said, casting a contemptuous glance back at de Villiers.

'The best manager in the business. I don't know what you're so upset about.'

'Don't you understand? I am not the champion. I have to prove it again.'

They passed a very ample-looking, dark-skinned brunette. She smiled knowingly at Ricardo, and Debbie recognised her immediately from the beach. She was furious. Ricardo was playing games with her.

He opened the car door for her. 'You want to go to the hotel?'

'I'd rather be on my own.'

Ricardo got into the car and drove away, leaving her standing in the car park. She would be back in his bed that evening, he was quite sure. Women were all the same.

Rod Talbot liked the spacious villa. From the patio, which was covered with luxuriant creepers and flowers, you could look down on the whole city of Rio, sprawled across the valley. In the distance a hang-glider floated gently towards the sea. Yes, he liked the villa. But he did not like Jules Ortega.

Jules came out onto the patio, wearing a Hawaian shirt and neatly pressed white pants. He was sallow-skinned, with a full head of greasy black hair. However, Rod reflected, with his money he hardly needed looks to attract women.

'Jules,' Rod Talbot said lazily, 'you live like a king.'

'I am the king,' Jules Ortega said.

Rod eyed the man directly. Their working relationship was good – but he did not want Jules to think that he, Rod, was the weaker party in the deal. He could crush Jules; he had connections through which he could control him. But right now, Rod needed Jules. He was about to collect the first big delivery from the factory in the Amazon.

'You have the merchandise?' Rod asked, keeping his eyes locked on Jules.

A smile crossed the sallow face. 'For a price.'

Rod tried to remain composed. He had underestimated Jules. Silently, he cursed himself. 'What's your game?' he asked coolly.

Jules spread his arms in a gesture of submissiveness that didn't fool Rod for a moment. He had invested a lot of money with Jules, he had built the new plant for him and got him the chemicals from Europe. Now Jules was trying to cut him out.

'I am greedy, Rod,' Jules said.

'We had an agreement.'

Jules laughed. 'You're going to call your lawyer?'

No, thought Rod, straightening his fingers. A lawyer is the last thing I need.

A naked woman came out on the patio and waited, head bowed. 'Marisa,' Jules said. 'Get Mr Talbot another drink. I think he needs it.'

'Bourbon and soda,' Rod said, and the woman took his glass and disappeared.

'Do you like naked women, Jules?' Rod said idly, looking after her.

The Colombian laughed, his pearl-white teeth glistening like an animal's. His teeth, reflected Rod, were the only decent part of his body. 'I prefer women as servants,' Jules said, 'and I prefer them without clothes. That way I can see what they've got.'

Marisa returned with his drink, and Rod took it, and waited for her to go.

'All right,' he said. 'What's the price?'

'One hundred million dollars.'

Rod bunched his fists. 'You're crazy! That's four times what we agreed. How can you overcharge me for drugs that come out of the factory I built for you and Antonio Vargas?'

'It is not overcharging. Remember, you can't get the raw cocaine. And if you don't pay, I will leak it to your government that you are laundering drug money in Europe.'

Jules grinned and stroked back his long, lank hair. He rose, and walked over to the edge of the patio. 'One hundred million, Rod.'

'No deal.'

Jules chuckled, and an ugly expression crossed his face. 'Then you're a dead man, Rod.'

Talbot got up. It had been a mistake to deal with Jules, he realised that now. The man was scum. Antonio Vargas was the only one with any brains – Antonio Vargas was the one who controlled Jules anyway.

And then Rod stopped in his tracks. He found that he was looking down the barrel of a .357 magnum revolver.

'Pay,' Jules said softly.

'No. The deal with Vargas was that you make me the first two deliveries for free, to pay for the new factory I built you.'

Jules laughed again. 'We thank you for the factory. Now please, no more of this. You must go from here.'

Rod looked round. The naked woman had reappeared, holding a pump-shotgun that was pointed at his stomach. He moved towards Jules and, as he had expected, the woman moved forward, an arm's length away.

'Pay up, Rod, or die,' Jules growled.

'All right. One hundred million, you bastard. Where can I make payment?'

'I go to the race-track tomorrow, to see the practice for the Grand Prix.'

'I'll meet you there, with the money.'

Jules relaxed, and as he did so Rod dropped slightly, swung his right foot out and round, and kicked the legs of the naked woman from under her. He straightened the fingers of his right hand and stabbed them like a blade into Jules's gut. He caught the shotgun as it flew through the air, and then slammed his right foot up into Jules's gun hand. The revolver spun uselessly across the tiled patio.

Jules clutched at his stomach. It was as if he had been jabbed with a metal rod. He couldn't breathe.

Rod grabbed the woman's arm, twisted the fingers back and forced her to sit on the edge of the balcony, facing the drop.

'Stand up, you silly bitch.'

She rose to her feet shakily, staring down at the drop below. Rod had merely to touch her and she would fall to her death. Then he gestured to Jules.

'Up, on the edge of the balustrade, next to her.'

Jules climbed up and stood on the concrete rail, Rio and the sea far beneath him.

'Drop your pants.'

Jules pulled down his trousers, which rested around his ankles.

'And your jockeys.'

The woman giggled nervously as she watched. An ugly expression crossed Rod's face, then disappeared. 'Amused, my dear?'

The woman shook with fear. Rod pushed the nose of the shotgun into the small of her back and tears ran from her eyes.

'No, no,' she whimpered.

'Your boss doesn't want to play straight.'

Jules was silent, scared of overbalancing and plunging into the void.

'You think you can threaten me, Ortega?'

Jules shook his head vigorously. Rod pushed the shotgun harder into the woman's back, and she screamed and struggled to hold her balance. He pushed her again with the barrel.

'No! No! No!' she screamed as she hurtled into the void.

Jules began to urinate uncontrollably. Rod raised the snout of the shotgun and brushed it under his testicles. 'You want to live?'

'P . . Please God.'

'I'll meet you tomorrow. I'll pay you ten dollars. Is that satisfactory?'

Jules nodded. It was eminently clear who had the real muscle.

The heat in the pits was stifling. Wyatt sat in his jumpsuit listening to Suzie as she read an article in the newspaper to him. She read Portuguese fluently.

'Last night, a maidservant of Jules Ortega, the well-known playboy, fell to her death from the balcony of his cliff-side home. Police say the cause of the accident is not known, but foul play is not suspected.'

Wyatt caught sight of Ricardo staring at him. He returned the glance, and for a few moments was conscious of nothing except the hatred in the Italian's eyes. The expression was mirrored in his own.

'Easy, boys.' Bruce's deep growl interrupted their mental battle, and Wyatt looked up.

'Take it easy today,' Bruce went on. 'The heat will be on tomorrow. It's sixty-one laps at an average speed of over a hundred and ten mph. That's over one hundred and ninety miles, and my guess is that the temperature will be over thirty degrees.'

'What happened to Ricardo yesterday?'

'Engine failure. The Shadow got too hot. That can happen easily on this circuit, especially if you're tailing another driver. There are going to be a lot more people jockeying for that front position now.'

Wyatt stared down the lane at the other pit crews and the long line of cars. The occasional umbrella indicated the presence of a driver. In the distance the Sugar Loaf wavered in the heat-haze, but Wyatt could never think of Rio as a holiday city.

'I was talking to Ronnie Halliday this morning . . .'

Wyatt's ears pricked up. Halliday was one of the most powerful men in motor-racing, the former boss of the Zanders team. He was president of the Formula One Constructors' Association and vice-president of FISA, the world governing body for Grand Prix racing.

'He thinks you've got the makings of a champion. But take my advice – don't let people talk, show them instead.'

Wyatt eased himself into the cockpit of the Shensu Shadow. Already he was soaking with sweat. He heard the other engines starting up, and pulled the helmet down. It was time to prove himself again.

Out on the track, he relaxed. He forgot about the heat. All that mattered was the car, the track and the other drivers. All other thoughts vanished, it was pure concentration. Everything had to be memorised, to be used the next day. His biggest adversary now was the circuit. It could catch him unawares, break him, even kill him.

He felt in control, but less anxious to push himself to the limit. Now he was exploring the track from an analytical perspective, preparing for the race.

He took Bruce's comments very seriously. He had to keep his front position from the beginning. Any dropping back would cost him dearly.

After ten laps he roared into the pits, happy with his performance. Bruce came up next to him as he pulled off his helmet.

'Nice going, Wyatt. Now relax. No one's coming close to yesterday's times, let alone yours.'

'Ricardo?'

'He's going like a bat out of hell, but doesn't know the car as well as you do.'

Wyatt felt good. So far, he held the race.

Ricardo was boiling. He could not extract more from the car. He was fighting her, not working with her. He felt the machine did not suit his style of driving. And he had never mastered the Nelson Piquet circuit – the heat and the anti-clockwise direction did not agree with him. It hammered every other driver as well, but some were better at coping with the change of direction than others.

Every other circuit on the calendar ran clockwise, so that for this one race the forces on the driver's body were reversed. This circuit always hammered Ricardo's neck muscles, as it did every other driver's, but for some reason or other it seemed to affect him more badly than the rest. He knew he was not handling the long, fast corners the way he should – and he was furious about blowing an engine the previous day.

He came off the main straight on his tenth lap feeling more confident, pushing the Shadow hard into the curve. The corner was sharp but he was determined to get through it fast.

Without warning, he overstepped the mark and lost control. The back of the Shadow shot round off the edge of the track. He saw the wall of tyres at the edge of the corner coming up fast. The next moment, he was into them and at a standstill.

He eased himself out of the cockpit, surrounded by marshals with fire-extinguishers. To his horror, he saw that the front suspension was badly damaged. He threw his helmet onto the sand in anger.

Bruce was on the scene in a matter of minutes.

'I don't believe this!'

'The car – she does not handle well.'

'Bullshit! You lost it.'

'You dare to insult me?'

Now de Villiers was right up close to him, squaring up to him.

189

'If you hadn't been such a bloody stuck-up fool, you'd have been in on the development of the Shadow from day one.'

Ricardo went puce. 'I will not drive for you!'

He turned his back, and Bruce said steadily: 'Chase will win this race. The press will say you lost your nerve, that you're over the hill. And so will every other constructor. Drop out on me, and you'll never be in the big money again.'

It was true. Ricardo turned slowly round. 'You fix the Shadow, I race.'

'Remember we have a spare Shadow.'

Ricardo knew what that meant – driving a car that had not been specifically set up for him.

'How can you do this to me?'

'You crashed the car, I didn't.'

Ricardo thought about this. It was a gamble that could go two ways. Either the car was better than the one he'd been driving, or she was worse. He saw the angry scowl on de Villiers' face. De Villiers wanted to win; de Villiers was under pressure from his sponsors. If Ricardo didn't drive, it would immediately put de Villiers in the losing seat as well. He hated de Villiers, but in the end, he also respected him.

'All right, I drive your fucking other car.'

Ricardo began walking back to the pits. He had no wish to talk to de Villiers any further; he would have to devote all his energies to inspecting the new car.

Back in the pits five minutes later, he saw that Phelps had arrived. Ricardo liked the big confident American, especially Phelps's special aura of wealth and power. Phelps was talking to Suzie von Falkenhyn, and couldn't resist touching her every so often; it was obvious that he wanted her. Good, thought Ricardo. That would upset Wyatt.

'Hi there, Ricardo – things are not going well today?'

'You judge correctly, Mr Phelps.'

'Jack, please.'

They shook hands and Ricardo returned Phelps's penetrating stare. Phelps averted his eyes and ran them over the pits, looking for Wyatt. 'Where's Chase?'

Suzie said, 'He's finished for today – now he's doing some promotional work.'

This pleased Ricardo. Such pointless activities would wear Wyatt down before the race. Ricardo had his own attitude to promotion – he would lend his name, but not his body.

Jack put his arm around Ricardo, who was conscious of expensive after-shave and a surprisingly taut body beneath the businessman's shirt. The grip was not kind, it was more an extension of Jack's power over him.

'Ricardo. I can see you're concerned about your performance here today. But you'll have to drive faster tomorrow. I'm paying you a lot of money and I expect you to deliver. I want you and Wyatt in the number one and number two positions. Get it?'

Jack's words fanned the fire that burned within him. He was not a loser, and he hated being treated like that. He could see Jack was trying to belittle him in Suzie's eyes, and he pulled away from Phelps and turned to face him squarely.

'I decide whether or not I drive tomorrow. No one else. I am not afraid. I am going to win.'

'Suit yourself, buster. Just remember who's the boss.'

Ricardo kissed Suzie on the lips, ignoring Phelps. His attractiveness to women had always given him the opportunity to rile other men, and as he had expected, he saw sparks of anger in Phelps's eyes.

'Just make sure you don't kill yourself, Ricardo.' There was a distinct snarl in Phelps's voice. 'I've heard that this isn't your favourite circuit.'

Several of the mechanics looked round, including Reg Tillson. It was unheard of to threaten a driver. De Villiers had also come into the pits, and Ricardo guessed that he must have heard the earlier part of their conversation: Bruce was obviously bristling.

'Ricardo,' Bruce said, 'why don't you go and talk to Mickey about the new Shadow? He's made plenty of modifications to her, based on what we've learnt already.' Brushing beads of perspiration off his forehead, he turned to Phelps. 'Jack, let's go over to the motorvan.'

'I've gotta leave,' Phelps said.

'No,' Bruce insisted. 'Come.'

Phelps followed him to the Calibre-Shensu motorvan, an

air-conditioned motor-home that the team used as a conference-centre at the track. Bruce closed the sliding door behind them as Phelps settled into one of the body-hugging chairs that were set into the floor.

'Bruce,' Jack Phelps said easily, 'just relax.'

Bruce felt as if he was being treated like an over-strung adolescent, but he kept his rage under control. 'Jack,' he said, 'we made an agreement. You supply the money, I do the racing. Your wires are getting crossed.'

Phelps stretched out and put his hands behind his head. He did not seem in the least put out. 'That doesn't preclude me making casual conversation with Wyatt or Ricardo.'

'Oh *ja* it fucking well does, man. Especially when you threaten them!'

'You don't need to shout, friend. I'm paying for results, not hot-headed behaviour.'

'Every goddam race counts. Every chance has to be taken. Of course I want two front-runners – just as much as you do. Even a fucking idiot would know that'd push your fag sales through the roof.'

'I've got the money. I don't need losers. Chase is doing wonders for Calibre Lights in America, and if Ricardo can't deliver, I'll order you to cut him.'

'And what about Shensu? Does he agree with your shotgun management?'

It was as if a cloud had passed over Phelps's face and taken the sunshine from it. He appeared agitated. Sensing his advantage, Bruce pressed on. 'Shall I tell Shensu what you said just now?'

He had Phelps now. He couldn't quite work out what sort of hold Shensu held over Phelps, but it didn't really matter. At least he had a way of controlling the American.

'Let's get on with the job. Are you unhappy with the Shensu relationship?' Phelps replied guardedly, changing the subject.

'I've got twelve Shensu mechanics working night and day on the engines. Cut the crap, Jack. What's your game?' Bruce deliberately played his hand hard. He was glad to have found something with which he could rile the usually imperturbable Phelps.

'I spoke out of turn, Bruce.' Phelps seemed to change gear as he was speaking; de Villiers could imagine the devious cogs in Phelps's brain turning over another well-oiled plan.

'Well, Jack, I'll be interested to hear Shensu's views on your attitude to racing.'

'What we discuss here is between ourselves.'

Bruce laughed. He wanted to smash Phelps in the face, wanted to pulverise him into the ground. 'No it's not. This isn't power politics. Anything that affects my chances of producing a winner is Mr Shensu's business.'

'You tell him a word of this, and you're gone.'

Bruce gauged the situation carefully. If Phelps succeeded in railroading him now, he would be under his whip for the rest of the season. It was all or nothing. Better to get it over with now.

'OK, Jack, I'll tell Shensu I'm out.'

Bruce got up. He felt like screaming. He knew this would probably destroy his career, but he wasn't going to be kicked around like a second-rate player.

As he was about to open the door, Phelps held his arm. To his surprise, Bruce saw a look of almost desperate concern on the American's face. He couldn't believe it. He had obviously touched some vulnerable spot in the man; made him feel threatened.

'Cool it, Bruce. Let's just . . . talk this out?' Phelps's tone was unmistakably conciliatory.

Bruce settled back into the chair facing Jack. He felt a surge of relief but didn't let it show on his face.

'I'm a businessman,' Phelps said. 'I tend to be abrupt; I'm just used to getting my own way. You were right, Bruce, and I was wrong.'

'OK. Then you agree to work with me, not against me?'

Phelps nodded his head reluctantly.

'All right,' Bruce said briskly. 'Then the first thing you do is phone Ricardo. I want you to apologise to him.'

He could see that Phelps was desperately trying to control himself – but he didn't care. Phelps had done the damage, now he must rectify it. He could see the blood suffusing

Phelp's face, the immaculate edifice looked as if it was about to explode.

'I'll phone him tonight,' Phelps said.

'You do that.'

Phelps stormed out of the motorvan in a blind rage. He had totally underestimated de Villiers. He could not remove him, and even worse, he could not manipulate him.

The chauffeur held open the door to the air-conditioned car, and he stepped inside quickly. Immediately he was in the cooler climate of the car he began to feel better and to think more logically. A plan began to form in his mind that could give him exactly what he wanted: the power to control and manipulate de Villiers. Of course, if it didn't work out there were other options, for there were plenty of other people in the team who could be effectively used to get at de Villiers.

And, Jack thought, he had one big advantage over Bruce de Villiers – because, in the end, he wasn't in Formula One for the racing.

Bruce de Villiers watched the jet-black executive jet coming in to land on what he estimated to be one of the worst runways in the world. An accomplished flyer himself, he admired the precision with which the pilot put the plane down. And as it taxied towards him across the runway, he thought about his two drivers.

Ricardo was still the better driver of the two, through sheer experience, but Wyatt was the young lion, anxious to make a kill. And what really set Wyatt apart from Ricardo was his attitude. Although Wyatt was ruthless in his determination to win, he knew that he relied on the team to get him first across the finish-line. And Bruce could see that the mechanics, and Mickey Dunstal, sensed Wyatt's respect for them. They wanted to help him – and there was no doubt that more care was lavished on Wyatt's car than on Ricardo's.

The tiny door in the fuselage of the plane swung open, and a team of ground-staff quickly pushed the mobile stairs closer to the door.

Bruce was feeling pretty good. He had figured out a few things about Phelps, and now he felt more in control of the team. He was pleased that Phelps had not come. There were one or two things he wanted to discuss in private with the Japanese entrepreneur.

Aito Shensu came quickly down the steps of the plane. Bruce was struck by the similarity between him and Wyatt in the way they moved – purposefully, with economy of movement.

'Bruce, it is good to see you. You did not have to come to the airport, you know.'

'Welcome to Rio, Aito.'

They walked together across the tarmac and through the customs area. A Shensu car was waiting for them outside the airport foyer, and the chauffeur drove them smoothly off.

'Is Jack here?' Aito asked, as if mirroring Bruce's thoughts.

'Yes. He was at the practice this morning.'

'Is he pleased?'

'I think so.'

Aito looked quickly across at him. 'There's something wrong?'

'Ricardo spun his car and damaged it,' Bruce said. 'He'll have to use an untried car.'

Aito weighed his words before he spoke. 'Ricardo is a superb driver,' he said. 'Why should he have an accident in a qualifying event?'

'A superb driver, yes, but he's also human. Wyatt achieved the fastest qualifying time – Ricardo was simply trying to better it.'

'Surely an easy task for the former world champion?'

'I feel Ricardo is less at home with the Shadow than Wyatt. But that's just a teething problem.'

'Ah! I understand.' He paused. 'And what about you? You are happy?'

It was odd, the way Aito asked the question. It sounded like something a psychiatrist might ask.

'I'll be happy once the race is over and we have two front positions.'

'And the engine?'

'Faultless. But then it's only in the race that it will really prove its reliability.'

'You find the back-up you are getting from my people OK?' Aito looked at him intensely, and Bruce could not help smiling.

'Relax, Aito. I've never had better back-up from an engine manufacturer. Everything from your side has been done in the best possible fashion. At this stage we just have to keep our fingers crossed and hope that nothing's been left out or forgotten.'

'I am sure you have done a fine job.'

The car pulled up outside the hotel, and the chauffeur leapt out and opened the side door.

'You will join Jack and myself for dinner tonight?'

'Thank you, but no. I have to be at the circuit. The last-minute preparation is critical. But I'll see you at the start tomorrow – and I look forward to bringing you victory.'

Bruce watched Aito disappear into the hotel, and then the chauffeur pulled off and headed towards the circuit. It was time to get down to the real business of racing.

Wyatt sat in the pits, enjoying the coolness now that the sun had gone down. He could feel himself tensing up. He tried not to think about the race, but it was impossible.

Memories came flooding back. He had been here in 1978, for the Grand Prix at the then brand-new circuit. It had been hot then; his father had been at the front of the grid, and was tipped to win the race by a wide margin. The day itself had been sweltering, and the Brazilians wild with excitement. James had led the field for twenty devastatingly fast laps. Then, without warning, his car had careered off the circuit and into a barrier of tyres. When they dragged him out, he was a wreck. The incredible heat had caused him to black out. He was lucky to be alive.

Wyatt could understand his father a lot better now, understand the constant tension he'd been under in those days.

He looked across at Reg. He could see the excitement in his eyes, and could feel it mirrored in his own. Here, competing in the intense world of Formula One, this was living. Reg met his stare.

'Relax, Wyatt, you're at the front of the grid.'

'I want to be first over the finish-line – it's sixty-one laps, it's hot, and it's hard on the car. Relaxed is the last thing I am.'

'I was there when your father went off as well – forget about it. The Shadow isn't as cramped as his machine was, you won't get as hot.'

Bruce walked in and looked around. His eyes lighted on Wyatt.

'You should be resting.'

He was right. 'All right. I'm turning in.'

'You're confident?'

'I feel in my gut I can do it.'

'You can.'

Wyatt walked out into the darkness. What happened tomorrow would determine his future.

It was four in the morning. Bruce sat next to the two cars and looked across at his mechanics. Everything was in place.

'Let's call it a day, gentlemen.'

Everyone filed out, dog-tired, leaving the garage empty except for Bruce and Mickey.

'Now it's up to Ricardo and Wyatt,' Mickey said. 'I know who I'll be putting my money on.'

Bruce sat down on a tool-box next to the machine. 'You're letting your heart influence your mind, Mickey. You know as well as I do how much experience counts for in this business.'

Bruce didn't want to admit that he also rated Wyatt higher than Ricardo. He remembered Ricardo years before – Ricardo had been better then, less cocky and a lot more professional. Still, a couple of poor finishes and the Italian would be back fighting. And of course, if Wyatt was out in front, Ricardo wouldn't be far behind.

'Do you know Ricardo's got the better car?'

Bruce swung round to face Mickey. Yes, he knew that the latest Shadow was the more refined car, the one in which they'd been able to incorporate every single thing they'd learned from Wyatt's testing work.

'Theoretically better,' Bruce said. 'She hasn't been put through her paces yet.'

There was a noise from the entrance to the garage, and they both looked up. It was Reg.

'Worried about something, Reg?'

'No. I didn't realise it was you two in here, I thought it might be someone snooping. It's pitch-black out there. The McCabe lads are looking tatty – they're still hard at work.'

Bruce was surprised. McCabe were obviously having problems. 'They must be worried about the new engine,' he said, voicing the thoughts of all of them.

'Well, they're certainly sweating. It's as hot as Hades.'

Bruce thought fast. They were experiencing a heat-wave. Perhaps McCabe weren't so disorganised after all; perhaps they were making some useful modifications to their engine. If it was this hot at four in the morning, when the race was run in the early afternoon tomorrow, the track would be a furnace.

He cast his mind back to the time when they were still testing at Kyalami. Wyatt's car had blown up from overheating. At the time he thought they'd solved the problem more than adequately.

He turned to Mickey. 'I'm worried. Reg has made a good point. Maybe McCabe are improving their cooling-system.'

Mickey had got up and was examining the ventilation ducts that directed air into the cooling-system of the car.

'I know what yer thinking,' he said slowly. 'But I think we should leave things as they are.'

Reg glanced apprehensively at Bruce. They were both mechanics by training, and they both knew the dangers of changing things at the last minute. Generally such changes weren't properly thought through, and caused other faults during the race.

It was Reg who broke the agonised silence. 'What about modifying just one of the cars? Ricardo and Wyatt are both bloody good drivers. It'd be a fifty-fifty gamble. Then if one grinds to a halt, at least the other's in with a chance.'

Bruce knew he would have to decide whose car they would make the modification to.

'Give me a minute. I'm going to take a walk.'

He got up and went out into the blackness. It was even hotter than he'd realised. Hell, he must have raced here every year for the past nine years, but it had never been this hot before. Both cars could be out of the race because of severe overheating.

Reg was right, you couldn't see a thing out here. He walked into a parked car and cursed silently.

Should he pray? He was, in a quiet way, a religious man. What was fair, that was the question? In the end it was a gamble. Mickey's modification would have been fine two days before the race – then they could have checked it out, refined it.

Wyatt deserved a good car for his first race, but he was the number two driver. An initial win for Ricardo would put the champion in great form for the rest of the season. And Wyatt drove hard, whereas Ricardo was smoother; Ricardo wouldn't hammer his car as hard.

After a few more minutes he walked back into the pits. Both Reg and Mickey were staring at him intently as he returned.

'So, what's it ter be?' asked Mickey, keen to get to work.

'It's in the hands of Lady Luck.'

Bruce pulled a coin out of his pocket, spun it in the air and caught it on the back of his wrist. Then he stared at Reg.

'Heads or tails?'

'Tails.'

'OK, we do it. It'll be Wyatt's car we modify. Gentlemen, let's get to work.'

They finished at seven in the morning. To an outside observer Wyatt's Shadow looked just as it had the previous day; only a careful examination would have revealed the enlarged air-cooling ducts. Bruce had called Professor Katana from the hotel – Shensu's head of engine development was here in Brazil for the Grand Prix. Katana had worked with them on the computer to calculate the exact dimensions of the enlargement, then he'd reprogrammed the chip that controlled the engine's electronic management system.

Bruce staggered over to the motorvan with Katana, Mickey and Reg. They were all on edge, and Bruce could see the sweat dripping from Reg's forehead.

'Wyatt and Ricardo have their final warm-up soon.'

Reg looked up, exhausted. 'Who's going to tell Wyatt?'

'And why are we talkin' so quietly?' Mickey interjected.

Bruce stared at the Irishman: Mickey was always fast off the mark. Reg had thought they'd just come into the van to relax.

'I don't want to say anything to Wyatt about this,' Bruce replied, his face betraying none of the tension he was feeling.

'You're the penultimate bastard,' Reg uttered softly, knowing that he would go along with Bruce, knowing that he himself wouldn't have had the courage to be so ruthless.

'It is dishonourable,' Professor Katana said quietly.

'Bruce, you're not being fair,' Mickey chimed in. 'Wyatt knows more about that car than any of us. Telling him that he's got better cooling would push him to drive a bit harder.'

'Dammit, Mickey, telling him there's been a last-minute modification will scare the shit out of him. He'll be driving as hard as he can anyway.'

There was a knock at the door, and they all looked at each other. Bruce allowed himself a thin smile, knowing they wouldn't betray him.

The door opened and in came Wyatt, looking fresh and relaxed. He ran his eyes over them – they all looked exhausted.

"Morning everyone. Didn't you get any sleep last night?'

'There was a lot to check,' Bruce replied evasively.

'Well, I hope you'll be able to keep your eyes open this afternoon.'

'Like some coffee?' Reg asked, moving towards the automatic dispenser in the corner of the cramped lounge, and hiding his worried face.

'Yes, thanks. The coffee's one of the few good things about Rio.'

Professor Katana looked at Wyatt directly and spoke in Japanese. Wyatt nodded a few times, then turned to Bruce. 'Why my machine and not Ricardo's?'

Bruce clenched his fist and snarled at Katana – and Wyatt was across the room and standing beside him in an instant. There was something in his eyes that made Bruce take a few steps back.

'Why my car, Bruce?'

'It's the hottest I've known it here – we're experiencing a heat-wave. I believe that the Shadow will overheat, but I can't be sure. The modification is a gamble. It could go wrong. But then Ricardo's car could also overheat.'

Wyatt spoke to Katana again in Japanese. 'What are you saying?' Bruce asked angrily.

'I'm telling him,' said Wyatt, 'that he has more courage than the rest of you put together.'

Bruce's knuckles were white, but Mickey nodded his head. 'He's right. I'll be takin' the blame as much as you. Wyatt, me boy, I'm sorry. I think it'll work, and it'll make you faster, by God.'

'Or it'll blow me up before I've had a chance to prove myself,' Wyatt said angrily.

They sat sipping coffee and talking over the exact details of the race as the air-conditioning hummed in the background. The incident wasn't mentioned again, but it was not forgotten.

Outside, the air temperature was rising fast, and a heat-haze shimmered across the track. Enthusiastic motor-racing fans were already packing in around the circuit – women in bikinis, dark-skinned men in shorts and little else. Already the ice-cream and cold drink vendors were doing a roaring trade.

The atmosphere was humid, the air desperately hot and still. The temperature in the shade was thirty degrees Celsius, and rising, and the day had hardly begun. The heat-wave was on.

Ricardo sat in his car at the entrance to the inside of the circuit, sweat running down his face. He'd told Debbie he wanted to come here alone, but he hadn't told her why, because she wouldn't have understood. Only he could deal with the enormity of it. He lifted his left hand from the steering-wheel and dispassionately watched it shake. He'd known fear before, but never like this. All he dreamed about was the accident, and every time he relived it the vision became more intense.

He didn't need the warm-up session. He didn't need the race. But he desperately needed the money to keep living the way he enjoyed. He'd phoned his bank in Rome two days ago, and the news hadn't been good. He had always spent wildly and without thought; a multi-millionaire, he reasoned, didn't need to worry about his financial affairs. But he'd been wrong. A big business venture had gone sour on him in the last few weeks, and he owed a lot of money, big money.

If he retired now he would be destined to a middle-class existence – and the idea of that revolted him. He had fought to escape poverty, and now that he had tasted the exotic life, nothing else would do for him. Perhaps he should marry money. He had never asked a woman to marry him. He didn't believe he could be faithful to one woman, because he loved challenges and a beautiful woman was always the ultimate prize.

Debbie had been easy to bed – he had lost respect for her because of that. And already he had cheated on her, the experience being peculiarly enjoyable. But he suspected that Debbie might be from a wealthy background, even if she was only Bruce's secretary. Little things she'd mentioned about her father's various business dealings led him to believe the man was a big wheel. Also, Debbie wore expensive jewellery, all of which she said she'd inherited. He'd do a little more investigating on that score before he dumped her.

He put the car into first, and showed his special pass to the marshal. He noticed that several cars had their bonnets up, steam pouring out of their radiators. It was going to be a very hot race, unless there was rain to cool the circuit down in the afternoon. But rain would make the circuit dangerous – deadly slippery after the heat.

He drew up alongside the Calibre-Shensu motorvan, and Wyatt stepped out as he arrived. Immediately, Ricardo's fear vanished. Wyatt was his enemy, the man who could beat him, humiliate him. But there was no way he was going to let Wyatt Chase do that to him.

'Is it always this hot?'

He wasn't going to reply, then he looked into Wyatt's eyes and saw that there wasn't a trace of animosity in them.

'No,' he said. 'This is very bad, my friend.'

'Bruce doesn't seem concerned.'

This last remark really got to Ricardo. Wyatt was always a jump ahead of him, getting close to de Villiers. Ignoring him, Ricardo walked across to the motorvan and went inside to escape the heat. The coolness of the air-conditioning was an immediate relief. Bruce was sitting in the centre of the lounge, his arms stretched along the couch. In the hazel eyes Ricardo thought he saw irritation. De Villiers had this silent power about him that could make you feel uneasy for no explicable reason.

'It is hot, eh?'

'Don't push it in the warm-up, Ricardo. Give your engine a chance.'

Ricardo raised his eyebrows incredulously. 'You're saying the engine, it cannot take the heat?'

'I'm saying, take it easy. Everyone else is facing the same problem. How you handle it could make all the difference when the race is on.'

'But when we get going, I'm not holding back.'

Ricardo hated the fact that he was under de Villiers' control, and he knew the only way out of it was to win.

Without saying any more, he left the motorvan and walked in the blistering heat towards the pits.

Jack Phelps drank another glass of iced water. He was enjoying the event. Everyone was asking him questions about the team. The publicity was positive, and he was seen as an innovator as well as a sponsor. The Shadow was attracting a lot of attention and comment.

He cast his eye around the huge Shensu pavilion that had been set up on the outskirts of the circuit. It was typical of the style in which Aito Shensu approached any task: none of the other teams' exhibition centres were anything near as good. In the centre of the display was the Shensu Ninja sports car – not a completed car but a model that looked like the real thing. This was the prototype that Mickey Dunstal was evolving in conjunction with Shensu. Jack had already put his name down to be the first owner of the greatest supercar to come out of the Orient.

The Ninja was attracting a lot of attention. Jack was cynical about it, though. He guessed these people had come inside to escape the heat, and were just looking at the new sports car to pass the time. He could think of another reason for coming to look – walking elegantly around the display were models dressed in some of Suzie von Falkenhyn's most stunning creations. An unexpected bonus of Suzie's involvement with the team was that the Calibre-Shensu gear she designed for the team was selling like crazy in department stores in Europe and America – Jack still could not quite believe the demand for it. Calibre-Shensu had not competed in a single race, yet the team was already labelled a success.

Rod Talbot walked out of the warehouse and listened to the wail of the Formula One engines. The warehouse was situated amongst many others at the back of the circuit.

Two huge container trucks thundered up outside. The side-door of one cab opened, and Jules Ortega stepped down, briefcase in hand. As expected, he had brought reinforcements, and Rod noted the two thugs step down from the cab of the other truck.

He backed into the warehouse, the noise of the Grand Prix cars echoing around him. He moved into the private office at the side of the open area. Perfect: no other doors and no windows, the only approach was from the front.

Jules's eyes were cold and emotionless. He dropped his briefcase to reveal an Uzi machine-gun which he pointed at Rod's chest.

'Now you pay for the death of my woman,' he hissed.

Rod laughed. 'You cock-sucker, where's my delivery?'

'No money, no nothing, you Yankee bastard.'

Those were the last words Jules got out. He never saw Rod's right foot come up and wind him in the side of the head.

The two strong men closed in. Rod straightened his hand and jabbed his extended fingers hard into one man's eyes, and his opponent dropped to the floor screaming, clutching his face. Then the other moved in in a classic boxer's stance. Rod laughed, and kicked him hard in the left knee-cap. The man hobbled forwards as Rod smacked his right knee-cap, and grinned in satisfaction as he heard the bone crunch. He slammed his right fist directly below the thug's nose, breaking the bone above his mouth and killing him instantly.

Rod smoothed out his suit as he looked at Jules's unconscious body, now lying at his feet.

'Cock-sucker.'

The blinded thug rolled around on the floor, screaming. Rod pulled out a cigarette, lit up, and waited for Jules to come round. Rod was going to take delivery on his terms.

The Formula One cars buzzed around the Autodromo Internacional do Rio de Janeiro – renamed the Nelson Piquet Circuit after his 1987 win there – like angry flies. A record crowd was in attendance, and all around the circuit people were in various stages of undress. The heat-wave was in full swing. It was a great honour, the local newspaper reported, that the first Grand Prix of the 1991 season should open in Rio.

Aito Shensu looked up at the mountains, far in the distance, with satisfaction. He was pleased. Jack Phelps had done a superb job – he could sense the spirit in the Calibre-Shensu team. He thought, too, of the Shensu Ninja, sitting proudly in the centre of the Shensu pavilion. No man could match the masterpiece Mickey Dunstal had created.

Aito knew his investment in Formula One had added to his stature as a leading car manufacturer. Almost overnight the Shensu name was being associated with performance: dipstick market research in Europe and the United States had proved it.

Aito wanted Shensu to become the world's top-selling cars; he wanted Shensu to be even more successful than Ford. He also wanted Wyatt Chase to win. Wyatt, who understood so much about Japan and its culture.

There was something else, too – even more important – that he had been grooming Wyatt for from the day he first met him. For that, though, Wyatt had still to prove himself.

Rod tightened the vice up another turn and watched the bleeding fingers locked in its jaws with detachment.

'No!' The Colombian's scream was lost in the drone of the Formula One cars blasting round the circuit. He was drenched in sweat, slumped across the bench next to the vice, his other hand tied up behind his back. On his face was a look of terror.

Rod sipped at his iced water, sitting on a collapsible chair slightly away from the bench. He said nothing, only occasionally getting up to increase the pressure.

Now the Colombian was sobbing, his right hand a pulp. 'Oh my God, what is it you want?' Jules's voice was almost a whisper.

'I like to be called Mr Talbot.'

'What is it you want, Mr Talbot?'

'Let's start with the delivery.'

After a moment's silence, Rod got up and started to tighten the vice again.

'No, please. I have the consignment.' Jules's voice was quavering. 'Please . . . my hand . . .'

'I want you to deliver it where I told you to.'

Rod yanked the vice handle upwards, tightening the jaws. The Columbian's scream sounded like a woman's, it was so high-pitched – then he passed out.

Rod walked over to a bucket of water standing in the corner. He picked it up and deftly chucked it over the unconscious Colombian. Jules came round almost immediately and started blubbing like a child.

'Why you hurt me?' The voice was pleading. All resistance had gone.

'Now listen,' Rod replied, watching Jules's eyes which were firmly locked on his hand. 'I want you to do something else for me.'

'Yes?'

'I want you to tell Vargas what I did to your hand. I want you to let him know that if there are any more problems, I will find him. And I will hurt him so badly that he wants to die.'

'Yes.'

Rod undid the vice, and the Colombian dropped to the ground clutching his hand.

'Now,' Rod said, 'I hope you will not be so stupid as to forget what you have promised.'

Bruce de Villiers wiped the sweat off his face as he looked at the bank of computer monitors. He wondered what the men of the 1950s, the oily rag brigade, would have made of the racing gadgetry of the '90s. Back then there had been just five teams contesting the championship, and only in the mid '60s had the number reached double figures. But what kept the whole team running hadn't changed, it was still raw human energy.

He looked again at the impersonal screen. He could see just about every engine-function displayed. But it was frustrating in some ways: if anything went wrong, the monitors weren't going to help him fix it – they would just tell him what had happened so that next time he could rectify the problem. In a few years' time he knew he'd be monitoring the drivers in much the same way – constant read-outs on blood-pressure, pulse-rate and perhaps even pupil movement and cerebral activity.

Two of the monitors covered Wyatt's car, and the other two Ricardo's. Bruce was pleased that Ricardo had speeded up. Even though he was number seven on the grid, it meant he was more in the running than before.

The outside temperature was now forty degrees Celsius. Bruce prayed it wouldn't rise much above that – it was far too hot already. He watched the engine temperatures of both the cars very closely. There was no doubt that Wyatt's modified Shadow was keeping cooler than Ricardo's machine.

'Good morning, Bruce. Is everything in order?' Aito Shensu's cool, crisp voice cut through the stifling heat of the pits.

Bruce turned as Aito looked over his shoulder. The Japanese magnate was dressed in an immaculate dark-blue silk suit and the usual black-framed glasses.

'Both cars are running well,' he said. 'Your engines appear faultless.'

Aito ran his eyes over the monitors and nodded. 'The changes you made this morning are working to good effect.'

Professor Katana was obviously in constant communication with Aito, thought Bruce. This irritated him, because it took away a measure of his control. However, he told himself to relax; Aito's input was always constructive. 'As you know,' he said, 'only Wyatt's car carries the modification.'

'And if it wasn't for Professor Katana, he wouldn't know about it.'

Now Bruce was really angry. It was his business to decide what his drivers were told. His face betrayed his thoughts.

'You are not angry with me – you are angry with yourself,' Aito Shensu said. 'I believe in being honest with people I trust. I know how, as a Westerner, you choose to run this team. But you are a shrewd man, Bruce. I think you are still prepared to learn.'

The grip on Bruce's shoulder now felt like a steel clamp. He had totally underestimated Aito's understanding of the situation.

'I took the decision,' Bruce said grimly.

Aito gave a faint smile. 'I want you to be completely open with Wyatt. You can trust him.'

Logic and ethics, thought Bruce. Yes they were fine in discussion, but on the track you operated by different rules.

'This is going to be a hard race,' he said. 'There'll be a lot of passing and overtaking, and that means some drivers are going to be tailing each other a lot of the time. The heat build-up for the following car is rapid; after a while the driver has to back off or risk a blow-up. So the increased cooling on the Shadow could give Wyatt the edge he needs to win.' The words were out of his mouth before he realised it.

'Ah, you favour Wyatt rather than Ricardo,' Aito remarked reflectively.

'Aito . . .' Phelps's voice boomed across the pits. 'I've been looking forward to this.'

Jack and Aito shook hands. The President meets the Emperor, Bruce thought to himself.

'I was looking for you earlier,' Aito replied in a slightly abrupt voice, 'but no one could find you.'

'Oh, I'm sorry. I met an associate and we went off for a discussion.'

Bruce looked anxiously over the pit crew. 'If you'll excuse me, gentlemen, I've got work to do.'

The practice was over and the cars were coming in. Bruce's important business now was making sure that Wyatt and Ricardo were well rested before the race. That was what the motorvan was primarily for, a place where the drivers could relax before the big event. The masseuse was in attendance in case either of the drivers had tensed up.

Wyatt was first in, his face bathed in sweat as he removed his helmet and fire-protection mask. Bruce was impressed that Suzie was nowhere to be seen; she obviously understood how the team worked, that it was important for him to be close to his drivers at this moment.

'Well, Wyatt, how did she go?'

'Beautifully, but the heat's worrying me.'

'Every driver's under the same pressure.'

'It's just like sitting in a microwave.'

'Just relax. It'll get cooler in the afternoon. Maybe there'll be rain,' Bruce added, looking up at the growing number of clouds in the sky.

'You'd better pray there isn't. It'll be hell out there in the rain. After this heat the surface'll be slippery in the wet.'

When there was a prospect of rain, each team approached the change of weather from its own perspective. Wet-weather tyres were far slower than the smooth slicks used in the dry. If a car came in too early before a storm, the driver's times would drop; but if he was still on smooth slicks when the rain fell, he'd really have to slow down or risk losing control of his car in the curves. He'd only be able to speed up once he'd been into the pits to have his wet-weather tyres fitted.

'*Ja*, you're right. We'll worry about rain when it happens. It's going to be competitive today.'

'It's always a fight, and I enjoy a fight.'

It was what Bruce wanted to hear. 'Take a break now,' he

said. 'I'm sure you'll want to talk to Suzie.'

'I'll see you in the motorvan.'

Ricardo was a different case altogether. When he got out of the car he was in a foul mood, and it was all Bruce could do to keep him from having a punch-up with the pit crew. He was clearly not at home in the new Shadow – obviously he needed more time to get comfortable with the car.

'Relax, Ricardo, your times are good.'

Phelps ambled over, all smiles. Bruce wondered how the American could handle wearing a double-breasted suit in the blazing heat. Jack shook Ricardo's hand warmly.

'How's the champion?'

Ricardo brightened. 'Very well, Jack. It will be a good race.'

'And you'll be at the front?'

'Of course.'

Out of the corner of his eye, Bruce watched Aito Shensu examine the engine of Wyatt's Shadow with his mechanics. Aito had changed out of his suit into an immaculate overall.

Ricardo stepped up closer to Jack Phelps. 'Wyatt is always getting more attention from the mechanics.'

Phelps slapped him on the back good-humouredly. 'For God's sake, Ricardo, you know that isn't true.'

Bruce felt his nerves were frayed, and did nothing to disguise the irritation in his voice. 'Cut the bullshit, Ricardo.'

Phelps came to the rescue. 'Ricardo, cool down. We're paying you a small fortune – Wyatt's earning peanuts. You've got the better car, by Bruce's own admission, and you don't have the advertising commitments that keep Wyatt busy between races. I should think it's obvious who we consider to be the front-runner.'

'Keep talking, Jack, I like your direction. Perhaps you should consider managing the team.' It was a direct dig at Bruce.

Bruce ignored it. He was pleased that Jack had got Ricardo into better spirits, that was all that mattered. He'd sort Ricardo out later, when they didn't have an audience.

*

Suzie felt uncomfortable in the constructors' tower – she wanted to be involved in what was happening in the pits. Instead she had to listen to some half-drunk Brazilian industrialist who was drinking in her body and not listening to a word she said. Wyatt would not have tolerated the man or his behaviour.

'If you don't mind, *señor*. I'd like to be by myself.'

The industrialist walked off reluctantly, and Suzie looked out of the huge windows and down to the pits. She could see Jack, Ricardo and Bruce in earnest discussion. She guessed Wyatt was in the motorvan.

The tension excited her. She made her way down the steps and then across the tarmac behind the pits to the Calibre-Shensu motorvan. She punched in the entry code, and hydraulics operated soundlessly, opening the door. She took off her shoes and walked along the carpeted interior in her stockinged feet.

The masseuse was working Wyatt's shoulders on the bed at the rear of the van. She looked up at Suzie, who held her fingers to her lips. Then Suzie gestured for the masseuse to leave, and she noiselessly took over working Wyatt's neck muscles. Once the masseuse had gone, she worked her hands down Wyatt's back and then over his buttocks. Her hand gently stroked the area between his legs.

'Hey, that's enough,' he muttered.

She continued, and he pivoted round and gripped her by the waist. The anger on his face turned to surprise, then satisfaction, as his eyes took her in.

She eased down his underpants and caressed him with her lips.

'Suzie,' he whispered.

Her name on his lips aroused her, and she felt his leg come between hers. She couldn't control herself, she came before she even realised what was happening.

'Wyatt, please, please . . .'

He pulled her forward, his hands firmly around her waist, under her skirt. She had nothing on underneath except her suspender-belt, and she felt him penetrating. Her head arched back and her thighs pressed hard against his torso. She felt

211

him thrusting, and the passion swept through her so that she lost control and screamed out again and again in ecstasy.

Then she felt the hotness as he burst within her, and she subsided into his arms.

'Oh my God, Wyatt, this is crazy.'

He held her tightly as the tears ran from her eyes. 'Oh Wyatt, I'm so in love with you. I'm so scared.'

Then there was the noise of the intercom. Someone wanted to come in.

'I love you. I love you more than I've ever loved anyone,' he said softly.

Suzie rose, and smoothed down her dress. She picked up the intercom phone.

'Yes, he's here.' She held her hand over the phone. 'A Mrs Ramirez?'

'Let her in.'

She activated the door, and Mrs Ramirez walked into the lounge. Immediately, Suzie was conscious of the aquamarine eyes watching her. There was something in that look, in those eye-movements, that reminded her of Wyatt.

'I see you 'ave company.'

The accent was faintly French. Suzie was confused. Who was this very attractive older woman – a lover she did not know about?

Wyatt got up, pulling on his jumpsuit. 'Suzie, this is my mother, Estelle Ramirez,' he said stiffly.

A thousand thoughts shot through Suzie's mind as she turned and kissed Wyatt hard on the lips.

'You win. I know you can do it.'

Then she was gone, and Wyatt was left staring at his mother, who sat down beside him.

'She is a very beautiful woman, very sophisticated. She is also in love with you. My God, Wyatt, you are like your father.'

He stared hard at his mother, seeing the emptiness and the bitterness in her eyes, still the same after ten years. Why had she come? He had hoped the bitterness might have been wiped out, but no, not even Carlos had achieved that much.

Then, of course, there was Danny's suicide – she blamed him for that as well. Maybe she was right.

'I want to win, just like he did.'

'Oh, Wyatt, what has happened to us?'

Everything he had done since his father's death – all the time in Japan – had been an attempt to cope with this. He would not let her upset him now.

'Is Carlos here?' he asked.

'Wyatt, listen to me.'

He felt the tears running from his eyes, he couldn't control them. The words she'd said so long ago echoed in his mind, the words that had driven him away from her, away from England, to the *dojo* and the discipline that had helped him to survive.

You killed him. You killed him.

Then another voice broke the spell and brought him back to the present. 'Estelle, leave him.'

Wyatt looked up as he saw his stepfather fold his arms around Estelle. Carlos almost lifted her up as he guided her from the motorvan. Wyatt stared emptily through the window into the heat-haze.

Carlos's hand on his shoulder broke his reverie. 'Wyatt. I am sorry.'

He turned to Carlos, whom he both loved and respected. The deeply tanned face, the dark hair in its long pony-tail, the suggestion of great moral and physical strength, gave the Argentinian a magnetic presence.

'Wyatt, she came to tell you she wanted you to win – that in spite of everything, she loves you.'

Wyatt got up and stretched.

'After all this time . . . Carlos, I loved my father.'

Carlos shook his hand and held it, his other hand pressing Wyatt's forearm.

'This is your race. Forget about the past – but remember that she cares about you very much. And Wyatt . . .'

'Yes?'

'Your lady, I like her.'

*

Suzie felt better back in the crowded atmosphere of the constructors' tower. Wyatt had never spoken about his mother. That was something she would have to come to terms with, but what really mattered was that he'd said he loved her.

Jack Phelps came over, and was very friendly. His company was fine, it was just that everything he did was calculated. She also knew he was one of the wealthiest men in the world – his yachts, planes, cars and houses bore witness to it. But what was extraordinary was his ability with people. He had an almost hypnotic effect on her. She was drawn to him despite the fact that she didn't feel at all relaxed in his presence.

Suzie almost did a double-take as Wyatt's mother walked into the room. For a moment, all conversation ceased. With her was a striking-looking man with a dark complexion and a pony-tail.

Phelps glided across the floor and kissed Estelle on both cheeks. 'Jack,' Suzie heard her say, 'it's been such a long time.'

Suzie backed away, seeking anonymity in the crowd. The next moment Vanessa Tyson closed in on her, along with a burly cameraman. Suzie felt the video-camera zooming in on her face.

'Suzie, how do you feel about your lover, about to risk his life in today's race?'

Suzie tried to remain calm. 'I think he will win.'

'But what if he dies?'

Carlos Ramirez shot forward almost imperceptibly – Suzie sensed movement though she didn't see it. The next moment, the video-camera crashed to the floor and the cameraman was bent double, wheezing. Carlos was holding Vanessa's wrist tightly, staring into her eyes.

'You have no manners. Get out.'

The journalist walked out of the room, red-faced, her cameraman limping after her.

Estelle came up and spoke softly to Suzie. 'Journalists, they come from the gutter and they drag one's life down into it.'

Suzie thought of the articles she'd read over the years. She remembered pictures of James Chase in his Formula One days – James in his car, James winning. James dying in a car accident in Monaco; then the society gossip when Estelle married the captain of the Argentinian polo side only months after her famous husband died. There had been rumours of a long-standing affair . . .

Carlos took her hand and kissed it. 'You are in love with Wyatt?' he asked directly.

'Yes.' As she spoke, Suzie watched Estelle, fascinated because now she knew where Wyatt got his courage and his looks from.

'He was born to compete,' Estelle said with a faraway smile, hardly registering what Suzie had just said. Then she seemed to come to herself. 'Please,' she offered, 'join us for lunch.'

Suzie accepted – there was nothing for her to do now. Wyatt was on his own, and that was the way he would want to stay till the end of the race.

She felt fear gnawing at her stomach. Yes, she did love him.

Wyatt felt good as he climbed back into the Shadow, ready for the race. He was at the front of the grid, his car was handling beautifully, perfectly set up, and he was in peak physical form. One of the mechanics held an umbrella over his head while Reg Tillson checked the blankets that were wrapped round the tyres to warm them up before the start. Even in this intense heat the blankets were still necessary to bring the tyres up to the correct operating temperature.

Bruce leant down beside Wyatt. 'Wyatt. Now it's up to you. I think, with the new compound we've been testing, your tyres should last you the race. The decision to change to fresh rubber will be yours. Good luck. I want you to win.'

Then he was gone. Wyatt felt the adrenalin pumping through him, the engine screaming behind his head. Strung out behind him were all the other cars, their drivers just as eager as he was to reach the chequered flag.

Wyatt, leading the pack, could just see Ricardo's car in his tiny rear-view mirrors. The Italian was placed seventh on the grid, but Wyatt knew that he would catch up and be breathing down his neck the whole race.

He kept the engine running smoothly. A stall at the start would destroy all the hard work of the practice sessions. He ignored the heat – it was his greatest enemy. The danger would come near the end of the race, when sheer exhaustion combined with heat-fatigue might cause him to make stupid mistakes.

Twenty-three cars sat poised on the grid. Of those, Wyatt estimated only five had a fair chance of finishing up front.

Suddenly the umbrella was gone. He put his foot down on the accelerator and the engine revved up with an ear-shattering crescendo. He shot forward for the warm-up lap.

He felt comfortable with the track – a fast anti-clockwise circuit with a long main straight. Tracking quickly round the first curve called Norte, he concentrated on bedding in the tyres, getting them up to the right temperature and making sure he was comfortable.

Just over three miles later, he was back at the start, in pole position. In front of him was the red light that was the focus of every driver's attention. In his tiny rear-view mirror he noted that there was one car at the side of the grid, the pit crew desperately trying to get it started. For someone, the race was over before it had begun.

It seemed like an eternity before the light changed to green. He was unconscious of the deafening roar of all the other engines around him. Round the first bend, and he was aware of someone trying unsuccessfully to pass him. There was no way anyone was going to get in front of him now.

Ricardo pulled off the steering-wheel and flung himself from the cockpit. Hoexter's car was just in front of him, smoke billowing from the engine. Hoexter, the young German ace, was the number two driver for McCabe and had finished third in the previous season after a neck-and-neck contest with Ricardo for second place. They were bitter rivals. They had tangled on the Carlos Pace bend and had gone spinning off the track.

Ricardo ran over to Hoexter, who had just staggered from his car and was pulling off his helmet to reveal his close-cropped blond hair. Ricardo smashed his fist into Hoexter's stomach and the German toppled forward, fighting for air.

Ricardo was about to hit Hoexter again when two marshals grabbed Ricardo, pulling him away.

'Fucking kraut!'

Hoexter was doubled up on the ground, gasping for breath. He gradually regained it and got up, spitting at Ricardo.

'It was your fault, my friend! I am sure FISA will not approve of your hot-blooded behaviour.'

'Fuck you, you fucking kraut!'

There were press photographers and video-cameras everywhere. Around the world, some ninety million viewers were treated to a close-up of the former world champion behaving like a common thug.

Hoexter still did not retaliate.

Bruce de Villiers felt curiously detached from reality. All around him people were talking, but he wasn't listening to what they were saying.

Ricardo must have miscalculated on the fourth bend – he was out of the race before it had really begun. Bruce wanted to cry. He was desperate to get the constructor's trophy, and in his first race he'd had a major setback in the first minute. Now everything depended on Wyatt, and the worst part of it was that Wyatt's car carried a last-minute modification. Maybe that modification would fail and destroy Wyatt's chances of winning. Or maybe, just maybe, it would give him the edge.

'Bruce . . .' Reg said nervously. 'It's Halliday.'

He turned round to see himself looking at Ronnie Halliday. The 'King of Formula One' had an ugly expression on his face. There were few people Bruce respected and feared as much as this man.

'Bruce. Do you know what Sartori's just done?'

'No. He's out of the race, that's all I know.' A sinking feeling descended on him. What was wrong? They never watched the TV coverage in the pits, they didn't need the distraction.

'Ricardo hit Hoexter in front of ninety million TV viewers!'

Now Bruce realised why Ronnie had come to see him. No man had worked harder at trying to improve and revamp the image of Formula One.

'Surely people understand?' Bruce said.

'It was Ricardo's fault – he cut Hoexter off.'

Bruce saw Reg gesturing for him to come over to the monitor. 'Please, can we discuss this after the race?'

Halliday shook his head. 'No. I'm suspending Ricardo. You know what this sort of thing does to a sport. It happened with tennis. It's the same with soccer violence.'

Bruce was ashen-faced. He would not find another driver of Ricardo's stature for the season, he knew it.

'Ronnie,' he said. 'I'm going to have to fight you on this.'

'It's my decision. And wait till you deal with Alain Hugo – you could be facing a big fine as well.'

Alain Hugo was the head of FISA, the world governing body of Formula One, a much tougher nut altogether than Ronnies. Often he and Ronnie were at loggerheads – but it was clear to Bruce that on this issue they wouldn't be.

Ronnie left. He didn't have to say any more; in his place, Bruce would have made the same decision. Ronnie had put an enormous amount of work into making the sport more competitive and more glamorous; he saw Ricardo's unspeakable behaviour as a disaster. Yes, it was a disaster for all of them, Bruce thought.

Suzie left the constructors' box, white with anger. How could Ricardo have behaved like such an animal? She must find Don Morrison and discuss how he would handle the press after the race. It was incredibly bad publicity for Calibre-Shensu in their first outing.

Then she caught sight of Ricardo walking out from behind the pits, looking like a wild man. He was getting into his car.

'Ricardo!'

He ignored her and started the engine. She wrenched open the door and he stared up at her.

'Leave me alone.'

'What do you mean? How can you behave like such a bastard?'

He was out of the car in a second, and facing her.

'Don't *you* tell me how to behave! You're just another fucking kraut!'

She held back her anger. 'You have the manners of the gutter.'

'Get out of my way, you German bitch.'

He got into the car and drove away, tyres squealing. Suzie felt the tears running from her eyes, her face aching from shouting so hard.

She heard a noise behind her, and turned to see the TV cameraman who had been with Vanessa Tyson earlier, smiling sweetly. He'd got his revenge. He'd obviously captured the whole shouting-match.

She turned and walked away, her head held high. How was she going to handle this? Somehow she found her way into the workshop that Calibre-Shensu had been using at the back of the circuit. She let herself in through a side-door and sat down behind a huge container, trying to regain her composure.

She was about to get up when she was startled to hear the main door to the workshop being rolled up. Now she felt embarrassed, she didn't want anyone to see her. She shrank behind the container and waited for whoever it was to go away. No doubt a mechanic, collecting a few spares.

She was wrong.

A big truck reversed into the garage and Suzie saw a lean, fair-haired man leap out of the passenger-seat. He started shouting commands in English, and five other men jumped out of the back of the truck, all dressed the same way in jeans and T-shirts. And they all carried guns.

'Move it!' As he spoke the fair-haired man pulled a stop-watch from his pocket.

Suzie shivered as she saw the driver get out of the cab and move in a semi-circle in front of the others. There was a sub-machine-gun in his hands. What type it was, she didn't know, but she could tell from his manner that he was quite prepared to use it.

They opened up the container and hauled out the tyres. She could see into the back of the truck. One of the men started lifting tyres into the back of the truck.

They were swopping tyres, she realised.

It must be some sort of sabotage. She thought of Wyatt and Ricardo. A blow-out at high speed could kill them.

The air was filled with the scream of Formula One engines.

219

Suzie summoned up all her courage and moved quickly towards the open doors of the garage, her heart thumping.

The blond man immediately stopped what he was doing and leapt down onto the concrete in one fluid movement. The sub-machine-gun was trained on her.

He will kill me, she thought, stopping dead in her tracks.

The man strode up to her and grabbed her. His grip was like a steel clamp on her arms.

She stared into his intensely green eyes. 'What do you think you're doing?'

He bared his teeth in a thin-lipped smile and firmed his grip. Then, before she could react, he had turned her round and twisted her arms behind her back.

She screamed.

His hand clamped across her mouth, and she bit it. He let out a groan and slammed his other hand into her kidneys. She fell, and almost blacked out as he pulled a thin nylon tie-back from his pocket. He completed the loop and slipped it over her thumbs, then he zipped it tight. He clamped one end of the nylon in one of the vices that lined the bench on the wall.

Suzie was about to start screaming again, but he put a piece of adhesive tape across her face. Meanwhile the other men continued working, hardly looking her way. They continued pushing tyres into the back of the truck.

What the hell were they doing? Suzie asked herself. Whatever he'd put round her thumbs was cutting off the circulation, and she could feel the sweat trickling off her body. She tried to move, but she was trapped. She could not see into the back of the truck. She prayed for time, but after what seemed a very short while they were finished.

The blond man walked up to her, turned his right hand palm-up and jabbed it, fingers first, into her stomach. She sagged, but as she did so the nylon slip-knot round her thumbs took her weight and it was agony. He loosened her from the vice and frog-marched her to the back of the truck, threw her onto the metal floor at the back and slammed the doors shut.

She started gagging. She could hardly breathe. She heard the big doors of the workshop opening and then the truck's engine thunder into life.

The heat in the back of the truck was unbearable, the adhesive tape was pressing into her mouth: she realised she was suffocating. Desperately she tried to manoeuvre herself amongst the tyres so that she could bang against the wall of the truck. Tears streamed down her face and her body was soaked with sweat.

No one would know where she was. There was no way they would know what had happened to her.

She couldn't breathe. She felt herself losing consciousness.

She was in the sea and she was sinking. The water enveloped her and she saw a hand reach out. It was Wyatt's, but she was too far away and she sank deeper. His face became more and more watery, and though she tried to swim upwards, it was no good. Then the blackness enveloped her.

Twenty laps had gone by and Wyatt was still leading. Behind him was the world champion, de Rosner, nick-named the Doctor because of the cold, calculated manner in which he drove. But the gap between de Rosner and Wyatt was widening all the time. Another five cars were thirty seconds behind them, and this distance too was increasing all the time. He had lapped all the other cars.

Bruce had told him over the radio link that Ricardo was out of the race. This did not please Wyatt because he knew it meant trouble for the team – less points for the coveted constructor's trophy.

He had to win.

The Shadow was handling beautifully. The engine felt strong and Wyatt was confident that it would last the race. But the Carvalho tyres were taking a hammering, and there was no doubt that he would have to come in for rubber soon. His concern was that the Doctor's McCabe was fitted with Pirellis, which had a reputation for staying power – the Doctor might go the whole race on one set of tyres.

Wyatt would have to get further ahead of the Doctor before he could dare go into the pits for a tyre-change. Still, the way he was going, he would be forty-five seconds ahead by the fortieth lap. If Reg and the rest of the guys were as fast as they had been in the practice sessions, he knew he could be out of the pits in under eight seconds.

The radio crackled into life again – Bruce telling him to try and take it easy. Several cars had already gone off with overheating problems. Wyatt listened, but did not respond; he had to stay in front; he could not afford to back off with de Rosner on his tail.

Bruce felt the sweat dripping down his face. He looked at the read-outs on the monitor that was radio-linked to the Shadow's engine, and saw that the engine was overheating – the last-minute conversion hadn't worked.

Someone touched his elbow. Aito. 'What is wrong?' he asked quietly.

No time for lies now. 'The modification isn't working.'

'Bruce, I also have a few things up my sleeve.'

Aito spoke quickly in Japanese to Katana, who sat hunched over the screen alongside Bruce. Katana tapped in a few commands.

Bruce whistled softly. 'If this is what I think it is, I don't fucking believe it.'

Aito rested a hand on his shoulder. 'It is as much a gamble for us as the engine modification was for you. We will always push the regulations to the limit.'

The seconds ticked anxiously by. The engine temperature started to drop. Katana typed in some more commands.

'You're remote-controlling the entire management system?'

Bruce noticed that Mickey was hovering behind them. There was an enigmatic smile on the Irishman's face.

'These fellas can teach us a thing or two, eh, Bruce?'

Bruce met Aito's eyes and felt his respect for the Japanese entrepreneur go up a few notches.

'I think they can.'

In the constructors' tower Estelle watched the television intently. She had come here to try and make things up with Wyatt, because she was beginning to feel guilty at the way she'd treated him. She understood, having been married to James, the pressure Wyatt was under, and she wanted to give her son as much support as she could. She knew that her being there would mean a lot to him.

At that moment James Hunt was handling the commentary, taking over from Murray Walker. As usual, Hunt wasn't pulling punches, but he was clearly excited.

'Out in front now at lap forty is British driver, Wyatt Chase, in his début Grand Prix for Calibre-Shensu. The question is, how much of this is the car and how much the driver? After Sartori's unspeakable performance just after the start, we'll never really know till next year. Sartori has been suspended with immediate effect for the rest of this season. This is a tragic blow for Calibre-Shensu. However, in Wyatt Chase I think I can predict we have the makings of a champion. And with the money Shensu are pouring into the Shadow, combined with the design genius of Mickey Dunstal, nothing is going to come near him. The back markers . . .'

Estelle felt the excitement coursing through her – the old excitement. She felt as she had done years before, watching James. She felt Carlos's hand on her shoulder.

'He will win,' Carlos said.

Estelle was silent. Then she said in a low voice, 'You know, although I try to, I will never forgive him . . .'

'James's death was an accident.'

'He was driving like a bloody fool.' Estelle's voice had risen in pitch. 'He says he can't remember, but I can see the guilt in his eyes.'

'It was ten years ago.'

'Don't you understand?' He could hear her desperation. 'I love Wyatt. That is why I am here. But he feels the guilt, I know that. That is why he has to take the same risks as his father. And as for what he did to Danny, that is another matter.'

Carlos stared away from her, trying to think of something to say that would ease her torment, yet knowing there was nothing that would help. Eventually he said, 'You cannot make a man turn away from his destiny.'

'Even if it means he might die?'

'Sometimes, only by confronting death can a man live.'

*

Bruce de Villiers went through the sequence that Wyatt's pit-stop would take. At zero seconds Wyatt's car would fly into the pits, running almost into Reg Tillson's shins at nearly thirty mph. Reg had a steady nerve – essential for this job. Bruce was in charge of the whole operation – in radio contact with Wyatt, and using hand signals. Wyatt would keep his right heel on the brake and blip the throttle occasionally with his toes.

At point-five of a second, the front- and rear-wheel teams would move in. The gun-men, operating pneumatic spanners, would whip off the wheels by three-point-five seconds and slip on fresh ones by five seconds. The gun-men would tighten up the nuts with their pneumatic spanners, raise their hands – and Bruce would give Wyatt the OK to pull away fast after just eight seconds in the pit.

That was how it was supposed to happen. That was how it was going to happen.

On the fiftieth lap Wyatt was still only thirty seconds ahead of the Doctor. Now he had to come in: the Shadow was not handling well – his lap times were dropping and the Doctor was closing in on him. Reluctantly he informed Bruce that he'd be coming into the pits on the next lap.

After the main straight came six bends in quick succession. He went through them as fast as he could, fighting the temptation to take the pressure off the tyres. Every second counted. He shot round the last bend and roared into the pits.

The Calibre-Shensu team swarmed around the car, the tyres coming off the wheels almost as he stopped moving, the new rubber being put on in seconds.

Great. Great. They were moving fast, very fast.

He could go.

Shit. What was happening? What the fuck was wrong! Where was the signal to pull out?

I don't believe this, Wyatt told himself. They've fucked up. Twenty bloody seconds! De Rosner's going to catch me!

No!

*

Reg was wrestling with one rear tyre which would not come off. Bruce started kicking it hard as the rest of the pit crew pulled. Then the tyre came loose and they had the next one on in a fraction of a second.

Bruce raised his hand and screamed at Wyatt over the radio to leave.

My God, thirty-one seconds. A total balls-up.

Fuck it!

Wyatt gunned the engine as hard as he could. As he emerged out of the pits, the Doctor's McCabe streaked past him.

Damn!

Thirty-one bloody seconds when it should have taken eight.

He wasn't going to lose – not now. He was going to win, whatever it cost.

Bruce couldn't say anything. The time spoke for itself. Wyatt had been over thirty seconds in the pits, and all because of a jammed wheel. The pit team of twenty men, including himself, Reg Tillson and the Shensu mechanics, were silent.

He could see the other teams looking over at them. He knew what they were thinking. The running of Calibre-Shensu was his responsibility; he had let his driver down badly, and he knew it.

He walked over to the monitor and Aito looked up questioningly.

'Aito, I fucked up.'

'Wyatt will catch him.'

'The Doctor isn't going to let go.'

'The Doctor hasn't got fresh rubber, he's not in the Shadow and he's not Wyatt Chase.'

Aito nodded to Professor Katana, who tapped some fresh instructions into the management system.

'Now, Bruce, we take a risk. Wyatt will get a little more power and the engine will take a little more strain.'

They both turned from the computer back to the track. The Doctor's McCabe shot past, hotly pursued by Wyatt in the Shadow.

Bruce's face broke into a broad smile. Wyatt was driving like a demon.

There was only one lap to go and Wyatt was right on the Doctor's tail. James Hunt's commentary reflected the excitement of the crowd.

'Chase has just set a new lap record. But the Doctor still holds the lead and he is driving incredibly fast. This is the final lap, and the question on everybody's lips is, can Wyatt Chase pass de Rosner to win Calibre-Shensu's début Grand Prix?'

Wyatt soared down the main straight after the Doctor. They had lapped all the other cars, and all Wyatt could think about now was how he could improve his speed through the corners. The McCabe was nearly as fast as the Shadow on the straight.

The Doctor took the right-hander after the pits at a perfect line. Wyatt was right behind him, looking for a gap which failed to materialise. The bends piled one on top of the other in dizzy succession, and all the time Wyatt was behind the Doctor. But the Frenchman did not relent.

The main straight saw Wyatt almost gaining on the McCabe, but he did not have the power to pass, and at the left-hander at the end, the Doctor was still in front. Now a bend to the right, and Wyatt was fighting for his life. There wasn't a chink in the Doctor's armour; the McCabe was moving faultlessly towards the finish.

A really sharp left-hander came up next. Wyatt laid down the power and surged level with the Doctor. It was an almost suicidal manoeuvre because if he lost it, he'd go flying out of control.

He felt the Shadow straining as she moved into the corner at the absolute limit of adhesion. Wyatt shot past the Doctor and accelerated into the next three bends.

He crossed the finish-line seconds later, in a blur of sound and colour, to a sensation of overwhelming heat. He felt his body almost levitate from the car as the emotion soared through him. He couldn't believe what was happening. He wanted this moment to last forever. It was everything he had dreamed it would be, and more.

He had won.

Bruce was crying. He had his arms around Mickey, and Reg Tillson was pumping Professor Katana's hand. The crew were embracing one another, Japanese and British mechanics finally united in the moment of victory.

Bruce pulled away from Mickey, searching for Aito. He stood at the edge of the pit bay, quiet, a faint smile on his face. Tears were running from his eyes beneath the black-framed glasses. Bruce stretched out his hand and Aito grasped it firmly, not letting go.

'I . . . I cannot tell you what this means,' Aito said. 'I had no idea it would be like this. I thank you from the depths of my soul.'

Bruce could hear the British commentary over the loud-speakers. 'This is incredible! A proud day for Britain – and what a start to Wyatt Chase's second season in Formula One! Without doubt, that is one of the finest drives I have seen in the last few years. The field was very, very competitive, yet Chase stayed close to the front and outmanoeuvred one of the most talented drivers on the track. Down in the pits, I can only feel that Bruce de Villiers must be a very happy man. McCabe must be very sore to be beaten by their former manager in his first outing.'

Estelle was stone-cold, tears streaming down her face as Carlos held her tightly.

'You know what could have happened on that bend? This is just the beginning. He will never give up.'

Carlos guided Estelle outside, into the maelstrom of supporters who were jostling around the pit enclosure. They had to fight their way through the mass of seething bodies to the area below the rostrum.

Carlos gripped Estelle's hand tightly. 'This is his moment,' he whispered. 'Do not take it from him.'

*

Wyatt was barely able to drive the victory lap, he was so exhausted. He tried to replay in his mind the last few minutes of the race when he had taken the lead from the Doctor. He could scarcely believe that he had pulled it off. The applause from the crowd at the side of the circuit was tumultuous.

He pulled back into the pits and saw the Brazilian fans leaping over the barriers. For a brief moment he was with Bruce and Mickey as they helped him out of the cockpit, then he was surrounded by the seething crowd.

A woman kissed him. Hands were tugging at his jumpsuit, ripping at it. He was shaking hands with his left and right hands, and people were thumping him on the back. It was incredible.

He kept expecting to see Suzie, fighting her way through the throng, but she was nowhere to be seen.

He moved towards the rostrum and his mother appeared through the crowd. She was crying as she kissed him. Then Carlos embraced him.

Around him Wyatt could see the track officials desperately trying to clear the crowd so that he could make his way onto the rostrum.

Where was Suzie?

The Doctor came up and shook his hand warmly. Next it was the turn of the third-placed Brazilian driver, Marco Herrera.

Wyatt staggered up to the top of the rostrum to be presented with his trophy by the Brazilian Prime Minister. He was so exhausted he could hardly lift it above his head.

After that there was the traditional bottle of champagne. Wyatt shook it vigorously, then the cork exploded out of it and the cheering crowd were sprayed with champagne.

And in that moment Wyatt knew he could take the world championship. Before, he had dreamed of it; now he knew that it could be his.

Ricardo sat in his hotel room, a half-empty bottle of whisky by the bed and a glass in his hand. Suddenly he hurled the glass through the centre of the TV screen.

He knew his contract backwards, every driver did.

Suspension by the governing body meant he lost all right to his earnings for the year. Of course there was next year, but he needed the money now. He had not paid his taxes for years, and the Italian receiver of revenue was onto him. He had not even worried about this before, but now his only source of revenue was cut off.

He hated Wyatt Chase more than anyone else in the world at that moment. Chase had shown him what was possible in the Shadow – she could take the championship. But Ricardo knew he was history. He took another drink from the bottle, unable to look the future in the face.

The phone next to the bed rang, but he ignored it, staring out of the window at the blue sea. He would lose his villa when the bank foreclosed on him. How dare they suspend him because he hit the German! Chase, Hoexter, they were all the same . . .

The phone kept ringing. He thought of throwing it through the window, but instead he picked it up. 'Yes!' he shouted angrily into the receiver.

'Ricardo . . .' The American accent was as smooth as Cointreau poured over ice. Jack Phelps. 'Aito isn't very pleased with you, nor is Bruce.'

Ricardo's drunken mind turned the words over very slowly. Something registered – Phelps did not appear to be angry.

'What do you want?'

'I know your circumstances, so let me be quite blunt. You're in serious financial trouble, Ricardo. You won't drive again this year. Bruce thinks he'll persuade FISA to change the ruling, but I have a contact on the inside – he spoke to Alain Hugo just now. FISA aren't going to budge. You're out.'

'Bastard!'

'He might speak of you in the same way.'

'I've heard enough, Jack.'

He was about to put the phone down when Phelps said the magic words.

'You need money, Ricardo. You need it desperately. I can give it to you.'

He put the phone down a moment later. Perhaps things

229

were not so bad. Whatever Phelps wanted, he would do. Providing, of course, that the money was right.

Aito Shensu was walking on air. He shook Wyatt's hand again for the press.

'I'd like to say that Ricardo Sartori's suspension will make no difference to our determination to win the Formula One championship,' he said. 'Wyatt Chase is a driver superbly qualified to take us to victory.'

Wyatt leaned back on the pit wall, exhausted. He whispered into Bruce's ear, 'Where the hell's Suzie? Isn't she supposed to be around for this?'

'I'm sure she's somewhere about. Don't worry. Now, I think you deserve a rest.'

Bruce guided him out the back of the pits and across to the helicopter. Wyatt slumped back into the seat and bade good-bye to Bruce, and the helicopter lifted up quickly from the ground. He looked out to see the long, curving lines of the track on which he had fought for the last one and a half hours.

The helicopter banked steeply so that he was staring directly down at the pits. Already it all seemed far away. Wyatt felt a sense of loss. He wished that the moment of winning would go on; he craved to have it again. He needed it more than anything else in the world.

Suzie came round very slowly. The tape wasn't across her mouth any longer, and she was in a white room without windows or doors. The only light came from recessed luminous panels in the ceiling. Where was she?

Perhaps it was just a dream. She thought that if she closed her eyes it might go away, but no, this was very real. Then she tried to move, and realised that her hands were still bound. The surface beneath her was springy – she was lying on a bed. Her watch and rings had been taken. She felt soiled and dirty.

Wyatt must realise she was missing now. He would be looking for her. But no one had seen her go into the warehouse, and she was sure that Ricardo wouldn't say a word about their argument.

These worries disappeared as one wall of the room slid

230

back, letting sunlight filter into the room. Suzie drew her legs up to protect herself. She looked up and saw a stocky man with dark, greasy hair. She felt utterly helpless.

'Don't be afraid,' he said. His English was accented, his tone friendly. 'You are my payment.'

She looked at him dumbfounded, not understanding what he meant. He sat down next to her on the bed and she noticed that his right hand was heavily bandaged. Suddenly, she kicked out with her legs, but the only effect of this was to make her fall on the concrete floor. He pushed her down against the cold surface, his left hand exploring her body.

'You are very beautiful,' he said softly.

His left hand was perfectly manicured and he smelt of expensive after-shave. On his right wrist, above the bandage, he was wearing what was obviously a custom-made watch. He must be wealthy.

'You have no right to keep me here,' Suzie said as forcefully as she could, holding back the urge to burst into tears.

'So you think I should let you go?'

'Yes.'

'And then you would tell someone about me.'

'I would keep my mouth shut.'

'You must think I am incredibly stupid!'

He pulled her back onto the bed and started to pace around the room. 'My brother is dead,' he said, 'and I was nearly killed. There have been too many mistakes so far. You will not be another, whoever you are.'

He stared at her for a few moments, then walked to the door. 'Now you must get cleaned up. I will have someone help you.' He disappeared into the sunlight.

A woman in a khaki skirt and top came into the room a few moments later. She was in her forties, and had a pitted, dark-skinned face.

'Get up,' she said in Portuguese.

Suzie shrank back, and the woman grabbed her hair and yanked her to her feet.

'Up, bitch.'

Suzie stood up shakily, and the woman went behind her and untied the nylon band that held her thumbs together.

'We go to bathroom.'

She led Suzie past the sliding wall and down a passageway constructed entirely of glass. On one side she could see a steamy jungle, endless green stretching off into the distance, far below her. Heart sinking, she realised that there was no possibility of escape. Then she looked to her right and found she was staring dizzily down a tremendous cliff face. How had she arrived at this incredible place? It was as if she had been transported into another world.

The bathroom was tiled with the finest Italian marble, and all the fittings were gold. The woman turned on the taps of the sunken circular bath and then grabbed Suzie's arm and tried to kiss her. When Suzie resisted, the woman slapped her, and Suzie fought back, raking her with her nails. As the woman staggered back, blood pouring from the cuts on her face, Suzie saw that the inside of her left arm was covered with red pin-pricks.

'Maria!' the woman called, backing away from Suzie.

There was the sound of feet running down a corridor, and an enormous black-haired woman appeared, similarly dressed in khaki. Before Suzie could resist Maria pulled her hands behind her back.

'Now, Julia, you may have the bitch,' she whispered.

Suzie closed her eyes as Julia began to fondle and then kiss her. Maria forced her to kneel, leaving her in no doubt about what she would have to do next.

Then there were shouts in the passage, and she felt the arms release her. She opened her eyes as the man who had spoken to her earlier came into the bathroom. He stared at Maria.

'Didn't I tell you she was not to be touched?'

Maria smirked. 'Mr Ortega, sir, she is a prisoner. Prisoners are for fun.'

An armed guard came up behind the man. 'Maria deserves to see the jungle,' Jules said softly.

Maria started screaming as the guard grabbed her by the hair and dragged her from the bathroom into the glass corridor. Suzie felt a wave of hot air come into the bathroom as the guard slid one of the glass panels back. Julia lay pressed against the wall, quivering.

Suzie stared down the passageway. The guard was now standing behind Maria, his pistol pushed into the back of her head.

'Jump!'

Suzie closed her eyes. There was a scream, and she opened her eyes again as Maria's screams echoed along the passageway. Then the glass panel was closed and there was an ominous silence.

'See, Julia, if you dare to touch the lady again you will follow your friend. Now, you will please help the lady to take her bath.'

As she lay in the scented hot water, Suzie stared out at the jungle. Her mind was in turmoil. She tried to think about Wyatt, tried to hang on to her sanity. Julia watched her without moving.

The man came back into the bathroom a little later and sat down next to the bath.

'I must introduce myself, I am Jules Ortega.'

He clicked his fingers, and a man in a white laboratory coat came in, holding a syringe.

'Dr Estevez, it is time to give her a tranquilliser.'

'No, no . . .' Suzie moaned. But Jules took her right arm and held it tightly, and Dr Estevez smiled and pushed the needle into her arm.

'Relax, my dear, this is perfectly safe. The hot water will improve your circulation.'

'What is it?'

'Just something to help you feel more at home.'

Suzie felt her head swimming and a series of kaleidoscopic images appeared before her eyes. She sank down into the hot water. It was going to be all right after all . . .

Antonio Vargas, alias Emerson Ortega, relaxed in his office, waiting for the phone call. He stared through the picture-window at the jungle below him, considering. No, Suzie von Falkenhyn would not be a problem. Life was so simple really – you either had the control, or were controlled. She was Jules's now, but he was not envious, he did not want her. That side of life had never particularly appealed to him. He thought of Jules and his harem, and decided that Jules would probably take Suzie immediately. But perhaps not. He might not feel like it after what Talbot had done to his hand. Jules had been stupid to try and cross the American.

The phone on his desk rang softly and he picked it up.

'Antonio, are you ready to make the next delivery?' Talbot was brisk and business-like.

'Yes, I have the goods.'

'You do not foresee any problems?'

'Your plan is brilliant – you have come up with the ultimate solution. I must apologise for my – er – partner's stupid behaviour.'

'No matter. Distribution can start immediately.'

'Payment?' asked Emerson, trying to keep the edge out of his voice.

'This, as you will realise, I discussed with Jules. He was a fool to try and play games. As agreed, your first two deliveries to me will be free, and after that I will pay you fifty per cent of the value. The other half will go to pay off the cost of the new laboratory. The money will be laundered in Mexico, then deposited in Zurich.'

'In Yankee money?'

'As you requested.'

'And there will be no problems concerning the rubber?'

'I will deal with that.'

The phone went dead, and Emerson smiled. Talbot had said he would kill Jules if he tried anything again. He, Emerson, felt a strong bond with Talbot. Life was so simple when you knew who your allies were.

Wyatt relaxed. Suzie's arms were around him . . . Then the alarm clock shattered the dream and he stared round the hotel room helplessly, knowing that Suzie had not returned.

He got up and took an ice-cold shower, then moved into his training routine. First the exercises to build up stamina, which included multiple press-ups and sit-ups, then the *katas*, the moves that were a fight against an imaginary opponent. Soon he was sweating freely.

The feeling of victory was gone, and he felt empty. He had wanted to share his success with Suzie, but there wasn't a sign of her anywhere.

As he moved into the third of the *katas* his mind cleared, and for an hour he was aware only of his body as it moved through the disciplined sequences.

By nine he had showered and breakfasted. Then he put on a black Calibre-Shensu sports shirt and a pair of matching cotton trousers. Finally he slipped on a pair of immaculate, hand-made Italian mocassins.

The press conference was scheduled for ten in one of the hotel's conference rooms. Many of the other drivers would already have left Brazil, but Wyatt had to take advantage of the publicity for Calibre-Shensu. He'd received a personal call from Phelps late the previous evening, and Phelps had spelt out, in no uncertain terms, how much was riding on Wyatt. The success or failure of the team, he had declared, was now Wyatt's responsibility.

He ran his eye over the newspaper that had been stuck under his door. He was on the front page. It was a typical picture – him on the rostrum, spraying the crowd with champagne. The headline, in Portuguese, was simple: 'Chase Takes Rio'. He saw a sub-head saying: 'Sartori Suspended.' The next two pages carried two big pictures, one of Ricardo hitting Hoexter and the other, to Wyatt's surprise, of Ricardo arguing with Suzie. The headline was as damaging as it could be: 'Raging Bull'.

What was Ricardo doing, fighting with Suzie?

The phone on the bedside table rang. 'Tell them I'll be down now.'

He arrived in the hotel foyer moments later, to be greeted by an explosion of flash-bulbs. Bruce was waiting for him.

''Morning, Champion.'

'Anything special you want me to say?'

'No. You'll handle it. Just field any questions they put to you about Ricardo. He checked out of the hotel early this morning and I don't know where he's gone. To be quite frank, I don't care.'

Wyatt went forward into the conference room and climbed onto the rostrum to face a field of microphones and cameras.

The questions started the moment he was up. He kept thinking of Suzie. What was going on between her and Ricardo? Where the hell was she? He answered the press questions in a daze. Then one brought him back to reality.

'There has been some question as to the legitimacy of the Shadow's design. How do you feel about that?' asked a hard-nosed reporter quite close to the front.

Wyatt felt a stab of anxiety, but he didn't show it. He looked coldly into the reporter's eyes. 'I haven't heard anything about that. Mickey Dunstal's design is so advanced that as a driver I'm only beginning to explore its potential.'

'You're predicting another victory in Monaco?'

'In Grand Prix racing nothing is predictable. I want to win, but like I did here, I want to win against stiff competition.'

That brought a wave of muffled applause.

The conference went on for over an hour – an overwhelming success for Wyatt. He left the room in a hurry; he wanted to start searching for Suzie. Bruce was waiting in the hotel foyer, and Aito Shensu was there as well. Wyatt was surprised that Jack Phelps wasn't present.

'Let's go up to my room,' Bruce suggested, seeing Wyatt's agitated face.

In the lift, out of sight of the reporters, Wyatt noted that the confident look on Bruce's face had dimmed. Wyatt knew what a blow it was for him to lose Ricardo. Aito looked tense, too, and Wyatt could understand why – Ricardo Sartori was hardly the sort of ambassador one needed to launch a new car range.

They all sat down in Bruce's room and he ordered coffee.

'First things first,' Bruce muttered. 'Wyatt, when we took you on, it was a gamble.'

Wyatt couldn't help smiling. The tables had turned.

'It's no longer a gamble,' Bruce continued. 'Both Aito and I feel that you deserve a better deal.'

Wyatt thought: you're scared of losing me. Then he was embarrassed because he could tell that Bruce knew exactly what he was thinking.

'This is the deal.' Aito spoke softly as he handed the

agreement to Wyatt. 'Fifty thousand pounds for every championship point you earn.'

'That means I have just made five hundred thousand pounds?'

Bruce nodded. 'I'd like you to read it through now,' he added.

A waitress came in with their coffee and they were silent while she poured for them all. Wyatt read the agreement. It put him right up in the first league.

'You're taking over from Ricardo,' Bruce said bluntly.

'I see there's a second contract?'

'Yes, that's correct,' Aito replied. 'I'd like you to think about that one. You don't have to take it up if you don't want to. Basically, you agree to drive cars with my engines in them for the next two years. You will see that for this you would be rewarded substantially.'

'OK.'

Both Bruce and Aito hunched forwards. 'Don't you want legal advice on the agreement?' Bruce asked.

Wyatt hadn't got time for all this, he wanted to start looking for Suzie.

'No. I trust both of you. After all, you both trusted me.' He took out his pen. 'Where do I sign?'

He left the room in a hurry and took the lift down to the ground floor. He wanted to find Suzie. The police? Should he contact them, or was that overreacting? As the lift door opened he was approached by a cameraman and a reporter, and immediately recognised Vanessa Tyson. There was no way he could avoid her.

She swept her hair back and stared into his eyes. It was a look that held something more than the cold analytical assessment of the dedicated reporter – but then it was gone, and the professional mask was on again.

'Wyatt, how do you feel about Ricardo's behaviour on the circuit yesterday?'

She wasn't pulling her punches. 'I think everyone is in agreement that it was excessive,' he said calmly.

She gave him a thin-lipped smile. 'Don't you think such violent behaviour reflects the danger inherent in motor-racing?

Doesn't it scare you that you might have to compete with a man who might assault you, or worse, kill you for first place?'

'Are you afraid of danger?'

She reddened, more from irritation than anger, he sensed.

'That's irrelevant,' she said. 'What we're talking about here is millions upon millions of dollars being spent on what is a very violent and dangerous sport.'

'If you're afraid, don't watch it.'

Her face was dead-pan. Wyatt sensed the cameraman was still filming and waited for her next salvo, relishing the challenge.

'It's not just the drivers,' she said. 'Spectators' lives are at risk.'

'People come to motor-races because they like the excitement. It's been said that some come hoping accidents will happen. I think you've been waiting for an accident.'

'That's totally untrue!'

He moved forward and before she could block him, kissed her softly on the lips. 'You know,' he said, 'I think you are the most beautiful woman I've ever met.'

He saw that the cameraman was smiling, almost laughing. He turned back to the lifts. He wanted to be alone now, to get to a phone and call the police. Where the hell was Suzie?

He got out of the lift on Calibre-Shensu's floor, to find Mickey in earnest conversation with Bruce.

'There's something wrong, to be sure,' Mickey was saying.

'Ricardo had a hell of a go at her. I'm sure she's just very, very upset and she doesn't want to show her face,' Bruce said.

'She wouldn't take being treated like that. I'm going to check Ricardo's room,' Wyatt set off down the hall but Bruce's voice checked him.

'It's empty. Maybe she's back in your room now, or has left a message.'

Wyatt's room was in chaos; Suzie's clothes were scattered all over the place. It was obvious that someone had been there during the press conference and rifled through everything. Suzie was in real danger, Wyatt was sure that something must have happened during the race. He felt powerless and disorientated.

The receptionist reported that Miss von Falkenhyn had not made an appearance since the Grand Prix. Wyatt couldn't understand it. It was Mickey who came up with a possible direction for their search.

'Let's find the reporter who took the picture of Ricardo arguing with Suzie. He's the last person who saw her, apart from Ricardo.'

There were plenty of reporters still hanging around the reception area, and Wyatt suddenly caught sight of Vanessa Tyson stepping into a taxi with her cameraman. He dashed over and grabbed her hand – and again, as her lips parted, had that sense that her interest in him might be more than professional.

'I'm prepared to give you a private interview if you can find out something for me,' Wyatt said tentatively.

'Well, ask away,' she answered in the deep voice he found so intriguing.

'Suzie von Falkenhyn has disappeared.'

'Scared your next win's not going to be in designer clothes?' Vanessa replied cynically.

'No!' Wyatt snapped. 'I happen to be in love with her.'

Now there was a crowd of reporters surrounding them, and Wyatt felt himself getting increasingly annoyed. Vanessa seemed to sense his mood. She led him to the lift, gesturing for her cameraman not to follow. When they were in the confined space of the elevator, she spoke again.

'I apologise. It's my business to provoke people because I need to get a reaction.'

Wyatt looked at her closely. About five foot five, she was petite yet voluptuous, with a strikingly unusual face. It had a restrained sensuality about it that appealed to him. He sensed she hid a lot of herself from the outside world; that beneath the steely exterior of Vanessa Tyson there might be another woman – a very different woman.

'I need this thing sorted out privately. I'm worried about Suzie.'

The lift doors opened on the top floor and Vanessa showed Wyatt to her room. Inside, it looked as if a whirlwind had hit it, papers and documents lying all over the place.

'I work in organised chaos. Find a seat.'

Wyatt moved a lap-top computer and sat down. 'We went up to my room just now,' he said. 'Someone had been through everything of Suzie's. Ricardo's gone, probably back to Europe.'

'Wyatt, are you sure she didn't have something going with Ricardo?'

'Definitely not.'

'So,' she said, sitting down. 'How can I help?'

'I believe that the cameraman who took the pictures of Ricardo arguing with her was the last person to see her.'

'That was Max,' she said, reaching for the phone.

Five minutes later, Max, a tall, burly man with a thick beard, was standing in front of Wyatt. From what Vanessa had told him, he knew that Max was one of the world's top video-cameramen.

'Yeah,' Max said, 'Ricardo really had a go at her. Struck me as the kind of woman you don't shout at.' Max paused to light up a cigarette. 'I got good footage and I took a couple of pictures. You obviously saw the one in this morning's paper.'

'Yes, but what happened after all that?' Wyatt asked desperately.

'Well, Ricardo stormed off. I was going to go back and watch the race, but Suzie interested me. She was cut up, walking away from the circuit, so I followed.'

Wyatt was hanging on every word.

'She disappeared into one of the workshops,' Max went on. 'I don't know what she was doing – probably pulling herself together. I decided to wait outside. Well, about five minutes later this truck pitches up. It was slightly obscured by the side-wall of the warehouse. I heard feet scuffling and a few commands.' He took a long draw at his cigarette, then stubbed it out and took another.

'I put my head around the corner and there's this lethal-looking blond guy who's obviously in command. I didn't wait for him to see me. They must have been loading up something important.'

'So what happened to Suzie?' Wyatt fought down his fury. Why hadn't Max taken the trouble to see that she was OK?

'I don't know. I pointed my video-camera round the corner and let it roll. After that, I left very quickly.'

'The videotape?' Wyatt asked desperately.

'I haven't looked at it. I sent it off ten minutes ago, by courier, to London.'

Vanessa went to the phone. 'We'll catch it before they put it on a plane. Max, you arrange it.'

The manager of the local courier service was very happy. Now he would be able to afford the holiday flat he'd been hoping to buy his mistress. He'd received a phone call earlier that morning, something about some videotapes. Well, he'd told his employees to be on the lookout for them. What a find.

A couple of phone calls, and they'd been across like a rifle-shot. He hadn't even had to barter with them, the money had been laid on the table. Now they had the videotapes, and when the cameraman, a Mr Max Senda, phoned, he would shrug his shoulders and say that these things happened. The videotapes were now officially 'lost'.

Max Senda waited in the reception area of the hotel, smoking his thirty-eighth cigarette of the day. Where the hell were his videotapes?

A tall, blond man in a Hawaian shirt strode in. He looked vaguely familiar, and under his arm was a batch of video-tapes.

'Over here!' Max shouted.

The man came over and looked him up and down, then he handed him the boxes. Anxiously, Max opened them.

'One's missing. Where the hell is it?'

'Must still be at the airport,' replied the man.

'Well, let's go there.'

He followed the man in the Hawaian shirt out of his car. There were two more men in it.

'My friends. You don't mind?'

Max couldn't have cared less. He got into the front seat with the blond man. 'Let's go!' he shouted.

The man drove very quickly, and had a surprising knowl-edge of the back streets. After a while Max looked down at his watch and saw that they had been travelling for over fifteen minutes. Still, he didn't know the area; perhaps this was the quickest route to the airport.

'Far to go?' he asked, after another five minutes.

The man ignored him. Max noticed that the streets they were travelling through were becoming progressively poorer. He began to feel uneasy.

'Where the hell are we going?'

The man didn't reply. Suddenly, Max remembered where he'd seen him – at the track, in the workshop.

He tried to open the car door – and received a blow across the back of the head, then felt something pass over his face. The next second the garotte tightened around his windpipe. He raised his hands to relieve the pressure, but it was no good. Then the other man in the back held a cigarette-lighter to his fingers – but he couldn't scream out for lack of air. The driver turned to him.

'Not too far now. Just relax.'

As he was about to black out, the pressure relented and he slumped forward, holding his neck. The man at the wheel grabbed the scruff of his neck and rammed his head into the dashboard.

They pulled up outside a tin shanty, and the two men from the back dragged him out of the car. He tried to run, but they kicked his feet from underneath him.

'What else did you see?' the blond man asked.

Max tried to answer but they started kicking him before he could get the words out. Blows struck every part of his body, knocking out some of his teeth, breaking his ribs. He tried to defend himself but he didn't stand a chance.

'Ready to talk?'

He lay on the ground, blood oozing from his mouth, and prayed they'd leave him alone. He tasted the dirt mingling with the blood in his mouth, and smelt sweat.

'What do you want?'

'Why did you take the pictures?'

'I'm a reporter.'

This answer was greeted by a heavy kick in the face. The

man in the Hawaian shirt then stood on his fingers and twisted his heel around.

'What do you want!' Max screamed.

'What did you see?'

'You. The truck. That was all. Where the hell's Suzie von Falkenhyn?'

'Did you tell anyone about this?'

Max hesitated. He thought of Vanessa undergoing this treatment. Who knew what these men might do? His interrogator spat on him.

'I think you should go for a ride to loosen your tongue.'

They dragged him round to the back of the car and tied his feet to the bumper, so that the rest of his body was lying on the ground. He heard the engine start, and the next minute he was being dragged across the ground at high speed. His clothes tore through in seconds, and his skin started scraping against the ground. When the car finally came to a stop he was barely alive.

'Does anyone know?'

'Wyatt Chase and Vanessa Tyson. They're looking for Suzie. I was following her when I saw you and the truck.' Max passed in and out of consciousness.

The blond man looked agitated. 'Is that all?'

Max nodded weakly.

'Put him in the boot.'

Max could do nothing. They tossed him into the back of the car and pulled away.

As they bumped along the road, he felt sick. He clawed at the edges of the boot. He could smell the exhaust fumes . . . Then he realised the exhaust was feeding directly into the boot.

He banged against the metal, but he was already losing consciousness. A kilometre later Max Senda was dead.

Wyatt had just about finished the packing, but there was still no call from Vanessa Tyson. He had a tough testing schedule lined up in England, which he needed to get back for, but he wasn't leaving till he found out what had happened to Suzie.

He would spend a few more days in Rio if necessary. Maybe it was time to contact the police.

He decided he'd talk to Vanessa. He took the lift and went up to her room, but the door was locked, and when he knocked there was no answer. Some sixth sense told him she was inside, and there was something wrong.

He took a run at the door, and kicked it down with a single blow. The room was empty, a picture of order, and Vanessa was nowhere to be seen.

Then there was a noise from the bathroom. Wyatt opened the door to see Vanessa suspended, naked and unconscious, from the shower-rail.

'My God!'

He put his arms around her and lifted her, taking her weight off the cord, then he reached up with one arm and unhitched it. He threw Vanessa onto the bed and gave her the kiss of life, but there was no response.

Breathe, damn you. Breathe.

He put his hand over her heart and hit the back of it with his fist. Breathe! He smashed the flat of his hand against her chest.

Suddenly she coughed, and then vomited.

Breathe!

She gulped in air as he held her head up. 'Oh God!' she coughed. 'For God's sake, help me!'

She vomited again – several small white pills. He reached for the phone next to her bed and dialled reception.

'Get me an ambulance and a doctor – fast!'

Detective Inspector Farina folded up his small notebook and stared hard at Wyatt Chase. 'Suicide.' Farina's English was good, with hardly a trace of an accent. 'Rio is a rough town. All we know is that Mr Senda and Miss von Falkenhyn have not been seen. Your lady friend's attempted suicide is probably unconnected with their disappearance.'

'So you're going to do nothing?'

'I will wait.'

'What, till someone else dies or disappears?'

'You may be an expert driver but you're not a policeman. I

haven't got a lead, and Rio is a big city. Vanessa Tyson is only one amongst over a hundred people who have tried to commit suicide today. If Max Senda or Miss von Falkenhyn do not appear in the next twenty-four hours, I will hand their pictures over to the TV network.'

'That's all you're going to do?' Wyatt muttered angrily.

'You want me to declare a state of emergency because your girlfriend has walked out on you?' Farina replied sarcastically.

Vanessa looked terrible. Her neck was in a brace and there were bags under her eyes. Her arms were held with straps to the side of the bed, as were her legs. She looked up at Wyatt as he came into the private room at the hospital.

'You all right?'

'How does it look?' she croaked. 'Give me a fucking cigarette. My handbag, in that cabinet, if there's anything left in it.'

He found the cigarettes, placed one in her mouth and lit it. She inhaled deeply and lay back.

'I thought you didn't smoke.'

'That's privileged information.' She paused, then looked at him squarely. 'You think I tried to kill myself?'

'No.'

The cigarette dropped from her mouth and she started coughing. Wyatt picked it up and waited for her to recover.

'They say I'm a drug addict,' she spluttered. 'It's quite incredible! All I know is that there's a lot more to this than meets the eye.'

'Vanessa, what happened?'

'There's a knock on my door, right? I say, "Who is it?". I hear a muffled "Wyatt". I open the door, and this blond-haired man in a Hawaian shirt bursts into my room, grabs me and rams a hypodermic into my arm. A day later I wake up here, diagnosed suicidal and a drug addict.' She took another long drag on the cigarette. 'Now tell me what's been happening to you.'

Wyatt knew he must tell her the truth. 'The police found Max's body this morning,' he said heavily. 'We were the last two people to talk to him, and we are the only ones who knew about that videotape. The courier company knows nothing, but Senda was picked up by some men claiming to be their representatives. Two hours later, you were almost dead.'

Vanessa stared at him coldly. 'My instincts tell me that you and I had better leave this place, or we'll both be in coffins pretty soon.'

Wyatt went through Vanessa's handbag, and found her passport and her credit cards. 'I'm taking you to the airport,' he said.

'You're not coming?'

'No. I have a few more loose ends I want to investigate.'

'Wyatt, you're in danger!'

'Listen, Vanessa, I'm taking you to the airport and you're in no condition to argue with me.'

Wyatt glanced across at Vanessa, securely strapped into the back seat of the taxi next to him. She winked at him. 'I think I can trust you not to take advantage of me. Let's go.'

The taxi-driver pulled out into the busy street and weaved his way through the traffic. It had taken Wyatt an hour to discharge Vanessa from the hospital, and a fight with the doctors, but he'd won in the end.

'I'll make sure Suzie's disappearance gets full coverage in the media,' Vanessa said. 'They'll have to mount a search after that.'

Wyatt grimaced. Suzie must be in big trouble. She must have seen something at the circuit. But what?

The taxi-driver turned off the busy street and took a side-road. Immediately another car drew up alongside them. Wyatt caught sight of a flash of metal and dragged Vanessa down to the floor.

'Jesus, Wyatt!'

At that moment the windows of the taxi exploded around them and the driver leapt out. Wyatt, forcing his way between the front seats, slipped the taxi into gear and pressed the accelerator. The taxi shot forward, bullets ricocheting all over the place. He heard Vanessa moaning, and eased himself into the front seat, weaving the car backwards and forwards now, praying that the bullets wouldn't find their mark. He swerved into another alley, and the gunfire stopped.

The sweat dripped from his face as he gunned the car on, desperately staring into the rear-view mirror. A car appeared behind within seconds, and more shots slammed into the back of the taxi. Wyatt swung to the right and followed another street that led upwards, towards the wealthier suburbs surrounding the Sugar Loaf.

Vanessa sat up to look out of the window. 'Get down!' Wyatt screamed as more bullets slammed into the boot. He turned again, and found himself on a road that clung to the side of the mountain, with a precipitous drop on one side.

He looked back again, and sure enough, the pursuing car swung into view. All right, you fuckers, he thought. Now let's see what you're made of. He gunned the taxi hard into the next corner, the wheels squealing as the machine reached the limits of its adhesion. He looked back – and saw the pursuing car fall away.

Vanessa saw a cold smile creep across Wyatt's face. He drew up the handbrake and the taxi screamed round, the cliff edge coming into view as they spun in a round-the-clock turn.

'No!' Vanessa cried as Wyatt accelerated downhill at a suicidal pace.

The attacking car was coming towards them. Wyatt slammed the taxi into second gear and drove at it head on. In the last millisecond before impact he wrenched the steering-wheel to one side and then back again, and slammed the taxi hard into the side of the attacking car. The car rocketed over the side of the cliff and into space.

Wyatt floored the brakes and twisted the steering-wheel again, and the taxi screamed to a halt, teetering on the edge of the cliff. Vanessa was sobbing. He dragged her out and they watched the other car smash into the rocks below.

The circuit felt different. No spectators. There was litter everywhere, and the only people in evidence were the crews from the various teams packing up their gear for the air journey home. Bruce and Wyatt headed for the garage where

Max Senda had last seen Suzie. Calibre-Shensu's equipment had been packed away and the place was almost empty.

'What was kept here?' Wyatt asked.

'Spare tyres – Carvalho over-supplied us.'

'Just the other day you were scared they weren't going to supply enough.' Jack Phelps's voice echoed around the empty garage.

Wyatt turned round to look at Jack. He thought of saying something, then decided against it. For some reason he couldn't explain, he felt that the less Jack Phelps knew about this, the better.

'Are you still looking for Suzie?' Phelps growled out.

Bruce looked up. 'We are. This is the last place she was seen.'

Phelps leaned against a work-bench and folded his arms. 'God knows what she was doing here . . . Personally, I think you should forget about her and concentrate on preparing for your next race.'

Wyatt felt the hair lifting on the back of his neck. He didn't like being ordered around.

'I'll do what I bloody well want to,' he said.

Phelps turned to Bruce. 'It seems our only driver is going to miss a few testing sessions.'

De Villiers smoothed back his hair and stared across at Wyatt. 'Jack's right. We should leave this to the police.'

Wyatt noticed a quiver about Phelps's right eyebrow. 'You've contacted the police?'

'Well, of course we've contacted the bloody police!' Bruce yelled. 'Suzie's missing!'

'Have they been here?'

'No. They seem to think she ran off with a man, bloody idiots.'

'Quite probable.'

With that parting shot, Jack walked outside – and baulked at he saw two police cars draw up. A short man with slicked-back black hair stepped out of the front car, pulling on a light-coloured sports jacket. He walked past Phelps with his hand outstretched and greeted Wyatt warmly.

'A pleasure to meet you again, Mr Chase. It was a great

race and you are a worthy champion. I am Detective Inspector Farina, as I think you know.'

Farina stared at de Villiers and Phelps, and Wyatt introduced them. Phelps looked distinctly uncomfortable. 'Is there anything the matter, Inspector Farina?'

'Two men dead after their car went over a cliff. An attempted suicide, and a dead cameraman. And the disappearance of a wealthy and beautiful woman. Yes, I'd say there's something the matter,' Farina muttered cynically, lighting a cigarette.

Wyatt smiled bleakly. Farina had clearly changed his tune since they last met.

'Well, I hope you find Miss von Falkenhyn quickly, otherwise you can expect a rough ride from the American Embassy, as well as the German one.'

Farina blew smoke in Phelps's face. 'I do not respond kindly to threats,' he said quietly.

'Then get on with your job and you won't have to worry about them,' replied Phelps, walking off smartly towards the helipad.

When Phelps was out of earshot, Farina raised his bushy eyebrows. 'That's one angry man.'

Bruce drummed his fingers on the side of the police car. 'Mr Phelps is our biggest sponsor. He pays the bills and he doesn't like bad publicity, inspector. With Sartori suspended and the disappearance of Miss von Falkenhyn, he's got major problems.'

'You stick to racing, Mr de Villiers, I'll find Miss von Falkenhyn. Now, a few questions . . .'

Suzie had lost all sense of time and space. Her world was filled with one simple desire – relief from the tension that racked her body. Sunlight drifted in through the plate-glass window, and below her steam rose from the dense greenery of the jungle.

The second experience had been better than the first, but once it wore off she had felt curiously deflated. Now that depression had been replaced by a growing anxiety. Her hands and arms were free but she felt no desire to escape. The door at the corner of the room opened and she leapt to her feet. Jules Ortega came in rubbing his hands.

'Ah, Suzie, you are pleased to see me?'

She nodded quickly, almost in spite of herself. 'I want some more,' she said as warmly as she could.

'Ah. You like it? I thought you would.' His voice was very soft, almost a caress. 'Today I'm going to teach you how to do the injections yourself. Then whenever you want another one, it will be very easy.'

He took the syringe from his pocket and removed the cover from the needle with his mangled right hand. She was shaking with excitement. He showed her how to bind up her arm correctly, and then how to draw the fluid from the vial into the needle.

'You must be careful not to take too much.'

Having shown her a number of times how to prepare the needle, he let her inject herself in the arm. Immediately she began to feel better. The feeling of freedom was incredible: there were no worries about money or the need to produce more designs – she felt she could cope with anything.

'Now, when you want some more, just ask me.'

She loved his voice now.

'There are people looking for you,' he said. 'They want you to go home with them. But of course, then there will be no more injections. You don't want to go home, do you?'

'No. I never want to go back.' She spoke earnestly, looking into his dark eyes and stroking his arm gently.

Jules Ortega felt very good. Just by holding back the supply he could get anything he wanted out of this German woman. But he also knew he must be careful – he didn't want her to die.

The cellular phone bleeped and he picked it up.

'Yes, Rod . . . Ah . . . No, I have not heard anything. But of course, should anything come to light I'll let you know. The Brazilian police? Yes, a few payments and it will all be sorted out. Yes, the next shipment will be ready on time. Yes, she will still be around when you return.'

*

They'd been up the coast, following a lead of Vanessa's. They'd talked to some migrant labourers who were working on a new hotel complex. Yes, the workers had said, a man had been there two weeks before, looking for men who were prepared to take risks for a good salary. But no, none of them had accepted and they couldn't give a decent description of the man who'd done the hiring.

Now they were driving back to Rio and it was terribly hot. They decided to pull off and go for a swim on the first deserted beach they could find.

Wyatt drove the hire-car under the palms, which swayed in the light breeze from the sea. He looked out across the glistening sands and switched off the engine, then he helped Vanessa out of the passenger-seat.

Once she was on the sand, she kicked off her sandals. 'Welcome to paradise,' she said gaily.

Wyatt opened a couple of beers, then looked up to see Vanessa running down into the waves, the wind blowing back her raven hair. She moved with a natural grace; the neck-brace had been removed the day before and she was almost completely recovered.

They'd ignored Inspector Farina's warning to leave Rio immediately; Wyatt wanted to find out what had happened to Suzie, and he sensed that this British reporter could help him. Vanessa Tyson was not an easy woman to get close to, but what Wyatt liked about her was her free spirit – her determination to go her own way. Like now – as she slipped off her dress and underclothes and dived into the water. He watched the full breasts swing in the foam, and felt himself stiffen.

He lay stretched out on the sand and she came up, water dripping from her, as if swimming naked on an isolated beach was the most natural thing in the world to do. He handed her a beer and they drank a silent toast, then continued to sip their beer while contemplating the waves that crashed against the shore.

'You're in love with Suzie?'

Her question hung in the air, lingering. The only way to deal with Vanessa was to meet her directly – any back off or evasion would be taken as a show of weakness.

'Yes,' he said.

She turned away, and watched the waves breaking on the sand.

Later, driving back to the hotel, she was strangely quiet. Wyatt sensed that she was as troubled by Suzie's disappearance as he was.

Bruce sat in his office, looking out into the darkness. He'd got back to Heathrow some hours before and had driven over to the Calibre-Shensu headquarters. There was a fax from Ronnie Halliday, the head of FOCA, waiting for him. It advised him in the strongest possible terms not to try and fight for Ricardo's reinstatement. The sport, Ronnie argued, could do without that sort of dissension. They wanted to keep Formula One squeaky-clean.

The fax now lay in one corner of his office, squeezed into a ball. Bruce had made up his mind: he was going to fight them to get Ricardo readmitted. It was worth the risk, he reckoned. He had nothing to lose and everything to gain. If he could get Ricardo reinstated, even if the Italian missed the Monaco Grand Prix they would still have a very good chance of winning the constructor's championship – he knew that, judging by the Shadow's performance at Rio, Wyatt and Ricardo could be amongst the front-runners in every race.

He picked up the phone and rang Don Morrison to get him to assemble a group of prominent motor journalists. Tomorrow he would give a press conference to get the ball rolling. There was nothing wrong, as far as Bruce could see, in getting public opinion on his side. Had he been present at a meeting in Paris that evening, he might have decided otherwise.

The meeting in Paris was tense. Ronnie Halliday took off his glasses and peered at Alain Hugo, who with him, controlled Formula One racing – the two of them held its future in the palms of their hands. They were constantly fighting, Alain Hugo very much the older and more conservative of the two, always seeking to apply discipline. Ronnie Halliday was responsible for the huge growth of the sport, its enormous TV coverage and its international scope. Ronnie was always scared that the Frenchman would so over-regulate the sport that he would kill it.

'Alain, let's just leave it for the moment. Calibre-Shensu have had one big blow already – with Ricardo gone, they've effectively lost the constructor's championship.'

Hugo waved his hands dismissively, but Ronnie wasn't giving up.

'No one has complained about the design of the Shadow. If they do, then we'll have to follow it up.' Halliday was persuasive, a natural businessman, known for his ability to get what he wanted.

Alain heaved a sigh and raised his bushy eyebrows, then held his large nose between his thumb and forefinger before replying.

'All right, Ronnie. I'll accept that.' He growled out his grudging acceptance of Halliday's strategy. 'But if there's any trouble from de Villiers about Ricardo, then I'll go ahead.'

'Most certainly.'

Wyatt didn't feel any better now that he was back in London. There was still no news of Suzie – she'd vanished off the face of the earth.

Vanessa had proved as good as her word, and had stayed in Rio, encouraging the TV networks to keep showing Suzie's picture together with the offer of a large reward for any information leading to her discovery. Wyatt had put up some of his own money, but it was Jack Phelps who had supplied most of the reward – $750 000.

Unfortunately, another journalist had seen Vanessa leaving Wyatt's hotel room in Rio late at night. The tabloids were now making a song and dance of it – *'Chase Loses One, Only to Gain Another'* read the headline.

He looked through a list of that night's TV programmes and saw that there was a motor-sport report about to begin. He switched on the set and sat back.

'Right now,' the commentator said, 'everyone in Formula One is talking about the newly formed Calibre-Shensu team. Their number two driver, Wyatt Chase, took the victory honours at Rio. Chase is undoubtedly championship material, and if this performance was anything to go by, he could be this season's front-runner. However, with that victory came defeat for Calibre-Shensu's number one driver, former world champion Ricardo Sartori, who was suspended after striking German driver Johan Hoexter.'

The camera pulled back to reveal Bruce de Villiers seated next to the presenter. 'In the seat next to me I have Bruce de Villiers, formerly manager of McCabe Racing, now part-owner and manager of Calibre-Shensu. He's the man people are calling the new force in Formula One. Bruce, how do you feel about Ronnie Halliday's and Alain Hugo's decision to suspend Ricardo Sartori?'

The interviewer, Robin Cox, was a seasoned professional, and he and Bruce were old friends. Wyatt sat back on the sofa and waited for Bruce to start punching.

'I think it's unfair,' Bruce said. 'A temporary suspension for one race, yes, but the whole season . . .?'

'So you're objecting to the decision?'

'Of course I am. It costs a great deal of money to put a driver on the circuit. Formula One's not like soccer where you've a whole team, and one suspension doesn't really have that much effect on your performance. We've just lost fifty per cent of our potential because the people who organise Formula One are afraid of bad publicity. What about all the good publicity Ricardo's given them?'

'On that note, Bruce, let's take a look at a documentary we've put together on Ricardo Sartori's racing career.'

It was an impressive film, both from an editing standpoint and from the overwhelming testimony it gave to Ricardo's genius on the track. Wyatt felt uneasy. Ricardo's behaviour had been unforgivable, and Bruce's arguing against his suspension was pretty pointless – FISA had said that they weren't going to back down on their decision. Anyway, the interview so far was totally one-sided. Wyatt suspected it might have unpleasant repercussions for the team.

The camera cut to a close-up of Robin Cox. 'But of course there are two sides to every story. Our second guest tonight, Vanessa Tyson, needs no introduction.'

Wyatt sat up as the camera swung across to capture Vanessa walking into the studio and sit down opposite Bruce de Villiers.

'Thank you, Robin,' she said. 'As my US viewers know, I conduct investigations on a regular basis into controversial matters. First, I'd like to show you a film I've put together over the past few weeks.'

The title of the film came up on the screen: 'The Way of Death: Cancer and Speed.'

Wyatt's blood froze as he watched: shots of people dying of lung cancer intercut with glamorous cigarette ads of Grand Prix racing, and then film of some of the gruesome accidents from the last twenty years of Formula One. It was all beautifully held together with a tight-lipped commentary from Vanessa. It was brilliantly done, but like Bruce's previous argument for Ricardo's reinstatement, it was totally one-sided. Wyatt felt for Bruce: Vanessa had nailed him on two counts, questionable sponsorship and the danger of the sport.

The documentary drew to a close with a shot of Vanessa stepping onto the track at Rio. So that was what she'd been doing in Rio – she hadn't given a damn about Suzie after all. She had used him.

'Millions and millions of dollars,' Vanessa was saying 'are poured into motor-racing by the big cigarette companies, whose ruthless entrepreneurs – like Jack Phelps of Calibre – can no longer use conventional advertising. It is a dangerous sport funded by a dangerous habit. Can we continue to support an activity that encourages the man on the street to drive irresponsibly, and to take up a habit that can cut twenty years off his life?'

The film ended, and the camera focused on Bruce de Villiers, who was icy cool. Out of camera, Vanessa's voice cut across the stillness of the studio. 'Bruce de Villiers, you are now challenging the governing bodies of Formula One. You want a driver who is dangerous on the track reinstated?'

Bruce gave a tight-lipped smile to camera. 'Everyone is entitled to their own viewpoint. I live Formula One. My drivers are in it because they want to be. They know the risks. Our sponsors are giving the world something it wants to see. Formula One is life at the sharp end. Only thirty men in the world can ever sit in the driving-seat of a Formula One car, and only about five of them can ever hope to feature high in the points. I'm in this business to win, so are my drivers. Yes, I do have a responsibility to my sponsors. I also have a responsibility to my team and to Ricardo. Suspended for one race – I couldn't argue with that. But a whole season? No way.'

Vanessa smiled demurely. 'How do you feel about the two drivers you've killed in the past ten years?'

Wyatt wanted to strangle her. She was baiting Bruce – de Villiers' temper was legendary.

Bruce replied, his face red and his fingers tapping on the edge of the chair. '*I* killed? They died where they wanted to live, behind the wheel. You take your risks with a TV camera, you never put your life on the line. Where are you at the start of a race? Where are you during the sweat of preparation, when my men work without sleep to make the car as perfect as possible? I suggest you get off your fat arse and get in the seat of a Formula One car, see if you can take it for one lap.'

Vanessa's eyes flashed and her face was white.

'You were born a bully, Mr de Villiers, and you have no manners. Drivers are for killing, are they? But no, don't ask any difficult questions, because this is a man's business, a man's gotta do what a man's gotta do.' Vanessa was shouting now. 'I don't buy it, Mr de Villiers, and I'm not scared of you or your sponsors. You don't care, but I do. It's time some questions were asked, and I'm going to ask them.'

There was a quick glimpse of de Villiers' angry face, then the camera cut back to Robin Cox.

'Only the men who run Formula One can decide if the decision they made against Ricardo Sartori three days ago is just. However, you the viewer can make your own decision, and then perhaps ask yourself a question: Is Formula One all that sporting? Thank you, Bruce de Villiers and Vanessa Tyson, for being with us here tonight on "Straight Talking." Next week's terview will be with Austrian climber, Reinhold Meissner.'

Wyatt switched off the set and walked about in a daze. The images from the documentary flashed through his mind. He thought of his mother by his father's graveside, then his

256

uncle's; he thought of the long, winding road in Monaco and the memories that refused to come back. *You killed him. You killed him.* The words echoed through his mind.

He felt he was losing control, cracking up. He changed into his karate-*gi* and moved into his training ritual. In half an hour the thoughts were forgotten and he went through the elaborate sequences of several *katas*.

The phone broke the inner peace. He lifted the receiver and heard Vanessa's voice.

'Wyatt, I'm sorry but . . .'

'Go to hell!'

As the first rays of sunlight passed through the window, Ricardo looked down at the blonde woman who lay sleeping on his chest. They'd made love passionately for hours. Earlier, the previous evening, she'd taken a line of coke to heighten the experience, and she'd exhausted him.

He pushed her away. He was still numbed, both by his suspension and the way Bruce had told him that without the right to race, his contract was null and void. But money would not be a problem, Phelps had spoken of higher earnings than he had achieved in Formula One. But at what price? Ricardo asked himself. He had lived to race.

In a day's time he would be appointed executive vice-president of Calibre Worldwide. His yearly salary wouldn't be close to what he was earning in Formula One, but with the perks it included, and the profit potential of the deals Phelps had hinted at, it could net him far more.

In the two days he'd spent so far in New York, Ricardo knew he'd been constantly assessed by Phelps's partners. He guessed that there was more to the deal than met the eye and he wondered when Phelps was going to enlighten him.

The phone next to his bed rang and he snatched it up.

'Sartori? The board-meeting will begin in thirty minutes.'

Ricardo felt a moment's hesitation. Maybe he should leave New York, sell his island villa and his jet, and pay off his tax debts. He could spend the rest of the year as a test driver, and then re-emerge on the Formula One circuit. But perhaps the other teams would be reluctant to take him on in case he lost his cool again? Anyway, he definitely did not want to lose the villa or the plane.

He looked at his watch. 'The meeting is now?' he said into the phone. It was six in the morning.

'Yes, at six thirty. We'll see you there – in a suit please. A chauffeur will collect you in ten minutes.'

Twenty minutes later Ricardo strode into the enormous foyer. The words 'Phelps Plaza' were emblazoned in silver over a huge waterfall that cascaded down over marble blocks piled four storeys high. He liked it. And he was sure that whatever it was Mr Phelps wanted, he could accommodate it. The lift took off like a jet, taking only a few seconds to reach the top floor. The doors opened and Ricardo was greeted by the smell of coffee – and a very attractive woman in a tailored suit.

'Good morning, Mr Sartori. Welcome to Calibre. First let me show you your office suite. Mr Phelps and his board have another matter to discuss before it will be necessary for you to join them.'

'That's fine with me.'

He followed her down a series of dark, oak-panelled passages, walking on a carpet that was as thick as uncut grass. He admired the line of her long, athletic legs in expensive silk stockings.

They walked into a large room with a curved ceiling, lit on either side by concealed neon lights. At each end of the room were double doors, and on the walls hung a series of original paintings by Salvador Dali. The receptionist's desk was Georgian with a black leather surface.

'This is your reception area,' the elegant woman said. 'Anyone coming into your office will be screened. Naturally, you will choose your own personal secretary. There is also a hidden TV camera at the back of the wall, so that you can always see who is in the reception area.' Her voice reeled off further information with computer-like precision.

He came up to her and touched her arm. 'Your name?'

She hesitated. 'Lauren, Mr Sartori.'

'How would you like to be my secretary?'

She moved discreetly away from him. 'I'm sorry, Mr Sartori,

but I'm Mr Phelps's personal assistant.' She spoke very quietly. 'I appreciate your offer very much, but I suggest you don't mention it to Mr Phelps.'

Lauren opened the doors to the main office area and Ricardo found himself looking out across the New York skyline. She switched on the lights and the room took on a different quality. The main desk was a giant marble slab perched on a granite pedestal, and there were two leather couches and a long, flat coffee table. The room had an over-all feeling of space, and suggested immense power.

'Hidden behind the mirrors along the wall are a bathroom and sauna, also a filing room and a walk-in safe.' As Lauren spoke she pushed a button underneath the desk, and two of the mirrors slid back to reveal a boardroom. 'This is for any private discussions you might wish to conduct.'

Another set of mirrors slid quietly back to expose a suite of private rooms. Sartori followed her through the doors. 'This is a self-contained living-area. If you wish to live here some of the time, you can, quite comfortably. A personal chef is on twenty-four-hour stand-by.'

'Where does this go?' he asked, pointing to another lift inside the private suite.

'To the helipad. There's also an entrance to it in the lobby. However, you might want to leave discreetly.'

Ricardo nodded his approval. He walked back out to the main office.

'Who used this office before me?'

Lauren appeared to be slightly embarrassed by this question. 'The office was completely redecorated for you, Mr Sartori. It has not been occupied for a while.'

'Yes, but when it was, who sat here?'

'Mr Ambrose. He held the position you are about to take-over.'

'Which is?'

This line of conversation was broken by the purr of a concealed telephone. Lauren went behind the desk and lifted out the receiver from underneath.

'Yes, Mr Phelps, I'll send him through now.'

*

Ricardo felt his confidence evaporate as he walked into the oval boardroom. There was a deathly silence as he contemplated the faces at the table, headed by Jack Phelps.

There was one empty place and he moved silently towards it. He felt he was being examined – quietly assessed. He was about to sit down when Phelps gestured for him to remain standing.

'Gentlemen. I stated last year that I would handle special operations myself, but now I have found a successor to our previous special operations executive. The man you see before you is Ricardo Sartori. With his assistance, over the next six months we will establish an unprecedented hold over the world market. He will take on the anti-tobacco lobby and win.' He paused for a moment, and surveyed the faces around the table before delivering his final sentence. 'Those in favour, raise their hands.'

Every hand at the table was raised. Ricardo guessed that anyone who didn't raise his hand would be looking for a new job.

Phelps looked over to him. 'Mr Sartori, you are now a board-member of Calibre. I will not ask you to sit in on this particular meeting as your full portfolio is still to be decided. I will speak to you later.'

Ricardo correctly interpreted this as an order to leave and walked smartly out of the boardroom. Immediately he was through the door he heard a heated discussion erupt.

Lauren was waiting for him outside. 'I've left some files on your desk as well as some videotapes. Mr Phelps would like you to look through them before he speaks with you.'

Ricardo walked back into the big office, beginning to feel in control and at home. His desk was covered with photographs and he moved closer to find out what they were.

Several minutes later, his hands were trembling. There were pictures of him with several women and a man in bed. Who had taken them? He smacked the desk with his fist and began to gather them up quickly.

Lauren came into the office.

'Get out,' he said quietly.

'I saw all the pictures before I met you, Mr Sartori. Relax.

260

Mr Phelps insists that you watch the videotape. The switch is the red one on the left inside panel of the desk.'

He sat down in the huge leather chair behind the desk and pushed the red button.

The film started with a wide-angle view of Milan, then dissolved to the face of the presenter. Ricardo didn't recognise him.

'This is where it all began,' the presenter said, 'the career of Ricardo Sartori – in public the world-class racing-driver, in private a violent and unhappy man. His mother, a part-time prostitute . . .'

He wanted to switch the video off but he couldn't. It was all there, all the worst parts of his life. As the minutes passed he was treated to interviews with his early girlfriends, details of the criminal record he had tried to have erased, and all the other dirt of his past.

He was aware of someone coming into the room and switched the recorder off quickly. The lights came up automatically and he found himself looking at Jack Phelps, lying back on the couch, smoking a cigar.

'You bastard!' he said.

Phelps smiled thinly. 'That's what the board said after they saw the film half an hour ago.'

Ricardo got up and made for the door. 'Forget your offer, Phelps. I'm out.'

Saying he was going was as far as Ricardo got towards achieving it. He found his way blocked by a tall man in a dark suit, and when he tried to get past him he received a roundhouse kick in the side of the head. In an instant Ricardo knew that this man could kill him – and wouldn't hesitate to do so if those were his orders.

He staggered back into the room, and Phelps dismissed the man, then returned his eyes to Ricardo.

'Relax,' he said. 'You can leave, never to see me again, if that is what you wish. All I want to say is that the tape will then go to every major TV network in the world, as well as to all the influential newspapers and magazines.' Phelps stopped and pulled another cigar out of his pocket. 'Care for one?'

'No.'

'Smoke it.' The command was icy.

'I don't smoke.'

'Lauren!'

Lauren came into the room with a sheaf of files. 'Give them to him, Lauren. You may stay.'

Lauren gave Ricardo the files and sat down. 'That's all the fine print on your financial standing,' Phelps muttered maliciously. 'I have it in my power to destroy you completely. So. Join me in a cigar.'

Ricardo took the cigar in his now trembling hands and placed it in his mouth. Lauren lit it.

'Ah. I see that you are not intractable.'

'What . . . what do you want?'

'Your co-operation. You will live very well, and I will not work you hard.' The words were precisely spoken, well thought out and full of menace.

'I want to return to racing,' Ricardo said almost pitifully.

'Next year. This year you will concentrate on your career with me.'

'But I need practice . . .'

Phelps got up and stared out of the window. He needed Ricardo because of his position, his public stature. He was the ideal front-man for what he had in mind.

'I give the commands. Now, listen carefully . . .'

Ricardo was tense when he stepped outside Phelps Plaza one and a half hours later. The Rolls-Royce that had come to collect him earlier in the morning rolled up with the precision of a Swiss watch, and the chauffeur opened the back door for him and he stepped inside. Being inside the car made him feel more secure again. He had read in a book many years before that every man had at least one major failing, and life was a process of overcoming one's weakness. Just when he had felt most secure, everything had been taken away from him.

The terrifying reality was that he had no choice. He had had to accept Phelps's offer. True, it paid very handsomely, but at the same time it enmeshed him in Phelps's carefully spun web. As long as Phelps lived, Ricardo would be in his power.

*

Jules Ortega felt remarkably good. Everything was in place for expansion; from supplying America they would move on to supply the world. But better, he now had a new love – Suzie von Falkenhyn.

Her picture was everywhere in Brazil, on television morning, noon and night. Even if he'd wanted to, he couldn't have taken her anywhere in public – she would have been recognised instantly.

Of course, he had been concerned, because some of his men must have seen her when Rod brought her to laboratory, and the reward for information leading to her whereabouts was close to a million dollars – too much of a temptation. So Talbot had agreed to dispose of them, quietly and professionally.

He went back into the bedroom, where Suzie had passed out. The needle was still in her hand, the inside of her arm a minefield of red pinpricks from the regular injections of heroin she had been giving herself. He sat down next to her and her eyes opened.

'Jules, where have you been?'

Such an expression of love. 'Don't worry now,' he said softly.

Her lips caressed his chest. 'You'll give me some more?' she murmured.

'Just carry on, and you'll get all you want.'

April

Monaco was the epitome of all that was best and worst about Formula One, Ricardo thought as he looked across the harbour at the yachts bobbing up and down in the moonlight. Monaco was glamorous, and the circuit demanding. But running a Grand Prix in the middle of a busy old city meant the track was narrow and bumpy, and a nightmare from a logistical standpoint – supplies and spares and motorhomes had to be kept away from the main pits which were too small to hold them. Every time something was needed it meant a long journey from the pits to the parking area.

That evening the principality was alive with excitement, everyone waiting in anticipation for the Grand Prix the following day.

Ricardo walked out of the casino and looked down towards the sea, trying to forget his losses at the roulette wheel. He remembered the contents of the Calibre-Shensu press-release that was neatly folded in his pocket – and was incensed all over again. Wyatt had got pole position. The Shadow was performing exceptionally well, and Ricardo knew that if he hadn't had the fight in Brazil, he could have been leading the championship. But now he was banned for a year and working for Jack Phelps, co-ordinating the Calibre-Shensu sponsorship.

Ricardo didn't find his new position easy going. Jack Phelps never left him alone – there were calls at night, and impossible deadlines to meet. On top of all that, the team members avoided him if they could. Bruce de Villiers was icy – he still hadn't forgiven him for his behaviour in Rio.

That afternoon Ricardo had bought a paper from a pavement kiosk. The leader on the sports page had filled him with a rage of jealousy. *'Chase Sets The Pace'*, the headline had read.

He looked down now at his watch. Just after two in the morning. He'd better get some sleep. It was strange how his life had began to revolve around the night – all those strange, secret liaisons he had to make with Phelps's associates. A cloud passed over the moon, and for a moment he felt nervous. Then he dismissed the feeling and walked off down the road, an elegant figure in his dinner-jacket, a white silk scarf hanging casually around his neck.

Estelle and Carlos arrived back late at the estancia, after a pleasant dinner with some members of Carlos's polo team. There was a telegram waiting for Carlos in the large wood-beamed hall, and something told Estelle that it did not bode well. However, he put it in his jacket pocket and walked up the stairs to their room.

She followed him upstairs, drew the curtains and looked out at the rolling grasslands in the moonlight, the distant mountains. She thought – not for the first time – of how lucky she was to have found Carlos after James's death.

Carlos was reading the telegram and his face had darkened. 'Darling, what's wrong?'

He looked across to her. 'It's from the man investigating my brother's murder.'

'David is dead, Carlos – revenge won't bring him back. Leave it alone.'

Estelle was scared. She thought of how gruesome David's murder had been. But it was in the past – she wanted Carlos to forget about it. She knew his brother had been playing with fire. David, as Minister of Justice in Colombia, had challenged the Ortega Cartel; he had liaised with the CIA and had had Emerson Ortega, the biggest producer and dealer, assassinated. But then David had been abducted and murdered, and a videotape of his dreadful death had been sent to his wife and children. It did not bear thinking about . . .

Carlos looked across at her. 'My contact says that Emerson Ortega is alive,' he said. 'That he murdered my brother. Emerson Ortega slowly hanged my brother to death.'

She felt herself shaking. She did not want Carlos involved in this madness. 'How do you know it's true?' she said.

'An associate of David's suspected that Emerson Ortega was still alive – that he'd been warned of the assassination attempt and had substituted a double for himself. Then, after his supposed death, Emerson Ortega murdered my brother in revenge.'

'Leave it alone, Carlos . . .'

'I cannot. I loved my brother.'

Estelle walked to the window and stared out, unseeing. She prayed with all her heart that this thing would not take Carlos away from her too.

The morning sunlight held Monaco in a warm embrace. Every available balcony had been commandeered to watch the event of the year. Policemen and officials were stationed at strategic positions throughout the city. No one was thinking about anything except the race.

Bruce de Villiers gazed out over the road circuit. He did not like this track at all. As far as he was concerned, it was an anachronism that should have been left off the Grand Prix calendar years ago. He was still amused by the rebuff he had received from Ronnie Halliday, the head of the Formula One Constructors' Association, after the TV appearance in which he tried to get Ricardo reinstated. He knew he'd got to Halliday.

Street circuits were kept in the Grand Prix programme because they had a romance and glamour of their own. They were less impersonal than the large, purpose-built circuits, and less accessible. More importantly, they heightened the exclusive nature of the sport.

'Something wrong, Bruce?' Wyatt's voice boomed out from across the pits.

'No, nothing. Are you feeling confident?'

'Yes.' Wyatt walked over and slapped Bruce on the back. 'As long as I can start in front, I'll stay in front.'

They were both silent for a few seconds. Monaco was hard on cars, it would be the ultimate test of the Shadow's reliability.

'Make sure Hoexter doesn't try to cut in.' Bruce was still scared of what had happened at Rio.

'It wasn't Hoexter's fault.'

Wyatt was excited. Hoexter was in second position in the McCabe. He was a driver who never held back, and Wyatt knew he would have to fight him the whole way.

'I haven't got a second driver in this race, Wyatt. Just remember that.'

Debbie caused a lot of heads to turn as she walked into the pits with Ricardo. She was wearing an excuse of a white dress that hardly covered anything. Seeing her, Wyatt was reminded of Suzie, and his happy mood evaporated.

Jack Phelps appeared from amongst the crowd that clustered at the edge of the pits like animals at a water-hole. He pumped Wyatt's hand warmly.

'It's great to see you on form again, Wyatt,' he beamed enthusiastically. 'Our noted recall scores are way up. You're advertising dynamite.'

Wyatt couldn't give a damn about noted recall scores. He stared at Phelps cooly. All the publicity was bothering him. He felt apprehensive, almost superstitious about making too much of a fuss about his victory in Rio. He knew the other drivers would be gunning for him now.

'It's one race so far, Jack. I need to consolidate to really make an impact.'

'Hell, you're a typical Brit. Isn't he, Bruce?' Phelps swung round to greet Bruce.

Bruce was looking drawn, and Wyatt understood why. It was the constructor's trophy that mattered more to Bruce than anything else, and with only one driver in the championship he hadn't a chance of winning it. Only two drivers, both getting high up in the points, would give him the points accumulation he needed to win the trophy.

'I prefer action to talk,' Bruce said softly, each word carefully emphasized to make his point.

'Modesty gets you nowhere in today's world. You know Andy Warhol said that everyone should be famous for fifteen minutes? That's the nature of the business – to ensure enduring fame. To put it bluntly, it adds to the pressure on you to perpetuate the legend.'

Wyatt laughed. Perhaps Phelps had worked in marketing for so long that he believed his own bullshit. He wasn't buying it, for sure, and he certainly wasn't going to let it affect his edge.

Phelps pulled them both away from the pit crew and took them into a huddle in the corner.

'Listen, guys, I'm taking flack from that bitch Vanessa Tyson. She's on an anti-smoking, anti-motor-racing drive. I'll have her taken care of, but for the moment watch out. Especially you, Bruce. I don't want any more interviews with her.'

Bruce coloured. 'I didn't know that bitch would be on that programme!'

Wyatt tensed up, and Jack winked at him. 'I don't want you worrying about this, Wyatt. She's history.' The big American slapped him hard on the back.

Wyatt never ceased to be amazed at Phelps's organisational ability. True, there were a lot of flags and banners for other teams, but Calibre-Shensu logos seemed to be everywhere.

Phelps concluded his discourse. 'Gentlemen, I can see you're busy, and besides, there isn't much room down here. Wyatt . . .' He stretched out his hand. 'I know you'll deliver. Just like your father did here, ten years ago.'

Phelps walked off smartly. He had hired an entire hotel for the Calibre-Shensu entourage – rooms and tickets had been given free to everyone who could be of influence in the cigarette or the car business. It was pure Hollywood.

Wyatt felt numb. Phelps's reference to his father had brought memories back. Memories of his father's victory, memories of the accident, and Estelle shouting at him: '*You killed him, you killed him . . .*'

If Bruce had been momentarily been taken in by the glamour of the circus, what was happening in the pits brought him back to reality with a bump. It was crazy racing at Monaco: there wasn't enough room. At every other track, safety and security standards were being constantly upgraded, but at Monaco life went on as usual. The track was narrow and bumpy, and it was almost impossible for cars to overtake one another. And once the race was on, you were stuck in the pits – there was no way out at the back, except on foot through the heavy crowds. Really, it was almost impossible to race effectively in such an environment. Yet Monaco endured.

There would be twenty-six cars on the starting-grid, all of them more competitive than the previous year. In fact, there was only seven seconds between the fastest and the slowest.

The Monaco Grand Prix was a gamble. Beautiful girls, idyllic setting, high stakes . . . and if a car went out of control in the wrong place on this circuit, it could be catastrophic.

He watched the cars whipping past him in the warm-up before the main race. Wyatt was keeping well in front, the tightness of the circuit not seeming to bother him at all. Twenty-six cars was too many as far as Bruce was concerned; he would have limited it to eighteen maximum. There just wasn't room for them all on the circuit.

As the cars rolled up onto the starting-grid, Bruce experienced a sense of foreboding. If Wyatt stayed out in front, he was safer, because it was in the pack – jostling for front position – that the true danger lay. At Monaco, if the front driver could maintain his pace he could lead the race from start to finish in an unassailable position.

The sound of the cars' engines rose into a collective roar, and as the starting-light turned green they burst from the grid, each driver determined to win.

So far so good, thought Bruce.

He waited for Wyatt's car to come round into view, ready to commence the seventy-seventh lap, and glanced down at his stop-watch. And suddenly he thought of Ricardo Sartori: yes, he could understand his bitterness at not being able to compete.

Where were the cars? They should be round again by now. He knew Wyatt still held the lead, but Hoexter was hot on his tail. For the crowd the main excitement was coming from the back-markers, where an unknown German driver, Kurt Kunstler, was doing battle with Italian veteran, Toni Vignelli.

Then the sirens erupted. Bruce could hear them in the

distance and felt his body go weak. The pit lane exploded into chaos as different reports started coming in, but no one could tell what had happened. Over the speakers it was announced that there had been a serious accident at the Virage du Portier, just before the tunnel.

Wyatt sensed Hoexter was dropping away as they came into the Virage du Portier. He saw the crashed cars and the flames, and he saw the gap between the crashed cars and the edge of the track. Only one lap left, one lap to victory.

He glanced in his mirror. Hoexter was pulling over. At this late stage, there'd been no flags to halt the race. One lap, and he would win. He had to win for James's sake.

Wyatt put his foot on the accelerator and powered on through the smoke and the devastation.

Bruce felt removed from the action. Two drivers in two races? Could his luck be that bad? The circuit was dangerous, everyone knew that, but what the hell had happened?

The sound of ambulances and police cars was louder, and he heard sirens from across the pit lane. It was Professor Sid Watkins, the London neurosurgeon responsible for overseeing all the Formula One medical facilities, and in the car with him was the Chief Medical Officer.

There must be fatalities. But they would not stop the race with only one lap left.

He glanced down at his stop-watch. If Wyatt was still in the running, he'd be round now.

The black shape of the Shadow shot past the pits, leading the rest of the pack by a lap. Hoexter was nowhere to be seen.

Wyatt came around the Loews hairpin. The smoke had cleared and he saw the first cars, the flames and devastation. He saw the back of Hoexter's McCabe in amongst the wreckage of a multitude of other cars – and he caught sight of a break in the Armco where several machines had careered into the crowd. There were stretchers everywhere. People were screaming.

He kept on driving. This was the final lap. He had to win.

*

270

Ricardo stared up at the crowd in the brilliant afternoon sunlight. This was what they waited for, he knew it. Not consciously, of course; no one would ever admit that the reason they watched motor sport was to see a serious accident. But danger was the magnet, all the same.

The arena, the gladiators, the blood . . .

Then, out of the flames and wreckage closer to the tunnel, came a man in a charred black jumpsuit. The face was black, the arms were carrying a body towards one of the ambulances. It was Hoexter.

Ricardo could not help himself, he just kept on shaking. He had pushed himself to the edge of the crowd and was looking down on the devastation.

You couldn't blame the circuit for what had happened, he knew that. It was the two drivers, Kurt Kunstler and Toni Vignelli, who had died. They had gone into the Virage du Portier neck-and-neck, each trying to pass the other. As they swept around the corner their cars had collided and burst into flames. Neither of them had had a chance. Then the car immediately behind them had turned the accident into a catastrophe: it hit the other two, vaulted the Armco and went straight into the crowd like a Cruise missile. The driver was fine, but four people in the crowd lay dead and another twenty-one were seriously injured.

Ricardo could remember the whole accident in meticulous detail, even though the actual collision had happened so quickly. The other cars had come round the corner with no knowledge of what had happened, and had ploughed into the burning wreckage. Most of the drivers got out, but there was one, Yves Courtauld, a Brazilian, who couldn't. He was trapped, and the crowd had watched in stunned silence as the flames advanced on his car.

Then Ricardo had seen the Shadow sweep round the bend. He had thought Wyatt would pull over, but he had carried on, determined to win. It was a cold-blooded, ruthless decision.

Hoexter had pulled over. He'd been out of his car in a second, and without waiting to consider the consequences of his actions, he had sprinted into the flames engulfing the Brazilian's car and with great difficulty pulled the man out.

271

Ricardo didn't want to see any more. He turned away, disappearing into the crowd, already late for his next appointment.

Vanessa clutched at the Armco as Sean kept filming. She felt sick. Why hadn't Wyatt stopped? They'd actually caught him on videotape glancing at the accident, then powering his car on past it with a roar.

Her campaign was gathering momentum like an avalanche rolling down a snow-covered mountain. The tobacco companies, especially Jack Phelps Co., were putting pressure on the network to drop the story, but the owner of her station, Jay Levy, knew that the world reaction against smoking was growing, and that the audience figures for Vanessa's show had rocketed higher than ever before. In his own words, she was media dynamite.

Vanessa breathed in deeply and then Sean started filming her, the flames in the background.

'Is this a war zone?' Vanessa began. 'Four people are dead and twenty-one injured. No, this is Formula One racing. And with one lap to go, the race isn't going to be stopped. Everyone agrees that Monaco is a potentially dangerous circuit, but no one in Formula One is prepared to take any action because the sponsors know that Monaco grabs the public imagination, grabs the public attention. The glamour is here. So this footage will no doubt notch up cigarette sales for those conscience-free entrepreneurs out there, but the question must be asked: Can we really support this? Should the cigarette companies be allowed to keep on sponsoring this carnage? This is Vanessa Tyson, live from Monaco.'

Sean gestured for Vanessa to relax, and she turned, gripped the Armco and leaned over the tarmac, sobbing.

What the hell was she doing? she asked herself. She should have gone for Wyatt. She should have exploited the fact that he hadn't stopped.

Wyatt powered across the finishing-line in first place, and there was a roar of applause. The crowd cheered as he took

the stand and showered them with champagne, the second-
and third-placed drivers at his side.

Then he stepped down, victory ringing hollow in his ears.

In the main operating theatre of the Monaco hospital, Dr Ian
Tremaine looked up at the clock and saw that it was seven in
the evening. He did not want to remember the Monaco Grand
Prix; all he could think about was the operating-table, and the
racing-driver, Yves Courtauld, who lay on it.

This had been the most difficult operation of his career. For
over four hours he and his team had laboured over the patient
attempting the impossible. Now Yves Courtauld hovered
between life and death, his spine broken between the seventh
and eighth vertebrae.

With Tremaine were two other doctors, an American anaes-
thetist, and one young, but extremely talented Scottish surgeon.

Tremaine leaned over Courtauld's body once more. Before
he began again, he muttered a silent prayer.

In Vanessa Tyson's hotel room the phone started ringing, and
reluctantly she picked it up. It was Jay Levy, the owner of
WWTN.

'Vanessa baby, it's three hours after the accident, what are
you doing?'

'I'm lying down.'

'But you said you were going to get hold of Chase.'

'Don't tell me what to do!'

'Hey, cool it, babe. Remember you're the one who's usually
pushing me. I've taken huge risks on this one – Phelps could
sue me and try to close us down. You've got a great story,
everything you wanted's been handed to you on a plate. Now
what's the problem?'

'All right, Jay. Relax. It just wasn't very pleasant watching
it all happen.'

'So? You're going to stop it from happening again. That's a
very laudable thing you're doing.'

'Oh Jesus, Jay, it's not that simple.'

'It's Chase. Is that true, that rumour you were seen leaving
his hotel room late one night in Rio? Are you lovers?'

273

'No, damn it!'

'Then get off your butt and get me some footage.'

Vanessa slammed down the phone, then got up off the bed and made for the door.

The men got up when they saw her, and she raised her hand. Sean O'Connor, her cameraman and editor, who'd worked for her for years, stared at her aghast.

'Vanessa? What's goin' on? This story of Chase going past the accident is the big story you've been looking for. It proves everything you've said against Formula One.'

She gestured for him to follow her, and the two of them walked out of the conference room WWTN had hired at the hotel for the Grand Prix weekend, and stood in the corridor. The other members of the crew knew better than to get involved; Vanessa and Sean were famous for their stand-up fights.

She turned to face Sean, her features set. 'I'm going to soften Chase up first,' she said. 'He'll be expecting me to corner him – and I want to catch him with his defences down.'

'Nail the bastard, he's a cold-blooded murderer! That footage of him staring at the accident and then accelerating away says it all.' Sean folded his big brawny arms. 'So, how are we going to play this?'

'You go to the hospital, get an interview with Hoexter. I'll soften Chase up on my own, and then you can join me later and really catch him off-guard.'

Sean gave a satisfied smile and lumbered back into the conference room.

Outside the hotel, Vanessa caught a taxi. The streets were jam-packed with people, taxis and cars, but the usual after-the-race hysteria was strangely absent. The accident had affected everyone in Monaco.

As the taxi made its way up towards Wyatt's hotel, she tried to think about how she'd question him. She ignored the many beautiful old buildings she passed, thinking only of what she'd got into. There'd been her so-called suicide attempt, then Max Senda had been murdered. There was something going on behind the scenes that she didn't understand . . . And she realised that there was more to Formula One racing than she'd ever imagined.

She was at the hotel before she realised it. She made short work of the guard Bruce de Villiers had placed on Wyatt's floor, who immediately took a fancy to her, and then moved quickly down the passage and tried the door to Wyatt's room.

He was naked, sitting on the floor with his legs crossed, reading a book. She caught a glimpse of his latticed stomach muscles, aware for the first time of the power of his body.

As Vanessa came in, he looked up, annoyed. He stood up and pulled a towel round himself.

'So,' he said. 'You've got what you wanted.'

She sat on the edge of his bed. 'No, Wyatt.'

'You'll interview me and I'll lose my cool. Your viewers will pass judgement on my actions, and . . .'

She broke into sudden desperate tears. 'You bastard, you complete bastard! Yes, I've got the footage and the story, but I can't do it . . .' She knelt down next to him. 'I can't do it because I'm in love with you.'

Sean didn't feel good about what he'd done, but Jay Levy had spoken to him over the phone and told him in no uncertain terms what he'd wanted. So Sean had broken into Vanessa's room and taken the videotape of Wyatt driving past the accident.

Later that evening, Sean confronted Dr Ian Tremaine as he left the hospital.

Tremaine's face was drawn. 'In spite of our best efforts,' he said, 'the operation has not been a total success. Courtauld is alive, but is paralysed from the waist down.'

Sean gestured to the crew to keep filming. 'Do you think the safety measures at the track were inadequate, Dr Tremaine?'

He looked at Sean a moment, and then replied, 'I think your question is most inappropriate at this time.'

Sean smiled pleasantly. 'And what do you think of Wyatt Chase's behaviour?'

'In my opinion, the man's little better than a cold-blooded murderer. His victory is a shallow one.'

Two hours later Sean edited the footage, using Vanessa's commentary from the race, then the interview with Dr Tremaine – and capitalising on the grim expression on Dr Tremaine's face. As the doctor pronounced his opinion that Wyatt was a cold-blooded murderer, Sean cut to the footage of Wyatt driving towards the accident, staring at it momentarily and then accelerating away. It was the most damning piece of reportage yet produced by WWTN on Formula One. And it looked as though it had been edited and co-ordinated by Vanessa Tyson.

A day later, a meeting was called between the Formula One Constructors' Association and La Fédération Internationale du Sporte Automobile. Although the meeting was deliberately kept secret, the press and television networks had been told to stand by at another venue for a press announcement concerning the Monaco Grand Prix.

Ronnie Halliday looked particularly concerned as he went into the conference room with some of the senior members of his association, and Alain Hugo also entered the room grim-faced.

The press headlines had been devastating, and the blame for the accident, most of the papers said, lay with the men who controlled Formula One. It was they who had let the Grand Prix be staged on a dangerous circuit, and clearly, they argued, Monaco should be scratched from the Grand Prix calendar.

The meeting lasted two hours, Halliday and Hugo leaving the room together and taking a car to the waiting press conference. It was Ronnie Halliday who made the announcement.

'As you know, both Alain Hugo and I have campaigned tirelessly for safer circuits and safer machines. The decision against turbo-charging was the result of our wish to make the sport more competitive but less dangerous.

'I am very upset, as we all are, by what happened here at Monaco. I cannot blame the circuit, because what happened here could have happened almost anywhere: you cannot stop drivers colliding with each other, that is an inevitable risk of the sport. However, we can move the crowds further back from the bends, and this we will do.

'We should like to take this opportunity to praise Helmut Hoexter for his act of bravery – for saving the life of Yves Courtauld.'

There was applause at this point, but Halliday and Hugo remained grim-faced. There was clearly more to come.

'As far as Wyatt Chase is concerned . . . we prefer to keep our views to ourselves. But concerning his team, Calibre-Shensu, we regret that we have to make two announcements.'

The reporters went very quiet. What could Halliday be going to say?

'First, we will not on any condition allow Ricardo Sartori to race again this year. There have now been two accidents this season, and we don't need any more. Sartori will be allowed to race again in the 1992 season.

'Secondly, the Calibre-Shensu Shadow, on examination, fails to meet the basic requirements of FISA. Until the car is modified to meet these requirements, she will not be allowed to race. In fairness, however, this decision will not affect the points won by the team in the first two races of the season.

'The next Grand Prix will take place in Belgium in two weeks' time, as scheduled.'

Halliday walked away from the podium with evident relief.

Ricardo was well satisfied. His first deal had been concluded without any real difficulty. The two Frenchmen he had negotiated with were clearly men of influence, and had not haggled over the price as Phelps had warned they might. The percentages were agreed without argument.

Not for the first time, Ricardo wondered why Phelps had employed him at all. He guessed it must be because of his international fame – wherever he went, he was recognised as a personality, and he knew that people liked to talk and be associated with him.

Phelps had explained his cash-flow problems and his tax problems – and Ricardo was pleased to learn that he was not the only one in financial difficulties. His task, Phelps had explained, was to handle the sale of large quantities of raw tobacco that Phelps had stockpiled.

Payments were made through a numbered Swiss bank account that was set up in Ricardo's own name. This did not concern him, especially as he received a straight one-per-cent commission on all monies 'laundered' through this account. From the Swiss account the money was transferred into other slush accounts. And the end result was that Phelps was getting large sums that did not have to be reflected on his balance-sheet, that were not taxable and that could be used for the acquisition and salvage of companies.

Ricardo knew that if his work continued to be as profitable as Phelps had promised, he would never have to race again. True, Phelps had a loaded gun at his head, threatening to release the video on Ricardo's past – but then Phelps had also not tried to underpay him.

Ricardo packed up his bags in the Monaco hotel room. For him it had been a most profitable Grand Prix.

Bruce de Villiers stood looking at the wall of his hotel room. He had been a fool, a complete fool in thinking he could take on both FISA and FOCA by enlisting the support of the media. He had misread Ronnie Halliday. And he couldn't blame the man at all – after all, he had been warned to watch it.

The only solution was to get back to Calibre-Shensu's headquarters in England and start reworking the design on the Cray Supercomputer. They would never make the Belgium Grand Prix, he knew that, but if they worked hard perhaps they would be able to go back onto the circuit for the German Grand Prix.

As she stood, the Shadow was the most competitive car on the circuit. A redesign might reduce that competitiveness dramatically.

There was a knock on the door, and when Bruce went to open it he found Mickey Dunstal, looking in much the same mood as himself.

'What a bunch o' bastards! I'm thinking about the redesign

already. I'll have to meet with the technical lads and get down to the bottom of it.'

'Mickey, it was because we tried to push them. We asked for it. I told you I was worried, but you and Phelps didn't seem concerned.'

The Irishman went over to the bar fridge and poured himself a generous Scotch, which he knocked back in one.

'They'll be asking for major changes,' he said bluntly. 'The car is radically different from any of the others on the circuit. There will have been complaints from the other constructors.'

Bruce walked across to the window and looked out over the harbour.

'I didn't like the comment Ronnie made about Wyatt. The press are saying Wyatt's a ruthless bastard. Perhaps if he doesn't drive in Belgium, it'll be forgotten about.'

''Twas a callous thing he did.'

Bruce went red. 'So would you have preferred us to lose? I know what he did and I agree with it!'

'Even if Courtauld dies?'

'Hoexter stopped.'

'And what if he hadn't?'

It was at that point that Wyatt walked into the room. He knew exactly what they'd been discussing, and spoke his mind.

'If Hoexter hadn't stopped and saved him, Courtauld would have died. But let me tell you, if I'd been Courtauld I wouldn't have expected Hoexter to stop. I'd have wanted him to win.'

Mickey stared into Wyatt's dark, restless eyes and was scared by the man inside. 'I'm not a driver,' he muttered, 'so I'm not saying anything more.'

'All right,' Wyatt said. 'Now let's forget about Monaco and me. What about the Shadow?'

'If we catch a flight this evening we can get down to work tomorrow with the basic design. It's all on the computer, so I can start working the moment we get all the details.'

At Mickey's words, Bruce felt the fight coming back into him. He had two Grand Prix wins under his belt, and it was a better start than anyone else had. And missing one race wasn't going to affect Wyatt's chances that badly. The man was a total professional.

He'd better get on the phone to Aito Shensu and tell him their plan of action. He wasn't going to get much sleep for the next month, that was for sure.

Phelps watched the TV sports report, completely dumbfounded. It was the one thing he had not calculated into his elaborately worked equation. Ricardo had been a big enough blow, but this was a total disaster. They *had* to race in Belgium, that was all there was to it.

As for Wyatt Chase, he just hoped that the negative publicity about his behaviour would die down fast.

Bruce was furious. He slammed the phone down. Who the fuck did Jack Phelps think he was? The ultimatum was quite clear – either they fielded a car in Belgium or he was withdrawing his sponsorship. And he wanted a second driver. He was very, very unhappy about the negative publicity surrounding Wyatt.

When Vanessa got back to her hotel, Sean was waiting for her in the foyer.

'I don't think Wyatt Chase is going to be talking to you again,' he said.

'Rubbish, Sean. Give me a couple of days.'

He held up a VHS recording-tape. 'Actions speak louder than words, Vanessa. So let's watch the action.'

They went up to her room and Sean slipped the tape into the portable video-recorder and TV screen that she always had with her. She watched the footage that Sean had edited together. She could hardly bear to watch Wyatt driving callously past the accident, and she noted that Sean had edited in some screams above the noise of the Formula One engines, to dramatise the whole scene.

'How could you do that?' she cried.

'Jay ordered me to. He said he couldn't trust you to do it. I'm sorry, Vanessa, but if I hadn't, he'd have fired me.'

She held her face in her hands. Wyatt would never speak to her again.

*

280

Jack Phelps gazed across the Paris skyline and then at the drink in his hand. Was his hand shaking? It wasn't – and this gave him a measure of reassurance.

Things were not going well. The negative publicity surrounding Suzie's disappearance hadn't helped the Calibre-Shensu image, and that had been on top of Ricardo's suspension; now there was the disqualification of the Shadow.

He remembered the argument he, Aito and Mickey had had with de Villiers. Perhaps they should have listened to de Villiers after all – he'd said they'd be pushing their luck, flouting the regulations so brazenly. At the time they'd all felt very confident, but now, with the tide of events turning against them, de Villiers' stand seemed justified. The man hadn't just been difficult for the sake of it.

And, Phelps decided, he'd totally underestimated Vanessa Tyson. The growing popularity of her investigation into Formula One was disturbing. Particularly worrying were her scathing attacks on cigarette companies like his, who sponsored individual teams for publicity purposes.

He switched on the video-recorder recessed in the wall, and watched the giant screen above it. A series of anti-smoking commercials rolled on. They made it clear that his game-plan of the last decade had been correct: it was only a matter of time before the cigarette business was subjected to heavier and heavier attacks from the media. The bans on conventional advertising meant he couldn't threaten the newspapers and TV networks with the withdrawal of his advertising spend if they broadcast anti-smoking commercials.

He picked up a glossy picture of Vanessa Tyson from his desk top and crumpled it in his fist. 'My dear, you are about to become history.'

Aito had been deeply disturbed by Phelps's late-night call. He agreed that missing the Belgium Grand Prix could be disastrous to their whole programme, and he also felt guilty about siding with the others against Bruce de Villiers in pushing to keep the more radical elements of the Shensu design.

The next morning saw him jetting into Heathrow in a chartered Boeing 747. With him was the entire Shensu design team. He didn't care what the board said to him, he was going to have the Shadow ready to compete in Belgium.

His dream was that Wyatt Chase should become world champion in the Shensu Shadow. But he also, like Bruce, wanted the constructor's trophy. Next to him sat a young Japanese with an expressionless face. Just over five feet tall, Charlie Ibuka was a national hero in Japan; the previous year he had won the Japanese Formula Two championship in his début season – a unique achievement. No one could argue, Aito thought, that Ibuka wasn't good enough.

Aito's greatest gift was to simplify seemingly complex problems and come up with immediate solutions – it was this ability that had enabled him to build Shensu into one of the most powerful motor manufacturers in Japan. Now he applied this gift to the current problem with his Formula One team. Appointing Charlie Ibuka as Calibre-Shensu's number two driver was his first move. He knew that Ibuka would be totally committed, and that was what the team needed. What Jack Phelps had told him over the phone made sense – they had to have a second driver. So now it was just a question of redesigning tne Shadow to fit in with the official regulations.

Aito was certain that, backed by the entire Shensu design team, Mickey Dunstal and Professor Katana could sort the problem out.

He glanced down at his watch. It was just after eight in the morning. Bruce de Villiers would be at the airport to collect him in person. There was not a moment to be wasted.

The plane touched down smoothly, and ten minutes later the door at the side of the cockpit opened, and the wind and pouring rain swept inside. Aito shivered, then hurried quickly down the gangway and across the tarmac towards the customs area.

He was through in a matter of seconds. The British Minister of Trade had made special arrangements – the head of the large Japanese consortium who was investing vast amounts of money in the United Kingdom was to be given top priority.

Aito hurried through to the reception area, closely followed by his team. He was pleased to see that Bruce de Villiers was waiting for him. However he had not reckoned with the huge entourage of reporters ganged up behind him.

The questions started as he shook hands with Bruce. 'Mr Shensu, is it true that you're thinking of withdrawing your sponsorship?'

Aito flashed a smile to the cameras. 'I would never let my team down. I have come here to assist in the redesign of the Shadow. We will be competing in Belgium with Wyatt Chase and Charlie Ibuka.'

He saw de Villiers squirm at this, and wished he could have told de Villiers in private about Charlie Ibuka, but there hadn't been time. He wanted to put an end to the negative publicity; Shensu's image was of paramount importance.

'Do you think the disqualification of your car is a reaction to the invasion of the American and European markets by Japanese technology?'

'Not at all. I think it's perfectly normal. At Shensu we play by the rules. That is why we are here to redesign the Shadow. I accept FISA's decision.'

'Are you disturbed by Wyatt Chase's callous behaviour at Monaco? Do you think he should have stopped?'

'I must support Chase's decision,' Aito replied with a frown on his face.

'Will you be talking to the Minister of Trade about further investment in this country?'

Aito smiled again. 'We have already had lengthy talks. My investment in your country has been approved. A new factory will be opened next year.'

Don Morrison sprinted across the arrivals hall and slid to a halt in front of the reporters. Bruce de Villiers glowered at him for his lack of punctuality. A hasty discussion ensued between Don, Aito and Bruce, and eventually Don turned to face the cameras.

'Thank you for being here to greet Aito Shensu,' Don said smoothly. 'There will be an official press briefing tomorrow at Calibre-Shensu headquarters.'

He guided Aito into Bruce's car, and the rest of the Shensu team bundled into the Shensu luxury bus parked behind it.

Inside the comfortable confines of Bruce's Aston-Martin,

Aito braced himself for the attack that he knew was coming. Bruce was red-faced and angry.

'What's this about Ibuka? Why wasn't I bloody consulted? You and Phelps had no fucking right to make that decision. Just like the time you didn't fucking listen when I said we were coasting a thin line with FISA on the design of the Shadow!'

'Bruce, please relax. Jack told me that you haven't been looking for a second driver.'

Bruce breathed in deeply. He was far too emotional about the whole business.

'All right, Aito, that's true. I've been more concerned about FISA's ruling on the Shadow.'

'You must realise that, for me, it is not the money in this venture that is my big concern. I want to build an image for Shensu.' His voice became tighter. 'The image of the team so far is not at all what I had desired. Wyatt's behaviour at Monaco might have won us the race, but it's done nothing for our image. And we have to have two drivers competing to win the constructor's trophy.'

Bruce was still trying to decide how he felt about Wyatt's behaviour at Monaco. At the time he'd been overcome with joy at a second victory, but having seen the video footage of the accident and Wyatt driving past it, he'd had his doubts. But he'd kept those doubts to himself.

'Wyatt has been our saving grace,' he said now. 'Ibuka's an unknown. For all I know, he could be right at the back for the whole season.'

'That's why he must drive in Belgium. The Shadow has to be ready. Then we'll know how competitive he is.'

'Doesn't my opinion count any longer?'

Aito was silent. He waited for Bruce to calm down before he spoke again.

'I want to win. Winning is the only way I know to live. That is why I didn't listen to you when you said we were risking it with FISA by pushing the design of the car too far.'

Bruce looked across at Aito, then back at the road. He didn't say anything for a while.

'Look, Aito,' he began at last, 'there are still a lot of

problems facing us. We've had some bad luck – and there's still no news of Suzie. You know that she and Wyatt were close?'

'No, I didn't know. Who's looking for her? What action has been taken?'

Bruce felt guilty. Since Monaco, he'd hardly given Suzie a thought – there had been just too much on his mind.

'To tell you the truth, in the last few days I haven't been able to contact the Brazilian police to see if there have been any developments. Wyatt is furious. He thinks they're covering something up. I mean, with the reward money he and Jack have put up, something should have come to light.'

'These things concern me. It is as if Calibre-Shensu is, as you would say, jinxed.'

Bruce stared out of the window at the cars on the motorway. 'I'm not a superstitious man myself – there has to be an explanation.'

Aito pulled a folder from his briefcase.

'I know your concerns about Ibuka. But I'd like you to study this.'

Bruce looked across at the document. 'You've just got to accept the guy's going to be on a learning curve,' he said. 'It's almost unheard-of for a driver to perform well in his first season.'

'You voiced the same concerns over Wyatt.'

Bruce thought about what he'd heard of Ibuka. The man certainly was determined. Maybe, just maybe, he was the right one for the job. Right now, he didn't have an awful lot of choice.

Wyatt sat behind Mickey Dunstal, watching the Irishman punch information into the Cray Supercomputer at a daunting rate. With every new command, subtle revisions to the Shadow design appeared on the screen. On the table next to them was FISA's document identifying the areas where the Shadow was out of line with the complex regulations.

'The problem is one of mental attitude, Wyatt. I can't let the fockers get to me. If Shadow Two is better than Shadow

One, you'll find the other teams will stop trying to criticise the design.'

Mickey was quiet for a long time. Then he started tapping the computer keys again.

As he worked, he was thinking about Wyatt. How could Wyatt have driven past the accident? It disturbed him. He admired Hoexter for pulling off – but then Wyatt had won the race. Perhaps FISA's disqualification of the Shadow had more to do with Wyatt's behaviour than the actual design.

After forty-five minutes he sat back.

'That's it. With the team Aito's brought in today, we'll get the modifications done. Quite quickly, too – but it'll cost a bloody fortune. And it'll be a better car.'

Wyatt studied the revised design. He was impressed by how simply Mickey seemed to have solved the problems. Now it was just a question of rebuilding the Shadow.

He had no real regrets about his behaviour at Monaco. He wouldn't have expected the lead driver to pull over for him. You had to accept the fact that you might die; that was the price you paid when you sought victory.

Wyatt had been training hard since Monaco, breaking pain-barriers as he pushed his body to the peak of physical fitness. However, the real pain came from within, from worrying about what had happened to Suzie. He sensed she was still alive – but where was she?

Manuel sat in the rickety wooden hut, shaking. It was over thirty-five degrees centigrade outside, and the humidity was intense. There was mould on the inside of the hut, on the chair he sat in and on his bed. The black-and-white television set buzzed angrily in the corner like a trapped bee. He glanced nervously at the flickering images on the screen and pulled his leather jacket a little tighter around him. Why did he feel so cold when it was so hot?

The advert had just appeared again – a flash of images of the woman, and then the offer of a fortune for a clue as to what had happened to her.

He knew.

The hut was one of many in a big clearing – a new, hastily

built township for the men who were building the motorway that would eventually cut across the greenness of the Amazon basin like a thin silver line. The men who worked on the road were unskilled labourers. When the job was finished, they would be unemployed again. They made good money, but they had little to spend it on because they were working in the middle of nowhere. So they spent their spare time watching television.

Manuel had heard them joking about the woman, Suzie von Falkenhyn, as they came home from working on the road in the evening. The jokes were about what they would like to do to her if they found her. But of course, if they did find her, or a clue as to where she was, they would be onto the police immediately, anxious to collect the reward.

There was a knock on the door. Manuel shivered again and then moved slowly forward to open it.

'Isabel.'

He recognised the woman and gave her an angry look. She had a dissipated look about her, with her long, greasy, black hair and heavily rouged face. She spoke in slurred Portuguese.

'You want to fuck? I can make you very happy.'

He moved to close the door but she barged in, stronger than he had realised.

'Don't you need a woman?' She stared at him incredulously, hiking up her skirt slightly.

'I have no money!' he screamed at her.

She laughed without mirth and then coughed for a long time, tears running from her eyes.

'I heard you did a big job,' she said, 'but then I should have known it was all crap.'

'I have spent all the money.'

'Oh yes, Mister Big. You told me you had so much.'

Manuel thought about how he'd gambled the money away – enough to have lasted him for a year. But there was always the possibility of more. He had information, priceless information.

'I can be a millionaire overnight.'

'How?'

'I know where the woman is, the one the police are looking for.'

Isabel spat in his face and laughed. 'Mister Big. You're all talk.'

She let herself out before he could strike her, and the door slammed in his face.

He lay in the chair for a long time, angry. His sister, Julia, had written him a letter. She had always had a big mouth. And there was no television where she worked, so she kept writing to him. Apparently the letters were smuggled out through one of the pilots. She told him about her fantastic new job, about the factory on a mountain in the Amazon basin and about this beautiful German woman the owner had as his concubine. She said the woman was a prisoner and that her boss had pumped her full of drugs.

Yes, when he had seen the ad on the television, he had looked again at the letter. He had sent a note back to Julia, asking her for a map of how to get to where she was working, and to find out if the woman's name was Suzie von Falkenhyn.

The reply had come two weeks later, and he knew that soon he would be a wealthy man.

Isabel spat into the bin at the side of the room, then looked apprehensively at Raoul, the large, fat man behind the desk. Along the wall was a couch on which sat two other women of similar appearance to herself.

'I do not believe you,' Raoul growled. 'Manuel must have money. He was away for over a week. He must think you are ugly. I will send another girl.'

Isabel looked at the other girls, seated on the couch. They looked better than she did – but then they did not have to look for work, the men came to them. She was scared. She did not want to be beaten, or worse, be kicked out and lose Raoul's protection.

'Why do you not believe me, Raoul?'

'Because you're a whore, Isabel, and all whores are liars.'

The other girls laughed nervously and he cut them a glance that shut them up, then looked again at Isabel.

288

'You can try again this evening . . . Maybe Manuel will be drunk enough to want to fuck you by then.'

He looked up at the television mounted on a shelf on the wall. It was the entertainment he provided for his women before they went out to work in the evening. Today was Friday – pay-day – and the men who worked on the road got paid in cash. The trick was to wait till they'd had a couple of drinks and then move in with his girls. They could turn a trick every fifteen minutes – if they were working properly.

Isabel knew she hadn't long to go. She'd lost her looks and even the most drunken of the men sometimes refused to sleep with her.

'It's her!' she cried out, suddenly pointing to the television screen. Then she was silent just as quickly. Raoul looked at the flickering images, saw the woman's picture and the reward. His attention was immediately caught.

'What do you mean, Isabel?'

Now she trembled. 'It's the woman they want the ransom for,' she answered a little too quickly.

'I know that, bitch, but why did you say "it's her"?' Raoul's voice was like a snake, slivering and worming its way towards its target.

He rose, and grabbing her by the hair, dragged her screaming out into the next room. Then he laid her across the dirty bed and took a rubber fan-belt that was hanging off a nail in the wall. She screamed, remembering the pain from the last time. He would not stop until he knew the truth.

He brought the fan-belt down heavily across her back.

'The woman they're offering the reward for – Manuel says he knows where she is,' she screamed out.

Manuel got back after dark. It had not been easy to score – he was not as well-known in the north. However, after a few phone calls everything had been sorted out, and now he had crack to sell.

Something about the hut aroused his suspicions. He was sure he hadn't left the outside window open. But then again, perhaps he was imagining things.

He stuffed the plastic packet deep into his jacket pocket.

He had grown up learning not to take chances, and nothing had changed. He pulled out the hunting-knife he always carried with him and proceeded cautiously towards the hut. It was so dark he could hardly see the front door.

A shot burst out as he moved towards it – he dived, but the bullet creased him on the shoulder. He rolled over to the side and waited patiently, like a cat.

A torch was shone in his face and another blow caught him unawares, so that he dropped the knife. The lights of a car came on and he saw Isabel standing next to a fat man.

'Is that him?' the fat man asked.

'Yes, Raoul,' Isabel trembled.

Manuel felt his arm being jerked further up behind his back. Raoul stepped forward and put his cigarette out in Manuel's face. His cry of pain tore through the darkness.

'Manuel, what's this you tell Isabel about knowing where the German woman, Suzie von Falkenhyn, is being held?' Raoul asked coldly.

'I know nothing,' Manuel groaned.

'Then my men will give you something to know about, eh?'

He was dragged to the rear of the car. He struggled to get away, but his captors kicked him in the knee-caps, then pulled him down so that his face was beside the exhaust-pipe.

'Talk,' Raoul said quietly.

Manuel's face was pushed against the hot metal, and there was the smell of burning flesh. But Manuel gritted his teeth and remained silent. He wanted the reward money for himself. He had been stupid to boast to Isabel.

'Ah, Manuel, you must know something. And yes, you are very scared to tell us. I think we must move to the front of the car.'

One of the men opened the bonnet and Manuel stared at the running engine, wondering what they would do. Then one of the men grabbed his arm and forced his hand into the cooling-fan.

'No! No! I'll tell you, please . . . She is in the jungle, held by the Ortega Cartel. My sister works at their secret factory. I have a map . . .'

'Ah, this is good, I will collect the reward money . . .'

'But if they find out, the Ortega Cartel will kill us.'
'No, you are wrong, my friend. They will kill you.'

Bruce rested his hand on Wyatt's shoulder. They were watching Mickey explaining a detail of his new plan to the Japanese design team from Shensu. Tall, forceful and wild, Mickey was a complete contrast to the pliant Japanese designers who surrounded him, noting his every move and gesture.

'He reckons he can have the new Shadow on the track in four days,' Wyatt said, 'and then have it air-lifted out to Belgium in time for the first practice.'

Bruce stared down at Wyatt. He knew Wyatt was angry at the press reaction to his behaviour at Monaco, but he was more worried by his reaction to Suzie's disappearance. He would have to have a private chat with him.

Bruce was now greedy for more championship points. And with Charlie Ibuka in the second car, they were suddenly looking very competitive again. Provided, of course, that FISA accepted the modifications.

Phelps had been driving Bruce particularly hard – the threat of his withdrawal was a real one. Bruce knew that if he didn't have a car on the track in Belgium, Phelps would cut him out of the team. He didn't want to think about that possibility.

'I'll send Reg over in advance with the rest of the pit crew,' he said now. 'You'll go with them, Wyatt, and the moment the Shadow Two arrives, you can start testing. But it'll be a very different car from the one you're used to.'

Wyatt listened, but Mickey had told him the machine would not feel different – that the basic design of the Shadow would stay the same, it would just sit a little lower on the tarmac and have slightly altered handling characteristics.

Aito Shensu came into the design centre, looking remarkably relaxed considering the circumstances. He went over to Mickey, whispered something in his ear and shook his hand warmly. Then he walked over to Wyatt and Bruce.

'Great news. We start full production of the Shensu Ninja tomorrow. I anticipate launching it at the German Grand Prix. Can you imagine the impact?'

'I'd rather see how Wyatt does in Belgium before you plan

your launch. If we're still winning, then yes, I think it's a good idea,' Bruce replied cautiously. There was enough pressure on Wyatt already.

'I am not the only one to have such faith in Wyatt's ability – Jack has already set his publicity machine in motion.'

Wyatt could only admire Aito. At seventy he still flew by the seat of his pants. He was taking one hell of a risk, basing his faith entirely on their ability to win the Belgian Grand Prix.

'You will be the star of the commercials that Jack plans to shoot for the Ninja, Wyatt. It will be launched with a live road-test. Imagine it, the world's top performing Formula One driver gives his first impressions of Japan's finest sports machine.'

'And what if I don't like it?'

'That is my gamble. You must say exactly what you think.'

'Then that's fine with me.'

'We'll set up the shoot after Belgium. I have told them that it is not to take up much of your time.'

'It'd better not.' Bruce was anxious that Wyatt should be given ample time to relax after the race.

Mickey came over, having finished his discussion with the Shensu design team.

'Aito,' he said directly, 'it is going to cost a lot of money, to be sure. But it'll be worth it. Your lads know what they're doing.'

'The money is unimportant. Just concentrate on doing your best, that's all I want.'

The lights burned continuously at the Calibre-Shensu head-quarters. The Japanese design team worked alongside the factory mechanics, rebuilding the chassis and fine-tuning the modifications.

After midnight, Mickey took a break and strolled round the offices. He found Wyatt hunched over the phone in his office, his face taut, his fists clenched. Mickey waited till the conversation was over, and Wyatt put down the phone. He saw the bags under Wyatt's eyes – and the look of total exhaustion and despair on his face.

'What's wrong?'

'Still no trace of Suzie. How the hell can someone just disappear?'

Mickey sat down and stared across at Wyatt. He wouldn't like to get on the wrong side of him, he decided; there was something very ruthless in his dark eyes.

'I pray to God you find Suzie,' he said quietly.

Wyatt clenched and unclenched his fists. If someone had taken her, if someone had hurt her, he wouldn't rest till he got them.

Jules Ortega felt Suzie's hand dig into his arm. She was lying on the bed, a gag through her mouth to muffle the screams. He knew she was going through hell and he thought she deserved it. She was an addict, and that made her his slave.

He glanced out over the rain-forest. Already the first rays of sunlight were beginning to appear, and thin pockets of mist drifted across the green horizon. He studied the mangled fingers on his right hand – all he could think of was revenge.

They had been stupid to deal with Talbot. Why had they allowed the American to control them? It was the Ortega Cartel who ran the drugs business, not the suppliers. His brother was running scared now he'd changed his identity, but Jules wasn't going to stand for it any more. He would kill Talbot.

Wyatt put the phone down, his hand shaking. He glanced across at the clock by his bedside. It was just after midnight. The call had come unexpectedly – a long-distance call from the Brazilian police. A man called Raoul had contacted them and said he could give them information that would lead them to Suzie.

Wyatt knew there was no way he could deal with this alone, but he knew someone who could help him – someone he trusted more than anyone else in the world. Suzie's life depended on it.

He dialled the number in Argentina. It rang for a long time and then was answered by a servant. Wyatt thought of the estancia, of the polo field and the mountains in the distance. What was he doing here in London?

'Is Carlos on the ranch?'

'*Si*, I call him for you.'

He waited patiently, hearing the faint calling and then the noise of feet across the floorboards.

'Wyatt. You are all right after Monaco? The press were unkind . . .'

He felt a surge of relief on hearing Carlos's voice.

'Yes,' he said. 'I will race in Belgium.'

There was a long pause.

'Estelle is concerned about you,' Carlos said at last.

'You know how it is between us,' Wyatt replied quietly.

'I know.'

Another long pause. 'Carlos,' Wyatt said. 'I need you to help me, but it might be dangerous. The Brazilian police have a lead on Suzie, a man called Raoul. You must make contact with him, find out what he wants and then get the money to him.'

'Don't worry, Wyatt,' Carlos's strong, reassuring voice came down the phone. 'I will handle this.'

Raoul put down the phone. He had spoken with Wyatt Chase, the man who had put up the reward money, and Chase had said he would send his stepfather, one Carlos Ramirez, to meet Raoul with the money. Ramirez would give him the money in exchange for information that would lead them to Suzie von Falkenhyn. Chase had emphasised that the information had to be good.

Raoul knew now that Manuel had been telling the truth. Manuel was barely alive, but he had talked.

Raoul understood why Manuel had been terrified to talk. This cocaine factory hidden in the bowels of the Amazon basin sounded incredible. And it was in this secret factory that Suzie von Falkenhyn was being held, supposedly for the pleasure of Jules Ortega.

Raoul lay back on the bedstead and stared at the discoloured ceiling. By late that afternoon he would be a millionaire. He would kill Manuel, then he would move on to another country. He wanted to be away from this hotel, the brothel and the town. Every minute was dangerous here. If the Ortega Cartel knew what Manuel had told him, they would have both of them killed.

It was just before midday when a helicopter buzzed noisily over the roof of the hotel. Raoul sank back behind the curtains. It must be Carlos Ramirez. It had to be – he didn't want to wait any longer. Thank God! He would supply Ramirez with a map showing the location of the factory where Suzie von Falkenhyn was held, then he would take the money, kill Manuel and run.

He moved back to the bed and pulled out the Uzi carbine, then let himself out of the window and onto the fire-escape.

Five minutes later there was a knock on his door.

'Who is it?' he shouted from outside the window, the Uzi lined up on the door, his finger stroking the trigger.

'A Mr Ramirez to see you,' said a voice from behind the door.

'Tell him to come up here.'

He was sweating now. He must be very careful not to give too much away. He wanted his million dollars.

There was another knock on the door.

'Come in,' Raoul shouted, and moved to the side of the window, out of view.

A man came into the room. He was over six feet tall, blond, and wearing an airforce jumpsuit. In his right hand he carried an attaché case.

'Put down the case or you die,' Raoul said softly.

The man walked forward and dropped the case on the bed.

'Who are you?' Raoul asked.

'Talbot. Rod Talbot.'

Raoul laughed uneasily. 'You lie. You must be Carlos Ramirez.'

'No. But I have the same amount of money as Ramirez.'

Raoul moved into view. 'What do you mean?'

Talbot flicked open the catches on the case to reveal wads of money. 'The rest is in the chopper.'

'You pay me the money so I don't talk to Ramirez?'

'You get the drift good, buddy. I have my contacts in the police force, and they put me onto you.'

Raoul stepped carefully over the window-ledge and into the room. 'We go to the helicopter to get the rest of the money. You walk, I follow.'

Raoul looked closely at Talbot's back. The muscles were rock-hard on the neck beneath the crew-cut.

They moved out of the hotel and into a field behind it. The helicopter stood on the grass, empty and forbidding.

'Show me the money that buys my silence.'

Talbot reached inside and pulled out a couple of bulky holdalls. Raoul felt his pulse racing.

'Take out the money.'

Talbot reached inside one of the bags, pivoted – and a shot exploded from his side, taking Raoul in the hip. Raoul staggered back, but before he could fire Talbot deftly kicked the Uzi from his hands in one fluid, lightning movement. Raoul writhed in pain on the ground.

'Where is the person who told you where she is being held?' Talbot asked. When he got no answer, he knelt down next to Raoul and pressed his fingers into his wound.

'No! No!' Raoul screamed.

'Where is the person?'

'His name is Manuel, it was his sister Julia, who works in the cocaine factory, who told him. He's in the basement with my men. Please let me go – it was his idea to claim the reward, not mine.'

'Turn over.'

Talbot bound Raoul's hands and left him face-down in the grass, then walked back into the hotel. Minutes later, Raoul heard screams. After what seemed an eternity, Talbot dragged Manuel into view, blubbering like a child.

'Why you call him?' he sobbed at Raoul. 'He works for the Ortega Cartel. He kill us both.'

Raoul looked at the blond man in terror. 'Let me live, please! I will say nothing.'

'Shut up, cock-sucker. I had to fly a long way to get here, and you've really upset me. Now, Manuel, be a good man and sit on the edge of the hold.'

Manuel obediently sat on the edge of the chopper, his feet resting on the landing-frame, and Talbot hauled up Raoul and deposited him next to Manuel. Then he climbed into the cockpit and took off. High above the ground, he tilted the machine to one side so that the two of them were almost falling out. The road in front of the hotel lay one hundred metres below them. Manuel was shaking.

'Talk, my friend, or jump. Tell me if anyone else knows about where she is,' Talbot said quietly.

Manuel stared into Raoul's eyes and remained silent. The helicopter tilted over a little more.

Raoul vomited. Then he talked.

Talbot relaxed. 'You are a wise man, my friend. You're sure no one else knows about the location of the factory?'

Raoul nodded.

'Manuel?'

'No. Only Raoul, I tell no one else. I gave you the only map showing the location of the factory.'

Talbot felt the map in his side-pocket.

'Then you may both die in peace,' he said.

He banked the chopper, and Manuel and Raoul fell screaming towards the ground.

Carlos arrived in the little village late in the afternoon. There was an eerie chill about the place, and he had the uneasy feeling he was being watched.

He checked into the hotel and was about to phone Wyatt when something warned him against it. He walked down to reception and confronted the manager.

'I am looking for Raoul.'

The manager swallowed, then said quickly, 'Who?'

Carlos grabbed the register and spun it round before the manager could stop him. A guest had checked out that afternoon. Carlos looked at the room number, then pushed the register back across to the manager and ran up the stairs to the top floor. The door to room twenty-one burst open with one well-aimed kick from his boot.

The place was a mess. A suitcase lay in the centre of the

floor, half-packed, and the bed was unmade. The window was open, a slight breeze blowing in through the curtains.

Carlos closed the door and began to search. He examined every piece of clothing. There were no papers and no money. Clearly, someone had given the place a clean sweep.

At the bottom of the suitcase he found a couple of paperbacks and a child's atlas. He sat down on an upright chair by the window and stared round the room. There had to be something he could find, some tiny clue.

He searched through the man's possessions again. When he came to look at the atlas, it fell open at a map of the Amazon basin. There were some scribbles on it and a few arrows – and a circle round an area that lay on the borders of Brazil and Colombia.

What did it mean?

The Dorchester was living up to its reputation as one of London's – if not the world's – finest hotels. He was contemplating the Waterford whisky decanter when the phone rang.

'Mr Sartori? I'd appreciate it if you could spend a few minutes with me. Perhaps we could meet in the lobby?'

The smooth American voice was disturbing. 'Who are you?' Ricardo said.

'Let us say that I know you've been laundering drug money through certain Swiss banks and that you are now in serious trouble.'

Ricardo felt sick.

'Are we going to talk, Mr Sartori? Or would you prefer me to speak to the authorities?'

'Please . . .'

'Meet me in the coffee lounge in five minutes. I'll be reading a book with a pink cover.'

Ricardo put the phone down nervously. Should he ring Phelps? Drug money? Jesus, so that was why Phelps was paying him so much! Then Ricardo put two and two together, and a whole lot of things he hadn't been able to understand about the Calibre-Shensu deal suddenly fell into place. With a sick feeling in his stomach, he went down to the coffee lounge.

He saw a man reading a book with a pink cover, a tall, lean, blond man who looked as though he might be an actor.

'Mr Sartori, the name's Talbot . . .'

Coffee with Talbot did nothing to improve Ricardo's spirits. He was clearly in very serious trouble.

'So, Mr Sartori, by rights I should have you arrested.'

'But . . . but what about Jack Phelps?' Ricardo stuttered.

'Come off it, buddy. That's your story. There's no mention of Phelps in any of the dealings I've investigated – and Phelps is a powerful man with influential Washington connections. I'd say you'd be signing your death-warrant if you accused him of anything.'

Ricardo sipped nervously at his coffee. What a fool he'd been to get involved with Phelps! Now he was out of his depth.

'What do you want?' he said. 'Who are you?'

Talbot laughed. 'I'm with Interpol – we want to cut a deal with you.'

Ricardo suddenly felt a little more optimistic. 'A deal?'

'Yeah.' He smiled. 'You see, we know perfectly well Phelps is involved, but we can't get a handle on him. So, you co-operate with us, you help us nail Phelps, and . . .'

'And?'

'We'll take a lenient view on the fact that you've been laundering drug money.'

Talbot looked like a bigger James Dean, thought Ricardo, but there was an air of menace in his turquoise eyes that was disturbing. He wondered what Talbot meant by 'co-operate'.

'So, Ricardo, old friend, is it "yes" or "no"?' said Talbot, getting up to go.

'You give me no choice.'

'There's always a choice.'

'I co-operate with you.'

Talbot leaned a little closer. 'Look, we know Phelps has master-minded a huge cocaine-smuggling operation that's being mounted across Europe. We just want you to let us know what's going on.'

Ricardo looked a little nervous and Talbot slapped him across the back.

'Hey, relax! Phelps totally underestimates your abilities – he'd never dream you could two-time him. I know you can do it, though. Besides, I'll always be around for you to consult. Really, there's nothing to worry about. With your help we can identify the dealers. We have to infiltrate the network, you see, to get all the big boys.'

'I don't know about this . . .'

'You want to spend the rest of your life in jail?'

'All right, I do it.'

The Belgian sky was grey and overcast, which suited Debbie's mood perfectly. The temperature had scarcely risen above five degrees centigrade, and the tall pine trees above the track looked strangely forbidding in the low light.

She sensed that Ricardo might be interested in someone else. He'd been so strange lately, so preoccupied.

The Calibre-Shensu team had arrived a few days in advance of the redesigned Shadows, but Bruce de Villiers had stayed at the Calibre-Shensu headquarters to help with the final stages of the rebuild. Wyatt would be coming with the cars.

Debbie knew how desperately Ricardo wanted to compete. She'd felt closest to him just before the Brazilian Grand Prix. He'd been at his most vulnerable – and, for once, he'd relied on her.

She wandered from the pits to the warehouse where the rest of the team's equipment was stored. There were the usual security guards, supplied by another of Jack Phelps's endless list of companies. One of the guards smiled at her, his eyes fixed on her breasts, which were plainly visible through her tight-fitting white polo-neck jersey. She stared him out and walked past, sensing his interest move from her breasts to her backside.

Inside, she looked around at the immaculately organised paraphernalia of equipment – all the miscellaneous accessories that travelled with every Grand Prix team. She knew the inventory pretty well off by heart. As usual there were plenty of Carvalho tyres. They'd probably brought more wet-weather tyres because it looked as though the entire race would be run in the rain – unless the conditions changed drastically.

She ran her hand over the surface of one of the tyres that

had just come out of the container – then felt a hand rest firmly on her shoulder and spin her round. Ricardo took her arm and guided her away from the tyres.

'Let me take you to lunch,' he said. 'It is a tragedy for a beautiful woman to be alone.'

The jet landed in pouring rain. Vanessa Tyson moved quickly through the customs with her crew and then out through the rain to a hired mini-bus. Sean, her cameraman, grinned at her ruefully. 'The glamour of international Grand Prix racing?'

'Cool it, Sean,' she answered good-humouredly. 'This is typical Belgian spring weather. Believe me, it can only get worse.'

They were at their hotel a few hours later, having driven through an intense thunderstorm. After off-loading all their gear, Vanessa suggested that they eat at a nearby restaurant – a well-known watering-hole of the Formula One circus.

Vanessa had arrived at the Spa circuit well in advance, to pick up on any difficulties the organisers might be having, and any gossip about the teams. Her pulse quickened when they got to the restaurant – she caught sight of several of the top drivers. A few people looked up when she walked in; it was because of her growing reputation, she was sure. Most of the diners had had a lot to drink and were talking freely.

To her surprise, Ricardo Sartori came up and kissed her on the cheek.

'The very attractive Vanessa Tyson? Perhaps you would care to join us for dinner?'

Vanessa prepared herself for an interesting evening.

The door to Vanessa Tyson's hotel room opened quietly and a man slipped in without switching on the lights. He looked carefully round the room, using a small flashlight, and eventually moved towards the aluminium camera cases stacked up in one corner.

After opening a number of the cases, he moved on to the suitcase that lay on the bed. He sifted through Vanessa's clothes and belongings, his hands exploring her underwear, then moving on through the rest of her wardrobe.

Ten minutes later he slipped out of the room, closing the door very quietly behind him and disappearing down the corridor.

Vanessa returned to the hotel after two. She had hardly drunk anything at all, unlike Sean, who could hardly stand up by the time they got back to the hotel. Wearily she picked up her suitcase and put it on the desk in the corner of the room. She was about to open it to look for her dictaphone when she saw that she'd left it next to the bed.

She spent the next fifteen minutes noting down what information she'd picked up during the course of the evening. She found this was the best way to order her thoughts – generally she didn't even have to listen back to what she'd dictated, just the action of doing it improved her memory.

Having finished her work, she showered and went to bed, and almost at once dropped off into a deep sleep. She dreamed about Wyatt. She was lost in the desert, staggering forward through blinding sand-storms, and Wyatt's face kept appearing on the horizon with a cynical grin. It was a strange, tormented dream.

She was woken by a loud rapping on the door.

'For God's sake!' she shouted as she got up, pulling on her silk dressing-gown. The knocking continued. 'Hold on! I'm coming!'

She opened the door and found herself looking at a stern-faced man, thin, in his early forties. Behind him were two Belgian police officers.

'Miss Tyson? I am Detective Inspector Tielemans. I have a warrant to search your room.'

He handed her the warrant, and the two policemen filed into the room and started rifling cupboards and drawers.

'I don't believe this!' Vanessa said, watching. 'I'll be reporting it to the British Ambassador.'

Inspector Tielemans didn't react, but guided her outside the door and stood watching his men move methodically through the room. Vanessa folded her arms and watched with growing irritation. She would make them pay for this.

One of the policemen picked up her briefcase and opened

302

it. He pulled out the files and then examined the lining. It came away, revealing a flat, transparent plastic bag, filled with white powder.

Vanessa sucked in her breath as the policeman chucked it on the bed. 'What is it?' Detective Inspector Tielemans asked, a distinct edge to his voice.

'I don't know.'

He pulled out a pocket-knife and slit open the plastic. Then he wet his finger, touched the powder and brought it to his lips.

'Heroin.'

'I don't know how the hell that got into my case, but it's not mine,' Vanessa stammered.

'Our laboratory will confirm my finding. You are under arrest.'

'This is ridiculous!'

Before she realised it, a set of handcuffs had been attached to her wrists and she was marched off down the corridor. It was early in the morning, so there was hardly anyone about, but the few people they passed stared at her incredulously. She was bundled into the back of a waiting police car which took off at once, lights flashing and siren wailing.

Detective Inspector Tielemans sat next to her. 'You're treating me like a criminal!'

'People like you make me sick,' he replied, staring out at the rain that streaked the windows of the car.

'But I'm not guilty! What would I want to smuggle heroin into Belgium for?'

'For the same reason you work for an American television network – money. You will be given an opportunity to make a statement, Miss Tyson, and I suggest that you tell the truth. It will make things a little simpler.'

Vanessa closed her eyes. Who could have done this to her? It was unbelievable. She would have to get a good attorney to represent her, because it seemed she didn't have a leg to stand on.

Chief Inspector John Tennant of New Scotland Yard put the phone down and gazed across the murky London sky. It was

303

strange how a lead would develop when one least expected it. Tielemans was well-known to him, a man dedicated to ending the drug trade not only in Belgium but in the whole of Europe. For Tennant, the news was a promising break after months of silence. Interpol had known for some time that someone was bringing large shipments of heroin, cocaine and other drugs into various countries in Europe, but no real pattern had emerged, and no leads.

Vanessa Tyson. Somehow he wouldn't have expected her to be involved in such a business, but experience had left him cynical. She was the ideal person to engage in the transport of drugs, after all; her business took her to a different country every couple of weeks, and her journalistic credentials would put her above suspicion. She travelled with a camera crew and a lot of luggage, and because of her reputation customs officials would leave her alone. However, someone had turned on her.

What they had on her was damning: ten kilograms of heroin in her briefcase, and then another one hundred kilograms found after a more detailed search, in the camera cases of her crew. It was enough to put her away for eternity. But he guessed she must be working with someone – by merely snuffing out Vanessa Tyson, they wouldn't stop the traffic.

Would she talk? he wondered. And if she did, how much did she really know? He knew in his gut that there was someone very powerful controlling the whole operation, someone singularly ruthless, who was not afraid to dispose of anyone threatening their network. The publicity that followed Miss Tyson's arrest would help, though. It would make whoever was behind her nervous, and nervous people made mistakes.

Ricardo hung over the toilet bowl, grasping the rim with his hands, and threw up again.

He wished he could die. He was in so deep he could never pull out now – and if he told Phelps he'd been found out, Phelps would destroy him. There were documents he had signed without thinking . . . It was he who was in the position of king-pin: he had been manipulated and used, an ignorant player in a sophisticated game.

But at least Rod Talbot had promised him a light sentence. It was Talbot who'd asked him to entertain Vanessa Tyson the previous evening. Now he had just heard the news on the radio. She had been arrested: a major drug-bust. What the hell was going on?

The phone rang and he shivered. Reluctantly he answered it.

'Ricardo, good buddy, you did well.' Talbot's voice purred from the receiver.

'Did you find drugs on her?'

'Yes. You gave us the time to search her room. We knew she was one of Phelps's main dealers,' he lied, 'but we've never been able to catch her.'

'But Phelps hates her!'

'The perfect cover.'

'So now you expect Phelps to approach me?'

'Exactly.'

Ricardo shivered again. He was caught between Talbot and Phelps. Either of them could destroy him.

'What will happen to her?' he asked in a small voice.

There was a moment's silence.

'First we will break her,' Talbot said. 'We will try to get her to confess Phelps's involvement. She'll only get twenty years . . . if she co-operates.'

Ricardo was shaking. 'But what do you want me to do?'

'Relax, buddy. You're working for Interpol. You're safe. I guarantee Phelps will make you take over where Vanessa Tyson left off. You will make the next delivery.'

The phone went dead.

Ricardo felt sick. What the hell was he involved in?

The new Shadow Two rolled out of the Calibre-Shensu workshops at Amersham that same morning. It was a glorious early spring day, the air crisp and fresh, the sun shining brightly. Vapour rose from the mouths of those who stood talking around the car.

Bruce de Villiers watched the official FISA scrutineers

warily. The inspection lasted over an hour, with much note-taking and discussion amongst the officials. Bruce could feel himself getting more and more worked up. There was nothing he could do about it, he really wanted to race in Belgium and it all hung on whether the Shadow Two complied with the stiff regulations.

Eventually the most senior official, a man with heavy-rimmed black glasses and unfashionably long side-burns, came up to him.

'I'm pleased to inform you that the Shadow Two meets the regulations. I can also give you Mr Hugo's word that there will be no comeback on this decision.'

Bruce wanted to say a lot of things, most of them rude, but he shook the man's hand warmly. Then Don Morrison brought the press reporters onto the track and Bruce stood proudly next to the Shadow Two.

'We intend to be at the front of the grid at Spa . . .' he began.

The formalities over, Wyatt took the Shadow Two out for an hour around the test circuit. His times were good but not outstanding. Something was holding him back. Bruce hoped to hell it wasn't the new chassis-design.

Both the Shadow Twos would be flown that evening direct to Belgium. The first practice was on the Thursday and the Grand Prix was on the Sunday. That gave them only three days to set both cars up. Worse, Charlie Ibuka would be competing in his first Formula One race in a car he hardly knew.

Later the same day, Bruce de Villiers experienced a curious feeling of quiet satisfaction at he looked at Vanessa Tyson's picture on the front page of his newspaper. He was unsympathetic. The bitch deserved everything that was coming to her. And he hated the world of drugs; he had seen enough people on the circuit succumb to the attractions of narcotics.

Anyway, at least he didn't have to worry about any more negative publicity.

He folded the paper up and turned to the file on his desk.

There was a lot of paperwork to clear before he set off for Belgium.

Carlos put the phone down and walked out onto the balcony. Rain had fallen an hour before, but now the sky was a beautiful turquoise-blue. In the distance he could hear his horses whinnying. He loved the pampas; it was as flat as a billiard table, the long horizon broken only by the occasional windmill. He stood staring for some time at the intensely yellow poplars that marked the edge of the estancia's grounds; then he left the balcony by a wooden staircase and walked through gardens filled with mock-orange and hibiscus to the drive, which was lined with blue-gums, their white trunks gleaming in the fading light.

He liked to be alone at this time of day. Estelle was sleeping. He had not told her the truth; she had enough to worry about.

Carlos looked back at the house, and the memories came flooding back. The laughter, the camaraderie. He had grown up here on the estancia with his brother. They had been best friends as well as brothers.

David had always been the thinker. Polo did not interest him. And to their father's despair David had left the estancia, to become a lawyer. Years later, he had fallen in love with a Colombian woman and moved to Bogota. That was when he became interested in politics and government. But the brothers had remained friends during that time; they spent their holidays together.

God, it was as if David was standing next to him. How could he have been murdered in that way?

Carlos couldn't let David's death go unavenged. He thought about the film the Ortega Cartel had sent David's wife – of David slowly hanging to death. She'd had to spend time in a mental hospital after that.

Carlos had always had the lingering suspicion that Emerson Ortega might still be around. Now, after the mysterious disappearance of Raoul in Brazil, he had become even more suspicious. It was as if events were leading him towards the Ortega Cartel.

The map he'd found in Raoul's hotel room was in a safe in

his study. Tomorrow he would meet a friend, an aerial surveyor who would perhaps know the place indicated on the map.

Carlos's instincts told him that he might have stumbled on something that would lead him to the heart of the Ortega Cartel.

John Tennant looked wearily at the woman facing him. Even in the unattractive prison uniform, she was attractive. Dark-haired and voluptuous, she had penetrating brown eyes that unsettled him.

There was something wrong with this case, and he felt it more and more as he proceeded with his questioning. He'd first suspected a plant when Tielemans had given him the details of Tyson's arrest: it had been just a little too easy . . . Still, bitter experience had taught him that nothing in the world of drug-trafficking was quite as it seemed.

'Mr Tennant.'

Her voice caught him unawares – he had drifted off on his own train of thought. He stared back at her.

'Do you realise what all this is doing to me, Mr Tennant?'

'Miss Tyson, I suggest we keep the discussion to what is relevant.'

'If my condition isn't relevant, then I don't know what is.'

He looked at her, but did not show pity. He could not afford to show weakness. Underworld contacts had indicated that there had been an enormous delivery of drugs in Monaco, and there was about to be one in Belgium.

He got up. 'I must advise you that it is in your best interests to co-operate.'

'Mr Tennant, I cannot tell you more than the truth. If you do not believe me, then that is your problem.'

He stormed out of the interrogation room. He was getting nowhere fast.

Ricardo reached for the compact for the second time that day. Talbot had given it to him and told him to take a snort if he was nervous. Talbot said he knew it wasn't ethical, but he didn't want Ricardo botching up the operation because of nerves. Ricardo found this ironic – that he should be taking drugs in order to help Talbot uncover a drug-trafficking racket. Still, if it worked . . .

Talbot had also told him to be very careful. He said that Ricardo was only to deal with himself; he must trust no one else, even if they claimed they were from Interpol. Talbot had repeated this instruction to him several times.

The rain was pattering against the outside window of his sumptuous hotel room – but at the moment he didn't have a thought to spare for his surroundings. His whole body was literally shaking with tension.

As Talbot had said he would, Phelps had approached him. But what was strange was that Phelps hadn't mentioned drugs. He'd just asked Ricardo to arrange the delivery of some merchandise for him.

Ricardo had made the contact – delivery would take place during the race.

Now he went into the bathroom and rested the compact on the top of the toilet cistern. He then poured out a thin white line of the precious powder – and looked down at it with satisfaction. The first snort he'd had made him feel a lot better. He could handle it. And he felt like he could handle some more.

He rolled up a dollar note and inserted it in his left nostril, then he bent forward and quickly inhaled the powder.

It didn't take long before he was feeling very much in control again. He had plenty of money, he was trusted by Phelps, and Talbot had told him he must just play the game. So what the hell did he really have to worry about?

Jack Phelps was very pleased at the way things were going. It was clear that Vanessa Tyson's career was over. No longer would he have to listen to her tirades against tobacco companies and their involvement in Formula One. Also, Bruce would be entering two drivers in the Belgian Grand Prix, and Aito was especially happy that one of them was Japanese.

And, above all, he now had Ricardo completely under his control. There was nothing the man would not do for him.

*

Detective Inspector Tielemans went through the facts again. It was all very logical. A dealer had obviously decided to get even with Vanessa Tyson and had informed on her. Maybe she'd asked for too much money, or she'd been invading someone else's turf.

He looked up to see John Tennant coming into the room.

'Well, did you get anything out of her?'

Tennant sat down and rested his head on the desk.

'Do you think I've gone soft, André?'

'No. I consider you to be as professional as ever.'

Tennant leaned back, his face taut, his dark eyes restlessly scanning the walls and then zeroing in on Tielemans.

'I believe her story,' he said.

The smile left Tielemans's face. 'Don't be an idiot! She's going to get twenty years, of course she's going to plead . . .' He stopped, realising that John would already have taken that into account. 'All right,' he said. 'Tell me what makes you think that she's not lying?'

'My intuition.'

'Your intuition's wrong,' André growled. 'With what we've got on her, it's an easy conviction. And we've got evidence she experimented with drugs at university.'

'Dammit,' John slammed his fist on the table, 'she was used. Some bastard wanted to shut her up.'

'I won't let her go. The evidence is conclusive.' André shrugged his shoulders and raised his eyebrows. 'But you're a good friend – I'll hold the heat off for a month.'

John Tennant had one vague hunch. Why, he asked himself, had Sartori asked Vanessa Tyson to join him the night before she was arrested?

He found Sartori's hotel quickly enough, but he had a lot of difficulty getting the receptionist to call Sartori – until he used his police identification. Let Sartori know it was the police: if he was scared, that would rattle him a little more.

When he knocked on the door it opened instantly, and John Tennant found himself looking at the former Formula One world champion, Ricardo Sartori. They shook hands, and Tennant saw that the Italian's eyes were shifting nervously.

'I've always wanted to meet you, Mr Sartori,' he said. 'In fact, if you don't mind . . .' he took out a piece of paper '. . . my son would really be overjoyed if he had your autograph.'

He didn't have a son, but flattery could loosen a man's tongue faster than almost anything else.

Ricardo smiled, 'My pleasure,' and scrawled his name. Tennant observed the cut of his suit, the quality of his watch and many other details which told him Ricardo was a very wealthy man. Nothing surprising in that, though. He knew that the top drivers earned astronomical sums.

'I'm on the Vanessa Tyson case, and I thought you might be able to help me,' John Tennant said. 'You're a man who knows the Formula One world better than almost anyone else.'

Ricardo shrugged his shoulders. 'That's not really true. Bruce de Villiers . . .'

'Ah, you misunderstand. I'm interested in the glamour, the life style, not the behind-the-scenes work.'

'So . . .'

'A large shipment of cocaine is rumoured to have been delivered in Monaco at the time of the Grand Prix.'

Ricardo coloured slightly. Who was this detective? Some smooth operator who had come out specially to investigate Vanessa Tyson? Then he remembered Talbot's directive: he must not talk or deal with anyone else from Interpol, Talbot must remain his only contact.

John watched the Italian and noted the nervousness. His instincts had been right. Vanessa Tyson hadn't pulled her punches when it came to attacking Calibre-Shensu, and now their biggest sponsor's representative was looking distinctly edgy.

'Mr Tennant, I have a very busy schedule.'

'I won't keep you long. I imagine your sponsor must have been very happy to see Miss Tyson arrested?'

Ricardo shifted his eyes away from Tennant. 'No more than other teams' sponsors. Formula One relies heavily on tobacco industry sponsorship, and Miss Tyson's investigations were very one-sided.'

'I can only agree with you on that,' Tennant replied

311

pleasantly. He realised he'd come on a little too strong. 'But she won't be bothering you for the next twenty years.'

He got up to leave. 'Thank you for your time. I hope your team enjoys another victory. And I almost forgot, here's my card. Cocaine is a very good bribe, so if you hear rumours that Tyson supplied it to anyone to get information, give me a call.'

'I will.'

'Oh, something else that slipped my mind – why did you ask Miss Tyson to dinner the night before she was arrested?'

'I wanted to sleep with her.'

A startling explanation, John Tennant thought as he walked from the hotel to his car, but perhaps, coming from Ricardo, an acceptable one. But still, his intuition told him to investigate the situation further.

Ricardo read the card. 'Chief Inspector John Tennant MSc Cantab., New Scotland Yard.' He supposed it was logical that there should be an exhaustive enquiry after Vanessa Tyson's arrest. Well, he'd remembered Talbot's instructions and had not told Tennant he was already working with Interpol. But still, the situation was precarious. And if Phelps found out, he guessed he'd be a dead man.

He put a call through to Talbot, telling him about Tennant's visit. To his relief, Talbot was not in the least bit worried.

'You'll make your delivery, Ricardo. Relax. Tennant's just a lower-echelon operator in Interpol, he's not in on the major drugs-busts,' Talbot lied.

'I did the right thing?'

'Yes. Tennant's blind, he doesn't operate in my league. But, my friend, there are other people you'll have to be more wary of.' An edge had crept into Talbot's voice.

'Like who?' Ricardo asked, anxious to avoid any more surprises.

'You'll know if you meet them,' Talbot replied evasively.

'Why do you bring this up only now?'

'Because the next Grand Prix is at Monza – your home country, and the home country of the people I'm talking about.'

'The Mafia?' Ricardo tried to hide the hysteria in his voice.

312

'If you back out now, I'll press charges against you.'

The phone went dead before Ricardo could ask any more questions. He paced up and down his room, trying to resist taking another snort. It was no good, he had to have it, he felt so tired and powerless without it.

He had always feared the Mafia like the plague. He knew little about them, but what he did know frightened him to death.

Jules Ortega put the phone down and looked at Suzie von Falkenhyn lying on the bed. She was naked and shivering, but the long blonde hair looked better now he had made her wash it, and the aristocratic features were as haughty as ever, even if her face was thinner. But it was just in her eyes that he could see the desperation. He laughed as she looked up at him, every square inch of her body pleading. The inside of her left arm was blue and dotted with red pinpricks.

'Lie over the bed.'

He unfastened the hand-tooled leather belt that held up his trousers, and took it in his left hand because his right was still too mangled to use. He brought the belt down hard, and she screamed as the leather grazed her flesh, bringing up a line of ugly weals. He felt the excitement surge through him.

'Don't scream. Enjoy it. Ask for it. If you behave yourself, you'll get another fix.'

Captain Tennant looked at the fax that had just come from Milan. Ricardo Sartori had been in a lot of trouble, it seemed. He'd been investigated for tax avoidance, and his expenditure was enormous. He owned a huge villa on Skiathos as well as an executive jet.

But the outstanding tax, and the fine, had been paid a month ago . . . A warning bell ran in Tennant's head. Sartori's contract had been cancelled after his suspension at the Rio Grand Prix, yet it appeared that his finances had improved dramatically.

He was now registered as a director and owner of Sartori PR, and this company had taken over responsibility for Zen, the world-famous design group owned and founded by Suzie

von Falkenhyn. Von Falkenyn had disappeared. Interesting
. . . It was especially interesting that Sartori reported to Jack
Phelps.

Tennant picked up the phone and rang a contact in the US
Internal Revenue. He wanted to know where Sartori PR got
paid from and how much. It would take time to find out, was
the reply. He sighed wearily, staring out of the window at the
steadily falling rain, then began to page through his notes on
Calibre-Shensu. To run such a team required an enormous
amount of money. Jack Phelps and Aito Shensu were the main
sponsors. But since Sartori had been suspended, there seemed
no reason why they should be paying him a particularly large
salary. So maybe Sartori was moving drugs.

It wasn't the small-time criminals John Tennant wanted, but
the big operators. In 1992 the emergence of a united Europe
would make the trafficking of cocaine much easier – there
would be a relaxation of border and monetary controls. It
would be hell to follow leads after that. He needed to catch a
big fish now, in 1991, and signal to the major traffickers that
Europe wasn't going to be the tea-party they'd been dreaming
about.

The door to the small side-office the Belgian police had
assigned him, opened.

'Monsieur de Villiers to see you, sir.' The junior officer was
nervous because John Tennant had a reputation for being
hard-arsed and ruthless.

'Send him in. We are not to be disturbed.'

He turned back to his work but was startled when the door
to his office was slammed hard. 'Why the hell have you pulled
me in here?' a voice growled.

'Sit down, Mr de Villiers. Would you like some coffee?'

'No, I'd rather get on with my job. I'd like to get the hell
out of here as quickly as possible.'

Tennant was furious. 'Let me get one thing straight with
you right now, Mr de Villiers. You may think the world begins
and ends with Formula One, but I've got news for you – it
doesn't. What I do for a living is also incredibly dangerous,
but unfortunately, unlike your chosen profession, it doesn't

314

pay very well.' Tennant narrowed his eyes. 'If I've a mind to, I can make your life hell.'

Bruce de Villiers rested his hands on the table.

'You *are* making my life hell. I've got a tight deadline, and with every minute I'm away from my team I stand a chance of missing it.'

'All right, I apologise. I know your work is demanding, Mr de Villiers. I have only a few questions to ask.' Tennant leaned forward. 'Vanessa Tyson, how do you feel about her?'

'I hate the bitch's guts.'

'She threatened the survival of your operation?'

'Yes. She chose us, out of all the teams on the circuit, as the focus for her attack. Jack Phelps is our major sponsor. He represents substantial business interests in America. He handles the sponsorship for Shensu Industries of Japan, as well as Carvalho tyres and Moulton who supply our oils and fuel. You understand what her attack on the tobacco companies and our safety standards does to our sponsors?'

John Tennant looked candidly at de Villiers. 'So you were scared you'd lose your sponsors? After the suspension of Sartori, you must have been on edge . . . So you arranged to have a quantity of heroin secreted in Miss Tyson's luggage.'

De Villiers snarled. 'You bastard!'

Tennant smiled and put his feet up on the desk. 'De Villiers, you arsehole, you're the number one suspect.'

De Villiers was breathing heavily. 'Listen, fucker, everything I own is in that team, my soul is there. But if you think I'd stoop to doing that, you're a pathetic judge of character.'

Tennant massaged the area around his neck and decided he wouldn't enjoy working for de Villiers.

'Do you know what the value of the heroin we found in Miss Tyson's luggage was?' he asked.

'Another trick question?'

'No. Take a guess.'

'Thirty, forty thousand pounds?'

'Try ten million.'

De Villiers whistled through his teeth, and Tennant smiled. 'No,' he said, 'I don't suspect you, Mr de Villiers.'

'So why are you wasting my time?'

315

Tennant scratched his nose. 'You've got more equipment arriving today?'

Bruce nodded. 'Then perhaps I should authorise customs to organise a detailed search – that should take about five days.'

Bruce froze. 'You bastard!'

'Look, I need your co-operation. You've been intimately involved in Formula One for over ten years, you have plenty of friends and contacts. If you hear one word about drugs, I want to know.'

'I haven't had a good year so far, Mr Tennant. I don't need more problems.'

'Relax. You co-operate with me, and you won't have to worry . . . Unless I find someone in your team is smuggling drugs.'

When de Villiers had left, John Tennant packed his briefcase. He was quite sure that de Villiers would mention their meeting to the other members of the team, which was precisely what he wanted to happen. He knew the South African would tell his people, in no uncertain terms, that if they were found using or carrying drugs, they'd be kicked out of Calibre-Shensu.

With Sartori he sensed he was close to the big lead he'd been looking for for the last five years. But now he would have to be quiet, watch and wait patiently.

If he got close to the big men it would be another matter. They were ruthless. If they knew he was onto them, he would be a dead man.

Suzie staggered to her feet. She could hardly focus on anything. She hadn't much idea what was happening to her, but she hadn't been this lucid for some time. Perhaps she had not injected herself properly.

She was desperate. She had to get help, that was all she knew. She wanted another fix. She made her way painfully through the darkness.

She hadn't forgotten where she'd seen the phone before he'd switched off the light. She wanted to cry out, the pain from where he'd hit her was so bad.

She found the push-buttons and tapped in the number. It rang ten times and then an answering-machine came on. She wanted to cry. These was a noise behind her – and then she heard the tone.

'Wyatt, it's Suzie . . . I'm a prisoner on a mountain, somewhere in the jungle. It's very hot. For God's sake, help me . . . I need a fix now!'

The blow sent her flying across the room.

'You bitch!'

Jules was naked, staring at her, panting hard. In his hand was the leather belt.

'You animal!' she screamed.

She picked up the first object that came to hand, a crystal decanter, and hurled it at him. It struck him in the groin, and with a strangled sob he staggered forward, his hands gripping his genitals in agony.

Suzie grabbed a glass ashtray and staggered towards him, aiming it at his head. He avoided it, and hit her hard across the face with the back of his damaged right hand. Then he was on her, hitting her again and again until she finally blacked out.

Jules felt the tears running from his eyes. If she had damaged his testicles he would kill her. He dragged himself over to the intercom and called the doctor.

He would make her pay for this.

Dr Estevez burst into the room. He stared across at Suzie von Falkenyn, naked and slumped on the ground.

'Bastard,' Dr Estevez murmured, appalled by Jules's brutality.

Jules turned towards Dr Estevez, tempted to strike him as well, but knowing that he needed the doctor's help.

'She hurt me here,' he said.

The doctor carefully examined Jules's blood-soaked groin. 'There's no damage apart from a cut on your thigh. You're very lucky. Now, I must examine the lady . . .'

'No. She doesn't matter. If Mr Vargas or Mr Talbot ask what happened to her, you will say she fell.'

Dr Estevez nodded and then left quickly, anxious to avoid any further displays of brutality.

Suzie started groaning. Jules pulled the hypodermic out the drawer and drew up twice the maximum dose, then he grabbed her arm and injected her.

He walked down the passage laughing, confident in the knowledge that Suzie was heading towards oblivion.

Wyatt knew that the Belgian Spa-Francorchamps circuit bore little resemblance to the original fourteen-kilometre track that had made its name a legend in the annals of motor-racing history. In 1950, the year of the first Formula One world championship, it had been the scene of an outstanding race. Juan Manuel Fangio had taken first place in an Alfa Romeo; an Italian driver, Guiseppe Farina, fourth place. At the end of that year Farina was World Champion, but Fangio went on to win more world championships than any other driver in the history of Formula One racing.

After a series of accidents the circuit was considered unsafe for Grand Prix racing, and was closed in 1971. It was opened again, completely rebuilt, in 1983 – a wide, sweeping, unforgiving circuit that demanded courage, concentration and a good car.

The Virage de la Source, the bend closest to the pits, was one of the only parts of the old circuit that had been integrated into the new. The record for the fastest lap was held by Roger de Rosner in the McCabe at 132.5 mph, breaking the previous record for the circuit.

Set in the wooded hills of the Ardennes, the new circuit's most fearsome corner was the Eau Rouge, where the cars sped down the old pit-lane straight, turned left-right, and at the same time faced a steep surge up the hill into a slight left-hander. The circuit was a favourite amongst the drivers in the championship because it provided them with exciting and competitive driving conditions.

With an umbrella held over the cockpit and the rain pouring down, Wyatt reflected on another side of the Belgian circuit's character that was not particularly popular – the weather. It was the beginning of the first practice, and wet-weather tyres were definitely the order of the day. Wyatt was disappointed because these tyres wouldn't give him much of an opportunity to explore the full potential of the Shadow.

Friday afternoon, he reflected, was when most people went home early from work. For him it was the hardest day of the week – first practice was always the toughest.

Suzie. Where the hell are you?

He kept on thinking about her, he couldn't get her out of his mind. He just hoped that Carlos had come up with something. The practice had been scheduled for Friday morning, but the Formula One officials had been unhappy about the medical facilities at the circuit and had asked the organisers to bring in more people. Monaco was fresh in everyone's mind and the season did not need another disaster.

Wyatt closed his mind to all these thoughts as the Shadow Two exploded into life. The Shensu engine always thrilled him with the deep, melodic sound of its smoothly running cylinders. He moved out onto the circuit and did a slow initial lap, to get a better feel for the new car.

De Rosner was driving expertly. He'd turned in a lap time in the wet that came close to his existing lap record. Wyatt knew he would have his work cut out just to keep up with the Doctor.

The spray was really bad, and Wyatt did not feel at all happy with the way the Shadow was handling. She just didn't feel like the same car; the suspension set-up was radically different. His best time by the end of the afternoon session was only good enough to earn him fifth place on the grid.

Bruce seemed unperturbed by Wyatt's relatively poor showing.

'Relax, Wyatt. You've got too much on your mind. You've got to forget about it and get into the spirit of the race.'

Wyatt got out of the car, still in the pouring rain. 'I wish we had more time to set up the Shadow. She's under-steering like mad, and I don't have the confidence yet, especially in the wet, to really push it.'

Mickey came forwards, anxious to find out Wyatt's problems.

'Wyatt, me boy, you've got to realise that this is basically

319

the same design. If anything, it's better. It'll be a fock sight faster round the corners.'

Bruce put his arm across Wyatt's shoulder. 'Charlie's a second faster than you.'

Wyatt felt his blood tingling. The pressure never let up. He had heard a lot about the Japanese driver – now he knew most of it was accurate.

Wyatt unzipped his jumpsuit, enoying the coolness of the falling rain.

'Have you spoken to that cop yet?' Bruce said.

'What cop?'

'John Tennant. Here's his number. He wants to talk to you about Vanessa Tyson.'

'That's all I need in my life.'

John Tennant wasn't what Wyatt had been expecting. He was younger, about Wyatt's own age, and smartly dressed in a dark-blue suit. Tennant looked as if he meant business.

'Count me as one of your admirers,' he said warmly, stretching out his hand. Then he laid his cards on the table.

By the time he had finished, Wyatt was on edge: He sensed that there was something going on over which he had no control, something very sinister.

John Tennant stared at him long and hard.

'What's on your mind?' he said.

Wyatt told him about Suzie's disappearance and the incidents in Rio, about the attack on Vanessa. Tennant made detailed notes, not interrupting him. Wyatt didn't tell him about Carlos's involvement.

Tennant looked up. 'I want you,' he said, 'to be my inside man at Calibre-Shensu.'

Wyatt felt his spirits sink. Why was Tennant so interested in the team? He wished he'd never set eyes on Vanessa Tyson. Besides, he needed every ounce of energy to hold onto his lead.

'No,' he said firmly. 'What you're saying could spell big trouble for us. If our sponsor heard about this investigation, he could pull out. That'd be Bruce and me finished for the year.'

'I'll do everything in my power to make sure that doesn't happen. I know you want to find Suzie von Falkenhyn.' Tennant leaned foward on his elbows, his eyes wide. 'This is a giant jigsaw puzzle and I'm trying to put the pieces together. Drugs are coming in in enormous quantities to each country that's hosting a Formula One Grand Prix.'

'It could be coincidence.'

'I doubt it. We've had the same problems with rock groups in the past. The people doing it always change – the people behind them never do.' He paused, and pulled a cigarette with his lips from a crumpled pack.

Wyatt felt a strange empathy with the policeman. 'I'm not against you,' he said.

Tennant picked up a file and tossed it over to Wyatt.

'Take a look through that.'

Wyatt went through the news-cuttings, every one of them about Suzie.

'It doesn't make any sense, does it?' Tennant said. 'It's positively bizarre. You've put up more reward money than most people ask for a ransom, and yet you've heard nothing.'

Wyatt closed his eyes as Tennant continued, 'You know what buys the silence? Big money. And my guess is it's drug money. The Ortega Cartel is at the centre of the drug business. Earlier this year, Emerson Ortega was assassinated by a CIA operative, and in the United States a lot of cocaine was recovered. We cut off the supply routes through Panama and the Bahamas, and we also cut off the chemical supplies that the producers need to refine the drugs. But it's economics that's actually nailed the producers. The street price is dropping, because the US is heading for a recession.'

A habitual chain-smoker, Tennant pulled out his packet of cigarettes again, offered one to Wyatt who refused, and then lit up himself. He smiled.

'I've seen ads of you smoking – yet you don't smoke?'

'You sound like Vanessa Tyson . . . That's what sponsorships are all about.'

Tennant coughed, and then continued. 'It's those two factors: the difficulty of supplying the US market and the lower street price there, that's resulted in the Ortega Cartel developing new markets. Like Europe . . . Japan . . . and even the Eastern Bloc.'

Wyatt sat back in his chair and put his hands behind his head. 'That makes sense. But are there really that many people who can afford cocaine?'

'The demand is certainly there. The street price is fifty-five thousand dollars a kilo here, compared with eighteen to twenty-five thousand in the States. You see, there's more money in Europe at the moment.'

'How much does that translate into for the man in the street?'

'About one hundred and forty dollars a gram – and that could have been cut. You know what I mean by that?'

Wyatt shook his head.

'Dealers cut other chemicals into the coke, diluting its quality but upping their supply. So you see, the profit could be even higher.'

Wyatt stared around the bare-walled office, then back at Tennant. He read the hard face beneath the dark hair, saw the faint bags under the eyes. Tennant's casual attitude was an act, beneath the surface he was deeply agitated. But Wyatt couldn't concern himself with Tennant's problems.

'I've got one life,' he said candidly. 'I've got one chance at the championship. I came into racing late, I haven't got time to help you.

'Yeah,' Tennant said, waving an arm. 'Who gives a fuck? Forget all the destroyed lives, sweep the dirt under the carpet and hope it'll go away. Is that what you learned in Japan? Is that your code of honour?'

Wyatt gripped the glass of water that was on the desk in front of him. His hands closed around it and it shattered, glass shards flying round the office.

There was a moment's silence.

'I'm sorry,' Tennant said, 'maybe I shouldn't have said that. I did a little research on your background.'

Wyatt stared at him coldly. 'I've got enough guilt in me to last a lifetime.'

Tennant coughed. 'So you're not going to help me?'

He scribbled a number on the back of an empty cigarette pack and then tossed it over to Wyatt.

'If you hear anything, ring me at this number. If you want help, for any reason, get in touch with me.'

The door slammed shut and Wyatt was gone. Tennant picked up a glass from the bookcase. He squeezed it. Nothing happened.

'My God,' he muttered.

He paced around the office, tossed his finished cigarette into the green waste-bin in the corner, and lit another. Then he looked again at the telefax from New York. Sartori was paid out of a company in Switzerland. Apparently it wasn't possible to discover who owned the company – but Tennant didn't have to guess why Sartori was earning close to half a million dollars a month.

'Mr Sartori, you're out of your depth,' he said, voicing his thoughts.

He picked up the phone and dialled a number in Italy.

Set a thief to catch a thief. Sartori was about to feel the heat.

The evening air was hot and muggy outside the villa. And it wasn't improved by the exhaust fumes from the chauffeur-driven cars that kept arriving. Each time a car pulled up, the door of the villa opened slightly and a large man in evening-dress looked out to ascertain the identity of the car's occupant.

The lush, opulent interior of the villa was in dramatic contrast to its bland exterior. At the end of the long hall was a dining-room, painted rose, with long rose curtains on all the walls. Around the antique dining-table sat six men – all of them over fifty years of age.

The ruling families of the Mafia had little reason to like each other, but this evening they were drawn together by a common threat. Romano Ciolli, *Il Capo*, a thin man with heavy black-framed glasses and a deathly pallor, stood up at the head of the table.

'Brothers. This has gone on long enough. We have to band together. Someone is moving in on our territory.'

All the faces remained impassive.

'I have received a tip-off that two large deliveries have already been made, one in Monaco and another in Belgium. The next will be here.'

An enormous man with grey hair that stood out from his scalp like porcupine quills, grunted.

'*Porca miseria*! The bastards must be taught who is in control!'

The other heads nodded slowly in agreement.

'You agree, then. They must be stopped.' *Il Capo* treated them to a tight-lipped smile

One of the men coughed, the others looked around. It was not done to speak so openly of such things.

'An informer has given us the name of one of their number. I have arranged for his death. *Finito*. Expensive, but then success is guaranteed.'

'Who is it, *signor*?' A big, fat man spoke softly. The speaker turned to him.

'*Madonna*, Leonardo! That is my secret – as it is also my risk.'

This comment obviously found favour with the others.

'Then it is agreed. *Finire*, for a million dollars.'

The men nodded grudgingly. Then *Il Capo* was gone and they all filed into the hall. Fifteen minutes later they had all disappeared, and the house was silent. It was as if the meeting had never taken place.

Romano Ciolli walked back into the room. He pulled back one of the rose curtains to reveal a very petite, red-haired woman.

'You are happy?'

'Yes, *signor*,' she replied, in the impeccable English spoken only by the very aristocratic or the very rich. 'I feel comfortable with the agreement. My identity is protected, and the fee is adequate.'

Il Capo breathed in but held his temper. Adequate! It was the most he had ever paid out for an assassination. But then this was no ordinary assassin.

*

Ricardo stood in the constructors' box and stared out at the spectators in the pouring rain. Then he looked across to the brightly coloured cars on the grid. His eyes reflected his total desolation, desperation. He wanted to be down there. He longed to spend the next two hours living on the edge. He wanted the feeling of winning again – and he wanted to be away from the fear that gripped him. He wanted to return to the arena, to the challenge of the Grand Prix. A challenge he knew how to handle.

The cars had been round once for the warm-up circuit, and now they lay poised to advance, the black livery of the Calibre-Shensu Shadow in the number four place on the grid. This time Wyatt was going to have to fight for his lead, Ricardo thought to himself. Charlie Ibuka was further back, in tenth place. Judging by his performance in the practices, Ricardo could tell Ibuka was going to make a name for himself very quickly.

He looked up and across to Estelle Chase, and his pulse quickened as it always did when he saw a beauty. Her husband, the Argentinian, was not with her. Why, he wondered? Perhaps their relationship was strained?

He turned back to the grid where the cars crouched like predators, their engines growling. He did not see the starting-light change to green, but he heard the engines screaming with excitement and saw the cars launching forwards, down the short straight that led to the formidable bend of the Eau Rouge.

Oh, to be with them, fighting it out for the lead!

Wyatt shot past Maupassant and Zito as he flew off the grid, ending up right behind de Rosner in the McCabe as they took the same line round the bend.

Ricardo watched Estelle's face. Her mouth had tightened – there was a paleness around her lips. She knew the danger. Wyatt had given them a brilliant display of tactical driving, dispelling any doubts that the Shadow Two was not as quick as its predecessor.

Conversation broke out amongst the various constructors. No doubt, Ricardo thought, many of them would be disappointed to see that the Shadow Two was as competitive as the Shadow One.

'And here we are, in possibly the wettest Grand Prix of the year, watching some brilliant driving from Wyatt Chase. I think we're soon about to see a very drawn-out fight between de Rosner and Chase for first place. De Rosner's McCabe is as competitive as ever. What a shame that Sartori blotted his copybook in Rio: who could predict how this race would be going even now, if the great Italian was also on the grid? Still, we are witnessing a level of competitiveness that we haven't seen on the circuit for a long time.'

Ricardo switched his concentration away from the BBC commentary and looked down at the pits. The Shensu team were clearly identifiable by their dark jumpsuits.

'Hi, Ricardo.' The big voice boomed through the box. Jack Phelps's presence was unmistakable. 'A great race for the team.'

Ricardo looked at Jack's superbly cut suit, the swept-back hair revealing the dramatic forehead. He was the image of the ultra-successful, wheeler-dealer American millionaire. Between his fingers he held a large Havana cigar which he sucked at viciously every few seconds.

'Everything OK?' he whispered in Ricardo's ear, the smell of cigar smoke filling the Italian's nostrils.

'It's OK.' Why was he so nervous, all of a sudden?

'It'd better be,' Phelps responded, and then pulled away to utter more loudly: 'You're lucky I gave you a job so you can continue living like a king – or should I say, count.'

A few people looked around. Jack had made his point. Without him, Ricardo would be nothing.

'Get me a whisky,' Phelps said suddenly.

Ricardo didn't budge. He'd had enough.

'Get it,' Phelps whispered softly, 'or perhaps I shall tell the papers a little about your background.'

Ricardo went and got the drink. He knew how Phelps liked it, a triple tot of Scotch with lots of ice.

He came back to see that the cars were on the third lap, de Rosner still leading, Wyatt right behind him. They had both broken de Rosner's previous lap record. Ricardo handed

Phelps his whisky, and saw that he had been joined by a female companion. He moved away, anxious to be on his own.

'Not so fast, boy. Amanda would like a drink.'

'A Perrier water.' The *Vogue* cover model on Jack's arm smiled without warmth.

Ricardo turned back to the bar. He could sense the eyes watching him, but he was trapped. Phelps could destroy him. Why had he allowed himself to be used like this? He would rather be poor than humiliated in this way. But then he comforted himself with the thought that Talbot was waiting in the wings to destroy Phelps. Life had been simple when he'd been in the fast lane.

In the pits, Mickey Dunstal stared at the computer screen alongside Professor Katana. He was worried. Wyatt's Shadow Two was overheating. If it had been a hot day, the Shensu engine in the Shadow Two would already have blown up.

He voiced his concern to Katana. He knew now that they could reprogramme the engine by remote control, as they had done in Rio – he was just scared FISA might find out about it and disqualify them yet again.

'No problem,' Katana replied, and tapped in a series of commands.

'What's up?' Bruce asked. He looked over Katana's shoulder, and saw from the read-outs that the engine was overheating. 'Bugger it. Don't blame yourself, Mickey, that was a record rebuild.'

Katana continued typing in instructions.

'What's going on?' Bruce asked, somewhat nervously, looking around to make sure no one was watching Katana.

'He's done it!' Mickey exclaimed, looking down at the changing readings on the computer screen.

'We reprogramme chip electronically. Very secret. You understand?'

'Yes, only too well,' Bruce muttered. 'For God's sake, don't let anyone else know about this.'

Bruce didn't need another FISA disqualification. He felt the hairs rising on the back of his neck as the Japanese engineer continued to reprogramme the chip on the Shadow Two's engine. Within minutes the engine temperature had dropped a couple of degrees and was back within the safe margin.

Katana turned to them. 'This is the result of ten years' work; it is the beginning of a revolution in car service. The next generation of Shensu cars will all benefit from this technology. It will be possible for a mechanic anywhere in the country to analyse a car's performance – and make corrections.'

Bruce was certain FISA wouldn't approve of Professor Katana's remote-control engine management system – Formula One was littered with the debris of great inventions that were not acceptable to its ruling body.

'Previously, the performance of the chip was built in at the factory. Now, at Shensu, we can adjust the performance when the chip is in the car. Thus, you buy a car in North America which we can adapt to comply with emission and performance regulations anywhere in the world.'

Katana stared down at the screen again. He punched a couple of keys.

'Here is a profile of Chase's driving style. We can assess the way in which he uses the engine, thus we make it stronger in certain places.'

'I don't bloody believe this!'

'The new engine fitted to the Shadow Two reflects this technology. I must also add that Chase's driving style is very hard on the engine. But, no problem, we have made it stronger.'

Bruce gripped the side of the desk. Charlie Ibuka was now in fifth place; he had two drivers in the points. They weren't just back in the running. They were winning.

By lap thirty-three Wyatt had had enough of de Rosner's dominance of the race. The rain had started pouring down and they'd both been in for a change of tyres; now the spray from the French driver's tyres made it nearly impossible for Wyatt to see a passing-gap. He knew that he could go faster in the Shadow Two, but he had to get past de Rosner to prove it.

He shot past the pits and braked late into the Eau Rouge.

He let his foot off the brake earlier than he had done before, then accelerated, shutting out from his mind what would happen if he lost control. Now he came inside the curve of de Rosner's line.

Shit! He was going too fast! The Shadow lost its grip and spun off the track onto the gravel.

He tried to get back on the track but it was useless, the wheels were stuck in the gravel. He smashed his fists up and down on the sides of the cockpit.

It was all his fault.

John Tennant walked down into the cell section, his nose twitching. Why did all prisons smell the same? In front of him the woman warder tramped noisily onwards, then stopped at a cell door and opened it carefully. John gestured for her to go away, but she stayed outside.

Vanessa Tyson was lying on a bunk, reading. They'd given her plenty of books as he'd ordered.

'So, Mr Tennant, what surprises do you have for me now?' She didn't look at him, but went on reading. He handed her a cigarette, which she took.

'Still not going to talk?' He lit her cigarette.

'I've said all I'm going to say.'

He sat down on the chair next to the bunk and picked up the book she'd been reading. It was on Formula One.

'Chase lost,' Tennant said. 'He spun off on the thirty-third lap. De Rosner won.'

He saw the flicker of despair cross her face, then she looked at him. 'Why did you tell me that?'

'You're his lover.'

She raised herself up and smoothed back her hair. Then she hit him hard across the side of his face.

'Get out of here, you bastard!'

Resisting the temptation to retaliate, Tennant quietly picked his cigarette off the floor and relit it; but his mouth was quivering.

Vanessa shifted on the bunk. 'I . . . I'm sorry.'

'You're in serious trouble. I hope you know that.'

'The first time I saw those drugs,' Vanessa said steadily, 'was when Inspector Tielemans found them.'

'I'd like to believe you. Everything adds up, yet nothing adds up. I can't work out why someone would spend millions of dollars to put you away.'

'Because I was threatening them.'

'Calibre-Shensu?'

'I don't know. There are a lot of cigarette companies in Formula One sponsorship. It could be any one of them.'

'There have been similar attacks in the past and there will be in the future. I don't think it makes sense. If they got found out it could be very, very damaging to them.'

Vanessa lay back on the bunk. 'You know what really frightens me?' She looked at the bars across the window.

'No,' he lied, thinking that she was scared of being denied her freedom.

'It's fine,' she said, 'watching those cars going round and round the circuit, as long as you're not emotionally linked to anyone inside them. The moment you are, the whole character of the sport changes.'

'Very touching. I sympathise.'

'Goddamn you! I'm terrified Wyatt Chase will kill himself!'

John got up, scratching his forehead, embarrassed. He was getting attached to Vanessa Tyson, and that was dangerous.

'Do you believe I'm guilty?' she confronted him.

'I'm afraid I can't answer that.'

The cell door closed, and he was gone.

Ricardo packed his case quickly. His mind was made up. He would sell the villa on Skiathos and his Lear jet. That would be more than enough to defray his expenses. Then he would start again next year. He could still win the championship one more time.

He would say nothing to anyone about Phelps – his discussions and dealings with the man would be taboo. He was going to close that chapter of his life altogether.

The phone rang, and he answered it reluctantly.

'No, Jack, I can't go on. I want out. Well, do your worst, but I'm out.'

He slammed the phone down. He could feel the sweat breaking out on his face. How had he got involved with Phelps? It would always be like this.

He pulled the card from his pocket and dialled the number slowly. The phone rang for a long time before it was answered by the sleepy voice of John Tennant. But as soon as the voice spoke, Ricardo remembered Talbot's instructions and lost his nerve. He put the receiver down, picked up his case and opened the door of his hotel room.

The doorway was blocked by Talbot. The fist hit him in the solar-plexus before he could react, and he toppled over, dropping his suitcase. But he was fit, and he was on his feet again like a cat – until Talbot's foot shot up and hit him hard in the side of the head. He flew across the room and slammed into the wall.

Ricardo realised he was out-matched. The phone began to ring again.

'Answer the phone, punk.'

He lay inert on the floor, scared to move. Talbot picked him up by the collar and dumped him on the bed, and Ricardo groped for the phone and picked up the handset.

'Yes?'

'Hallo, Ricardo. You haven't left yet?' There was more than a hint of menace in Phelps's voice.

'No, Jack, I'm staying,' Ricardo replied with difficulty, staring nervously at Talbot.

'Has anyone been asking questions about me?'

'No.'

'Just remember, I have the power to destroy you.'

The phone went dead. Ricardo stared at Talbot.

'Who was it?' Talbot snapped, and when Ricardo didn't immediately reply, he hit him hard across the side of the head.

'It was Jack Phelps,' Ricardo said, almost inaudibly.

'If I were you I wouldn't try that again.'

Slowly Ricardo nodded his head.

The first-class section of the plane was almost empty. Wyatt sat down, but he couldn't relax. He was in a quiet rage. How could he have been so stupid as to lose control of the Shadow in the wet? He had lost the race and it had been his own fault; he hadn't scored a single championship point. And he was torn with guilt, too, over his brief involvement with Vanessa Tyson in Monaco. Why the hell had he got involved with a woman who was trying to destroy him and the team?

A hostess offered him a glass of champagne and he waved her away. He wanted to keep his mind clear: the pressure was on him all the time now. Two victories and one total failure. The continuing comments about his driving past the accident in Monaco infuriated him. It had been his choice and it had won him the race.

He switched his mind back to Suzie. Had Carlos followed up his lead? Wyatt hadn't heard from him since the call a week before. But Carlos must be up to something because he had not flown out with Estelle to watch the Grand Prix. Wyatt knew he should be helping Carlos, but the hectic pace of the Grand Prix calendar demanded all his time and energy.

He would call Carlos the moment he got back to London.

John Tennant looked directly at Vanessa. 'I want you to go through the whole sequence of events before you were busted.'

'Again?'

'Yes. Every last detail.'

He made notes as she went through the whole story of her arrival at the hotel and subsequent jaunt to the restaurant. She was suffering, but he wanted the bastard behind the racket. God, he'd make them pay. He'd be as ruthless as they were.

Later, in his office, he enjoyed a steaming cup of cocoa and watched the rain falling from the overcast sky. Then he read through his notes. Vanessa had used her briefcase on the plane as a work-table, so there was no possibility that anyone had placed anything in it before she arrived at the hotel. After booking in at the hotel, she'd driven out to the restaurant with her cameraman, Sean O'Connor, and Ricardo Sartori had got up from his table as they entered and invited them to join him for dinner. Vanessa and Sean had then driven back to the hotel in the early hours of the morning, and Vanessa had dictated her observations made during the evening, before turning in, exhausted. She'd been woken up by Monsieur Tielemans and his men.

John Tennant decided that the heroin could only have been planted in the briefcase in her room while Vanessa was at the restaurant.

Maybe, just maybe, someone in the hotel had seen whoever had gone into Vanessa's room and planted the heroin. Unless, of course, the man had got in through the outside window of her room.

Tennant got up and put on his raincoat. It was only a short drive to the hotel.

Wyatt woke up as the plane touched down at Heathrow. He'd fallen into an uneasy sleep, thinking about Suzie, and what he wanted to do now was to get back to his house and get in touch with Carlos. He went quickly through customs and walked out into the vast open foyer of Heathrow, glad to be back in England.

Flash-guns exploded, and a pack of reporters descended on him.

'Do you take drugs?' a voice called out.

The question ricocheted round Wyatt's head. Then he remembered a newspaper article based more on wild speculation than fact, and his mind moved into focus.

'Drugs? Never. They'd interfere with my concentration. Formula One driving is about concentration – and anything that interferes with that can kill you.'

Another reporter burst in: 'Have you and Vanessa Tyson been involved for a long time? What did Suzie von Falkenhyn think about it?'

In an instant, the rage he felt at throwing away the Belgian Grand Prix was let loose. He straightened his hand and jabbed it hard in the reporter's solar-plexus. As the reporter crumpled with a groan of pain, Wyatt closed the same hand and in one flowing movement smashed the back of it against the man's head, knocking him flying across the floor.

Another reporter blocked his way.

'Move,' Wyatt said, but the man pushed a camera forward

– and Wyatt shifted back, and upward blocked with his left arm. The camera flew through the air, the reporter crashed to the floor – and Wyatt brought his heel hard down on the man's neck.

The whole crowd drew back in fear. Wyatt stared at them angrily, then walked across the foyer to the parking garage. He shouldn't have lost control, but he'd had enough. Quite enough.

Jack Phelps gripped the edge of his desk tightly as he watched the WWTN broadcast. Why had Chase been balling Tyson?

He pushed the button on his intercom. 'Lauren, get me de Villiers!'

'Sir, it's two in the morning in Britain.'

'I don't give a flying fuck. Get him now!'

Anna handed the phone to Bruce, who was desperately trying to orientate himself. He'd only got back from Calibre-Shensu headquarters after midnight – he was dog-tired and desperate for sleep. And he was furious about Wyatt's spinning off the track because of a hare-brained overtaking manoeuvre.

'Jack?' he said. 'What's wrong?'

'It's Chase.'

Bruce went cold. Drivers had a knack of getting killed on and off the circuit in the most bizarre circumstances. 'Is he all right?'

'Haven't you seen the fucking papers!'

'No, I've been working on the Shadow.'

'He smashed up two reporters at the airport. He nearly broke one guy's neck!'

God, thought Bruce, had Wyatt been on a drinking spree? Obviously, losing the Belgian Grand Prix had got to him.

'What the fuck do you expect me to do about it?' he shouted back.

'Do you know how much money I've got riding on Chase? Do you know what people will be thinking? That he's a callous thug, a killer. Especially after Monaco.'

Bruce held the phone away from his ear and waited till Jack had finished. 'He's under a lot of pressure,' he said, when at last he could get a word in.

'They've got goddamned photographs of Wyatt fucking up that reporter! And evidence that he was balling Vanessa Tyson.'

This took Bruce completely by surprise.

'Jesus!' he said. 'What do we do?'

'Bullet Chase. We'll use Ibuka. I mean, the guy finished third in his first race. Wyatt didn't even finish!'

'No!'

'Listen, de Villiers. Bullet Chase or I'll bullet you.'

Everything had changed within a matter of minutes. The call had been entirely unexpected. At first Ricardo had thought de Villiers was about to raise another problem with the Carvalho sponsorship, but he soon realised from de Villiers' tone that it was a lot more important than that.

Would he be prepared to drive for Calibre-Shensu? What a question! But how? The ban was still in force.

De Villiers told him not to worry – though he did stress that at this stage the matter was very, very confidential.

Alain Hugo raised his eyebrows for the fourth time in as many minutes. He liked Bruce de Villiers, even after the constructor's disparaging remarks about FISA. De Villiers was a fighter, and Hugo, who had come from a similar background, respected this man who'd clawed his way to the top of Formula One.

Sitting next to de Villiers was Ronnie Halliday. They'd both flown over to Paris that morning.

'You have spoken to Sartori?' Hugo said.

'Yes,' replied Bruce. 'Naturally, he's as keen as I am. I can honestly tell you that there will not be another incident. He agreed to abide by what I have recommended to you.'

'A public apology and a personal payment of half a million dollars to FISA?' Hugo raised his eyebrows.

'Yes. You understand that I am in an impossible position. If I cannot get Sartori, Calibre-Shensu will be finished.'

Ronnie Halliday gestured for de Villiers to leave them. 'Bruce, I must speak to Alain alone for a few moments.' De Villiers got up and walked smartly from the room.

Ronnie waited till the door was closed.

'Alain, I have made Formula One what it is today. Now, I know that Ricardo's behaviour in Rio was excessive, and so was Bruce's after the event, but let's look at the realities. Bruce has the backing of two major sponsors – and I think that if he fails, they may well leave Formula One alone. You know the cigarette companies are taking a hammering – there's pressure to stop them sponsoring the sport. That would be a disaster. Now, Jack Phelps of Calibre wants Chase out; the bad publicity about Chase smashing up reporters, and the relationship with Vanessa Tyson, isn't helping his company. But that puts Bruce in an almost impossible position.'

Alain Hugo pursed his lips and stared at the picture behind Ronnie's head. Charles de Gaulle had been a friend of his father's, a man he respected and admired for his courage and strength. As always in a crisis, he asked himself the question, what would de Gaulle have done in such a situation?

He turned his eyes back to Ronnie Halliday. 'The money and the apology. By tomorrow morning.'

Halliday broke into a smile, but Hugo held up his hand.

'Ronnie, now you owe me. Please don't forget it.'

Wyatt arrived at the Calibre-Shensu headquarters at seven thirty in the morning, in a state of high agitation. He hadn't been able to get hold of Carlos, but he had found a tortured message on his answering machine from Suzie – a message that had been interrupted in mid-stream. She'd talked about a mountain in a jungle where she was being held prisoner. It could be anywhere.

He just had to get hold of Carlos. He'd kept phoning the whole night, leaving messages with people he thought might see him. He'd been so agitated he hadn't trained that morning.

Now he was exhausted and very irritated. Mickey Dunstal had already discussed the latest modifications to the Shadow with him after the Belgian Grand Prix. Slight alterations to the anhedral wings at the front would increase the downforce, giving slightly better stability in the corners, which would help

336

the Shadow Two to exploit the tremendous power-output of the Shensu V12 more effectively. There would be a slight drop in top speed, but the increased cornering capability would more than make up for it.

As he got out of the Lotus, Wyatt was struck by the quietness – the place seemed almost empty. Usually at that hour most of the mechanics had arrived, and Mickey would already be discussing the day's testing with the team of Japanese engineers from Shensu. Where was everyone? What was going on?

He looked around. The only other car outside was Bruce de Villiers' Shensu saloon; it was pitch-black, in keeping with the team's livery.

What the hell was wrong?

Wyatt went quickly inside and dashed up the stairs to Bruce's office. Bruce was looking out of the window as he came in.

'Bruce, where is everybody?'

De Villiers swung round, his face ashen, the hard features set rigid.

'Wyatt. Take a seat.'

He sat down, trying to fathom what was happening. De Villiers leaned forward, placing the palms of his hands firmly on the desk.

'You are a survivor, Wyatt. I've always known that. It takes a lot of courage and a lot of guts to get into Formula One.'

Wyatt felt the fear creeping through him. What was de Villiers saying?

'Has this got something to do with my losing at Spa?'

'Wyatt, you've brought an avalanche of bad publicity down around our heads. You're reputedly involved with a woman who's trying to destroy us, and you've assaulted two journalists. And there are even rumours that you're on drugs. God knows what's going to come out next.'

'Bruce, I don't believe this. I helped get Vanessa Tyson out of Rio after she was nearly killed, that's all there is between us . . . I'm winning races. Spinning off was an error, and I won't make it again.'

'It's over, Wyatt. I am genuinely sorry.'

337

The blood was rushing to his head, he had a breathless, horrifying feeling that this couldn't really be happening.

'What's over?' he managed.

'Your drive. You're out. Jack wants it. Aito doesn't know, but he'll have to agree. And I can only wish to God it hadn't happened.'

'I'll sue you.'

De Villiers exploded. 'Don't be a fucking fool! Read your goddamned contract. This business is about racing, but to race you have to have money, and if I keep you I lose all our sponsorship. Phelps wants you out now!'

Wyatt breathed in and prepared to fight.

'You can't race without a driver,' he said.

'FISA have agreed that if Ricardo pays a half-a-million-dollar fine, he can race.'

He couldn't speak. He got up and walked out of the office. Behind him he heard de Villiers' voice: 'Wyatt, wait . . .'

Wyatt felt tears come to his eyes as he quickened his pace. His whole world was collapsing around him.

Outside he started up his car and accelerated away.

It was over.

He drove, foot flat to the floor. Drove hard and fast, not thinking, because that was too painful. He wasn't going to let anyone do this to him ever again. All his life had been geared for this year, for the possibility of taking the championship. Now, when he had it all in his hands, it was taken from him.

It was like that other time. The accident – coming round, finding his father dead. Then the hospital, and Estelle shouting at him.

You killed him. You killed him.

He'd been powerless against it, but in Japan he'd learned to fight the emptiness he felt inside. Now that hollowness threatened to return, and to destroy him.

No, he would not be beaten.

There was more to this business than met the eye . . .

He had to find Suzie. That was all that really mattered now.

*

When John Tennant arrived at the hotel, it was full of delegates checking in for a business conference. John waited patiently on the sidelines for a few moments, then he walked round the building and worked out that it would have taken an acrobat to climb the wall and get into Vanessa Tyson's room on the seventh floor.

The foyer had cleared when he returned. The concierge looked him up and down as he approached, but he wasn't fazed by this.

'Hallo,' he said, 'I'm from the Belgian police.'

The concierge looked put out. 'I hope this case of the drugs is sorted out. And now Wyatt Chase is dropped from Calibre-Shensu.'

'What?' This was news to Tennant.

'Oh yes. It was on the television.'

Wheels started turning in Tennant's mind. 'Perhaps you can help me?' he said. 'I can't believe the decision against Chase is fair, but I'm sure it's linked to his involvement with Vanessa Tyson.'

The concierge smiled. 'I admire Chase. If I can do something that would help . . .'

'Well, first of all . . . Who was on duty at this desk the evening before Miss Tyson's arrest?'

'I was.'

'Did you see anything remotely suspicious that evening, after Miss Tyson had gone off to dinner?'

The man looked up reflectively. 'No, not really. The hotel was empty.'

'When do you finish today?'

'In five minutes. I've been on since midnight.'

'Well then, I wonder if you would have lunch with me?'

After a couple of drinks the concierge had loosened up considerably.

'So,' Tennant said again, 'there's nothing that comes to mind about that evening?'

'Ah, yes. At ten thirty, I remember, a man walked out of the lounge to the lifts.'

'How do you remember the time so well?'

'My girlfriend always phones me at ten thirty to say hallo.'

A smile crept across Tennant's face. 'But why didn't you remember this earlier?' he said.

'It didn't seem important. But thinking about it now, I was aware of . . . well . . . the way he moved.'

'Moved?'

'In control. Almost like one of the Formula One drivers. In fact, I thought he might be a driver, but I didn't recognise him. He was about six feet tall, with short blond hair, dressed in a dark suit. Confident – like an American. And he was carrying a black leather document-case.'

John Tennant walked out into the pouring rain and moved along the street towards the centre of the town. The new information was disturbing. Who was the blond-haired man? What was the purpose behind the framing of Vanessa Tyson? Maybe the man had been making a delivery to her room.

Tennant was still none the wiser about what was going on, but he sensed that Vanessa Tyson was a small pawn in a very big game. It was a game he meant to put a stop to, once and for all.

Wyatt moved into the ring. His opponent, Dan Bugner, was twice his weight, and those extra kilograms were all solid muscle and bone. Bugner was the highest-graded *karateka* in Britain – Seventh Dan, equal in level to Wyatt.

Wyatt liked the concentration demanded by direct contact karate. He needed to clear his mind, get rid of the weakness, and combat was the only way to do that.

The *karateka* in London knew about him. They'd been asking him to fight Bugner ever since he'd moved there from Japan, but he'd always declined. Now he'd taken the challenge.

This was their third round. They were both dripping with sweat. Dan Bugner moved in, fast and sure, and the blow hit Wyatt hard under the heart. He didn't back off, but moved forward, disconcerting Bugner with his lack of fear.

The next blow contacted Wyatt's skull. Stars flew in front of his eyes, but he didn't lose his balance or his concentration. He squared his hips and dropped low as Bugner moved in again. He didn't block a hard kick that landed in his solar-plexus; instead he ignored the pain, swivelled his hips and drove his fist hard into Bugner's face.

Bugner's mouth opened up, the skin split up from his lips to the left of his nose. He staggered back, and then collapsed backwards, unconscious.

There was no applause from the ringside, just an intake of breath.

Wyatt walked off the floor. He knew there would be no more challenges. He felt sick. But he'd needed to expel the rage that was threatening to destroy him.

Wyatt inserted the key in his front door. Before he had a chance to turn it, his arms were gripped and pulled back. He dropped and pivoted: two quick kicks and the men were sprawling on the drive. He focused, and saw the distinctive uniforms of the London police. Damn. From the shadows another man appeared, not in uniform.

'We've got you for assault with intent to do grievous bodily harm, Chase. Frank Johnson, the journalist, is pressing charges, and believe me, they'll stick. And now it's assaulting police officers as well.'

Wyatt breathed in deeply. He knew he was in serious trouble. 'I need to change,' he said.

'OK,' replied the detective, 'but no tricks.'

He got into the police car five minutes later, and the detective handcuffed him.

'Let me tell you, Chase, it's bastards like you I particularly enoy nailing.'

Wyatt pressed his hands together and fought against the temptation to smash his right elbow hard into the detective's face. He was in enough trouble already. He stared at the police driver's head and wondered how the hell he was going to extricate himself from the mess he'd got into.

The campus of the University of Buenos Aires was empty. The buildings stood silent in the darkness, and the pavements that rang to the sound of students during the day, were deserted. In the corner of one building, however, a solitary light burned. Inside it, Carlos Ramirez sat opposite Professor Durate, who was poring over a map.

'Yes, Carlos,' he said excitedly, 'there's even a bearing scribbled here to one side. But you see, the problem I have is that there's nothing there.'

Carlos pointed to the position on the map. 'But what's that?'

'Mount Roraima.'

'Well . . .?'

'It is one of the most inaccessible places on earth.'

'Good. Excellent!'

'I don't understand,' the professor replied, taking off his reading-glasses.

'An inaccessible place is just what I have been searching for.'

Professor Durate got up, stretched and then slapped his old friend hard on the back.

'You are the most enigmatic man I have ever met, Carlos. This woman, she is a prisoner?'

'Please, it is better that you do not know.'

He drove home very fast, but it was still two hours from the university to his estancia. After forty-five minutes the concrete turned to grass and the paved side-streets to dirty lanes. At the side of the road were little outdoor grill restaurants – sometimes no more than card-tables and a portable kitchen. He breathed in deeply, enjoying the smell of grilled meat.

Then came the first pastures, dotted with cattle. In this area many people owned holiday houses where they came from the city for the weekend. Another hour, and the air smelt fresh. Now in the moonlight he saw the typical scenery of the pampas, a landscape of endless grass pastures broken only by trees and the occasional house.

He smelt the air again as he came onto his land, and felt very good. A long drive, lined with blue-gums, led up to his estancia.

He pulled up outside the long, sprawling courtyard and turned off the engine. He listened to the noise of the cicadas.

Estelle came out, a shawl wrapped round her shoulders, and he embraced her and felt the tears on her face.

'Oh God, Carlos,' she sobbed.

'What's wrong, my love?'

'They've arrested Wyatt for assault.'

Tennant landed at Heathrow and took a taxi to New Scotland Yard. He had been delayed a day in Belgium whilst arranging Vanessa Tyson's deportation to London. Rain lashed against the windows as they crawled at a snail's pace through the early-morning London traffic.

'Sorry, guv'nor, but the bleedin' place is a continuous traffic jam. There's talk of banning cars from the city centre,' the cabbie said apologetically.

Tennant nodded, sifting through some urgent paperwork. It was certain that Tyson would receive a long sentence – but he sensed that he was close to the bigger fish and he didn't want it to get out of the net.

When he'd finished, he paged through the paper he'd bought at the airport. The header on the sports page brought him up short. 'Chase Out, Sartori In.'

He devoured the article. Wyatt Chase's career as a driver was over, the article said – after the incident at Monaco, his assault on two journalists at Heathrow and now the rumour of his involvement in drug-trafficking, no one would want to give him a drive in Formula One.

He knew Chase had been arrested for assault, and he was looking forward to interrogating him about his involvement with Tyson, amongst other things. He also now suspected Chase might, just might, be involved in the drugs business.

The cab pulled up outside New Scotland Yard, and John paid the fare and dashed inside. An hour later he was shaking with fury.

'How the hell could you let Chase go!' he yelled.

'Now listen, sir. Bail was set at fifty thousand pounds – so he's hardly likely to jump the country. Chase's stepfather knows some very influential people through his polo connections.'

He whispered a name in Tennant's ear. 'You must understand, sir, I didn't have any choice.'

'So, where the hell is he?'

'At his house, I suppose.

'I want an immediate run-down on his stepfather. We'll probably never see Chase again. Fifty thousand pounds, my friend, in that league is pocket-money.'

Bruce de Villiers shifted uneasily in his chair. Aito Shensu had flown in the previous night, anxious to find out what was going on.

'Bruce, I do not like this at all,' he said now, taking off his glasses and staring directly into Bruce's eyes. 'Jack Phelps had no right to order you to dismiss Wyatt without consulting me. At Shensu we stand by the people we employ. Wyatt was provoked. By dismissing him, you have dishonoured his name.'

Bruce cursed silently to himself. He ran a tight team, and he kept complete control of all areas. Sartori's dismissal, and now the assault charge against Chase, were taking his focus away from the team. He said defensively, 'Jack said you'd both withdraw all your support if Chase was kept on.'

Aito was silent for a moment. Then he said, 'You remember how I helped you before?'

De Villiers nodded, reddening at the same time.

'Then I would think you could have learned from that,' Aito said quietly.

'Aito, I thought you and Jack were in complete agreement!'

'And what if I had been? You should have stuck up for Wyatt.'

De Villiers turned and looked out across the test circuit. 'All I care about is winning in Formula One,' he said. 'These things are getting in the way.'

'No. Winning is commitment, but it is the individual who counts. If a person is your friend, when he strikes hardship or is in trouble, you cannot walk away from him.'

'So, what do you want me to do?'

'Continue. But I will find Wyatt, and he will drive for Shensu again, no argument.'

The door slammed shut and Bruce sank back in his chair. Aito was right. He'd taken the coward's way out.

Wyatt stood in the estancia's big lounge and waited for her, and she walked in, wearing a simple black dress. He could never quite picture her in his mind, she was always better-looking in real life than in his imagination. Her face was serious.

'So you come here a criminal . . .'

'I didn't mean to punch up those reporters. They caught me at the wrong moment.'

Estelle didn't sit down, just focused her eyes on his.

'And the drugs . . .?'

'You know I'd never deal in drugs.'

'And that bitch, Vanessa Tyson?'

'Just the once.'

'My God, Wyatt, how can you be such a fool? She used you!'

He came up to her, tried to touch her arm, but she brushed his hand away.

'Everything you do is emotional,' she said. 'You drive like a lunatic and kill James. You lose your cool with Danny and he blows his brains out. Now you beat up innocent people.'

He gripped her wrists and pulled her close to him.

'You think I do those things deliberately?'

She burst into tears. He had never seen her lose control before.

'Goddamnit, Wyatt, what the hell are you doing with your life? Everything you do hurts me!'

She turned from him and left the room, and he heard her sobbing in the distance. Inside he felt hollow. There was nothing he could do to change anything.

Wyatt studied the maps and the photographs. Carlos's study was lined with books and trophies: the Ramirez family had played polo for three generations, and each had produced a ten-goal player. Carlos rested his hand on Wyatt's arm.

'I leave this estancia to you.'

'No, Carlos, there are your brother's sons.'

'You are my son, in spirit if not in body. You continue the blood-line. I want you to forget this Formula One, and I want you to forget about your father.'

'I cannot. I will never shake off this terrible guilt. I race because I know that's what he wanted me to do.'

Carlos got up from the desk and walked across to a black-and-white photograph that hung on the wall. He handed it to Wyatt.

'It is the remains of the Jesuit mission in San Ignacio mini.'

Wyatt looked at the dry-stone walls covered in vegetation, the trees growing out of roofless buildings. There was a feeling of emptiness about the place, a sense of desolation.

'In 1609,' Carlos said, 'at the request of the Governor of Paraguay, the Spanish king gave the Jesuits permission to set up missions in Paraguay, to convert the Guarani Indians to Christianity. This was the first such mission. Had these missions survived, they might have established an independent theocratic state and altered the whole course of our history.'

The picture lay still in Wyatt's hands. 'What happened?'

'In 1750, by the terms of a treaty between Spain and Portugal, seven missions were handed over to the Portuguese in exchange for the colony of Sacramento. When the Indians and some of the Jesuits refused to move, they were decimated. But one of their descendants still lives today – one of the priests had broken the Holy Order and had been having an affair with the daughter of the Governor of Paraguay.'

He handed Wyatt a hand-painted portrait of a beautiful girl with raven hair.

'Her name was Eva Ramirez. When her priest-lover was killed, she was on the verge of committing suicide, but somehow she carried on. It was later that she discovered she was pregnant with the priest's child. Amidst great scandal, she gave birth. Her father died soon afterwards – from shame, it was said. She inherited his farms and estates. She raised the child herself, then sent him to the Jesuits for his education.

'The child was christened Carlos Ramirez – taking the first name of his father. The name has been handed down from generation to generation in our family, along with the diaries and the picture of Eva. So you see, I carry on a tradition; I

346

carry a burden, as it were – to honour the courage of Eva Ramirez and her lover . . . Perhaps my brother David did more good than I. Nevertheless, like you I carry a sense of responsibility about the past.

'That is why I understand you so well, Wyatt. Yes, unfortunately, you are right, you cannot forget the past – just as I must honour that long-ago Jesuit priest whose blood and name I carry.'

Carlos went over to a map of South America that covered most of one wall of the study.

'The man who I was supposed to meet, Raoul. The man who said he knew where I could find Suzie . . . I searched his hotel room and I found a map. There were markings on it, and with the help of a friend of mine at the university, I located this place.'

Wyatt slid forward on his chair. 'She is alive,' he said. 'I got a message from her on my answering-machine – a message I couldn't make out.'

'You must understand one thing, Wyatt. There are few men who would build a place at the most inaccessible point of the Amazon basin.'

Wyatt studied a picture of Mount Roraima that Carlos had handed him.

'It is my guess,' Carlos said, 'that she is being held somewhere in the area of this mountain.'

'But that was what she said to me! That she was being held a prisoner on a mountain in the jungle!'

'It must be the place. We will find her.'

Carlos did not mention the real reason for his interest, the possibility that Emerson Ortega might still be alive, and that a place like Roraima might well be his sanctuary. That he hoped to kill Ortega to avenge the death of his brother.

'But Carlos, what would anyone be doing there?'

'I have a pretty good idea already, but we will find out for sure when we get there.'

John Tennant studied the contents of a large box-file on his desk, and whistled. It all began to make some sort of sense. After all, South America was a major drug producer.

Carlos Ramirez. His brother, the former Minister of Justice of Colombia, had been assassinated in the most barbaric fashion by members of the Ortega Cartel. Perhaps, mused Tennant, David Ramirez had been supporting a rival cartel. On that assumption, Carlos Ramirez could well be a major producer and trafficker.

Wyatt had grown up in England, the son of the great James Chase. Wyatt had developed an early fascination in motor cycles, then moved on to go-karts. He was also a keen climber. Both interests had been encouraged by his father.

Then had come the accident, with James Chase killed and his son carrying the blame. After that, it got hazy. Wyatt had apparently spent ten years in Japan, studying karate at some obscure *dojo*. He had reached the level of Seventh Dan. Wyatt Chase was a walking weapon.

Then, following his sudden departure from Japan, he had been given a seat in a car in his uncle's Formula One team. This year it was Calibre-Shensu, and Wyatt had been set to win the championship.

Money might well have been a problem: Wyatt had got next to nothing when his uncle sold the team to Jack Phelps. That was a good enough motive. So could Chase be the drug-pusher he was looking for in the Calibre team? Tennant asked himself. Moving cocaine he'd obtained from his stepfather? It was unlikely that Chase was an addict; he was a fitness fanatic, and rarely even drank. So Chase might well have been selling the coke to raise funds to buy a drive in Formula One. And he might have planted the drugs on Vanessa Tyson, just to shut her up and stop her tirade against Phelps, his employer.

Wyatt Chase was in very serious trouble. Evidently he had jumped bail and caught a plane to South America. That, and the link with Ramirez, would seem to indicate that he was guilty.

After all, Chase had the right South American connections.

Jack Phelps dived into his pool and looked out through the clear blue water at the New York horizon. He rose to the surface, watching the vapour come off the warm water and dissolve into the sky above.

He was feeling good. Things were working out perfectly. Sartori, as the new number one Calibre-Shensu driver, was firmly committed. Several more teams had also expressed interest in Carvalho tyres, and as a direct result, two of the world's major tyre manufacturers were making interested noises about buying Carvalho out. Jack stood to make a lot of money on that deal alone.

He'd never liked Chase; the man could not be bought or controlled, which meant he was dangerous. He was glad Wyatt was out. He was surprised that Aito was cut up about it, but then the Japanese did have some funny ideas about morality and other outdated concepts.

He pulled himself out of the water and felt the cold air making his skin tingle. He reckoned they'd take the first two places in the Italian Grand Prix. Things couldn't be going better.

May

The plane dropped from the sky and winged its way lazily over the rolling greenness of the thick jungle below. Below them, the river coiled its way through the blanket of dense foliage like a silver snake. Then from the green broke a dirty scar, the isolated town of Manaus.

Carlos touched Wyatt's arm and shouted across the noise of the engines. 'You disappear in the Amazon basin and no one will find you. We are going into the unknown.' He laughed loudly, and Wyatt smiled. Carlos was always confident . . .

A day later they were in a motorised launch with two local Indians, travelling up the lazy waters of the Amazon. They had told everyone they came into contact with in Manaus that they were botanists looking for a rare species of plant.

Wyatt looked uneasily at the crates stowed in the centre of the boat. He hadn't been surprised when Carlos explained they contained machine-guns, hand-guns and grenades. There were also three huge rucksacks packed with an assortment of climbing gear.

He let his hand drift in the water.

'Hey, Wyatt, that's not a good idea. The piranhas like the taste of raw flesh,' Carlos shouted.

Wyatt withdrew his hand quickly. He thought about the testing he would have been doing now if he'd still been with Calibre-Shensu. In another week it would be the Italian Grand Prix at Monza. It really didn't bear thinking about.

'Hey, Wyatt.' Carlos broke into his thoughts. 'We get to the bottom of this thing, my friend, don't you worry.'

He turned to face Carlos, who was tying up his pony-tail, strands of hair blowing in the breeze.

'I wanted to race at Monza,' he said. 'That was where . . .'

350

'Forget about the accident. Forget about Formula One. If you were in London, you'd be in jail. This way, we might find Suzie. You are in big trouble, Wyatt, don't forget that.'

Wyatt lay back and looked at the trees lining the edge of the river. 'Imagine,' he said, 'if someone told you you couldn't play polo any longer.'

Carlos flashed him a grin. 'But no one can! This Formula One racing is a crazy business.'

Ricardo sat looking out across the Paris skyline. He wanted out, now that he'd got his drive back. Opposite him, Talbot leaned back in his chair and put his hands behind his head, watching the other people in the hotel's top-floor lounge. The American was always looking, Ricardo thought; he was never completely relaxed.

'Ricardo, good buddy,' Talbot said, 'I don't know why you get so nervous. We're partners. I think I made that very clear to you in Belgium. There is no going back.' He was quiet, but firm.

'But I can't sleep at night. Tennant keeps phoning me. Why can't we tell him what is going on?'

'Because Tennant is a stupid British cop and he'd blow the whole operation. He's probably wasting his time trying to work out the truth about the Tyson case, and find out what's happened to Chase.'

'Tennant told me he's already been talking to the *Carbinari*, in preparation for Monza,' Ricardo replied, looking at a leggy blonde walking past. 'But if you're not worried . . .'

He did not see the muscle on Talbot's neck quiver.

'Ricardo, I must be on my way. I have some urgent business to sort out.

Talbot disappeared into the dining-room, breathing heavily. Tennant, he thought, was becoming a nuisance.

John Tennant walked away from the house in the first light of the morning, feeling very good. The lady he had taken out the evening had proved better company than he'd expected, and coffee at her flat in Holland Park had progressed to cognac –

by which stage they had both known they felt the same way about each other.

The streets were almost empty. It was only after about five minutes that he had the uneasy feeling that someone was tailing him.

He increased his pace. He was now in an isolated access road, lined with gates and full dustbins.

He tripped over something – and then felt a cold metal object impact against the side of his head. He rolled over into a ball, and out of the corner of his eye caught sight of a tall blond man. He went for his gun. A kick in his back caught his kidneys and he screamed out in pain, but the gun remained in his hand: the instinct he'd developed during his years in the SAS saved him.

He rolled over, centred the bead on the blond head, and fired. His attacker staggered back, then recovered. He bounded up onto some rubbish-bins, and vaulted over a concrete wall before Tennant could fire again.

Tennant dragged himself to his feet. One thing was certain, he was getting a little closer to the men who dealt in drugs. But he still had a very long way to go.

Ricardo lay on the mattress in his hotel room, sweating. It was two days since they'd begun testing, and he was slow, very slow. Charlie Ibuka's times were always faster.

He desperately wanted a snort of cocaine, but he knew that was the pathway to death because it would slow down his reaction-times. He had to get back to the level of fitness and concentration he'd been at the previous year. The Shadow Two was extraordinarily fast, and he knew that if he could just get his edge back he could win.

But the pressure was getting to him. Talbot had insisted that he spearhead the Italian delivery. He'd argued that he needed to focus on the race – but he guessed that Talbot didn't give a damn what position he finished in.

At least the publicity was getting better. There was no more talk of drugs, and after the initial furore Chase had been forgotten.

*

The general straightened his uniform, looking up at the American flag on the wall and the picture of his President. He felt horrified at what he'd found out.

He hadn't liked Talbot from the beginning, but he'd had instructions from the highest level that he was to co-operate with him. The plan was that Talbot could land his planes and dump their cargo at his airforce base, and in return Talbot would ship special cargo out of the country for them. That cargo was guns and ammunition for anti-government forces in Colombia. The objective, he'd been told, was to overthrow the Colombian government, install a pro-American regime and stamp out the drug cartels. The general had thought then that the plan was excellent.

Only after a few months had he begun to wonder exactly what it was Talbot was exporting from Colombia. It didn't take him long to discover it was cocaine.

So he'd confronted the man.

Talbot had smacked him around. The general had thought he was the one in control till then. As he'd lain bleeding on the floor, Talbot had explained the bottom line: if the general wanted to go public, they'd accuse him of using the money from the sale of the drugs to fund the whole operation.

The general realised he'd been used. He could not raise any objections – he knew what would happen if he did: Talbot would disappear, and he would be regarded as personally responsible for the whole stinking plan.

Talbot held the trump card.

The general pulled his eyes away from the President's picture and back to the list of men and equipment Talbot had requested for a special mission. The question in the general's mind was, what exactly was it that Talbot was planning to attack?

Much to his irritation, the Concorde flight the next morning was fully booked – but then a last-minute cancellation allowed Ricardo to get a place. Two hours, he thought now, and he would be exactly where he wanted to be. He always liked travelling in the sleek-bodied plane that looked more like a giant bird of prey than a supersonic airliner. Inside, it felt quite different from an ordinary passenger plane; not the cavernous interior of a wide-bodied 747, but a narrow fuselage that could only accommodate two pairs of seats on either side of the aisle.

He relaxed back into his seat and studied the newspaper. The sporting page carried the story of his reinstatement at Calibre-Shensu, his progress in developing the Shadow Two; the writer predicted a win for him at Monza. Ricardo grimaced. If only he could be so certain! At least Charlie Ibuka was not in the same class as Chase – and he sensed that de Villiers thought the same.

The massive engines hummed as the plane raced down the runway and then leapt into the air with a carelessness that belied the technology beneath its metal skin. The thrust pushed Ricardo gently back in his seat. In two hours he would be in New York. His mind was quite made up: there was only one way for him to proceed.

Jack Phelps liked to rise early. Lauren would bring him coffee and the morning papers. There would a short dictation session and then Lauren would leave, allowing him time to dress. His suit was always selected the day before and subjected to a rigorous inspection. It was more than Lauren's life was worth to present him with clothes that were not immaculate.

He had just started to dress when his intercom sounded. Lauren's hushed tones announced: 'You have a visitor, sir.'

'Yes?' he asked irritatedly. He had told Lauren on numerous occasions that he didn't like to have his early-morning routine interrupted.

'Mr Sartori is most insistent that he see you.'

'Show him into the lounge, then, and offer him something to drink.'

'Very good, sir.'

Phelps snickered as he dressed. He knew Sartori's problems were only just beginning. He was going to pile on the pressure now – that way it would be all the easier to control him. He'd made sure that the Italian Receiver of Revenue didn't let Ricardo off the hook – and he also knew Ricardo was facing a heavy fine for tax avoidance. And he'd made quite sure that though he paid Ricardo a lot of money, it was never enough to pay off his debts completely.

Phelps straightened his tie and walked into the room. Ricardo was sitting on one of the hand-made leather couches, looking distinctly ill at ease.

'You bastard!' he said when he saw Jack.

Jack looked blankly at Ricardo. 'I don't know what the hell you're talking about.' He selected a thin cigar from a humidor on the table and offered one to Ricardo, who refused it.

'You cannot expect me to take a drop in my earnings because I am driving for Calibre-Shensu!' Ricardo burst out.

Phelps inspected the sole of one of his shoes. 'Why not? You are working for Bruce de Villiers. I should think the twenty million dollars we're paying you is quite adequate. The fine wasn't that much.'

Phelps knew that Bruce had renegotiated Ricardo's contract, but he preferred to pretend ignorance.

'I'm not getting twenty million dollars! Bruce paid my fine, but now he says he'll only pay for the championship points I score. I need money now! Do you know what it takes to drive a Formula One car? Do you? I tell you, I need to devote all my energy to it. I do not need these problems. I want my original fee.'

Phelps laughed loudly, then his face turned deadly serious.

'I hate people who waste my time,' he said. 'You caused us a lot of trouble, and I'm not going to ask Bruce to pay you any more than you're getting. And I know there's no way you can handle my affairs capably if you're racing, so I'm dropping your salary.' He got up and stretched. 'Lauren has booked your return flight,' he said.

'Bastard!'

Phelps held his chin between his thumb and forefinger. 'No more money,' he said.

'Whatever you want, I do it!' the Italian begged.

'Anything?'

Ricardo nodded.

Phelps returned to his desk, sifted through a few papers and then looked up.

'All right, Ricardo. I'll speak to Bruce about upping your

fee. But I want you to sign a new contract for your other services to my company. You will fly to Zurich.'

Ricardo sat in the small but immaculately decorated room. It had no windows, and he had been assured that it was swept twice a day for bugging devices. A tall, thin man with a receding hairline came in through the door on the left and sat down opposite him.

'Mr Phelps has decided, for reasons unknown to us, to make you responsible for his entire financial laundering operation outside America. Naturally, this arrangement also includes a majority share-holding. All that is required now is your signature.'

The man pushed the document over to Ricardo.

'I would like to read it,' Ricardo said.

'That is fine. You can have as much time as you want. Please push the buzzer when you have finished.'

The man got up to go. Ricardo did not like the Swiss, they were almost as emotionless as the English.

'Hey!' he said. 'Hold it! I won't take long.'

The man sat down again and folded his arms in front of him, staring at the table while Ricardo paged quickly through the document. He couldn't make head or tail of half the clauses – but still, they didn't really interest him. It was just the money that mattered. He stopped at the list of the other shareholders.

'Why aren't there any other names here except mine?'

'This is a typical arrangement,' the man said. 'The other interests are held by nominated holding companies. You appreciate the need for secrecy.'

Ricardo nodded.

'If you would sign here, here and here.'

Ricardo did as he was instructed. When he had finished, the man gathered up the papers.

'I would like a copy,' Ricardo said.

'Mr Sartori. Documents of this nature never ever leave this office.'

Five minutes later Ricardo was walking along the immaculate pavements of Zurich. He felt as if he was walking on air.

His financial problems were over, and now he could concentrate on driving again.

Estelle put down the paper and stared across the empty lounge. It was a large room, the huge terracotta-tiled floor scattered with Persian carpets. Outside, through the beech-framed windows, she could see the rolling grasslands of the estancia that seemed to stretch out endlessly into the distance.

Emotions tore through her. She had already lost one husband; now Carlos and Wyatt were in the thick of something she did not even want to try and comprehend. She looked at her reflection in the wall mirror. She would be forty-eight in a month's time. Carlos was two years older than her, and the best-looking man she knew.

She touched her face. There was nothing the matter with her, everyone said she looked like a woman in her twenties. Her body was still firm from the hours she spent in the saddle every day. But she wanted Carlos to love her with passion; she wanted to exhaust him in bed, so that he would always be thinking of her body. He must always desire her. To hold him through their wedding vows and the memory of what she had been, was not her way and never would be.

It had been like that with James. The intensity of their love had been frightening, his death unbearable. If it had not been for Carlos, she would not have survived. Carlos had an energy, a passion for life like James's. She would always compare him with James, she could not avoid it. And in the depths of her heart she knew that it was James she loved the most.

Tears sprang to her eyes. She still vividly remembered the call from the police and the trip to the hospital where the doctor told her that it was Wyatt who had been driving.

God, so much pain. What had she done to deserve so much pain? And then Wyatt had left. He'd gone to live in Japan, cutting himself off from her and everyone else. Then Danny had gone this year, by his own hand.

Estelle looked out of the window and felt how powerless she was against the train of events that had always seemed to dictate the course of her life – even though she tried to resist them.

It was then that she picked up the paper again, and saw the name of the man from New Scotland Yard who was handling Vanessa Tyson's case – John Tennant.

She picked up the phone and got hold of directory enquiries in England. 'Yes, madam, I have the number for New Scotland Yard.'

She took it down, and dialled quickly.

'*Allo*, New Scotland Yard? I'd like to speak to John Tennant.'

'It's two in the morning, madam. He's not here.'

'*Merde*!'

There was a momentary silence on the line. Then: 'Is it urgent? I do have a home number . . .'

'Give me the number.'

The phone rang for a long, long time. Eventually it was picked up and she heard a very English woman on the other end of the line.

'Who is it? Do you know it's two in the morning!'

'I'm sorry, I am phoning from Argentina, I did not realise.'

There was the sound of another phone being picked up, then a male voice. 'Who is that?'

'Estelle Ramirez . . .'

'Who are you?'

'Estelle Ramirez . . . Wyatt Chase's mother. I know where my son is.'

She briefly explained what she knew of what had happened, and that she thought Wyatt was innocent of the drug-trafficking allegations.

'Where is he now?' Tennant asked.

'Somewhere in the Amazon basin. Mr Tennant . . . something else. I . . . want to speak to Vanessa Tyson.'

More silence. 'Are you prepared to come to London . . .?'

'I believe Vanessa Tyson is guilty. I think she knows more than she's letting on. I want to talk to her.'

'Look, really, I can't . . .'

'You want my son, I'm the only person who can lead you to him.'

There was another long silence. Estelle held the receiver anxiously.

358

'How . . . How soon could you get here?'

'Tomorrow.'

'Phone me your flight and arrival time at this number, and I'll meet you at the airport.'

She saddled up her favourite horse and went for a long ride. Carlos and Wyatt were taking one hell of a risk, she knew it. But they had sworn her to secrecy, and she would never break her word.

But there was nothing to stop her from doing some investigative work on her own. She would use John Tennant to find out a few things. Once, long ago, she'd trusted Jack Phelps, but a few days before his death James had said on several occasions that he'd changed his mind about Phelps. Ever since that time, she'd wondered about Jack.

She touched down at Heathrow a day later. Dressed in black, her blonde hair piled high, she wore a simple choker round her neck. It was cold, and she pulled her fur coat tightly around her as she walked through customs.

'Mrs Ramirez?' the customs official asked, peering at her passport.

Oh my God, not problems now?

'Would you mind stepping this way? Your luggage will be taken care of. Please, don't look so worried. There is nothing the matter.'

She was shown down a series of corridors and then into an underground parking garage. A dark-haired man in his late twenties, early thirties was standing next to a white police Rover.

'Mrs Ramirez, I'm Chief Inspector John Tennant.'

She liked him immediately. He was different from what she'd expected.

John Tennant sucked in his breath. It was as it had always been – he couldn't resist an attractive woman. He liked the way Estelle Ramirez carried herself, her back perfectly straight, yet all her movements fluid and sensual.

'I am pleased to meet you, captain,' she said. 'I hope I can help you and you can help me.'

Once they were in the car and moving, he began talking.

'I work in drugs. I know your son was arrested for assault – but we suspected he might be involved in drug-trafficking.' His face lost its animation and his features became stony. 'He is now in serious trouble. He has broken his bail conditions, and has, in short, vanished. Do you know where he is?'

'He is with my husband. More than that I cannot say.'

John gripped the wheel tightly. He had to play her out. He could tell she was no fool.

'Look, I've managed to get permission for you to see Vanessa Tyson. She's been transferred to England.'

'I know she's guilty,' Estelle said. 'I'm not asking you to believe me, all I want to do is speak to her.'

John looked directly into her eyes. 'You know the facts. But to me it looks as if she was framed, the victim of a plant, a very elaborate plant. However, there's not a shred of evidence to support that view.'

'She is guilty, of that I have no doubt.'

'There's something very strange about this whole business, Mrs Ramirez. You were involved with most of these people ten years ago . . .'

'I think the past is best forgotten. But my late husband, I think he knew something about Jack Phelps, something that changed his relationship with Jack. Whatever it was, it made him realise that he couldn't trust Jack any longer.'

Wyatt's clothes stuck to him. Impatiently he pushed his shirt-sleeve above his elbow and chopped away at another tall vine – and suddenly sunlight streamed down, and he was staring up at a rock wall that soared into space.

Carlos staggered up next to him and pulled out the binoculars, combing the edge of the cliff. The sheer rock face was filled with fissures and cracks; left and right it seemed to stretch off into eternity. Pockets of mist drifted past it, adding to its unreality.

They must be mad coming here, thought Carlos. He quartered the cliff-top with the binoculars, looking for evidence of human activity, all he could see was buttresses and overhangs of rock.

Wyatt stared upwards, saying nothing.

'What are you thinking about, Wyatt?'

'How a Japanese person, someone like Aito, would relish the *mu* – the nothingness of this place. It is a lost world.'

'It's incredible, isn't it? Apparently only one party of climbers has ever attempted it, an insane group of Britishers.'

Wyatt took the binoculars from Carlos and felt a wave of despair. How the hell were they going to find the place, even if it existed?

They cleared a rough camp-site from the thickly matted vegetation and stripped off their sodden clothing. Carlos lit up the portable gas cooker, and they soon had a billy-can boiling. The jungle around them was dense, a green abyss that threatened to engulf them at any moment.

Carlos made the tea and handed Wyatt a mug. 'Now we wait. Six-hour watches each, while the other sleeps.'

Wyatt looked at him quizzically. 'What the hell are we waiting for?'

'If there's something up there, we'd never find it by plane. No one would know about it, and whoever built this place would make sure you couldn't see it from the air. And from the ground? What maniac would ever approach this hell-hole from the ground?'

'I still don't understand.'

Carlos laughed. 'You, who are so clever? Wyatt, it is very, very simple. The only way these people get in and out is by plane. Sooner or later we will hear one approach.'

'But what about the other side of the mountain? What if they come in from that side? We wouldn't see them.'

'You're nobody's fool, are you? You see, this is the only possible direction that a plane can approach Roraima from, according to my learned friend at the university. The other side is too broken up, and there is far too much air turbulence.'

Wyatt gestured to the massive line of cliffs that disappeared into the distance.

'And what if they are at the other end? It will take days just to cut our way through to the base.'

'Not so fast. We also studied every available map of Roraima, and this area above us is the most logical place to position a building and an airstrip.'

Carlos lay down in his hammock. God, he felt wet and uncomfortable. 'Now,' he said, 'after asking so many questions, you can take the first watch.'

Carlos fell asleep in minutes, and Wyatt was left alone with the noises of the jungle. He scanned the cliffs above him with the binoculars, but could find nothing of significance. The whole place – the geography of it, the atmosphere of it – made him feel deeply uneasy.

Vanessa couldn't understand what was happening. She had been woken up in her cell, told to dress, and was not being taken up to the ground floor. She kept running her hands through her hair – she felt shabby and disorientated. Was she to be subjected to more interrogation?

She was shown into an office with a new detective who looked drawn and tired. She felt like crying, but she wasn't about to give him the satisfaction.

'Where is John Tennant?' she asked forcefully. 'And why are you holding me? You're wrong, you know that? I am not guilty, and I intend to prove it beyond a shadow of doubt.'

'How?' the detective asked cuttingly.

'I am innocent till proven guilty.'

'Innocent? You're a fine one to talk, Miss Tyson.'

'What the hell you are talking about?'

'Let me spell it out. Money can buy you a lot of things, Miss Tyson, but it won't buy you freedom. We hardly ever get hold of you bastards, because you always slip out of our reach and we get left with small fry. Well, let me tell you, now I've got you I'll make sure you get the maximum sentence if it's the last thing I do.'

'I am not guilty you fool!' Vanessa screamed out hysterically – and then, in spite of herself, burst into tears. 'You fucking bastards! Do you know what it's like to sit in that cell and know that there's nothing, absolutely nothing, you can do about it? Do you?'

He looked at her without a trace of pity.

'Your boyfriend got out on fifty thousand pounds bail. Then he skipped the country. We're not about to make the same mistake with you.'

'You're wrong, and you won't accept it,' Vanessa replied very quietly.

'You're going to London for further interrogation. A police officer has your clothes ready in the next room, and once you've signed for them someone will escort you to London to see John Tennant.'

She went through to the next room and signed for her clothes. They were creased, and hadn't been washed, but she was glad to put them on anyway. They made her feel like a human being again.

Fifteen minutes later, followed by another plain-clothes policeman, she walked disbelievingly out of the front door of the station and into the darkness. The falling rain landed softly on her face, and she started to cry again.

Ricardo watched his hands shaking. This had never happened before. He had always managed to remain aloof from people, totally in command. Now that control was slipping. He had planned to be in peak form by the time he was back in Italy, but things hadn't worked out that way. He was still taking cocaine. He needed it, especially now that everyone was after his blood. The competition was harder than ever before.

Phelps was maintaining the pressure, of course – but then Phelps had delivered on the financial side and was entitled to make demands. And Talbot was phoning him every twelve hours, giving him commands and making sure that he was controlling the delivery.

He was not driving well in the practice sessions. He was not handling Monza's daunting combination of long, quick straights and slowing chicanes at all competently. And this was his home ground, Italy, where he should have been most comfortable.

He was angry, which only made his driving worse. Angry that he should have allowed himself to get into this position; furious at the way both Phelps and Talbot kept hounding him. But worst of all, he was angry with himself – enraged by the knowledge that he hadn't been spending enough time on the track.

The first official practice was the next day, and he knew that he stood little chance of a position near the front of the grid if his present performance was anything to go by. De Rosner, the French ace driving for McCabe, was going all out; the speed at which he was lapping meant that he stood a very good chance of leading the race. Charlie Ibuka was almost equalling those times, gunning for first-place honours.

Ricardo pulled in after twenty lacklustre laps. Bruce was waiting for him in the pit lane.

'What the hell's wrong?' he bellowed as Ricardo climbed out of the Shadow.

Ricardo pulled off his helmet. He couldn't tell Bruce that the car was perfect, that it was he who was pulling it down.

'I don't know,' he said. 'I just can't seem to get my act together.'

Bruce gestured for Ricardo to follow him out of the pits, and it was only when they were in the air-conditioned confines of the Calibre-Shensu motorhome, out of earshot of the rest of the team, that he gave Ricardo a piece of his mind.

'What the fuck are you doing? Everything's resting on you. Mickey says you tell him less than fuck-all about the car, so how the hell can you expect to have it set up perfectly for the race? I mean, Ibuka's lapping faster than you!'

'You 'ave got a cheek.'

'Aito and Jack are relying on you, Ricardo. It's not their fault you can't get your act together. You know Ibuka can't be expected to deliver throughout the race, he just doesn't have the experience.'

Ricardo turned his back on Bruce de Villiers and let himself out of the motorhome. The hydraulic doors closed softly behind him. He was bristling with anger. He'd had enough of Bruce, he was sick of his demands. He had to get away from the trace and relax. He drove back into Milan feeling desperate. Why had he let other people interfere with his life?

Later, in the gigantic bath in the presidential suite of the Milan Hilton, he tried to relax. This was the town where he'd grown up, where he should have felt the most at home.

Instead, he was terrified and his fear was not unfounded. Talbot had warned him that the Mafia might start putting pressure on him.

The phone rang and he almost leapt in the air with fear. He picked up the receiver apprehensively.

'Hello, Ricardo, it's Rod.' The voice hissed down the line like an angry snake. 'Are you comfortable?'

'No. I think that somebody is onto us.'

There was a laugh that sounded like water running down a drain. 'Just concentrate on making the delivery.'

Shit, shit, shit! He didn't need this pressure, not on top of the driving. But he forced himself to concentrate. He had to co-operate with Talbot.

'The consignment, when does it arrive?'

'Early tomorrow. It coincides with the time of the first practice, as we agreed.'

'Fine. You will arrange a contact for me?'

'It is done. You will receive the delivery instructions in the same way.'

Ricardo wasn't feeling any better when he put the phone down. He got out of the bath and poured out a line of the white powder on his shaving-mirror, then he took out the special gold tube and pushed it up his nose. He sniffed up the powder and almost immediately felt his old confidence return.

He decided he was going to have a night on the town – after all, he had money to burn. It was now time for him to enjoy his new-found wealth. He dressed casually and then took the lift down to the foyer, chucking his key across the counter and making his way towards the revolving doors that led out onto the street. It was dark outside, and Milan was just starting to buzz. As he came out he bumped into a redhead who was going the other way.

She stumbled, about to fall, and he caught her elbow. His eyes registered the fact that she had good legs, then that she had a superb body, and finally that her face was ravishing.

'My apologies.'

'You should watch where you're going,' she replied in Italian.

'Perhaps I can make it up to you?'

365

'I don't think so.'

''Ow about dinner?'

She smiled. All he knew now was that he wanted her.

'You are very forward,' she said, 'whoever you are.'

'Dinner tonight?'

She ran a hand through her hair. 'All right, I will cancel my other arrangements. I'll meet you here in half an hour.'

Then she was gone, before he could say anything more.

He went back to reception and slipped the concierge a generous supply of notes.

'Yes sir. Can I help you?'

'Perhaps you can. The redhead. She is staying in which room?'

'Ah, let me look.' The man ran his finger down the print-out for that evening's bookings. 'She is in one of the suites on the top floor, right next to your own if I'm not mistaken.'

'And her name?'

'Mrs Jones.'

At the entrance to the airport cargo centre in Milan, two white minibuses awaited the arrival of a Lufthansa 747 freighter – their blackened windows revealing nothing to the outside world. In the distance, standing on the roof of a warehouse and looking through high-powered binoculars, a lean man with long drooping moustache scanned the outside of the cargo centre. He looked closely at the minibuses, then barked a swift series of instructions into the portable phone next to him.

Four pallets of Carvalho tyres from the 747 passed quickly through customs, since special clearance had been arranged. Half an hour later they were loaded into a container on the back of a forward-control truck, which pulled out of the centre and headed for the Autodromo Nazionale di Monza. The two minibuses tailed the truck at a distance.

Five minutes later, the truck was forced to stop at a police road-block. The driver stepped down from the cab – and collapsed as two bullets were pumped into the side of his skull. His assistant leapt down, shotgun in hand, but was cut down by a burst of automatic rifle fire.

The minibuses drew up, and armed men piled out. In the distance a large black limousine waited. One of the armed men went to the back of the container and cut through its locks with a set of bolt-cutters.

The black limousine rolled forward. A large old man with white hair stepped out. He lit up a cigar and gestured for the man with the bolt-cutters to open the doors of the container.

From inside the container a sub-machine gun erupted into life, spraying tracers across the tarmac. The old man was lifted up in the air as the bullets described a diagonal line across his torso and then threw him to the ground. He groaned, blood oozing from between his lips, and he died clutching the still burning cigar in his left hand.

There was a moment's silence.

The men moved forward, thinking that whoever was inside the container must have run out of ammunition. Just as they got to the door, a man rose up from beneath the packing-cases in the container.

Time seemed to slow down. Intense sunlight and birdsong filled the air. Then the sub-machine-gun in the man's hands erupted.

They had no time to react: the bullets smacked into them. One of them screamed, clutching at the holes in his stomach; another's knee-cap splintered. One man managed to get off a shot that went far wide of its target, who pivoted, and pumped him full of bullets.

Then there was silence again.

Rob Talbot stepped warily out of the container. He took out two jerry-cans, leaving the doors of the container open behind him. Then he moved round to the front of the truck, pulling the bodies of the driver and his assistant away.

Behind him, one of the men, still half-alive, his eyes covered in blood, pulled out a grenade and tossed it into the container, then rolled over dead.

The explosion knocked Talbot flat on his face.

'Fuck!' he screamed as the container erupted in flames, destroying its cargo of tyres.

He went over to the minibuses and tossed a fragmentation grenade into each. Moments later they erupted into flame.

He took the jerry-cans, poured petrol over the bodies and set light to them. Then he jumped into the limousine and drove away. It had all taken less than three minutes, and the road behind him looked more like a war zone than a public highway.

That evening, in a backstreet of Milan in a deserted villa, a special meeting was called. The men arrived at different times, all old, all immaculately dressed – and all very angry. They sat around a bare wooden table, and Romano Ciolli addressed them. He took of his dark framed glasses to reveal his eyes, the colour of grey steel in his dead-white face. He spoke more through his nose than his mouth.

'My friends. You know why you are here. Georgio, may he rest in peace, intercepted the consignment at Milan airport. He and his men were gunned down.'

He paced around the table. 'I have instructed my assassin. *Finire!*'

The men round the table laughed uneasily. They all lived in fear of death, especially the kind of death that was now being ordered by *Il Capo*.

'This is our territory,' Ciolli went on. 'We must set an example, otherwise the world will think we have gone soft.'

One of the men from around the table spoke.

'*Signor*. You are sure he is the one?'

'*Madonna!* He even has the nerve to appear in public in our country.'

'You are quite sure?'

'I have connections in Zurich. His money is laundered through Panama and deposited in Switzerland.'

The men all stared down at the table, as if they were praying in church.

'He will die painfully,' Ciolli said. 'And he will tell us the name of the man who killed Georgio.'

Ricardo staggered into bed at three in the morning – tired and very frustrated. Elvira Jones had led him a merry dance. Right through the evening she had left him in no doubt of her intentions, and he was hard with excitement as they took the taxi back to the hotel. Then, outside his room, she had switched him off like a light-bulb. It was as if she had never given him the come-on.

She agreed to go with him to the Grand Prix the next day, and to dine with him the following night. Taking a woman out a second time before he had slept with her went against all his principles, but he had to admit that he was impressed by her tactics. Besides, he argued, she was a pleasant break from the pressures of the track.

Of course, he should not have gone out. He should have rested, mentally prepared himself for the race. Only lying tenth on the grid, he was going to have to fight to get to the front.

There was a knock on the door and immediately he was on his feet. Perhaps it was Elvira. Maybe she had changed her mind. He slipped on a silk dressing-gown and opened the door – then threw his hands in the air.

'What do you want?'

Talbot ignored Ricardo's histrionics. He sauntered into the room, sat down on the sofa and starting picking the dirt from his nails with a toothpick. Ricardo noticed an ugly scar on his forehead that had not been there during their previous meeting. He closed the door and remained standing.

'What's wrong?' he said.

'There have been problems.'

Ricardo's right eyebrow twitched. He did not need this now. He needed to rest, to relax.

'Someone knew about the delivery,' Talbot went on. 'They tried to corner me, but I killed every one of the bastards. It must have been a rival group.'

Ricardo went over to the bar fridge and poured himself a whisky. The glass shook in his hand. He never drank much before a race – but now he needed it.

'You want me to make the delivery?' he said.

'Yes. But after the race.'

Ricardo wanted to get it over with quickly. He did not relish the prospect of hanging around Milan after the Grand Prix – it would arouse suspicion, because drivers always liked to get away as quickly as possible after a race.

'I'll do it tomorrow evening,' he said.

Before Ricardo could react, Talbot was up from the chair and had stabbed his right foot hard into his groin. The Italian topped foward in agony, dropping his glass.

'Just remember who's in control,' Talbot grated.

'Please! Tell me when, and then go. I have to rest.'

Talbot left the hotel five minutes later, and Ricardo limped back to his bed – exhausted, drunk, and totally despondent.

Bruce de Villiers left the circuit at two that morning. Both cars were perfectly set up, but he knew in his gut that Ricardo couldn't win. The Italian had lost his edge.

He got into his car and didn't notice another vehicle, further back, start up as he pulled away. He drove out of the circuit and then towards his hotel. He cursed as the traffic-lights turned to red at an intersection. He was tired, and desperately wanted to rest.

Suddenly, his door was wrenched open and he was dragged out of his Shensu Fuji. Before he could react, a sack was dragged over his head. He tried to struggle loose, and received a vicious kick in the kidneys, that made him crumple. Then he felt a jab in his arm. His head started to swim, and he had time to feel terribly sick, before he blacked out.

He came round in a room that smelt of damp. He was naked, and tied to a chair without a seat. In front of him, on an easy-chair, sat a redhead who looked as though she'd just returned from an evening out on the town. Bloody hell, what was happening?

'OK, Mr de Villiers, what are you doing in Milan?'

Bruce hadn't got a clue who she was or what she represented. 'I'm here for the Grand Prix,' he said. 'I think you might have the wrong person.'

She laughed coldly. Next to her were a couple of cylinders and a welding torch. She picked up the torch, released the gas and lit the nozzle. Bruce stared at the white flame.

'You know what this is?'

'Oxy-acetylene.'

'Very good. But then you're an engineer.'

Bruce steeled himself. 'And you're a welder?'

'Very funny. As you'll know, the flame burns at three thousand three hundred degrees centigrade.'

She brought the nozzle down and inverted it between his legs. He felt the heat against his testicles, smelt the hair burning. He gritted his teeth, tears running out of his eyes.

'What's your real business, Mr de Villiers?' the redhead asked.

'Running a Formula One team.'

'You'll have to do better than that.'

He felt the heat. He would not show weakness. She moved the torch away and he recovered slowly, the tears still running down his cheeks and his body shivering.

'Come on, Mr de Villiers . . .'

'You've got the wrong man.'

She lowered the torch and brought it under him. 'This time I'm not playing.'

'Nor am I.'

His eyes focused on hers. He felt the flame go out and he sagged forward, hyperventilating. She lit a cigarette and held the glowing tip close to his face. He pulled away, trembling.

'Now, Mr de Villiers, tell me your real business in Milan.'

It was an all-or-nothing situation.

'I run Calibre-Shensu,' Bruce said. 'I'm telling you, you must have the wrong man.'

He talked quickly, willing her to believe him. The silence was terrifying. He was playing for his life. She reached for the nozzle again and he urinated with fear. Then he sobbed at his weakness.

'You're a lucky boy. I believe you.'

She pulled a hypodermic syringe from her pocket and jabbed it in his arm.

'Goodbye, Mr de Villiers.'

Bruce came round in his hotel room. Had it been a dream? But as he staggered painfully to the toilet he knew it hadn't, and he lifted the lid and vomited into the bowl.

What the hell was going on?

*

Vanessa was shown into a pleasant room with two easy-chairs and no bars on the windows. What on earth were they playing at? she asked herself, totally bewildered. Perhaps this was some elaborately conceived ruse to extract a confession from her? All she knew was that, despite the cordial surroundings, she was still a prisoner.

Estelle Ramirez walked into the room. She was the very last person Vanessa had expected to see.

'Vanessa, please sit down.'

Vanessa drew herself up to her full height. 'If you think Wyatt and I are drug-traffickers, you're wrong. And if you've been sent to get me to talk, you won't get anything out of me,' she said angrily. She'd be damned if she was going to sit down with the bitch.

Estelle, however, did sit down. 'My husband's brother died in Colombia recently,' she said. 'He was the Minister of Justice. He was slowly hanged to death by members of the Ortega Cartel who videod the entire event and then sent the tape to his wife . . . Please sit down. I just want to talk.'

Vanessa took a chair. 'Are you trying to make me feel sorry?' she said. 'Everyone thinks I'm guilty, but the fact is, I was set up.

Estelle smiled bitterly. 'I am not here because I care about you or what happens to you. I am here for my son's sake. I sense a conspiracy within Calibre-Shensu.'

Vanessa tossed back her hair, regaining her confidence.

'And you think I know more than I'm letting on?'

Estelle nodded.

'You bitch!' Vanessa said.

The morning air was cool on his face as he came up the stairs and stared across the rooftops of Milan. He ran out across the concrete, his head bowed to avoid the swirling helicopter blades. Normally he would have taken over the controls from the pilot, but today he waved his hand, indicating that he did not want to.

The helicopter took off from the roof of the hotel. He felt desperately tired, and tried to block out the thoughts that kept filtering back into his mind. He'd been woken up at five.

There'd been a mix up with the containers at the airport and a batch of Carvalho tyres had gone missing. As Phelps's agent, he was responsible for sorting the mess out.

Now the track appeared in the distance, and he felt the fear creeping over him. It was a new sensation. Monza had always excited him before; it had been the scene of some of his greatest victories. Like three years ago, when he had taken the lead from de Rosner in the final lap and the crowd had risen to their feet, cheering him over the finish-line.

They came in low over the pits. All the teams were at the track. The chopper nosed its way down into the car park, and then they were down. The pilot held out his hand and Ricardo shook it. Every red-blooded Italian would be behind him today, looking forward to another great performance from their hero.

Then the chopper was gone, and he felt quite alone in the car park. The air was warm, the sun burning brightly in the intense blue sky.

He had passed over long queues of cars on his way to the circuit. The crowd would be big and enthusiastic, as they always were at Monza.

Bruce came out from the pits. He was walking with great difficulty, keeping his legs wide apart. The Italian police had sniggered when he told them about his abduction, and after that he hadn't felt like telling anyone else.

'How are you feeling?' he asked Ricardo.

The look on Ricardo's face told him more than words ever could.

'Not too 'ot,' he muttered. 'But I will do my best.'

'What the fuck have you been doing? I know you were out late last night, and I can smell you've been drinking. And now you're taking twenty-five-million-pounds worth of investment onto the track.'

Ricardo bowed his head. 'Bruce, I'm sorry.'

There was nothing Bruce could do. He just had to hope Ricardo might pull himself together.

They walked together towards the pits, the hustle and bustle of pre-race activity all around them. The pungent smell of

373

petrol felt good in Ricardo's nostrils as the various teams swarmed like angry bees over their cars.

Ricardo breathed in the excitement. He was back in the circus, that was what really mattered. He had to concentrate, and forget about all the problems.

They walked into the Calibre-Shensu bay and Bruce looked over Mickey Dunstal's shoulders at the display on the monitor. Mickey was running through the Shadow's internal diagnostic systems.

'It's looking fine, to be sure. But how's the number one driver?'

'I'll be fine by the time of the race.'

Again, Bruce wanted to explode, but realised he didn't need to push Ricardo over the edge – he was there already.

'Listen, Ricardo,' he said, 'we don't need you yet. The car is absolutely perfect, so why not go over to the motorhome and catch some sleep. I think you need a little time to unwind.' He spoke calmly, keeping the anger out of his voice. He had so much that he wanted to achieve, and with Wyatt out of the running Ricardo was the man he had to bank on.

Ricardo let out a sigh of relief and walked back to the motorhome. He passed Charlie Ibuka, who gave him a searching glance. He didn't like Ibuka one bit, and he hadn't been shy about letting the Japanese driver know it.

He climbed eagerly into the bus. The air-conditioning system that ran continuously from a separate motor on the outside kept it beautifully cool. He went over to the bunk and climbed into it, and almost immediately dropped into a deep sleep.

Wyatt woke with a start. God, how long had he been asleep? He glanced at his watch. A few minutes, that was all. He frowned, trying to focus, to pinpoint what it was that had woken him. Then he was on his feet and peering into the blueness of the sky. In the distance, and getting steadily louder, was the drone of an aeroplane.

Perhaps it was nothing, just someone slightly off course. Then he caught sight of a Lockheed Hercules and realised that they might finally be in luck.

He shook Carlos awake and they both peered upwards.

The noise of the plane became deafening as it flew right overhead and then seemed to disappear into the top of the cliff.

'How long would you estimate to get to the top?' asked Wyatt, breaking the silence at last.

'Three days minimum.'

'I worked it out at two, but perhaps that's pushing it.'

They hoisted their gear onto their backs and hacked their way towards the base of the rock face. It was going to be a hard, dangerous climb.

It was cool under the shade of the umbrella. It seemed strange to be in the centre of the pack rather than at the front. He looked up at Reg Tilson – the chief mechanic was running his eye over the car for the umpteenth time before the start.

'What do you think?'

'You can pass the lot of them, Ric. That's what I think.'

Ricardo felt much better. He'd got four hours sleep in the motorhome, and felt stronger than he had done in the last week. Now he'd need every ounce of energy he possessed to fight his way to the front.

Bruce came up, and wished him good luck. Then he took the umbrella.

Bruce felt the burning sensation again between his legs as he sweated in the heat. He wanted to hold a gun to Ricardo's head, to tell him that if he didn't win he'd kill him. But what was the point? He knew Ricardo's ego would be doing that for him.

All the engines fired up in unison, and the angry screams of wailing machinery filled the air. This was it, thought Ricardo; the point of no return.

He kept his position through the initial warm-up lap. The car felt good, she was responding beautifully. The quick straights and narrow chicanes passed by quickly.

Suddenly he was back on the grid, amongst the pack, the engine now warm and free-revving. The red light above him glowed ominously, then it flicked through to green, and in the midst of the screaming pack he shot off down the straight, through the Variante Goodyear and into the Curva Grande.

He focused on the cars in front of him, twelve in all, with nine others behind him.

He took two out on the straight and went into the curve in tenth place, screaming after the ninth man. He put everything he'd got into keeping the car moving smoothly. He knew the Shadow would be put under immense strain with the constant overtaking he was going to have to do to get ahead. He'd have to tail every car he was going to pass, and that meant the Shensu V12 was going to get really hot. It also meant that he'd be hammering his tyres with the constant manoeuvring to get into the first place.

The strength of Dunstal's design showed in the corners, and Ricardo knew that through the bends she was faster than any other car on the track.

He heard the crackle in his headphones and then Bruce's voice. De Rosner was leading the field, with two other front-ranked drivers right behind him. Then there was a three-second gap, and the other five cars ahead of Ricardo were packed together, each intent on giving no advantage whatever to any of the others.

It was going to be a very hard race to win.

Bruce de Villiers sat looking at the bank of TV monitors, smoking a Calibre cigarette. Reg came up behind him, ill at ease.

'What's the matter?' Bruce barked.

'Fucking tyres. One container caught fire. I'm not sure about the wet-weather tyres – they were salvaged in the blaze. The Carvalho guys are examining them now, but they look fine to me.'

A Carvalho official ran up behind him.

'The tyres, they are OK,' he stammered.

Bruce turned to the pit lane and breathed a sigh of relief. There would be tyres for Charlie Ibuka when he came in. As for the Carvalho bugger-up, he'd have words with Ricardo after the race.

But he quickly forgot his anger as he watched Ricardo

fighting his way towards the front. It was as if the whole focus of the race was upon the Italian. There was a feeling that Ricardo was the true challenger, and that till he was right behind de Rosner, the race for first place had hardly begun.

Bruce was cooling down. He was glad he hadn't shouted at Ricardo on the grid, because the Italian had obviously recovered his style. It seemed almost inevitable, the way he passed each of the cars in front of him. Bruce knew Ricardo could do it. He also knew that, for Ricardo, every second in the cockpit was a lifetime.

Each time he heard the thin, shapeless noise of the Shensu V12 he felt his heart beat faster. The noise would rise in volume, and it would become the centre of his existence. Then it would come close, the scream of twelve pistons straining to the limit as they tried to go even faster; and then the black shape would rocket past and the sound of the engine would be more pure, lingering on until the Shadow was out of sight.

By the twenty-fifth lap Ricardo was placed just behind the fourth man, and ready to start catching the front-runners. Bruce looked up at the sky. The clear blue expanse was gone, now filled with patches of ominous dark cloud that were mustering in intensity every minute.

He glanced at the timer. Ricardo had set a new lap record. He had passed the fourth man. Now he was ready to do battle with the three front-runners.

Ricardo felt himself on a high. He had never driven this fast at Monza, and was using all the tricks of his lengthy career to keep going faster. The Shadow was holding in the corners like a magnet. He could feel himself moving in towards de Rosner, actually see the back of the McCabe in its distinctive red and white colours.

This was his best race yet, everything was happening magically. The engine sounded beautifully strong behind his neck.

The crowd were clearly excited. Italians have always been passionate about two things – *la donna e la macchina* – women and cars.

He was going to win. He knew it.

*

He heard Bruce's voice bark in the headphones as the rain started, telling him to come in for new rubber on the next lap. He couldn't argue. He held his position right behind de Rosner and whipped into the pits on the next lap.

The old tyres were off and the new ones on in a record 7.8 seconds. He roared back on the track with the quiet satisfaction of knowing that the others had to come in, and that they couldn't have their wheels changed any faster than that.

He concentrated on reeling in de Rosner. One lap later de Rosner went in for rubber, but the Frenchman was out of the pits before Ricardo could gain the lead. The spray from the water on the track was making things very difficult.

Now, with ten laps to go, Ricardo knew he'd have to push himself harder. De Rosner was driving like a demon – the Frenchman was inspired, there was no other word for it. As fast as Ricardo went, de Rosner went faster.

Bruce felt his pulse quickening as Charlie Ibuka came in for his wet-weather tyres. Ibuka was out in under eight seconds. Everything was going splendidly.

Ricardo decided to push for the lead on the Curva Parabolica. He braked late, coming towards the inside of the track, aiming to cut past de Rosner before he switched to the inside.

Now. Now. Foot off the brake. Flat down on the accelerator.

Fight it. Don't let him in. God, we're going to smash. No, I'm not going to give way.

I'm out. I'm in front.

Senses reeling, he swept out of the corner in front. The roar of the crowd was in his ears. His people. His victory.

He screamed down the straight, pushing the Shadow as hard as she would go.

He braked as he approached the Curva Grande, and the car began to break away. He fought with the wheel and the accelerator to regain control. What the hell was going wrong?

Then he was spinning uncontrollably across the track at over 150 mph.

Everything slowed down for him. The Armco on the corner

came up too fast. The car broke into splinters. He was flying through the air, terrified and unable to do anything.

He struck something, and blacked out.

Charlie Ibuka was lying in third place as he screamed down the main straight. He felt the instability start to develop as he was travelling at nearly 180 mph.

He went cold as he lost control of the car. He couldn't understand what was wrong. Then the wheel was wrenched from his hands and he flew off to the side.

The impact was deafening.

Estelle just kept looking at the television screen.

'This is a terrible tragedy,' the commentator was saying. 'Fortunately, Ricardo Sartori has only minor concussion.

'But I am reminded of the death of the late Jim Clarke – though this is perhaps far more unfair. Charlie Ibuka had yet to complete his first race. De Rosner's victory seems curiously irrelevant.'

Estelle felt unsteady on her feet. It could so easily have been Wyatt.

Bruce smashed his foot through the computer screen in anger. He bunched up his fists in fury, and tears of rage ran from his eyes.

Mickey went cold. Both cars at once. It could only be a design fault. His fault.

He looked out across the wet tarmac. Inside his soul he felt an emptiness, a void.

Although he was walking down the hotel corridor with Elvira Jones, it was Charlie Ibuka Ricardo was thinking about – that hard oriental face that gave nothing away. It was difficult to believe that Charlie was dead. What if it had been him? Jesus, he had been lucky.

Outside his room, Elvira Jones's hand traced a line across the inside of his thigh.

'Dinner was wonderful,' she said.

He made to kiss her on the cheek, but she shifted her lips

379

to meet his. A little later, she led him to her room and undressed slowly in front of him. He looked at the red bush between her legs; he had never had a redhead before.

'I want this to be a special experience for you. I know you are a sexual athlete and I think we should try something a little different.'

The excitement surged within him. He had had many women, but never a woman like this.

'Why not?' he replied softly, intrigued to know what she had planned.

He took out the flat silver compact that contained his supply of cocaine.

'Join me?' he asked casually.

'Of course. However, first I must prepare things.'

She went to one of the cupboards and took out long pieces of braid rope. At the end of each was a hangman's noose. She stood on a chair and attached the ropes over the beam that ran the length of the room, knotting them expertly in place so that each noose hung approximately a metre and a half above the double bed.

Ricardo looked on, intrigued. 'You propose we hang ourselves?'

'Yes. You know what happens when a man is hanged?'

'He dies?'

'Not immediately. It is all a matter of timing. Just before death he experiences an erection – and a woman experiences the same surge of excitement.'

'Fascinating,' Ricardo said softly as she began to unbutton him.

'With this technique, we both hang while making love. It is an experience that is like nothing on earth.'

He moved away from her and poured out a thin line of coke. Then he handed her the golden tube, and she took it from him and inhaled deeply. When he had done the same, she led him over to one of the nooses. He felt himself getting an erection as she passed it over his head. The excitement of the unknown, he thought. She tightened the noose expertly.

After that, she passed the other noose over her own head and hung from it, her legs apart as she straddled him. He penetrated her, and felt a soaring sensation as the noose tightened around his neck. This was like nothing he had ever experienced.

For five minutes he rocked backwards and forwards with her in sheer ecstasy. Then she shifted her weight, resting more heavily on him, and the noose tightened even more.

He tried to pull away. He could not, his erection stayed rock-hard and he stared into Elvira Jones's eyes in terror. All her weight was on him now, the tension was off her neck altogether.

He could not speak. She rocked backwards and forwards in a series of intense orgasms, and he began to choke. She lifted herself up slightly.

'The Mafia do not like you,' she said.

He went cold, his arms were powerless. She shifted again, so that his choking increased.

'I work for *Il Capo*,' she said. 'I am killing you for smuggling cocaine into our country. You have been a naughty boy. At least, however, you will die happy.'

His body began to convulse uncontrollably now, and she was laughing. He reared up, choking, desperately – and as he did so, she slipped and sagged on the noose. The weight came off his legs and he managed to raise himself, coughing and wheezing. Desperately, he pulled the noose off his head and stared at Elvira – she was limply hanging from her noose.

He staggered back and ran into the bathroom. Grabbing a towel, he ran back into the room and started to clean everything – frantically, frenziedly, obsessively.

Then he began to think logically again. He forced himself to breathe deeply, and stared around the room. Then he took the towel again and dusted wherever he might have left any fingerprints. After that he dressed slowly, dreading that the phone might ring or that there'd be a knock on the door.

Then he went out, closing the door behind him, and walked unsteadily back to his room.

The suicide of the redheaded Mrs Elvira Jones did not even make the front page of the local paper.

*

Talbot straightened the fingers on his right hand. The attack on him had been disastrous: when the grenade went off inside the container, the entire shipment had been destroyed. And Ricardo did not seem to be even remotely concerned about the loss of the merchandise. He doubted if the Italian realised its true value.

Ricardo's usefulness, he decided, was at an end. But Talbot could not dispose of Ricardo. Those were his orders. Because now, with Ibuka dead, Calibre-Shensu only had one remaining driver – Ricardo.

Talbot turned from these thoughts to the open folder on his desk. The grand plan he had been ordered to implement was falling into place. In twenty-four hours there would be a revolution in Colombia and a military dictatorship would be established. The end of the Ortega Cartel would be announced and the new military rulers would launch a war against drug-smuggling that would be applauded by the rest of the world.

Talbot would become a multi-millionaire overnight. After that, his orders were to establish a new and very secret cartel, from which each of the new ruling generals would draw an astronomical salary. For this they would prevent any other cartels from operating in Colombia.

The street price of cocaine would rocket because of the short supply. His orders were then gradually to expand his supply monopoly – supplying smaller quantities for a bigger profit.

Talbot looked down at his watch. In twenty-four hours he would have his fee – and to his employer he would hand over control of the most advanced cocaine manufacturing plant in the world.

Wyatt felt the sweat trickle down his forehead as he looked up at the barren rock wall above him. They were almost at the top.

'*Choto!*' he heard Carlos exclaim. 'There is no way we can get past that.'

Wyatt stripped off most of his equipment, including his shirt. The rope dangling slenderly from the harness round his waist, he inched himself slowly upwards.

'You come off, my friend, and you die!' Carlos cried out. 'Wyatt, come back!'

Wyatt moved up, his fingers caressing the cold rock, searching for hairline cracks. The two days of almost continuous climbing had brought him up to the level of awareness that he needed for this.

The rubber-soled climbing-boots pressed against the smooth surface at the outer limits of adhesion. He paused for a moment and glanced down at the rope that connected him to Carlos, who was belaying him. Eighty feet of rope stretched between them like a thin umbilical cord. If Wyatt came off, it meant one hundred and sixty feet to fall – eighty feet down to Carlos, and then another eighty feet before the rope took the strain. The impact would most likely wrench Carlos from the face, hurling them both to their deaths in the leafy jungle far, far below. And Wyatt still had at least another twenty feet to go.

This was living. Life at the sharp end. The blood ran from his fingernails as he clawed onto the rock. Far from easing, the level of difficulty had intensified and he wondered if it was possible to continue. But there was no possibility of retreat now.

His lips caressed the stone. The smell of lichen was strong, the rock cool against his cheek. He smoothed his way slowly upwards. There was no thought in his mind save the position of his four limbs and the fine balance that kept him pressed to the face.

He felt himself about to fall off, the void beckoning. Then the realisation of why he was doing this came back to him: a vision of finding her, and telling her he loved her more than anyone else in the world.

He clawed on upwards, forcing himself to ignore the closeness of death.

A memory came edging back – pushing itself into his consciousness. A memory of losing the car on the mountain road above Monaco all those years ago, of the terror in his father's eyes as they plunged over the edge . . .

He hung in the air, Estelle's face in his mind, the way she had looked as she stared down at his father's grave . . .

Then the memory of what had happened before the accident – the memory that had eluded him for all those years – came back, frighteningly real.

He screamed out in anger. Why had he not remembered it before?

As they'd left the villa in Monaco that day, he and his father, laughing and joking, Jack Phelps had bumped into them. Phelps had been using his father's car. He'd said he'd found the steering a little tight and he'd had it looked at – but it was all right now, and he wished them a good drive. The bastard.

Wyatt drew himself into the face and fought his way up the rock. Another foot, and he found a thin crack that he followed quickly to the top. Two tugs on the rope, and Carlos was ready to follow.

The guilt for his father's death was gone for ever. But the need for revenge had just begun.

A soft rain was falling, and Aito Shensu looked through it, and up at the slopes of Mount Fuji. This was an annual pilgrimage for him. He had first come to this mountain as a young boy with his mother. So young and innocent then, so filled with ambition. He had achieved far more than his dreams.

He remembered the coffin sliding into the furnace, then looking into the eyes of Charlie Ibuka's wife. He had wondered if he could go on after that moment.

He walked slowly upwards through the trees. All his life he had trusted his instincts, and now he knew there was something very wrong. He had not been able to contact Mickey Dunstal. He had wanted to speak to him, to tell him that the accidents, the tragedy, were not his fault.

He had made so many sacrifices to be where he was. He had no wife, no children, no grandchildren. He had been married to the business and to karate.

And now there would be no peace for him until the voices that plagued him were silenced.

*

Mickey Dunstal looked up at the light-fitting on the wall above the bar. Ugly, he thought to himself, definitely ugly. He pushed the glass across the counter.

'Make it a treble.'

'You've had enough, sir. Go home.'

Mickey raised himself up, shot out his hand and gripped the barman by his shirt-collar.

'I said make it a treble, man. Didn't you hear me?'

The barman poured the drink, the bottle shaking in his hand. Then, when his customer had settled down, the barman went to the back and made a discreet phone call.

Mickey felt his world spinning. He kept seeing the car, turning and flying through the air. 'Fock!' He didn't know what time it was, and he didn't care. The barman had left the bottle in front of him and he noticed that it was empty, as was the rest of the bar.

'Get me another focking bottle!'

Someone tapped him on the back and he spun round.

'Don't you do that,' he grunted, and then stared aghast at Aito Shensu. The Japanese businessman was clearly the last person he'd expected to see in the Dublin pub.

'Mickey,' Aito said, 'it's time to go home.'

'You focking Nip!' Mickey screamed, flailing his fists. He struck air, and crashed to the ground. Then he was pulled to his feet, his arms held in an iron grip. He had not expected either the strength or the speed.

'Mickey, we go outside.'

'Fock off!'

The grip intensified, and the pain shot through him and he vomited.

'Outside.'

Out in the cold air, he regained his energy.

'Leave me, get out o' me life.'

Aito maintained his grip on him.

'Now we'll go to the hotel.'

Mickey broke loose and Aito's left foot shot up, hammering into the side of his head. He crashed to the floor in agony.

'We'll go to the hotel.'

*

He lay in the hot water and looked across at Aito, now in his shirt-sleeves. For the first time he noticed the tight sinew of the muscles and the line of callouses at the edge of the hand.

Mickey touched his own ear. It was tender, and his whole head still rang from the blow he'd received. His neck-muscles screamed.

Aito handed him some tablets and a glass of water. 'Take these, they will make you feel better.'

Mickey gulped down the tablets and the water, then he sank back into the bath. 'Why did you come here?' he asked.

'We had a contract. You broke it,' Aito said coolly.

'I killed your focking driver!'

Aito shook his head. 'No one blames you. The only person who is against you is yourself. We have a saying in karate: "The hardest battle you fight in life is the battle against yourself."'

Mickey pulled himself up and held out his hand. They shook.

'Man to man, Aito.'

'I am sorry about your head.'

They sat in the viewing-room and watched the videotape for the twentieth time.

Bruce hunched forward. 'Let's look further back . . .'

Mickey shuttled the tape in slow motion, then actuated the start button.

In Ibuka's car there'd been a front-mounted video-camera, a source of additional film material for the sponsors, which was relayed to the broadcast cameras.

'No, Mickey. Further back.'

'What? To the pit stop?'

'No, even further.'

'What is it, Bruce?' Aito asked.

'Wait and see.'

The tape played on and Aito and Mickey stared at the screen.

'Bruce, I dunno what you're getting at.'

Bruce sat back in his chair and switched on the overhead light.

386

'While you were drowning youself in Dublin whisky,' he said, 'I was doing some hard thinking. I've never, ever known two cars to go wrong in the same way at the same time.'

Aito shrugged. 'Statistically, it is possible.'

'No! I survive in this business on detail: everything has to be right. My cars don't just self-destruct. Why has it never happened before, Mickey? Why?'

'I focked op.'

'No. Look at the footage on this tape.'

Mickey slipped the cassette into the recorder and Bruce switched off the light.

The first cut was of Ricardo driving, so was the second.

'I don't understand,' Aito said frankly.

'What difference do you notice between the two cuts?'

'Well, in the first he is driving smoothly. In the next he is using the wheel more . . .'

'The first clip is taken just before the tyre change. The second is taken at the identical bend, one lap later, *after* the tyre-change.'

'He was getting used to the new tyres,' Aito suggested.

'Yes. But the new tyres should make it easier in the bends, not harder,' Bruce expanded. 'Now let's look at the next two cuts.'

The footage was of Ibuka driving through the same bend. Mickey sucked in his breath. In the second sequence it was as if the Japanese was imitating Ricardo's movements after his tyre-change.

'These were taken before and after Ibuka's tyre-change.'

Aito frowned. 'Were the pit crew at fault?'

'Once maybe, but not twice.'

'The tyres! The focking tyres!'

Ricardo was sweating heavily. One of his responsibilities, as Phelps's agent, was the supply of tyres to the Calibre-Shensu team. And he had messed up. He knew what had happened in the ambush – that most of the tyres had gone up with the container.

The Carvalho factory had been quite specific in their instructions. Certain tyres were only for testing – and they had told

Ricardo the order in which the tyres had to be delivered to the pits, and the order in which they had to be used.

He hadn't checked the wet-weather tyres he'd salvaged from the container against Carvalho's instructions. Each tyre was carefully numbered, and if he'd seen the list, he'd have known they were for testing only.

Phelps had screamed down the phone at him soon after the race. The bugger-up, Phelps had told him, was his responsibility alone. Then Bruce de Villiers had also found out about the supply of the wrong wet-weather tyres, from watching footage of the accidents on video.

Now Ricardo was sitting alone in his car, down a deserted lane near the Calibre-Shensu test circuit. The passenger door opened and Talbot got in beside him. He put his arm around Ricardo's shoulders and whispered into his ear.

'Relax, buddy.'

Ricardo felt terrible. Every day was a battle to keep his weight down. Since the coke habit had started, his face had become puffy and his whole body had taken on an almost bloated appearance.

'You realise now that the accident was entirely your fault?'

Ricardo coughed and tried to free himself from Talbot's arm – but the grip intensified.

'*Porco Dio*! Are you out of your mind!'

'You killed Charlie Ibuka. Yes . . . it was your incompetence in handling the delivery of tyres that killed him.'

Then Talbot whispered something else in his ear, and Ricardo went white.

Bruce de Villiers stared around the huge laboratory, then back at his old school-friend. Dr Max Weiss had a cadaverous face and slow black eyes. His reputation as one of Britain's top forensic scientists brought him an endless stream of interesting work.

'What are you looking for, Bruce?'

'I don't know. It's just that something's not right with this business. I just want you to examine that video footage and then the pieces of the tyre I've given you.'

'Are you suggesting sabotage?'

The black eyes rested on him. Bruce felt unsure of how to reply.

'I don't know,' he said. 'It might be a wild-goose chase.'

The doctor sat down on a high chair and stared at the contents of a test-tube.

'I don't believe in chance. You know that. Everything happens for a reason.' He swept back a lock of his long black hair. 'Suppose I find evidence of sabotage and someone's to blame. What are you going to do?'

'I don't know.'

'If it's murder, I'll have to involve the police – ånd I know that your team has a lot of problems already. Would you give me a couple of weeks' grace?'

'Yes, but that's all.'

'Let's see what turns up, then.'

Wyatt couldn't quite believe what he was staring at. He felt Carlos's hand on his shoulder.

'Jesus! That is for making drugs – why else would someone hide a factory in this place?'

The buildings were all painted the same shade of green as the jungle. So was the landing-strip that stretched off like a giant tennis court over the edge of the cliff.

The Hercules transporter was backed up against one of the buildings and there was a swarm of activity surrounding it. The cargo was being unloaded by men who looked like laboratory technicians.

Carlos sank back into the greenery and drew out his knife.

'*Vamos.*'

Wyatt nodded. 'Let's find Suzie.'

They moved slowly through the foliage till they were behind the longest of the buildings. Big picture-windows ran along its side, and Venetian blinds kept out the sunlight. It looked like the in-house laboratory of a giant pharmaceutical manufacturer.

Carlos focused his binoculars on the interior.

'I do not believe this. Look . . .'

He handed the binoculars to Wyatt.

'See the transparent packets at the end of the room?'

389

'Yes?'

'It can only be cocaine. Tons of cocaine.'

Estelle leaned forward as a photograph of her dead brother-in-law appeared on the BBC evening news.

'Since the brutal slaying six months ago of David Ramirez, the controversial Argentinian-born Minister of Justice,' the newscaster said, 'Colombia has been in a state of agitation. Now rebels have seized command of the Houses of Parliament and have imprisoned the ruling party. The Colombian army is reported to have suffered heavy losses in the fighting that has broken out across the country. General Miguel Santos, the rebel leader, has announced that he will form a new government that will co-operate with the United States to stamp out Colombia's huge trade in cocaine.

'Rumours that the revolution was engineered by the CIA have been vehemently denied by the US President, but speculation continues.'

Estelle grimaced. She knew Santos, and that was why she could believe the rumours. She knew that he was no knight in shining armour. He was an opportunist who had worked for the Ortega Cartel as a hit-man, reportedly dumped when his employers discovered he had been taking charge of large shipments for his own personal benefit.

Perhaps the CIA was using Santos to establish a puppet regime under their own control. It was possible.

It had always been a relief to her that Carlos had never wanted to get involved in politics like his brother. He concentrated on his first love, the game of polo. But she knew that Carlos would not rest now until he found David's killer.

And where had Wyatt and Carlos got to now?

Having worked out the layout of the buildings, they had waited until nightfall before launching their assault.

Carlos handed Wyatt the knife with the blackened blade.

'These men will stop at nothing, believe me. There will be no second chances when they realise we have discovered their factory.'

But Wyatt handed the knife back. 'I don't need it,' he said.

'You are crazy.' Carlos slid the knife into its scabbard, slung the Uzi over his shoulder and pushed the pistol into its webbing holster.

They approached a side-entrance in the moonlight. A guard stood casually against the light, smoking a cigarette and staring into the darkness.

Wyatt crept through the foliage. The hours and hours of karate training, the years of hardening, condensed into a single fluid moment. He moved without noise, modulating his breathing, a coldness creeping through his body; he came up the side of the building, a leopard stalking his prey. Then he was behind the guard. His left arm pulled the guard back off balance whilst his right clamped over the guard's mouth. He twisted the guard's neck in a rapid movement and heard his spinal column snap.

The guard slumped forward, and Wyatt dropped him into the foliage.

Carlos was up next to him in a second. 'Jesus, that was quick.'

Wyatt gestured for him to be quiet. Then they opened the door and stepped into a clinical white corridor . . . and looked up to find themselves staring at a TV camera.

A second later the alarm sounded.

'*Choto!*' muttered Carlos.

Wyatt moved on the balls of his feet down the glass-walled corridor, and a burly man came towards him, smiling. Wyatt stood back, dropping his weight onto his left foot. A deft movement with his right foot sent the man reeling forward, and Wyatt's right hand chopped hard against his neck. There was a sickening crack as the man slumped across the floor. Carlos sucked in his breath.

They moved quickly down the passage – and another guard came up without warning, pointing a gun at Wyatt's torso.

Before the guard realised what was happening, his right hand was yanked forward and a blow came up from beneath the elbow, breaking his arm. As he gave a cry of pain, Wyatt twisted him round, applying pressure behind the left elbow.

'Where is the German woman?' he asked quietly in fluent Portuguese.

'I don't understand . . .'

Carlos heard the other elbow snap and watched the man's face explode with pain.

Wyatt twisted the man round again, placing his knee in his back and holding up his face by his hair.

'Where is she?'

'Down the corridor, second on the left.'

He lifted the man up, slammed his face hard into the wall and let him fall. As Wyatt moved down the corridor, two more men appeared. Carlos drew his gun, but waited as Wyatt appeared to dance between his two adversaries, slamming his fists and then elbows into them before they had a chance to react.

Wyatt opened a door. He caught sight of a big woman lifting a machine-gun. He dived under the burst of fire and rolled towards her, gripping her ankles with his hands and toppling her over. His main finger and little finger extended, he rammed his right hand into her eyes. Just within his field of vision he saw a man coming at him with a gun. His left foot shot out, took the man in the stomach and sent him flying hard against the glass window. The man's skull smashed against the glass and left a bloody patch as he sank down unconscious.

The woman was writhing on the floor, clutching at her eye-sockets.

'Jesus, oh Jesus!'

He turned to see Suzie lying on the bed, expressionless, wearing just a T-shirt and a pair of panties. The inside of her left arm was a mass of ugly red pin-pricks, and on the table next to her lay an empty syringe. Wyatt noticed her skin was a patina of bruises.

She looked up at him, no reaction in her eyes.

'Please, don't let her,' she pleaded in Portuguese, her eyes resting on the woman writhing on the floor. Wyatt pivoted round and his right heel came down hard on the woman's skull.

He lifted Suzie up gently. Behind him Carlos said, 'Wyatt, we must get her to a doctor.'

There was the noise of voices in the passage, and the sound of weapons being armed. Carlos unslung the Uzi in a single movement, rested his left hand on the barrel and moved towards the doorway. He opened fire as a man appeared in the passage and Wyatt heard the screams as he followed behind his stepfather. He was scarcely aware of Suzie in his arms, she was so light. The bullets coursed out of Carlos's gun as the trio made their way out of the front of the building, towards the landing-strip.

Then an ominous sound came from the air above – it must be a helicopter, closing in under cover of darkness. Then Wyatt heard a voice screaming in Portuguese: 'Lay down your weapons! We are coming in to attack!'

Carlos looked across at Wyatt, his eyes asking the same questions. Gunfire erupted, then bullets pumped into the concrete floor around them. There were screams in the distance.

They moved back into the building and ran down the passage, heading for the door through which they'd first entered. Every instinct told them to get out of the place.

Wyatt shifted Suzie to the other shoulder, and suddenly he and Carlos were out of the door and plunging headlong into the greenness.

Wyatt lay safely at a distance from the buildings, hidden beneath the green canopy of thick vegetation. He held Suzie tight, looking across to the factory.

The noise of the helicopter blades above sounded like distant thunder. At first he could see nothing, but then the Hughes Apache helicopter burst out of the darkness and into the range of the factory's lights. From its belly a machine-gun spat out bullets against retaliatory fire from the ground.

High above, another helicopter angled its spotlights around the factory complex, leading the Hughes Apache. Two more Apaches came in from the darkness and landed on the airstrip, their guns trained on the buildings. Then a Sikorsky H-53 Stallion dropped from the darkness like a vulture and touched down on the landing-strip, disgorging thirty-eight combat troops, who dashed into the factory.

Gunfire erupted, and there were screams as men died.

A tall, fair man in combat fatigues stepped down from the cockpit of the Sikorsky and surveyed the scene. His men regrouped and stood to attention in front of him, and he ordered them to conduct an intensive search of the area and to take up defensive positions.

Wyatt stared at the man in horror. It couldn't be. No, it couldn't be . . .

The years of training together, the competitiveness. And they had both been chosen, Wyatt to head the *dojo* in Japan and Rod to head the one in the United States.

Talbot. Rod Talbot.

He had disappeared, Aito had said – disgraced the *dojo*, just as Wyatt had done.

What was Talbot doing here?

Wyatt sank back down into the foliage. He had not been prepared for the change in Suzie. One moment she was as docile as a young puppy, the next her body was rigid. Now her eyes darted round anxiously.

'Please, I need a fix,' she cried out in Portuguese.

He held his hand over her mouth and she bit it.

'Suzie, it's me. It's Wyatt.'

Carlos laid his hand on Wyatt's shoulder. 'She won't recognise you.'

Wyatt stared at him for a moment, then nodded. 'We have to get out,' he said, 'and there is only one way.'

They started cutting their way through the undergrowth towards the airstrip.

Jules Ortega felt the pain creeping up from his stomach. He could hardly breathe and he wondered if he might be dying. In his mind the pieces of the jigsaw-puzzle refused to go together. There had been one attack and then another. The men who had taken Suzie were not the same as those who were now storming the factory. He remembered the face of one from somewhere, but he could not place it.

Every movement brought fresh pain, but he knew that he must remain silent. These men who were taking over the plant would not hesitate to kill him if they found him.

Ortega tried to put himself into the minds of the two men who had taken Suzie – and it didn't take him long to calculate their course of action. Without a fix, they'd have a hard time trying to cope with her.

He grabbed the intercom with his good hand and tapped in the number. His brother answered instantly.

'Jules, what is going on? I hear gunfire.'

'Some men came and took Suzie. Talbot has landed with Yankee soldiers. He has betrayed us.'

'Ah,' Emerson said. 'But he does not know about the bunker or my own bodyguard?'

'No. Emerson, help me. I am wounded.'

'Pretend you are dead. First, we must find Suzie and shut her up for good.'

Jules put down the phone and lay on the floor, feigning death.

Wyatt lay in the darkness, holding Suzie's body's close to his. Rod Talbot – so many memories and so much bitterness. They had been groomed to continue the teaching of their style of karate.

After nine years at the *dojo*, the *Shihan* had told them that there were no Japanese pupils who matched them in ability. Now they were to travel to the island of Okinawa, to meet the originator of their style. Only he was sufficiently experienced to teach them at the highest level.

On Okinawa, Wyatt had guessed he was to be given the highest honour – to become the *Shihan* in Japan when his master retired. Talbot had realised this as well. He could not accept that Wyatt had been chosen – he could not come to terms with not being first in line.

So Rod had left. He had sold out.

Wyatt felt a nagging sense of doubt. Could he just walk away from this?

He whispered a few words to Carlos. Carlos looked at him. 'Wyatt,' he said, 'she will die.'

'There is something I must do – I can't explain it to you . . .'

'I can fly the helicopter. Just help me get to a helicopter with her.'

'We must get back to the runway, then.'

*

Half an hour later, Wyatt was edging his way towards the side of the runway. It was an all-or-nothing situation. The pilot of the Sikorsky was standing next to his machine, calmly smoking a cigarette. His helmet lay in the cockpit and he was not expecting an attack.

In the distance came the sound of another helicopter. The pilot put out his cigarette and moved back towards the cockpit.

Out in the darkness, Wyatt cursed softly. What in God's name was happening now? They would have to wait till the new chopper landed before they could make their next move. Behind him, Suzie moaned softly in Carlos's arms.

The chopper circled several times, and to Wyatt's immense relief, landed close to the front of the factory, nearly eighty-five yards away from the Sikorsky. Combat soldiers filed out of the building and stood to attention as a man in a suit stepped down from the helicopter. For the second time that day, Wyatt did a double-take.

It was Jack Phelps.

Deep inside his bunker, Emerson Ortega felt the rage building up inside him. First the revolution in Colombia, now this attack. Phelps was destroying his life's work. In one lightning manoeuvre he had ousted the Colombians, and now he was about to take control of the trade.

Emerson knew he was not safe here. He must get away before Phelps launched a search. Phelps would know that he must be hiding somewhere in the complex – it was only the day before that he'd discussed the latest consignment with him, over the phone.

Leaving Carlos with Suzie, Wyatt made his move as Phelps stepped inside the building. He padded up slowly behind the pilot and smashed his hand down hard against the man's skull. Then he dragged him down into the jungle next to Carlos and Suzie.

The pilot came round ten minutes later, the nose of Carlos's Colt 45 rammed in the roof of his mouth.

'One shout, my friend, and this goes off,' Carlos said. 'Nod if you want to co-operate.'

The pilot nodded, peering nervously at his strange assailants. Wyatt whispered to him: 'Tell him the take-off procedure.'

The pilot rattled off a list of complex instructions, and Carlos went over them again and again, memorising the procedure. Then they left the pilot, lying face down, his arms bound behind him, with a primed hand-grenade in his hands. One wrong move and it would spring loose, blowing him to pieces.

They moved out across the tarmac, moving quietly, watching the building. Carlos slipped down behind the controls of the chopper, and breathed a sigh of relief: they were just as the pilot had described them.

'Wyatt,' he whispered, 'we're going to make it. Lie her on the seat next to me and strap her in.'

When Wyatt had done this, he kissed Suzie on the lips, then drew away. Carlos looked up. 'Come on!' he said urgently. 'We must get out of here!'

Wyatt stepped out onto the ground. 'Go,' he said. 'I have an old score to settle.'

'Don't be a fool! They'll kill you! We must get out of here, now!'

Wyatt looked round nervously. Carlos was running out of time.

Carlos stared into Wyatt's eyes. 'All right,' he said. 'I go. But I will come back for you.'

He eased the controls of the chopper back and felt the machine lift off from the tiny launch-pad. He looked down, seeing Wyatt leap into the green jungle and disappear.

God, Estelle would never forgive him for this.

Suzie started moaning hysterically, and he powered the chopper away. The bright lights of the factory buildings faded as they disappeared down into a sea of blackness.

Then suddenly, without any warning, he felt the cold steel of a gun-barrel, thrust up beneath his right earlobe.

'Yes,' a voice said, 'we are all going to make it.'

Carlos sat uneasily in the pilot's seat, with Suzie lying next to him, moaning.

'Let me introduce myself, Carlos Ramirez. I am Antonio

Vargas. I suppose I should count myself fortunate that you paid me a visit. At least, thanks to your assistance, I was able to leave my other unwelcome American visitors behind. And I am a generous man. I will give the young lady a shot of what she craves.'

Carlos turned, but stopped as the metal pressed hard into his ear. Vargas stuck a hypodermic into Suzie's arm, and within a few minutes her moanings had ceased.

'My friend, I suggest that you stick to playing polo. You are out of your depth, just like your poor brother.'

As Carlos listened, the hair stood up on the back of his neck. Memories came flooding back; memories of his brother David and the tape-recordings he had played him of the sadistic pleasures of a certain Mr Emerson Ortega. The voice was the same. He wouldn't have realised it but for the darkness masking the features of Antonio Vargas.

'You are Emerson Ortega,' Carlos muttered quietly.

He felt the pressure of the barrel on his cheek lessen. The silence was chilling. All he could hear was the steady hum of the helicopter's turbo-shafts.

'You have just sealed your death-warrant, my friend.'

'And you think that will save you life, Ortega? Jack Phelps has very powerful connections, not just in the United States military, as you've seen, but also in the CIA. So you're a dead man as well, my friend.'

'OK, Ramirez, I think you are right. A dead man, but right . . . Yes, I must eliminate Phelps. Take the chopper back to the base.'

'But they'll kill us before we land,' Carlos said, holding the cyclic tightly.

Ortega laughed.

'My special bodyguard will probably have killed most of them already. But we'll just make sure that Phelps is permanently silenced.'

Talbot spotted Jules Ortega's body lying next to the phone. He leaned down and held the palm of his hand against Jules's face, and smiled.

'Ah. Not so dead.'

He pulled out a cigarette lighter and flicked it on, toasting Ortega's ear, and as Ortega rolled over, clutching his singed ear lobe and screaming, Talbot kicked him hard.

'Where's Emerson?'

'Who?'

'Your brother Emerson. Or Antonio Vargas, if you want to continue the charade, buddy.'

'I don't know.'

'Yes, you do. Now talk.'

Talbot ripped the waistband off Ortega's pants and yanked them down. He pulled the Colombian to his feet, flicked the lighter on and held it to his penis.

Jules gave a cry of agony, and the uncontrollable flow of his urine put out the flame. Talbot swore, adjusted the lighter and flicked it on again, this time with a long flame.

'Please!' Jules Ortega begged. 'My brother is in the bunker just to the west of the main installation. I will show you.'

Phelps admired the layout of the factory complex. Talbot had done a good job, using the Ortegas. Now it was just a matter of tidying up the loose ends, and the business would run itself.

The new military junta in Colombia was successfully destroying all the cartels, so that his would be the only one left functioning. Talbot would run it well. Talbot was a killing-machine fuelled by money.

He heard screams and gun fire outside, no doubt Emerson Ortega's elite personal bodyguard were still putting up some resistance. They stood no chance against Talbot's men.

Jack Phelps was now the world's sole supplier of cocaine.

The door burst open, and he found himself face to face with Wyatt Chase.

'Phelps, you bastard. It was you who took Suzie!'

'I don't know what you're talking about,' Phelps said. 'I don't know what you're doing here either, but you're way out of your depth.'

'You had her put away because she found out too much. Just like you did my father.'

Wyatt moved towards the desk, and Phelps raised the Uzi carbine from between his legs and point it at Wyatt's stomach.

'Try me,' he said. 'I practice every day – just like you.'

Wyatt stopped in his tracks. He saw Phelps's finger brush the trigger. He shouldn't have been so stupid, shouldn't have allowed himself to get into this position – but he was tired and angry.

'Sit down, Wyatt. Enjoy the last few moments of your singularly purposeless existence.'

Talbot's men cut down the last of Emerson Ortega's elite bodyguard. Then they moved into the bunker, throwing a grenade into each room and blowing it apart before entering. The entire clearing operation was over in less than four minutes. A soldier ran up to Talbot and whispered something in his ear, and an ugly expression appeared on the American's face.

'The bastard's flown!' he screamed at Jules Ortega. Talbot dragged Jules still naked from the waist down, close to his face, and flicked his lighter on.

'He was after the two men who took Suzie von Falkenhyn,' Ortega stammered. 'Before you came, we were attacked, and two men took her. They must have escaped in the helicopter with Emerson. He cannot fly.'

Talbot barked out orders to his men and they ran from the bunker towards the airstrip. He turned back to Ortega.

'Let's go down to the patio.'

Jules walked nervously in front of Talbot through the lounge and out onto the patio that looked down over the darkness of the Amazon jungle.

'Stand on the ledge.'

'No! Please, no!'

Talbot dropped his weapon, moved towards Ortega, then turned and delivered a side-kick into his stomach that lifted him into the air and out into the void.

The screams echoed in the darkness.

The door of the room opened and Talbot stepped in alone.

'The operation . . .'

He stopped speaking the moment he saw Wyatt sitting beside the desk in front of Phelps.

'You are surprised, Wyatt, at our visitor?'

Rod and Wyatt stared at each other. So many years, so much, since then – since they'd first been together in the *dojo*.

Wyatt looked from one to the other. Talbot and Phelps. Phelps and Talbot. A trail of evil winding back in time to Talbot, winding its way forward to Phelps.

Where did it begin and where did it end? Where was the eye of the cobra? Was he looking at it here, in this room?

Wyatt saw the challenge in Talbot's eyes and knew he was ready for it.

'Chase . . .'

'The operation is a success?' Phelps asked, wondering what the connection between Talbot and Chase might be.

'We'll commence full-scale production in twenty-fours hours.'

'Very good,' said Phelps, rising to his feet. 'Then I'll take my leave of you. I trust you'll take care of Wyatt?'

'Oh yes, very good care.'

'Thank you, Rod. Just make sure he's dead before the night's out.'

'I'll get you, you bastard,' Wyatt said softly to Phelps.

'You're just a pawn in the game, Wyatt, nothing more. Just like James.'

'What do you mean?'

Phelps settled on the edge of his desk. 'Seeing as you're going to lose your life, I might as well let you in on one of the facts that shaped it. Your father was like you in a lot of ways. Naive, I think, is a good word to sum you two up. You remember, of course, that I was his biggest sponsor? Well, he discovered, completely by accident, that I was using his racing operation to smuggle heroin into various European countries. He refused to take a cut, which is what I thought he wanted, and then he very stupidly told me he was going to the police.'

'You killed him!'

'Well, not specifically me, but an associate of mine – rather like Rod. Let me unlock your memory. You were going for a drive after the race; an associate of mine actuated your steering-lock by remote control as you drove round the bend.

You just couldn't avoid going over the edge of the cliff after that. It's actually a miracle you survived.'

Wyatt tried not to think about it – the hell that his life had been after the accident. He felt the hatred burning in his soul. Phelps had killed his father; Phelps had caused Danny to commit suicide. And Wyatt had taken the blame.

Wyatt looked up to see the barrel of the gun Talbot was now pointing at him. He knew that if he so much as shifted his body-weight, Talbot would kill him.

The door closed, and Phelps was gone.

Talbot put the pistol down on the table and Wyatt moved into the centre of the room. In a moment they were both back in Tokyo, and the intervening years vanished as if they had never been.

'Why?' Wyatt asked, moving into the fighting stance.

'Why?' Talbot laughed. 'You're a fine one to talk. You're the one who got the highest honour. That's why I left the *dojo* first, because the highest honour went to you and you would have taken control. I didn't want to spend my life in a sweaty old *dojo* knowing I was second choice.'

Talbot moved closer, poised to launch his attack.

'There was no favouritism, you know that,' Wyatt said.

Talbot smiled a chilly smile. 'Now we will find the truth.'

Wyatt looked into Talbot's cold green eyes and saw the madness there.

'I have used my talents as you have used yours,' Talbot said. 'To make money.'

Wyatt was waiting for the blow that must come. 'You kill for money,' he said. 'You fight against men who are weaker than you. That is no challenge. You have betrayed everything that you were taught.'

Talbot was faster than he'd expected and the kick caught him in the side of the head, even though he tried to block it. The steel toe-cap of Talbot's boot impacted against the side of his skull and sent him flying across the floor. Talbot whirled after him, piling blows into his kidneys.

Wyatt raised himself up and dodged the blow aimed again at his skull. He cartwheeled backwards to the centre of the room, his eye on Talbot the whole time. He spun round, and chopped the American hard below the neck.

Talbot screamed out in agony, then launched another series of blows which Wyatt deftly avoided. Wyatt launched a kick forward which smashed into Talbot's stomach.

Talbot sank to his knees, gasping, but then sprang up again. Wyatt drove his open right hand hard into Talbot's abdomen, spun round and drove a kick into his head.

Talbot reeled forward, blood bursting from his mouth. For a moment Wyatt hesitated, then the words of his teacher came back to him.

Bushi no michi wa shinu kotomo osorete inai. The way of the warrior is not to fear death.

Wyatt spun round again and drove his flattened hand hard into the bone between Talbot's mouth and nose.

Talbot collapsed.

Wyatt bowed, rose, and breathed in smoothly; in control.

The door handle turned, and there was shouting outside. Wyatt came to his senses and stared down at Talbot's bloody body. He side-kicked the window and the pane shattered on impact. Then he dived into the greenness below.

Carlos felt the sweat run down his forehead as he saw the lights of the landing-strip in the distance. He had thought they were lost. As he came in closer, he glimpsed a figure running between the helicopters on the runway.

Wyatt.

Emerson Ortega was further back in the cockpit, keeping the gun trained at Carlos's head.

'OK, Carlos, put her down. We kill Phelps, then we leave for good.'

Carlos realised that Emerson could not have seen Wyatt on the ground. He moved in to the landing-point, keeping Wyatt out of Ortega's view, easing the chopper in lower.

Emerson had moved towards the door and was about to open it when Carlos switched on the public address system.

'Wyatt,' he roared, 'get in the chopper!'

The glass of the cockpit exploded as gunfire erupted from

the edge of the runway. Wyatt wrenched open the door – and Emerson Ortega raised his gun and fired, grazing Wyatt's shoulder.

Then Wyatt was on him, smashing his fists into Ortega's face.

'Take off!' Wyatt yelled to Carlos above the noise of the gunfire.

They rose up, were off into the blackness and away from the dark mountain.

The explosion caught Carlos totally unawares. The missile struck the top of the chopper and put out all three engines. He'd been so exhausted, he'd just concentrated on getting to Manaus, the closest town in the Amazon basin – forgetting that the other choppers still on the mountain would give pursuit.

He wrestled with the controls as the helicopter pitched downwards into the blackness. Ortega was screaming, but Wyatt held Suzie, bracing himself, cradling her head.

Carlos managed to restart one engine and arrested their downward course, but the engine began to misfire almost immediately. They were losing height rapidly, and he tried to glide the chopper in on its rotors. The next moment they crashed into branches with a sickening noise as the helicopter tore open. Something came up without warning and struck Carlos hard in the face. He fell back from the controls and blacked out.

Carlos came round to the smell of wood-smoke. Wyatt was sitting in front of a small fire, staring across at the horizon. Emerson Ortega was trussed to a large tree, shivering uncontrollably.

'Where's Suzie?' Carlos asked, then caught sight of the parachute cloth to his left.

Wyatt looked ashen. It was as if the life had been drained from within him, and that he hovered on the edge of an abyss, unsure if he had strength to go on.

Carlos wished he had never regained consciousness. He

walked over to the parachute cloth and pulled it back slightly. Suzie's face was perfect in death.

Wyatt did not say a word, but Carlos saw the tears running from his eyes and he knew the hurt that Wyatt felt deep inside.

The silence seemed eternal.

Later, towards the end of the afternoon, Carlos rose and went up to Emerson Ortega, drawing his knife.

'I saw the film of what you did to my brother,' he said.

'It was a lie.'

The knife in Carlos's hand shifted. 'You killed my brother,' he said.

'No! It was not my doing!'

'I want you to tell me you killed my brother. I will make you stand up in court and tell a jury what you did to him.'

Ortega chuckled weakly. 'You Ramirez, you are all the same. How long do you think you would last if it was known you had threatened me? Do you know what they'd do to your wife? Think about it, and let me go. I am a reasonable man. All this will be forgotten.'

Carlos walked over to the fire and rested the blade against a flame. Then he lifted it up, went across to the tree and pressed it against his own arm. Wyatt smelt sweetness. But Carlos did not cry out, instead he spoke, gritting his teeth.

'You know that I have learned to live with pain. To die is easy. You are not going to die, Ortego. You are going to live, and you are going to pay the price.'

'Go fuck yourself.'

Carlos walked back to the fire and sat down, staring at Emerson. 'I will never sink to your level,' he said.

Wyatt rose to his feet. He spoke for the first time that day.

'It would be better to kill him.'

'You do not understand. You will need this dog to convict Phelps.'

Wyatt walked down to the side of the river. He sat there for a long time, and then he felt Carlos's hand on his shoulder.

'Come. She must be laid to rest.'

They worked with their hands, digging a simple, shallow

grave. Then Carlos took Suzie's body to the river and washed it carefully. Wyatt collapsed on the ground by the grave, his sobs mingling with the noises of the jungle.

Carlos wrapped her carefully in the parachute cloth and laid her body in the shallow grave. Then he went across to Wyatt.

'Come. It is right that you should cover her.'

Wyatt scraped the black earth over the shroud. He felt empty, unable to go on.

Carlos carved a simple cross and placed it over the grave. The orange sun disappeared beneath the green horizon.

Wyatt felt a part of himself had died with Suzie.

They got Emerson to his feet at dawn, broke camp and started to cut their way through the foliage, heading towards the east.

A heaviness lay on Wyatt's soul. He did not care whether they got out alive or died in the jungle.

Bruce got the message to contact Dr Max Weiss when he came into the office after the testing session, and it was with considerable anxiety that he drove up to the scientist's house. He sounded the intercom, and looked up at the TV camera that was focused on him.

'Come in, please,' a digitised voice purred.

'Bruce, I'm sorry to drag you out all this way,' Dr Weiss said apologetically, looking up from a computer screen as he came in. 'It's just that my findings are odd, to say the least, and in view of what happened with Wyatt Chase, I thought your phones might be tapped.'

He gestured for Bruce to take a seat and handed him a sheet of test results.

'Both tyres definitely burst. As to why, I can't work it out. There aren't enough pieces to rebuild the carcass. But I did do a few other tests, and guess what I found?'

'Defective material?' Bruce suggested, hating the very thought.

'No, nothing wrong with the tyres at all. But I found minute traces of cocaine on the inner rubber. I think you should have a close look at your pit crew.'

Bruce felt rage building inside him. It was a rule of his that there was to be no drinking while working – but drugs, he hadn't even thought about drugs. Maybe he'd been naive. Maybe he should have paid more attention to Tennant that time. Shit!

'I'm suggesting that one of the men who fitted the tyres to the rims could possibly have been as high as a kite. That would account for the repeated mistake. I realise it's the last thing you'd like the press to get hold of.'

In the back of Bruce's mind another incident replayed itself. The redhead with the blow-torch. Of course, she'd been after something, something he didn't know about. Now he knew what. Someone on the team must be using cocaine – probably smuggling and selling it as well.

There was a deathly silence in Bruce's office. He eyeballed each of the pit crew and the team from Carvalho, only avoiding Reg Tillson.

Reg was not on the suspect list.

He coughed, then got up from his desk.

'As you know, we've been trying to work out what happened at Monza. The results now appear pretty conclusive: the tyres were not at fault. However, a forensic scientist has found traces of cocaine on the inside of the tyres involved in both accidents. One of you has been taking coke – perhaps more than one. I want to know who.'

The silence continued. Every face was red. He could understand why. Anyone admitting guilt would be admitting to responsibility for the death of Charlie Ibuka.

Bruce slammed his fist on the desk. 'Own up! Because I'll find out who it was, and when I do, I'll crucify you. I can understand if you don't want to come forward in front of the others, I can understand that very well, so I'm going to let you all go back to work. But I want whoever is guilty to contact me. This way, it'll be hard . . . The other way, I'll have to call in the police, and that'll be terrible.'

They all filed out of the office except for Reg, who sat down in front of Bruce's desk.

'Did you have to be so tough? I mean, is the evidence that conclusive? The guys have been under a lot of pressure. It could even have been one of the men at the Carvalho factory, for all you know.'

Bruce coloured and ran his hand through his hair.

'Yes, it could be. But you know, I have to start at the most obvious place, and that means the pit crew.'

Reg laid his hands on the table. 'What you're saying is that you don't trust them.'

'Well, you tell me how else to handle it. Or do you want Ricardo's death on your hands at Silverstone?'

Reg got up. 'I'll watch my guys like a hawk. If I suspect anything, you'll be the first to know.'

'Reg, if I'm wrong, I'm sorry, but there's no other way.'

Jack Phelps stood on the US Airforce runway in Texas and looked up at the sun. What he'd just been told wasn't good news. They'd got Talbot to the hospital, almost on the verge of death, but somehow the man had recovered.

Talbot had never mentioned Suzie von Falkenhyn, never told him they'd taken her. Talbot had been a fool, playing with fire.

Then there was the story about the helicopter that had come back out of the darkness. About the man with dark hair and a prominent chin who had leaped on board as it took off. A man who was lean but incredibly strong. Jesus, how the hell had Wyatt got out of there? And how had he got to the mountain in the first place?

History repeats itself, he thought. At least Chase was now dead. They'd rocketed the helicopter and seen it plunging, covered in flame, down into the vastness of the Amazon basin. Probably better that way; no evidence. Still, he had demanded they launch a search. No point in taking chances.

He walked back and shook hands with the general before getting into the helicopter. Now word would get out in the underworld that the Ortega Cartel was finished and that cocaine supplies had dried up. Then he would wait for the price to rise.

In a year he would be the wealthiest man in the world.

Estelle was at the Dorchester in London when she heard that Jack Phelps was in reception to see her. She looked at her face in the mirror as she checked her make-up.

The tension she was under was terrible. She still had heard no word from either Carlos or Wyatt. Both she and John Tennant wanted to talk to them – to try and get to the bottom of events.

Jack Phelps looked better than ever, she thought, as she made her way across the lobby to greet him. He kissed her on both cheeks and guided her into the coffee shop.

'I wanted to see you when Wyatt was arrested, but there was a lot of business pressure on. However, now I'm free from commitments, at least for the next twenty-four hours, and I want to try and find Wyatt. I must talk to him. I feel responsible, as the chief sponsor of Calibre-Shensu.'

Estelle felt the fear growing inside her. She decided to play along with Phelps. That was what she'd agreed with Tennant.

'Jack, I'm glad you came to me. I know where Wyatt is, and he's not in a good way. He doesn't want to give himself up.'

Jack rested his hand on her arm. 'I can help, I know I can. If you just tell me where he is, I'll go and talk to him.'

'But Jack, once you know where he is you'll be committing a crime if you don't let the police know.'

'Estelle, James was good to me. I want to help.'

A waiter came up to the table and Phelps ordered a coffee and a cappuccino. Estelle was touched that he remembered she always drank cappuccino in the afternoon. She softened.

'Jack, I don't want you in trouble as well.'

'I'm not scared of risks. Tell me where he is.'

She decided that a bit of the truth was all right. 'With Carlos,' she said.

'And where's Carlos?'

She moved closer to Phelps, anxious to see his face as she imparted her next piece of information.

'This is for your ears only,' she said softly, and Phelps leaned in towards her. 'As you know, his brother David was the Minister of Justice in Colombia. He was killed by the Ortega Cartel. Carlos was planning to bring back the man who killed him, Emerson Ortega.'

Phelps's face went white.

'Ortega's dead,' he blurted out a little too quickly. Then he recovered his wits. 'I'm sorry, Estelle, but that sounds like garbage.'

Estelle remained unruffled, watching the American. 'Carlos,' she said, 'was certain that Ortega was still alive.'

Phelps staggered up. 'Estelle, would you excuse me for a minute?'

He got up and strode away between the tables. Estelle gestured to a waiter, who was one of Tennant's men.

'Follow him. He's up to something.'

'But what?'

'Just watch what he does. Now go!'

Phelps staggered into the toilets, wrenched open one of the cubicle doors, hung over the bowl and vomited. Ortega still alive – it was too terrible to contemplate! Everything would come out!

It must have been Carlos with Wyatt, Carlos who'd captured the helicopter and rescued Suzie. But what had happened to Emerson Ortega? Was he still alive? Had they all survived? The pilot had assured him that no one could have got out alive from the chopper when it was rocketed.

He went over to the washbasins and cleaned himself up. One of the waiters from the coffee shop was busy washing his hands, and seemed to take forever – they left the toilets together.

Phelps went over to the maître d'hôtel. 'I need to make an international call immediately.'

He was shown to a private cubicle and handed a phone, and in five minutes he was through to a contact at the Pentagon. He barked out a series of instructions rapid-fire, and then slammed the phone down.

Estelle looked at her watch. He had been gone ten minutes. She looked up to see him hurrying back.

'Estelle. I'm terribly sorry but I bumped into an old business associate who wouldn't leave me alone.' He rested his hand on hers. 'Please, when you know where Wyatt is, get him to contact me.'

Then he was gone.

Tennant's man came up to her and recounted Phelp's behaviour over the previous ten minutes.

'You are sure that he did not meet an old friend?'

'The only person he spoke to was the maître d'hôtel.'

Out in the lobby, Tennant's man showed the hotel manager his police identity, and the manager got a print-out of the number Phelps had direct dialled from reception.

It was a United States number. Back in her room with Tennant's man, Estelle asked the telephonist to put her through to the same number.

'Good afternoon,' said a woman with an American accent.

'Who is that?'

'Who do you wish to speak to?'

'I want to know if I'm through to the right number.'

'Who do you wish to speak to?'

'Someone in authority.'

The phone went dead.

When the call came through, Jack Phelps was still trying to persuade himself that Estelle had been bluffing.

'Yes?' he said into the receiver. 'From the Dorchester? What? Estelle Ramirez, yes. She rang the number?'

He put the phone down and dialled another number. He barked a series of commands down the line.

'Talbot, I don't care how bad you are, you sort it out.'

Estelle met Tennant himself a little later, and he scribbled down the number she'd dialled.

'It's probably some financial brokerage service that has private lines for its more exclusive clients.'

'So you don't believe he's the one?'

'Mrs Ramirez, people always have a motive. Now why should Jack Phelps, already one of the wealthiest men in the world, want to get involved in drugs? Besides, the cocaine business is pretty much dead after the coup in Colombia.'

'But he lied to me.'

'I'm sure a man like Phelps is under constant stress. He's probably got an ulcer he's not talking about. And as for the phone call, well, he probably doesn't like to let anybody know what he's up to most of the time.'

'Perhaps I've been letting my imagination run riot.'

'I think we've been taking Vanessa Tyson too much at her word.'

Estelle got back to the Dorchester just after midnight. She took her key from reception and went up to her room. She remembered she'd left the light on, but now it was off. She searched for the switch and put it on.

A man with a bandaged face held a gun to her head.

'Good evening, Mrs Ramirez. One word, one gasp, and I'll put a bullet through your head. This gun is silenced, so don't make the mistake of trying me out.'

She turned for the door, and he gripped her arm and twisted it hard up her back.

'Come on,' he said. 'It's time for your bath. Take off your clothes.'

She undressed as the gunman looked on. After all she'd been through, she thought, she now had to run into a rapist . . . She pressed the panic-button the police had given her, then hid it under her discarded dress.

'Very good. Now I've run the bath for you and the water's nice and hot.'

As she moved to the bathroom door, his leg shot out and he pushed her forward so that she fell head-first into the water. She tried to scream – and then the door to her room burst open and two policemen ran in. The man with the gun swivelled, pumped shots into each of them. Estelle rolled into the bathroom and locked the door.

Bullets smashed through the wood, narrowly missing her. Then she heard sirens outside, and the shooting stopped.

John Tennant replaced the phone with a grim expression on his face. He thanked God he'd given her the panic-button – but he felt sick when he thought of the two men who'd died saving her life.

Then he remembered the number she'd given him, and

phoned headquarters and dictated it over the phone. Five minutes later he had an answer.

It was classified. A direct line to a general in the Pentagon.

John Tennant opened and closed his hands. It was worse, far worse than he'd dreamed.

The shadow crawled over the green carpet of foliage and threw up a whirlwind of leaves – and Wyatt buried his face in the mud and prayed to God they hadn't been seen. He gripped Emerson's hand, forcing the Colombian down; Carlos was out front, scouting ahead. He guessed the chopper was conducting a grid-pattern search, moving out from where they'd spotted the helicopter wreckage.

The three of them had been on the move for five days now, living off fish from the river they were following upstream. It would have been easy to construct a log raft and paddle their way along, but it would also have been suicide, because the helicopter conducting the search would have picked them up in minutes.

The helicopter disappeared into the distance. Emerson laughed out loud.

'You think you will get away from them?' he grinned. 'You are crazy. I tried to get away from the Yankees. Then I let them think they'd killed me and had plastic surgery.'

Wyatt yanked Emerson to his feet. In the distance he could see Carlos staggering towards them. He looked completely different now that a dark beard covered his face, almost like the legendary guerrilla, Che Guevara.

'We are there. Manaus is over the rise,' he gasped, and sank to the ground. 'We will wait for darkness and then take a boat from the harbour.'

'You will never get away,' Emerson mumbled.

'Carlos, maybe we should kill this bastard.'

'Wyatt, killing is *their* way.'

Wyatt stared across the flowing waters of the Amazon and thought that maybe killing was the only way.

Phelps looked out at the Calibre-Shensu test circuit and watched a flock of geese fly over the tree-line. He breathed

413

out, watching his breath hang on the cold air. He felt very secure. After a thorough search lasting five days, there seemed to be no trace of the three fugitives. If his men found Wyatt, Ramirez or Ortega alive, there would be a short interrogation and then they would be killed.

A police van drew up outside the offices and Phelps watched two constables step out. They went round to the back of the vehicle, and two Alsatians emerged.

Bruce de Villiers walked up to him. 'Jack, I know this may seem ridiculous, but we've got to cover every possibility. Morale is pretty low amongst the team members. Perhaps we'll find it was someone at Carvalho who was taking drugs.'

Ricardo came out of the building just as Jack put his arm around Bruce's shoulder.

'Well, buddy, if there's anything in there, I'm sure those dogs will find it.' He turned to Ricardo. 'Open the door up and let them in.'

Ricardo felt his heart fluttering as the sniffer-dogs moved into the tyre-fitting area and then into the warehouse behind. He realised that even the minutest amount of cocaine would be enough to alert the dogs.

Jack was trying to relax, trying not to show how tense he was. His team had been over the premises a week before with high-pressure vacuum cleaners; then they'd used their own techniques to make sure the place was clean. But there was always the chance they'd missed something.

The dogs started barking furiously in one corner. Bruce ran over and pulled back a case to reveal a comatose rat on the floor. The policeman closest to him shrugged his shoulders.

'Mr Villiers, I think you can relax. There have never been any drugs in this place. Towser's a good dog, he would have picked them up in a flash.'

The Alsatian barked as his name was mentioned.

'Will that be all, sir?'

De Villiers nodded.

Ricardo locked the doors to the warehouse as the police van disappeared into the distance. He felt the sweat on his hands. Phelps was a sharp operator, he must have had the place cleaned out – though he hadn't told him about it.

'Bruce,' Jack said now, 'I think you should stop worrying about Wyatt Chase. The police will get him. There won't be any more problems with drugs now.'

Bruce had organised the police search because he thought there might be more drugs hidden on the Calibre-Shensu premises. Earlier that morning, the sniffer-dogs had been right through the headquarters and workshops. Nothing had been found. Maybe, he thought, Dr Weiss had made a mistake.

'I think you should concentrate on racing,' Jack added unnecessarily. 'Silverstone is a big crowd-puller, and another Calibre-Shensu victory will put paid to the rumours that Ricardo has lost his nerve.'

Wyatt moved along the wharf like a cat and found a small fishing-boat lying tied up, in amongst the larger vessels. It looked ideal for their purpose. He climbed down the side of the pier and stepped onto the rocking deck. At once a man sprang from the shadows, and Wyatt saw a blade flash in the moonlight. Wyatt dropped back, took the man's arm and pulled him forward, chopping his right hand down hard on the man's neck. He toppled forward, hitting his forehead on the front of the boat, and collapsed on the deck. Wyatt checked his pulse – good – he was out, but still alive.

Wyatt climbed back up to the top of the wharf and whistled, and Carlos came out of the shadows, frog-marching Emerson. In a minute they were down in the boat, with Wyatt staring at the unconscious fisherman. He pulled out the oars and cast off, rowing steadily into the middle of the water. The force of the current pulled them away from Manaus, and as soon as they were well clear Wyatt fired the outboard motor.

The prow of the boat cut smoothly through the water as they headed upstream.

Wyatt was half-asleep when the first light of dawn broke across the boat. Carlos was sleeping on the deck, and Emerson lay wide awake against a pile of coiled rope. His eyes darted around nervously.

'Where are we going?'

'To repay some debts,' Wyatt answered quietly.

June

Ricardo could not remember the last time he had been to church, the last time he had made confession. But as he walked away from the austere building, he felt a kind of peace.

He was at the heliport within fifteen minutes, and took the chopper up on his own. He did not want the pilot with him. He looked down over the sprawling expanse of Silverstone and saw the long queues of cars snaking off into the distance. It would be a good race for them, he thought, and he would be in a fine position to win it, starting in pole position.

Silverstone was one of his favourite circuits. An old airfield, it looked unremarkable from above, but on the ground it was a totally different story. Most of the corners were very quick and could be taken in top gear at speeds between 150 and 165 mph.

He did not move immediately towards the landing area, but instead swept around the circuit, his eyes searching carefully. He passed over the Express Bridge.

Eventually, he put the chopper down in the landing area in the centre of the circuit. He made his way quickly to the Calibre-Shensu garage and was greeted by Bruce de Villiers.

'How're you feeling, Ricardo?'

'Very confident. It'll be a good race.'

Bruce nodded, watching him closely. 'I think the Shadow will come into her own here. Are you still worried about what happened at Monza?'

'No. It will not happen again.'

No, it will not happen thought Ricardo. Only I know why Ibuka died. Only I have to live with that.

'Jack would like to have a word with you,' Bruce said. 'He's in the motorvan.'

Ricardo walked over to the huge mobile palace decorated in the arresting black Calibre-Shensu livery. He wondered, not for the first time, where Suzie von Falkenhyn had disappeared to. He had a funny feeling that Phelps might know. Anyway, it didn't matter. Nothing mattered any longer.

He stepped into the air-conditioned silence of the motorvan and made his way down the thickly carpeted aisle to the lounge. Phelps was sitting on a couch in front of the rear window.

'Ricardo, it's good to see you.'

They did not shake hands, and Ricardo remained standing.

'Sit down, my friend, we need to talk.'

Ricardo sat on the edge of the couch. 'What is it you want to know?' he asked.

'I wondered, maybe, if Chase had been in touch with you?'

'Chase? He hates me.'

Phelps smiled. 'I don't want you involved in any of this drugs business,' he said.

Ricardo leaned against the back of the couch. God, what was Phelps playing at? What would happen if Phelps found out about Talbot?

'Have a good race, my friend.'

'It will be my greatest victory, you will see, eh?

Ricardo left the motorvan with his mind in turmoil. What the hell was Phelps getting at?

Bruce de Villiers waved to him. 'Ricardo, there's someone to see you. He's in the car park. You can't miss him, he looks as if he's just had a major head operation.'

He made his way out to the car park and saw a man sitting in a Mercedes-Benz with his head swathed in bandages.

'You want me?' Ricardo asked, going up to the window.

'Get in, arsehole.'

Ricardo gripped the roof of the car as he heard Talbot's distinctive voice.

'Get in.'

Ricardo opened the passenger door and slid down onto the leather seat next to Talbot.

'You read about the revolution in Colombia?

'Yes?'

'We organised it. We've just about cornered the market.'

'But you, you are with Interpol.'

'That was a lie. Interpol gathers, collates and disseminates information – it doesn't have field operatives. Wise up, buster. You're in deeper than you think.'

'I want nothing to do with this.' Ricardo was shaking.

Talbot smiled. 'The street price has doubled already.'

Ricardo tried to open the passenger door, but it was locked. 'The genius of modern electronics, my friend. I decide when you leave the car.'

Ricardo was trembling. 'I will not make another delivery,' he stammered.

'I have statements from two Carvalho employees that you arranged for Ibuka's car to be fitted with defective tyres. A mistake was made, however, and one was fitted to your machine with near-fatal consequences.'

'You lying bastard!'

'Yes, that's exactly what every motoring journalist in the world will be saying about you if they ever learn the truth.'

The 120,000-strong capacity crowd waited patiently for the start of the Foster's British Grand Prix. Thousands of banners and flags were held high by the supporters of the different teams. There wasn't a cloud in the sky – it was as perfect as only an English summer's day can be.

The five-minute signal came up, and the race director checked that the cars were in their correct positions on the grid. Ricardo sat in the cockpit, waiting for the opportunity to prove himself again. To prove that he could still win.

The three-minute signal came up and everyone, except for the most important team members, cleared off the grid. Bruce whispered some last-minute instructions to him. The one-minute signal came up. There was the crazy roar of noise as all the cars on the grid fired into life.

The thirty-second board and the green flag were held up to indicate the commencement of the warm-up lap.

Ricardo pulled off, careful neither to over-rev nor to stall the engine. He liked this circuit. God, it felt good to be leading the pack.

The Shadow felt perfectly set up – she was handling with the minimum of understeer – just how Ricardo liked it. The Carvalho tyres were bedding in nicely – constructed from a slightly tougher compound than before. Ricardo knew that, with copybook driving, they would last the race.

The warm-up lap over, he lay in first position on the grid and observed that the race director was in position on the starter's gantry. The overhead start-light changed to red. Ricardo felt his heart pounding.

The start-light turned to green. The Shensu V12 screamed out as he punched down hard on the accelerator and felt the tyres bite into the track.

A choir of twenty-six unleashed engines united in a single, deafening chorus. Their tyres gripped hard, leaving thick black smears across the track. The cars weaved and dodged their way towards the Foster's Bridge.

De Rosner tried to out-accelerate him as they went under the Foster's Bridge, but the McCabe was no match for the Shadow. Ricardo shot down the straight and headed into Copse, out in front of the pack.

It was an electrifying start.

Bruce felt the excitement growing. Ricardo's lead was increasing all the time, and he was now six seconds in front of de Rosner's McCabe. The Italian was driving flawlessly and had already broken the lap record by almost a second. He was taking a perfect line through the corners, obviously delighting in the performance of the Shensu automatic gearbox, and thrilled by the roars of applause from the crowd.

Bruce glanced down at the computer read-out. The Shadow was without fault, a testament to the perfect match of engine, gearbox and chassis achieved by Professor Katana and Mickey Dunstal.

By the fifty-ninth lap, Ricardo had lapped the second-placed McCabe driven by de Rosner and had twice lapped the rest of the pack. Calibre-Shensu's chances of winning the constructor's championship were looking good. To win it, the points of both drivers were added together to form a cumulative total. No other team had taken as many first places as Calibre-Shensu, and even with just one driver at Silverstone they were leading the points.

Ricardo came round Club, then through Abbey, and accelerated up to 132 mph as he closed on the Express Bridge. He sailed under, went into the Woodcote chicane, and took an easy line through Woodcote to cross the finish moments later.

Ricardo stepped down off the podium, flushed with success. He noticed John Tennant in the distance, and suddenly Alain Hugo appeared at his side.

'Sorry to do this to you, Ricardo, but we believe you were driving under the influence of cocaine.'

There was nothing he could say. Tennant stepped forward, guiding him by the arm. The press moved in, thrusting microphones towards him, focusing their lenses on his tense face.

He was shown to a small room at the back of the pits, and Tennant, Halliday, de Villiers and another man wearing a white coat, entered with him.

'Dr Weiss, will you examine Ricardo Sartori? We suspect he took cocaine just before the commencement of today's race,' Alain Hugo said coldly.

De Weiss conducted his examination with detachment. Ricardo could sense compassion in the doctor's eyes. 'He was driving under the influence of cocaine,' Dr Weiss said quietly.

Ricardo broke down.

'They forced me! Phelps, Talbot, they used me to smuggle in the cocaine. I couldn't do without it . . .'

Tennant looked on with horror. Every turn unfolded a new dimension to the business.

Bruce left the room, and Phelps followed him. 'Bruce, what's . . .?'

Bruce's right hand clenched into a fist and he swung a pile-driver blow into Phelps's gut.

'You fucking bastard!'

They scuttled the boat at the port of Obidos and waited for darkness before heading for the airfield.

It took Wyatt the whole night to commandeer a suitable plane, and an hour before the sun rose, with Emerson securely gagged and tied up in the back, they took off and headed south. They refuelled in Salvador and landed in Rio that evening.

Carlos booked two rooms for them in a backstreet hotel – as anonymous a place as possible. They trussed Emerson up and left him on the bed in one room, then they went into the other room and Carlos called his bank and asked them to advance him some money through their Brazilian associate. Then he called his estancia. He felt terrible at having left Estelle without news of him for so long.

Almost at once Wyatt could see that something was very wrong, for Carlos's face went white. Eventually, he put down the phone.

'Estelle is in London,' he said. 'She has been in contact with the detective who was investigating Vanessa Tyson. Someone tried to kill her.'

Jack Phelps read the morning paper with growing concern. True, Vanessa Tyson had been found guilty of trafficking heroin and was now awaiting sentence, but Ricardo's Silverstone Grand Prix win had been taken away and given to Roger de Rosner, the second-placed driver. An independent jury coordinated by FISA had found that Ricardo Sartori had been using cocaine, and further that, as the official representative of Carvalho, he had been negligent in the supply of tyres for the Italian Grand Prix. This negligence was found to have caused the fitting of defective tyres to his own and Ibuka's machine halfway through the Italian Grand Prix.

CONI, the controlling body of Italian sport, had suspended Ricardo from driving indefinitely. He was being held for questioning by the British police.

The Calibre-Shensu team were now fielding two new drivers for the French Grand Prix: Mike Young, sponsored by Calibre Lights, a top American driver, and Danny Yoshida, sponsored by Shensu.

Jack noted that the new government in Colombia had already signed a diplomatic accord with the United States government. A key member of the Ortega Cartel had been abducted and sent to the United States to face drug manufacturing and smuggling charges. His name could not be released for fear that attempts would be made on his life.

Jack put the paper down and decided that he would instruct Talbot to resume supply through Carvalho in another two months' time. By that time the factory in the Amazon should be producing at full capacity.

He changed quickly and dived into his swimming pool. He swam a length, looking out across the New York skyline, then turned – and saw Wyatt Chase staring at him from the edge of the pool, dressed in climbing-gear.

Jack started to swim back to the side of the pool. His mind was in turmoil. Chase was supposed to be dead! He moved to pull himself out – and a rubber boot pressed against his fingers. He moved away from the side and began to tread water. Above him, another man appeared next to Chase, a dark-skinned man with a long pony-tail – Carlos Ramirez. The Argentinian smiled and adjusted one of the bronze bracelets on his wrist.

'Mr Phelps, I think we have met. But let me introduce myself again, in case you have forgotten. Carlos Ramirez.'

Wyatt stepped forward to the edge of the pool.

Phelps discreetly pushed a button on his wristwatch.

'I think you might be surprised to know,' Wyatt said, 'that we have captured Emerson Ortega, alias Antonio Vargas, alive. I remember you paying a visit to his factory in the Amazon basin.'

Phelps lay back in the water and laughed. 'What is it you want, Wyatt? You can have your drive back if you want it.'

'I want revenge.'

'Touch me and you'll die.'

'Your threats are meaningless, Phelps.'

Jack was silent for a moment. Then he said, 'Like your father, you now know too much. Like your father, you are a little soft on certain issues. He threatened me, as you are threatening me now. I sorted him out in Monaco and I'm going to sort you out now.'

Wyatt went cold. Memories of the accident that had never

surfaced till now, flooded back to him. The car going over the cliff; his father taking off his own seat-belt and pulling himself over Wyatt, shielding him from the rocks and the debris . . .

He felt the metal pressed against his spine.

'Don't turn round, either of you. My men are now in control.'

Wyatt was perplexed. How had they known? Carlos and he had climbed up the side of the building under cover of darkness.

'My watch, you jerks, contains a micro-transmitter. I never travel alone, even when I'm almost naked. I must say, Wyatt, I'll enjoy killing you almost as much as I enjoyed disposing of your father.'

Wyatt breathed evenly and watched Carlos. The Argentinian was in a similar predicament to himself, with the barrel of a sub-machine-gun pressed into his back.

'And you, Carlos Ramirez. Pity about your brother, but then he learned a little too much for his own good.'

'You were responsible for his death as well, you bastard!'

'Well, let's say I had an interest in it. I really enjoyed the video, by the way, just as I shall enjoy watching the accident you two are going to have a few moments from now. It's never a good idea to climb up tall buildings, you can so easily fall off . . .'

Imperceptibly, Wyatt eased his hand across the webbed belt of his climbing-harness and pulled the pin out of the grenade that was attached to it. The guard training the gun on him didn't see the slight movement.

'You're an evil man,' Wyatt said softly. Phelps smiled at him as he swam towards the side of the pool.

In one flowing movement Wyatt whipped out the grenade, skimmed it across the surface of the pool and dropped down, kicking the gunman's legs from under him.

Wyatt knew what he was doing. The grenade would create an incredible amount of pressure on the outer wall of the pool – that was the weakest section of the structure.

Phelps laughed, then ducked under the water as the grenade bounced against the side of the pool and exploded under the water, blowing a little over the side. Carlos took advantage of the other gunman's surprise and wrestled with him for the gun.

Phelps was pulling himself out of the water now, as cracks exploded across the glasswork on the outer side of the pool where the force of the explosion had been greatest. Water started to pour out of the cracks and down towards the street far below. The cracks got wider, and the water was sucked out. Phelps tried to grip the side of the pool but lost his hold. Then, screaming, he was sucked with the water through a huge crack that had now developed in the wall. He plunged into the void.

The *New York Times* the following day noted the tragic death of Jack Phelps. He had died when his roof-top pool burst open without warning.

In a shock revelation, Chief Inspector John Tennant of New Scotland Yard linked Phelps to illicit business activities in Europe, including the laundering of drug money. Phelps's name was also linked with a Colombian drug-trafficking ring making inroads into the European market.

The suicide of General Hal Wright caused some concern in the Pentagon. A congressional commission of enquiry was established to investigate allegations that the CIA had been involved in drug-smuggling operations and supplying weapons to pro-United States groups in South America.

Ecologists criticised a practice exercise by the Brazilian air-force which had involved the shooting of missiles at Mount Roraima, deep in the Amazon basin. Investigation of the damage to the environment was unfortunately impossible, due to the inaccessibility of the location.

The Brazilian government issued an official apology and promised that the exercise would not be repeated.

Formula One sponsors, Carvalho Tyres of Brazil, went into provisional liquidation. A spokesman for Calibre-Shensu said that the company had signed a five-year contract with Pirelli.

*

A memorial service was held for Suzie von Falkenhyn in Munich. The fashion designer had been presumed dead after efforts to locate her in Brazil had failed. Formula One ace Wyatt Chase attended the ceremony, along with controversial British reporter, Vanessa Tyson, who had been found entirely innocent of the drug charges pressed against her earlier in the year. New findings had resulted in Vanessa Tyson's re-trial, and she had been acquitted.

The charges of assault against Wyatt Chase were withdrawn.

Carlos Ramirez, whose wife, society beauty Estelle, had been attacked in the Dorchester hotel, London a month previously, was elected President of the International Polo Federation.

Ricardo Sartori was found guilty by a Milan court on twenty-two different charges relating to drug-trafficking, the laundering of drug money, and income tax avoidance. He was sentenced to a total of twenty years' imprisonment.

November

Wyatt stood in the pits on Saturday afternoon, feeling distinctly down at heart. It was now four months since Phelps's death. It had been four months of fighting for him. He'd got back his place as the lead driver for Calibre-Shensu but it had taken him a long time to recover his form. Suzie's death still haunted him.

He was lying in tenth place on the grid. The Shadow that had performed so well for him throughout the season had been behaving erratically. There were problems with the engine management system that defied the continued attempts at diagnosis by the British and Japanese engineers. Mickey Dunstal was close to tearing his hair out. Aito Shensu maintained his characteristic calm between long chats with Professor Katana, his head of design.

The Suzuka Grand Prix circuit was actually a Honda test circuit, situated on Ise Bay, south-west of the industrial town of Nagoya on Honshu Island. Designed by the Dutchman, John Hugenholz, it combined an amusement park with a training facility. Wyatt felt it was a bit like staging a race in Disneyland.

That Sunday the weather was cool and the air filled with exhaust fumes. Already long lines of cars snaked back along the outlying roads around Suzuka, and outside the turnstiles people were queueing to get into the circuit. When the circuit was filled, the crowd would number over 100,000.

The Japanese, thought Wyatt, were crazier about motor-racing than any other people on earth. But what made them different was the dedication and dignity with which they pursued their passion.

He stepped out of the pits and walked across to the helipad. Vanessa was waiting for him beside the chopper. It seemed strange to see her without her assistants or her cameraman: she had come alone to Japan. He kissed her on the lips and felt her tongue caress his own.

They parted, and Wyatt slipped into the pilot's seat, having done his pre-flight inspection. Vanessa buckled in next to him, her dark skirt riding up to reveal her shapely legs. He ran his hand over them.

'Are you going to break your own rules?' she asked teasingly.

He never made love the night before a race. He felt that he needed to conserve every ounce of energy for the challenge that lay ahead. He thought of the one time with Suzie, in the motorvan, just before the race began. Why couldn't he just forget her?

They hovered over the circuit – a figure-of-eight, with one section of track crossing the other over a bridge. Wyatt was psyching himself up for the race, and pictured himself leading for the full fifty-three laps. The Suzuka circuit was fast – the top drivers clocking in average times of over 120 mph.

This was the final race of the year. Wyatt had missed two races, but had fought his way to second place on the championship ladder, just one point behind Roger de Rosner in the McCabe. To win the championship Wyatt had to win this race, or hope that de Rosner might break down, with Wyatt finishing in the points. But de Rosner's McCabe had never broken down before, so the chances of that happening at Suzuka were negligible.

De Rosner had taken pole position on the grid, and he held the lap record for the circuit. Lying tenth on the grid, Wyatt knew he could catch and pass de Rosner, but he knew it wouldn't be easy. De Rosner, the previous year's champion, was hungry to make it two in a row.

The number two driver for Shensu-deVilliers lay right behind Wyatt on the grid. If Danny Yoshida could finish in the points and Wyatt could win, then Shensu-deVilliers would take home the world championship and the constructor's championship.

When Wyatt had been brought back as the number one driver, de Villiers had had to ask Mike Young, the talented American driver who had taken Wyatt's place, to stand down.

Fortunately Young hadn't made too much of a performance about it – he'd already been talking to another team and they took him on. Danny Yoshida had been retained in the number two slot on Aito's firm instruction.

It had been a hard year for all of them. Bruce was determined that McCabe wouldn't take the driver's championship; he wanted the constructor's trophy and the driver's trophy for Shensu-deVilliers.

Bruce had a lot to prove, as well as a personal score to settle with McCabe. Bruce's name had taken a hammering, what with disqualifications, accusations that he couldn't control his drivers, the fatal accident involving Ibuka, and his links with Phelps and Sartori – both implicated in drug-trafficking.

Wyatt and Vanessa were back at the hotel as the sun set. It was quite cold, and they enjoyed a simple meal in their room. A knock on the door interrupted them, and Wyatt opened it to find Carlos outside with Estelle. They embraced, and he showed them into the room. Carlos kissed Vanessa on both cheeks.

'Still as beautiful. You are not covering the race?'

Vanessa looked at Carlos and Estelle. 'No, I chose not to. I'm too involved personally this time. A lot of people have died, and there is more at stake here than just a simple race – especially for Wyatt.'

Carlos took a parcel from inside his overcoat and handed it to Wyatt.

'This is from Estelle and me. Unwrap it now, please.'

Wyatt stripped the cover-paper off the parcel and uncovered an old rosary.

'The Jesuit priest I told you about – the one who had the affair with the woman from whom I'm descended – it was his. I do not have a son, so it is yours. I hope it brings you luck tomorrow. I know that many things are against you.'

Wyatt handled the string of faded beads and then looked up into Carlos's eyes.

'I know what this means to you – and I can't thank you enough.'

They talked for a little while longer, then Carlos and Estelle got up to leave. Estelle hugged Wyatt long and hard.

'When the season is over, I would like you to come and stay on the estancia. I have . . . Oh Wyatt, I have so much to make up to you, I feel so guilty . . . It was not your fault. Will you forgive me?'

'I always forgave you. I could never forgive myself.'

The door closed and they were gone.

Vanessa held the rosary between her fingers. 'You must carry this with you tomorrow.'

He took the rosary from her, laid it in its box and slowly, very slowly, began to peel off her clothes.

'But what about tomorrow?' she said, smiling.

'Rules are made to be broken.'

He rose in the first light of the Japanese dawn and showered in cold water. Then he put on the simple white jacket and trousers, the *karate-gi*, tying the folds of the jacket together with the thin black cotton belt that was worn and faded with use.

He caught the lift down, walked out of the foyer of the hotel and into the chill morning air. He started to run on bare feet, turning down the narrow streets and eventually heading upwards toward the mountain.

The *dojo* lay on the slope. Already the place was alive with the noise of students in training, the *sensei* putting them through their paces. Wyatt went through the open doors and joined them.

It was as if he had never been away. His body reacted instinctively to the commands of the *sensei*, and soon he was sweating profusely.

Wyatt stood a foot higher than the *sensei* and his students, but this gave him no feeling of superiority, for in the *dojo* all else is sublimated into the quest for perfection of control over mind and body.

Aito ordered the class to kneel.

'We have a visitor,' he said. 'Someone who left us, and has now returned.' Wyatt stood up and felt the eyes of the class move to the embroidery on his belt, the markings of the holder of the Seventh Dan.

429

Aito continued: 'Today our visitor faces a great test. With me he will now practise *kihon-kumite* to hone his senses.'

Wyatt moved forward, conscious of the years he had spent away from the *dojo*, yet knowing too, that during all those years he had continued training.

Aito's black belt was similar to his own, yet the markings were subtly different. Aito Shensu held the highest grade, the Ninth Dan. Some said it was an honorary grade, but those who worked within the tight disciplines of karate knew that it was only conferred on the most expert.

They moved forward onto the wooden floor, in the centre of the class, and bowed, looking each other in the eye. Then Aito moved in, his closed fist striking Wyatt in the solar-plexus. If the blow had been full-strength it would have permanently crippled him. Wyatt staggered back and looked into Aito's eyes. There was no mercy in them.

The next blow came across his feet, but now he was ready, leaping into the air and aiming a kick at Aito's skull. His opponent had moved a millisecond before connection. The roundhouse caught Wyatt by surpirse, sending him sprawling across the floor.

The anger flared through him. He was up again and moving in, every sense keyed up. Now Aito's blows failed to make contact, yet every counter Wyatt made was blocked. Then, suddenly, he caught an opening, and landed a blow to Aito's chest.

The *sensei* drew back, smiled and bowed. The *kumite* was over.

Later, alone in the sauna, Wyatt felt the energy coming back. He had not realised how slow he had become, and how arrogant.

The door opened and Aito stepped in, his body naked, reavealing the tightly-knit muscles of a man who looked as if he was in his thirties rather than his seventies. He offered his hand to Wyatt, then sat down next to him.

'You thought you were as good as when you left.'

'I thought I was better.'

'Why did you come?'

'You asked me to.'

'I have asked many times before and you have not come.'

'I was afraid. That was why I left. I am not Japanese.'

'My friend, that is irrelevant. You had a problem that you could not solve, a thing you could not live with. I think you have worked that thing out.'

'You are right, Aito.'

'You will train with me again?'

'Let me win the race.'

'You can still race, but when you are forty it will no longer be possible.'

'Why?'

'I will sponsor you every year till you are forty. Then you will come back here. You will eventually be my successor.'

'After I let the style down? It would not be fitting.'

'You are more like us than you realise. It would be most fitting.'

Wyatt nodded.

'Then you agree,' Aito said with quiet satisfaction.

'I do.'

'Come, I will take you back to the hotel.'

It was comfortable in the cockpit of the Shadow. The cool weather meant that, for once, the fireproof suit was pleasant to wear. In front of him was the portable computer screen, giving a last-minute read-out of all the essential engine functions.

Bruce leaned over. 'Good luck, Wyatt.'

Then the monitor was gone and the one-minute signal came up. The Shensu V12 fired into life and Wyatt's mind focused on the start. The green flag appeared, and he moved off with the pack for the warm-up lap. In tenth position he didn't have any room for complacency – the entire race was going to be a fight for survival.

Just over a minute later he was back on the grid, his eyes focused on the starting-light. With the first flash of green he was off, moving down the straight and heading for the first curve. He moved in on the car in front, but the driver swung over to block him, striking the nose of his car. Pieces flew up into the air and debris was scattered round the edge of the track.

The damage was not critical, but it would slow him down. Wyatt powered on through the curves, sick in the knowledge that at the end of the first lap he was going to have to come in to have a new nose fitted.

Bruce was pushing the pit crew to the limits of their ability. The nose was out and ready, along with a fresh set of tyres.

The dark livery of Wyatt's car shot down the pit lane and the crew swarmed over it. In twenty seconds the new nose and tyres were fitted, and the car blasted off, back into the race, Wyatt now lying sixteenth.

There was no way he could win.

Aito took off his jacket and walked down to the pits. He exchanged worried glances with Bruce, then gestured for Katana to move aside from the computer control-system.

Aito punched in a series of commands. Bruce hunched over him.

'What are you doing, Aito?'

'You think he has little chance of winning?'

'It will be the fight of his career – unless half the cars in front break down, and at this stage of the season that's highly unlikely.'

Aito looked at the different read-outs. 'We have never allowed the engine to be stressed to its absolute limit. At the moment the electronic management chip is programmed to peak at 13500 rpm . . . But I can change that through our remote-control system.'

Bruce knelt down and stared at the figures.

'But the engine could blow up.'

'It could. But Professor Katana has had her up to 17000 rpm on the test-bed.'

Bruce got up and stared out across the pit lane. It was a hell of a risk. If there were a few retirements, Wyatt could well end up in the points, and though the team wouldn't win the championship, they'd be in second place. But if he chose to change the engine settings, they could be out of the running and be much further back in the points.

432

He clenched his fist and walked back to Aito.

'All right. Reprogramme the engine management chip.'

It was the twenty-seventh lap, with twenty-six to go, and Wyatt was getting desperate. He'd made it to tenth place, but even though two of the front-runners had dropped out, he knew that at his present pace he could not possibly pass the cars in front of him.

In the headphones, to his surprise, he heard Aito's voice.

'Wyatt, we're going to reprogramme the electronic management chip in your engine – you should be able to push the engine another 2000 revs – maybe even 5000 if you're prepared to take the risk. Don't hold back now. I'm with you all the way.'

Wyatt felt the difference almost immediately, and the engine developed an uncanny snarl. In the first corner he was up to 15000 and passed the tenth car. A vague noise intruded and he guessed it was the crowd cheering.

He pushed the car harder into the next bend, tracking the ninth-placed driver in the distance. Now he had the power to reel him in and put on the pressure. His hand worked the wheel continuously and he felt his neck taking the strain of the increased G-forces. He was going very, very fast.

On the thirty-third lap he passed the ninth car on the straight. He heard the headphones crackle into life. Even the distortion couldn't hide the excitement in Bruce's voice.

'You've just broken the lap record! Keep it up.'

He was a long way behind the eighth car, and it seemed like an eternity before he finally started tailing it on the fortieth lap. He was running out of time.

The driver kept blocking him, shooting out to the side whenever he tried to pass. But Wyatt hadn't got time for these games. He came up on the inside, saw the car moving in towards him. He held his line, going straight for the side of the car. At the last minute the driver panicked and lost control.

Wyatt felt a lot better after that. The seventh car, driven by former world champion Nico Marx, was just in front, and Wyatt breathed a sigh of relief as the professional made way for his charge – the only driver who had done so.

Six cars to pass and thirteen laps to go. It was a formidable task.

The BBC commentator could feel the tension in the crowd, the growing excitement. There was not a single spectator who did not know of the relationship between Wyatt Chase and Aito Shensu – that Chase had lived in Shensu's country for ten years, and that this had created a special bond between them.

'This is without doubt the most exciting race of the season,' the commentator said excitedly. 'De Rosner has been leading the race, the other two front-runners having dropped out, and the world championship is his – unless Wyatt Chase can catch him.

'Till lap twenty-five, it looked as though Chase was out of the running. But then, on lap twenty-six, he suddenly recovered the form that has made him the most talked about driver on the circuit this year. In only his second year in Formula One, he could win the championship at the age of twenty-eight . . .'

'And here we are, he's moving into the Casio Triangle, and yes, he passed Rolf Steiner in the Kraftwork before Steiner could even work out what was happening. But it's now only ten laps to the finish and the question on everyone's lips is: "Can Chase do it?".'

The camera closed in on the Degner Curve, where Wyatt was already challenging the fifth-placed Andrews driven by Mort Hume, the only American in the race. Wyatt moved far out on the corner and crossed past Hume in an incredibly risky manoeuvre that could have sent him spinning out of control into the underpass.

'I have never, never seen driving like this. The Shensu-deVilliers Shadow is certainly putting paid to any criticisms of Mickey Dunstal's controversial design. If anything, the revised design, produced after the FISA disqualification following the Monaco Grand Prix, has made this machine even more competitive . . .

'And here is Chase coming down the straight, passing the fourth-placed Marrington-Ford driven by Michel Rotteglia. This is incredible! Chase is driving faster than any driver I've ever witnessed. The lap record is now down to one minute, thirty-nine-point-seven seconds. How Chase's tyres are handling all this is what's bothering me . . .

'And now he's heading for the leading pack, de Rosner up front with the two Ferraris close behind. They're six seconds ahead of Chase, with nine laps to go.'

Wyatt felt as if he were in a hypnotic trance. He could not hear the commands that came through over the headphones. All he was aware of were the two red cars coming up towards him. He was now down to eight laps and running out of time. De Rosner was six seconds in front of the Ferraris, and he'd need at least four laps to catch him.

Seven laps to go, and he was in a rage as the Ferraris blocked his path. There was no way they were going to let him through, and he knew why: if they took second and third places, second place in the constructor's championship was theirs. Well, if they weren't going to fight fair, neither was he.

He moved into the Casio Triangle at the highest speed he'd yet risked, and immediately the rear Ferrari moved out to block his path. He cut inside the red machine and, as he expected, she tried to force him off the track. The leading Ferrari then braked, and together they pushed him towards the edge. He forced the Shadow hard across to the left, wondering if he was going to come out of the corner alive. He nipped between the front of the rear Ferrari and the back of the leading one by a hair's breadth – and both drivers lost control and spun off the side.

Now he was after de Rosner. It was going to be very, very close.

'. . . And this is simply incredible. No one can criticise Chase's expertly timed break through the blocking manoeuvres of the Ferraris, but who would have expected both cars to spin off at the same moment? Shensu-deVilliers now only have to finish in second place to win the constructor's championship and the way Wyatt Chase is driving, there seems no doubt that he'll make that easily.

'But as we move into the final lap, it looks as though the driver's championship is going to go to de Rosner!'

The camera cut to de Rosner's machine pulling out of the Casio Triangle and into the last lap. A second later the black-bodied Shensu-deVilliers Shadow charged out, hot in pursuit.

The crowd were screaming as both drivers prepared to do battle.

Wyatt felt the car was not responding as comfortably as she had done earlier. He felt sick in the knowledge that his tyres were probably close to breaking-point. But he had to pass de Rosner.

He hung onto de Rosner through the bends, waiting for an opportunity, but none occurred. He just could not risk putting too much strain on his tyres.

As they accelerated round the Spoon Curve he realised that it was all or nothing. He came out neck-and-neck with de Rosner, and they flew towards the Casio Triangle. Wyatt knew the Shadow was at maximum power, but he could not outhaul de Rosner. His only chance was the Casio Triangle, where he might just pass him.

Both men refused to brake, and they entered the corner at a suicidal pace. Just when he thought it was too late, de Rosner's nerve went and Wyatt shot past, flying over the finish-line seconds later.

His car slewed round and round as the rear end exploded. He saw the side of the circuit come up with sickening speed, and the Shadow smashed hard into it.

Vanessa was running across the track, ignoring the shouts of the marshals, caring only about the black car that was being bathed in foam. The breath burst from her lungs as she pushed herself harder and harder.

She saw them lifting the body out of the car and started screaming.

Aito stood in the pits. Everyone had gone. He looked at the black computer screen again, then got up and walked onto the circuit. A man sat alone in the grandstand, staring into the evening sky. Something drew Aito towards him. He was a tall man with a pony-tail. Carlos Ramirez.

Aito walked slowly up the steps and then across to Carlos, sitting down next to him. Carlos turned.

'It is a tragedy.'

'No, it is not a tragedy. He won. And in life that is all that matters.'

Narita Airport was packed with people. Talbot looked at his ticket again and moved towards the boarding-gate. It had been a remarkably simple exercise, planting the bomb and the transmitter under the engine cowelling of the Shadow.

He had planned to explode the device within moments of the race starting, but something had stopped him. His training dictated that a warrior be given the chance to prove himself in combat and then die an honourable death.

But now the final score had been settled, and with Phelps and Sartori out of the way, he could retire comfortably. It was going to be pleasant flight to Europe. He decided to pay a final visit to the toilet before boarding.

Two smartly dressed Japanese executives followed him into the toilets. Oriental yuppies, he thought to himself – but the blow across his head changed that perception in an instant and he crouched down into a fighting stance.

He launched a flying kick at his first attacker that sent him reeling into the cubicles. As the second approached, he caught sight of an older man who had come out of one of the cubicles. It was Shensu.

The blow took him out before he saw it coming, and the next moment he was bundled outside. No one took any notice of his struggles.

In a matter of minutes he was manhandled into a light plane, gagged and blindfolded.

Talbot awoke naked, the sound of the sea in the distance. He lifted himself up from the futon and donned the black *gi* that was lying beside him.

He opened the door and walked outside to see the sea. In an instant he knew where he was. Okinawa.

Aito Shensu was sitting on his calves on the hard sand of the beach, looking out to sea, also dressed in a black *gi*.

He heard a voice behind him. The language was Japanese.

'Now you fight Aito. You have disgraced our style. You have murdered his successor.'

Talbot felt unsteady on his feet. He looked at the old man with the closely cropped hair. He must be over ninety. He had never been privileged to meet the head of the style before. He bowed.

'Do not bow. You dishonour me. The only honour that can come from this is that you fight Aito.'

Talbot turned and walked out onto the sand. It would only take a matter of minutes. Shensu was nearly seventy.

They bowed, and Talbot closed in. Two blows hit his skull in sharp succession and he collapsed to the ground. His mouth felt bloody. He hadn't even seen the blows coming.

He staggered up, and received a hammering side-kick to his skull. He collapsed again.

'Up!' screamed Aito.

Talbot did not know how long it continued. He could not strike one blow in retaliation, and his body became a field of pain. All he was conscious of was Aito: the old man, and the sea.

As the sun began to set across the horizon, he experienced a degree of pain he had never thought possible.

'Kill me,' he begged.

'I accept your request. You must die in the knowledge that you are nothing. That you have disgraced our teachings. That you have used what you were taught to harm weaker people.'

Talbot swayed on his feet.

'I beg to die.'

The blow took him without warning and smashed the life from him.

Estelle followed Aito to the mountain top and stared out across the fragile landscape. He handed her the box and she sprinkled the ashes in the wind. He took her hand.

'*Kanashimuna korega bushino michi*. Do not be sad. He accepted the way of the warrior.'

She looked into his eyes, not understanding. He turned away and stared across at the horizon.

'To die of old age, that is dishonourable. To die in combat, that is the greatest achievement. He understood that. That to fear death is the greatest weakness. He was not afraid when he died, he was victorious, for the way of the warrior is death.'

A Selected List of Fiction Available from Mandarin

While every effort is made to keep prices low, it is sometimes necessary to increase prices at short notice. Mandarin Paperbacks reserves the right to show new retail prices on covers which may differ from those previously advertised in the text or elsewhere.

The prices shown below were correct at the time of going to press.

☐ 7493 1352 8	The Queen and I	Sue Townsend £4.99
☐ 7493 0540 1	The Liar	Stephen Fry £4.99
☐ 7493 1132 0	Arrivals and Departures	Lesley Thomas £4.99
☐ 7493 0381 6	Loves and Journeys of Revolving Jones	Leslie Thomas £4.99
☐ 7493 0942 3	Silence of the Lambs	Thomas Harris £4.99
☐ 7493 0946 6	The Godfather	Mario Puzo £4.99
☐ 7493 1561 X	Fear of Flying	Erica Jong £4.99
☐ 7493 1221 1	The Power of One	Bryce Courtney £4.99
☐ 7493 0576 2	Tandia	Bryce Courtney £5.99
☐ 7493 0563 0	Kill the Lights	Simon Williams £4.99
☐ 7493 1319 6	Air and Angels	Susan Hill £4.99
☐ 7493 1477 X	The Name of the Rose	Umberto Eco £4.99
☐ 7493 0896 6	The Stand-in	Deborah Moggach £4.99
☐ 7493 0581 9	Daddy's Girls	Zoe Fairbairns £4.99

All these books are available at your bookshop or newsagent, or can be ordered direct from the address below. Just tick the titles you want and fill in the form below.

Cash Sales Department, PO Box 5, Rushden, Northants NN10 6YX.
Fax: 0933 410321 : Phone 0933 410511.

Please send cheque, payable to 'Reed Book Services Ltd.', or postal order for purchase price quoted and allow the following for postage and packing:

£1.00 for the first book, 50p for the second; **FREE POSTAGE AND PACKING FOR THREE BOOKS OR MORE PER ORDER.**

NAME (Block letters) ....

ADDRESS ....

....

☐ I enclose my remittance for ....

☐ I wish to pay by Access/Visa Card Number ☐☐☐☐☐☐☐☐☐☐☐☐☐☐☐☐

Expiry Date ☐☐☐☐

Signature ....

Please quote our reference: MAND